THE LAST PEARL

1879, York: Greta Costello works as a Saturday girl for an old jeweller, Saul Abrahams. Her long fingers and appreciation of beauty persuade Saul to train her as a pearl stringer, which leads her to a new life. 1879, Scotland: Jem Baillie knows the immense power of a perfect pearl. His father was a fisherman in Scotland, and together they found the rarest of pearls, a great white pearl they call Queenie. When this is stolen, they seek revenge. This is one woman's journey to open the shell she has built around herself to reveal the true beauty within.

THE LAST PEARL

by

Leah Fleming

Magna Large Print Books
Long Preston, North Yorkshire,
BD23 4ND, England.

British Library Cataloguing in Publication Data.

A catalogue record of this book is
available from the British Library

ISBN   978-0-7505-4319-4

First published in Great Britain by Simon & Schuster UK Ltd., 2016

Cover illustration © Rekha Garton by arrangement with
Arcangel Images Ltd.

The right of Leah Fleming to be identified as author of this work has
been asserted in accordance with sections 77 and 78 of the Copyright,
Designs and Patents Act, 1988.

Published in Large Print 2017 by arrangement with
Simon & Schuster UK Ltd.

Magna Large Print is an imprint of Library Magna Books Ltd.

Printed and bound in Great Britain by
T.J. (International) Ltd., Cornwall, PL28 8RW

There is just one piece of jewellery that is equally becoming to everybody...

Long live the pearl necklace, true or false from first date to our last breath.

Genevieve Antoine Dariaux, *A Guide to Elegance*

Part 1

THE PEARL

The pearl mussel of the British Isles *(unio margaritifera)* has a thick coarse and unsightly shell ... it is sometimes twisted, distorted and barnacled.

Kunz and Stevenson, *The Book of the Pearl*, 1908

Prologue

Perthshire, July 1879

The boys on Glencorrin green were hard at their evening football kick around, stripped to the waist with backs tanned like leather, their dusty shirts used for goalposts. The tallest of them by a head was standing poised in goal, his curly black hair damp with the heat of the day, when a voice called from the cottage gate down the lane summoning his attention.

'Jemmy, away and fetch yer pa in from the river,' shouted Jean Baillie, his mother. 'Supper's in the pot and it'll no keep till he graces us wi' his presence.'

Many folks in the village of Glencorrin wondered why Jean Guthrie had taken such a man as Sam Baillie to her bed. Sure enough, he was a fine-looking man with a head of wild jet curls and a dark winsome eye. His son took after him. He wasn't afraid of hard graft in the forests, but in village eyes Sam was one of the tinker kind, and folks knew there was no holding them when the spirit put wanderlust in their feet.

'I'm away this minute,' Jem shouted, turning to answer her just as the ball flew past him and the opposition roared in victory. He grabbed his shirt with a shrug. 'Sorry, see yous all tomorrow.' His mother's word was law.

11

It was high summer in the forests around Perth and almost the shooting season, but there was a brief gap for haymaking and river fishing on the estate where the Baillies were employed. It was the nearest the villagers got to a holiday season. The banks of the river were full of campers and locals scouring the water for those special pearl mussels that might make them a fortune.

Running down to the water's edge through a secret path hidden by the tall Scots pines with their scented needles and cones, Jem Baillie knew just the spot where his father had fished for pearls every summer, hidden from the travelling folk in their bendy tents and vardos. It was the dry season, when the river ran deep and calm in the centre and the camps used by the log floaters in the winter were now filled with pearl hunters paddling in the shallows in search of treasure.

Jem loved the silence of the dark forests. His grandfather had worked those hidden places, hewing down the great pines while supervising the other river rats jumping the floating logs that were carried by the water in full spate to the lumber mills. That was autumn work when the season picked up, but until the beaters went out on the Glorious Twelfth, there was nothing to do but join his father in searching the riverbed for the secret hoard that would bring honey for their coarse oaten bread and provide them with strong boots for the snows to come.

Jem was an only child. When Sam Baillie, an itinerant traveller stopped for the season on the laird's estate to be a hired hand, little did he know his wanderings would soon be over. When his tribe moved on he had already fallen for the quiet charm of Jean Guthrie who cleaned and served food in the shooting lodges. She'd borne him a fine son in her forties, a son they were trying to keep from the forest and the laird's employ by enrolling him in school as a pupil helper. Once school was out, Jem was away with his father fishing until it was dark. Sam Baillie was the undisputed king of the pearl fishers and Jem loved to watch him at work. He had the old way of doing things, the gypsy way. 'The right way,' he was told.

'Never forget, son, yon pearl is a gift of nature, it's God's bounty and not to be squandered. You have to tease the shell open a wee bitty, not crush it, killing the creature inside like the farm boys do. Some of my own are no better. All those piles of rotting shells on the shoreline, kicking up a stink. Why kill the goose that lays the golden eggs?'

Jem caught sight of his father bent over, peering into the water using the wooden bucket with a glass bottom, searching down into the clear water. He was chest high in cold water.

'Any luck, the day?' Jem yelled but his father was too busy to answer at first. He looked up and smiled.

'Give us a hand, laddie.'

'Ma says its time you were out or you'll catch yer death.'

'Ach away ... she's in here, I know it in ma bones. I had a dream last night. She's waiting down there. Come in and see. Your young eyes are sharper than mine and my back is awful weary.'

Jem rolled up his britches, barefoot he waded in, taking hold of the shaft of the scraper with its

13

hooks bent backwards to dislodge the mussel from its berth. He fished around with his feet through the stones and mud and sand, scraping up mussels to the surface, giving them to Sam to shove into the bag slung round his body, already weighed down with shells to be opened.

'Come on home, the stew's in the pot.' Jem was hungry.

'Howd yer whisht,' Sam replied, coughing with a rasp that Jem hated to hear. 'What's that down there, can you see, to the left of yon stone?'

'Just an old twisty thing.' Jem was feeling with his toes.

'Bring it up then.'

'But it's an old battered shell.'

'Twisters are the best. Have I taught you nothing, son? They misshapes is there for a reason. Bring it up.'

The boy and the old man sat on the tussocky riverbank as Sam carefully opened up each mussel in turn, one by one, but there was nothing of note, just glistening molluscs. Some were useless and not worth opening so Jem threw them back. Two had small seed pearls, like tiny shot pellets. There was one shaped like a minute acorn, a type they called a barrel pearl. They would all go in Sam's baccy tin to be sold in a job lot.

'I'm starving, Pa. Let's away home or I'll get a row.'

'Wait, it's here, I know it is. I dreamt it.' Sam forced open yet another misshapen shell with a hump on its back, fingering inside to see if there was anything hiding in the folds of flesh.

'There's nothing.' Jem was bored and his

14

stomach was rumbling as he ferreted into the old shell he had brought out last, but then feeling something he pulled out what looked like a large white marble. His father took one look, crossing himself with a whistle. 'Praise be. Have you ever seen anything like that in all yer born days?'

Jem held the pearl in his palm. His heart was racing. Even he knew this was special, bigger than anything they'd ever found before. It was a perfect sphere and in the sunlight all the colours of the rainbow glinted from its smooth surface. 'Wait till Ma sees this.'

'No, you tell no one. This is our secret. You know she can blether with the other wifies and then they'll all be wanting to know where we found this gem of gems. You can fish all your life and never find such a beauty. It's worth a king's ransom, lad-die. I know it in ma bones and where there's one there'll be others. The Lord be praised for he told it to me in a dream. This wee darling will change our lives, sure she will.' Sam kissed the pearl.

Jem could see the excitement on his father's leathery face but he could also hear his breathless-ness and the rattling cough in his chest. Pa was getting too old for standing in rivers and lugging logs. If this pearl would buy them warm winter clothes, a horse and cart then it would be worth-while.

Yet as they trudged back through the path and the needles scrunched under his bare feet, Jem sensed the thrill of the search. All the disappoint-ment of finding empty shells was forgotten when you had such a miracle in your pouch. Did this mean their fortunes had changed for the better?

15

1

York, 1879

The dawn light peeped through the hole in the curtain. It was Saturday again, the best day of the week for Greta Costello as she rolled off the bed board, trying not to wake her sister Kitty. She'd slept in again, leaving no time for a lick and a promise in the wash bowl as she threw on her thin striped shirt and cotton skirt, wrapping her crocheted shawl across her chest and pinning her thick black plaits over her head. She crept down the steep wooden stairs in her stockinged feet. The boots would be waiting, polished, or her brother Tom wouldn't be getting any spice.

The tea was stewing on the embers of the banked-up fire but there was no time to linger. Mother was sleeping on the camp bed, she stirred as Greta lifted the latch of the door that opened straight out onto the darkened street. She hoped that Mr Abrahams had remembered to unlock his door.

Greta scurried up Walmgate to the house of the old watchmaker, who lived across the River Foss in Aldwark, trying not to shiver in the dawn air. It was creepy in the first light; prostrate figures lay snoring in the doorways, mangy dogs scavenged for scraps. At least the laundry had been delivered before his Sabbath; a clean shirt, underclothes neatly pressed and mended. Mother always took care with his washing, keeping it separate, thankful for work at the end of the week rather than Monday. Living alone now, he always received them as if they were the Crown jewels, nodding his head in gratitude.

Sometimes when she delivered them he was busy at his bench, curled over a watch repair with a candle lighting a globe of water acting as his magnifying mirror, looking up with tired lashless eyes and heavy lids. 'Ah, Margareta, is it that time already?'

She loved the special way he called her Margareta.

'Do you know it is the Greek word for a pearl,' he told her umpteen times.

Here she was thinking she'd been named after the Blessed Margaret Clitherow of York, pressed to death between doors for sheltering a Jesuit priest in the bad old days, or so her father had once told her. Margaret was her Sunday saint's name but Dad always called her little Greta and that's what she liked best. Today she was the Saturday girl who could escape the poor Irish quarter of the old city. Later she would make her way to Parliament Street, to the bustle of the market stalls where helping behind the scenes brought welcome treats for the family.

But first she must attend to Mr Abrahams as his gentile Sabbath girl who lit his lamps before sundown on Friday night, made up his fire and lit it again on Saturday morning, made sure all his 'Sunday best' was laid out while he slept and then topped up his special soup on the range to warm through. Mother had been happy to do this for a while but had been even happier to pass the task onto her eldest daughter when Greta turned fourteen.

Saul Abrahams belonged to another world, a world of book learning and foreign languages. He was of the Jewish race and spoke Yiddish with his friends. He was a widower, frail and tired, who worked all day in his workshop room full of ticking clocks, some chiming at different times, others sitting silent and dusty, waiting for his magic touch.

Greta lifted the latch and opened the door to Mr Abrahams's house. She revived his fire, making sure it was well stoked, and tidied round a little of the clutter. The house smelled of chalk, spirit, oil and polish. His bench was cluttered with eyeglasses, brushes and tools of all sizes. She liked to linger over his repairs, fingering the delicate files and instruments he used, examining a box of broken jewellery, bracelets and chains labelled for repair beside soldering irons and burner which she mustn't touch. She knew he would be doing no work today or any cooking until after sunset.

Satisfied that the first task of the day was finished she left the house.

It was time to rush to where the market stretched down the whole length of Parliament Street to help with the setting up of stalls. There was a blind basket maker who always needed a hand and some country butter makers who asked her to mind their babies while they set out their cheeses and butter pats. They knew she could be trusted behind the stalls. The vegetable growers also found her jobs: pulling off rotten cabbage leaves, unpacking boxes of fruit and putting the best specimens to the front of the stall.

If she was lucky there were mugs of tea and buns, or perhaps a hunk of Wensleydale cheese which she slipped into her apron pocket along with the few pennies she gleaned for helping out.

She avoided the drunks, who thought any lass fair game. Costellos might be dirt poor but Mother warned her not to give any men the eye or they might think they could take her down the back alley and mess with her private parts. Some of her school friends had already gone down that slippery slope so on Friday nights, when the men had their pay packets, they were out on the town with painted faces.

Greta knew she looked older than her years with her hair tied up. Her Irish colleen looks, with her tumble of black curls fizzing in the damp air and her bluebell-coloured eyes, often brought unwelcome attention. Nothing would make her go down such a seedy path. She had a nose for danger.

As she watched the young shoppers with their mamas, wearing their fine gowns, and sporting perky hats from the smart millinery shops, it was hard not be envious. They didn't have to rise at the crack of dawn or spend the week with hands doused in scrubbing soap.

The preacher at the Mission Hall told them that everyone was equal in the sight of the Lord, but not in York, they weren't. You knew your place just by your address. Living off Navigation Road, Walmgate, might be within the city walls but it was a rat-infested, warren of back courts and dilapidated houses, full of Irish immigrants who came after the terrible potato famine years ago. Brendan Costello had worked as a navvy, building railways in Yorkshire. He'd earned a decent wage and found an English wife. They'd been respectable, well shod and fed, living in clean rooms but his dying of the cholera fever changed everything. Now Greta's mother rented two flea-bitten rooms close to the wash house and the stand pipe so Mother could boil water in the copper and take in washing.

Two of Greta's brothers died as babies and now there was just Tom and Kitty to feed and keep clean. It was hard in those damp rooms but let no one say Mother didn't try her best to keep them as they once were. There had been no chance of Greta staying on at St Margaret's School when she was needed at home. Tom went out with the street boys collecting dog muck in pails to sell to the tanneries and he stunk to high heaven if they got in a silly fight. Even Kitty had to mind babies for a few pennies. That's how they survived to the weekend.

There were skivers like Nora Walsh who made her living reading palms and tea leaves, telling stuff and nonsense to wide-eyed biddies. Only the other day she'd plonked herself down at their table to cadge a mug of tea and a bit of a craic while Mother was trying to press shirts.

'What can you see?' Kitty asked, watching as the old woman swirled her mother's tea leaves round.

'Whish't ... I'm seeing. You'll no have far to find yer sorrows, Sadie, my girl.' Nora sighed.

'I don't need you to tell me that. A husband taken before his time, two bairns dead of the fever, a house full of damp and vermin.'

'Oh, it'll get better, in time, I promise. You'll find comfort. Look.'

Greta was curious to know more. 'Read mine, then.' Greta held out her cup. Nothing could be worse than the last years. Perhaps there'd be good news for her too.

'And me,' Kitty added, looking up from her chores.

'You're both too young for such capers,' Mother snapped. 'No tea leaves for them.'

'No, it's never too young to know your fate,' Nora replied, putting down the cup. 'Let me look at the big'uns hand. I'm good with palms.'

'I don't hold with tempting fate, putting ideas in her head. Leave her be.'

Greta stood up in a sulk. 'I never get any fun. My hand's as good as anyone else's or is it all a trick?'

'Oh, give the girl a go or there'll be no peace.'

Widow Walsh examined Greta's long fingers, looking up at the girl. Greta's face was pink with expectation. The widow opened her mouth as if to speak and then shook her head. 'I can't see nothing, dearie. It's all gone cloudy. Perhaps another day.'

Greta knew Nora had seen something from the way she had changed the subject before turning away.

'Am I going to die young, then?' Greta whispered, staring at her open palm.

'Of course not, look at that long lifeline and those fingers.'

'Then what can you see?'

'Nothing for you to be bothering about, just live out your span as it comes to you, but make good use of those long fingers. What's for you will no go past you, child, so don't be in such a hurry. Thanks for the cuppa, Sadie, I'll be away to my own midden.' With that Nora rose, leaving Greta and her mother staring at each other.

'That's what comes of meddling in things that are not our concern,' Mother said.

Greta was busy searching her palms, wondering whether Nora knew something she didn't or if it all was just blarney, when she felt a hand on her shoulder.

'Hurry up there, lass,' shouted a farmer's wife, pulling Greta back from her daydream. 'There's a customer waiting to collect her basket.'

'Sorry, what do you want me to do next?' The long day was dragging.

'Sweep and tidy up in the back, lift the crates on the cart. And sharp about it, girl, while it's quiet.'

By packing-up time, she was bursting to find the convenience in Silver Street and be free to wander round the ancient streets with coins jangling in her pocket. She was in no hurry to go home for bathtime in the zinc tub. They had to be scrubbed up for Sunday school and spotless no matter what it cost Mother in soap and elbow grease.

Greta took her usual zigzag route along the back streets to the heart of the old city. If you lived in York, you lived in many worlds, poor folk by the river, parsons by the Minster, soldiers in the barracks and shopkeepers open all hours. The walls of the city were like arms enclosing everyone and Greta loved going through the ancient city gates, shuddering at the thought of heads stuck on spikes for all to see in the olden days. There was the famous castle and parks to play in but it was the rows of higgledy-piggledy shops under the watchful eye of the Minster towers she was making for now; the shiny shops in Low Petergate and Stonegate full of beautiful hats, pictures, pretty pieces of furniture and, best of all, the shop windows full of sparkling jewels, ticking clocks, rings and necklaces.

Greta knew every one of those windows and how their displays changed from season to season. It was hard not to stare as the elegant ladies and gentlemen arrived in their carriages, gliding through the hallowed doorways, waited on by men in dark coats and starched white shirts. She was invisible to them in her short grey cloak and patched skirt, stained from a day's market work. She melted into the stone walls, letting them pass as she lingered by the windows, imagining what she would choose if she could have anything she wanted.

Dreaming cost nothing but sometimes she stared at a window display for so long that an assistant would wave at her to move on. 'You're blocking the view, girl.' There was one jewellery shop in Stonegate where she never stopped, ever since that time when the owner had taken her by the arm and said, 'Don't think I don't know your little game. Off with you before I call the police for loitering with intent.' Had he thought she was part of a gang sent out to spy on goods in the window when all she was doing was drinking in the pretty pearls and gold bracelets? Her face had flamed with embarrassment. She didn't choose to be poor.

If only I could be a part of this world, she sighed, imagining a magical world far from the squalor of Walmgate's back-to-back houses and noisy neighbours. Greta stared at her callused hands. Who would want hands like this? She recalled her daydream and wondered again what Widow Walsh had seen but had refused to tell her? Was there a better future waiting for her if only she could find it, a future where one day she would walk through those fine shop doors in furs and finery? The very thought of this made her ache with longing.

She wanted a house with a proper fireplace with plenty of coal to warm them through, a bedroom of her very own and somewhere soft to sit of an evening, a larder full of food. It was this longing that was like a grit inside her. All that glitters isn't gold, went the proverb she'd embroidered for the nuns. All that mattered was that Mother and the others were fed and strong enough to find work when the time came for them to leave school. She'd been taught that hard work and duty was its own reward, but there had to be more to life than that, some sparkle to lift your spirits out of these dung-covered streets. Beautiful objects that dazzled her eyes with colour and starlight, that's what she needed to brighten her life. How was she ever going to find those living off Navigation Road?

It shouldn't matter, but in her heart she knew it did. The Costellos, through no fault of their own, were poor, backstreet poor. Mother deserved more than what she'd suffered and it was up to Greta to make something happen. Staring into shop windows wouldn't alter anything. Perhaps, she thought, her future was in these hands of hers. Perhaps if she tried to better herself, these hands would open a path to a better life for all of them, if only she knew how.

2

Perthshire, 1879

On a bright July morning, Ebenezer Slinger was a young man on a mission to make his fortune securing the finest of Scottish pearls. *Search and ye shall find, knock and it shall be opened up to you* was his mantra. There was a spring in his step as he stepped off the train north for he sensed in his very bones they were here for his taking.

Two days later he was having a bad day. Nothing had gone to plan and he hadn't made one decent purchase yet, just a few misshapes suitable for brooches and some dull sleepy pearls fit only for backing up cameos and mourning jewellery. Ebenezer's sandy complexion did not suit the heat from sun on water. His face was covered in freckles and his moustache itched over burnt lips. It was too hot to be tramping along the River Tay in his thick tweed overcoat so he sat soaking his blistered feet in the cool river shallows, smarting at his lack of luck. He'd left his London shop suit in the lodging house in Perth in favour of britches and a large straw hat that helped him mingle in the pearling camps without attracting much attention.

He could pass himself off as a surveyor on the railway taking a well-earned break in the hills. His coat he wouldn't part with so he rolled it up to use as a pillow to rest under a tree but if the weather changed it kept out the harsh easterly wind.

Ever since the pearl fever of the 1860s, many of the Scottish rivers were being fished out of mussels. He saw banks of broken shells piled up on the shingle that told their own tale of reckless fishermen gouging out the estuary beds in search of a quick sale. He cursed the Edinburgh dealer Moritz Unger who'd picked up gems cheaply but then disappeared, bankrupt and owing thousands. Now everyone was wary of pearl dealers and demanded top prices in advance. It was better for the moment to disguise his intentions.

The season was short in the summer and he recognized other pearl dealers tramping round the traveller camps for a quick exchange of cash for pearls. Farm boys and town lads with tents were lining the inland rivers hoping to make a fortune on their weekend jaunts.

Eben was not downhearted. He was one of the best in the business. There was not a pearl of note that passed him by. He had learned his calling the hard way during a London apprenticeship, examining, selecting, grading pearls to be drilled through and strung into the finest of necklaces. He'd endured years of hard slog, constantly at the beck and call of a tyrant jeweller, but now he was ready to strike out on his own. He needed stock, quality stock, but more than that he needed a clutch of priceless pearls to warm his heart and set him up in business. So far these precious gems were illusive.

He sat dangling his feet in the clear water, recalling his earliest memories of clutching at his mother's string of pearls. He had fallen in love with their lustre and subtle hues. They reminded him of her before she died, leaving him to the mercy of those two cold aunts. No mention was ever made of his father who'd abandoned them before Eben was born. The only thing he had bequeathed him was his second name, Alfred.

As a boy he'd loved to read the legend of how the pearl oyster rose to the surface of the sea once a year to catch a drop of moon dew. His head told him this was unscientific nonsense but in his heart he wished it could be true. Out of such an ugly casing came the gift of a teardrop from the gods. In his eyes, the pearl was the queen of gems, which reminded him of his mother, and from those earliest years had grown his desire to know more about their history.

Eben could repair a timepiece, solder gold links. He could assess a fine Ceylon sapphire, a Burmese ruby or a well-cut African diamond but there was only one gem that lifted his spirits. Now he was back in his old hunting ground ready for the chase.

He smiled, knowing in the deep recesses of his old coat lay a nest of pearls in a chamois leather pouch that no pickpocket would ever reach without having his throat cut.

It never paid to look prosperous. Scots were a suspicious lot and his Sassenach accent raised suspicion. He was still young enough to look like any other office boy off to chance his luck in the fast-flowing rivers of Perthshire. It was his intention to take lodgings not just for the season but to stay on and wander around the farmsteads in the winter months when trade would be easier to come by. Housewives needed shoes and tweeds, coats for their offspring, he reckoned. Selling a few good pearls was an easy way to augment the family coffers. That was the time to get a bargain.

He consoled his conscience with the thought that he was only doing what others in the trade were doing. He was what they called canny. He struck a hard bargain but his prices were fair enough, though woe betide any fool who tried to foist fakes on him: alabaster beads covered in salmon skin paste. He recognised the dull shadings of a 'sleepy' pearl fit only for background decoration or ground up for medicines in the Orient to treat yellow eye and snake bites. He could also spot the real thing so it wasn't his fault if the seller had no idea of the value of what he held in his hand or if the pearls had been mishandled. Ignorance was no excuse in his trade. Ignorance was stupidity. If someone spent all day fishing these river mussels and gave them no respect, then he didn't enlighten them.

How could anyone treat a precious pearl with careless abandon, scratching the surface, squashing them together in a tin? He had heard one of the greatest pearls ever to see daylight was ruined because it was baked for a meal and only found when eaten. How Eben yearned to find a rarity so fine all the world would come to his door; kings, maharajahs, empresses, all coming to be in its presence and buy from his emporium.

He'd learned early that no jewel could bring warmth to a cold heart and an unloving embrace, that no pearl ever cured his mother's madness or stopped his father from deserting them. Yet in the calm beauty of a fine pearl there was cheer and the opportunity to become rich and respected in the trade. Now the search for such treasures was taking over his life.

In his mind, pearls were symbols of love and perfection, purity and wisdom. Even the Bible said the same thing and he'd read that those who were born in the pearl month of June were the luckiest in life. He sighed, hoping this was true as it was also the month of his birth. Suddenly he jerked his attention back to the riverbank. Sitting daydreaming wouldn't make his fortune so he dried his swollen feet, gathered his knapsack and coat and headed onwards to find the nearest inn. He smiled, knowing that thirsty campers full of strong ale were always in need of silver and not too fussy about the price they got for their day's pearl fishing.

3

As the summer faded into golden-leafed autumn, Sam Baillie's cough grew worse and no amount of Jeannie's hedge doctoring could shift the phlegm or the shivers. Jem feared for his father. They had told no one of their rich find and Sam, like a man possessed, returned again and again to the same spot just in case there was another gem to be found but his hoard yielded just a few button-sized pearls, nothing to compare with the dream pearl Jem had found all those weeks ago. The winds blew over the river, swirling up the silt and making it run brown with mud. Sam took to his bed and Jem was afraid his father would not see another summer.

The laird's guns were out in the bracken and Jem skipped school to help out, much to the school master's dismay. He knocked on the door demanding an explanation. 'Young James should be at his desk not tramping the forest. I had him for college in Dundee or Edinburgh. He would then see you in comfort, Mistress Baillie.'

'I'll see what I can do,' Jean promised in a whisper knowing full well that Sam would not last the winter and there'd be precious little to be spending on books and education. She covered her husband tenderly but it brought him no comfort from the shivering.

'Send for the doctor,' Jem ordered.

'He'll no come out this far to see him. We'll take him into town.' But both of them knew Sam was too ill to travel in a cart.

When his mother left the room, Jem sat by the narrow bed and whispered to his father. 'It's time to sell yon pearl. We have to buy you medicines. Then next summer you'll be back by the river and I'll do the fishing for you.'

'I've done my last fishing, son. It's enough to have found such a queen of the river. All yer life you can tramp and never have a moment like ours.' Sam smiled up at his son's worried face, his eyes glassy with fever.

'I'm for the next journey to Tir Na Og, the land far away. You must take care of Queenie, she'll be yours when I'm a goner.'

'Don't talk like that.' Jem tried to protest but he could see his father fading away before his eyes.

'Look after yer mother and see her right. Then go and see the world for yourself, go travel and find Queenie some mates. You're the lucky one, Jem. This is yours by right, you found her and she will bring you good fortune.'

'Ach, away with you! What good is it sitting in the pouch when she can buy medicines and cures.'

'Too late for all that, as you know fine. I want you to have an eddicashun so no one will cheat you. There's a few more good pearls in ma box. Promise me to get yerself some learning, you never know when it will serve you well.'

'What's he blethering about now, Jemmy?' His mother was now hovering in earshot.

'He's away with the faeries. His fever's up and I'm afeard for him.'

That night Jem and his mother took turns to sit with Sam, covering him with plaids and blankets, anything to sweat out the fever, giving him sips of feverfew tea which he spat out for its bitterness. His mother felt Pa's feet and legs. They were cold as ice and she shook her head. Jem sat by his side into the wee small hours, his eyes heavy, until he woke in the dawn and his father's hand was cold. His mother was weeping.

'It's just the two of us now,' she cried. 'How will we get by?'

Jem sat holding her hand, knowing he must see

to his mother. 'There's some pearls in the chest. We'll get by. I can work on the estate, lopping branches, barking logs and building up the banks for the log rolling. We won't starve.'

'But what about yer schooling?'

'That's over and done with.' He sighed with relief that he could take over his father's work but there was a sadness too. His chance to travel and see far off places was gone now. He would have to wait and see his mother safe and warm. When she left the room he searched in the wooden press for the little tin of pearls but it wasn't there. His father must have put them in his old wooden travelling box with the lock. All he found in his pa's jacket were a few coins and a clay pipe. He touched the pipe, knowing it would never glow by the camp firelight again, and wept for the loss of such a good man. The heaviness of grief covered him like a blanket. Jem sobbed, knowing that at sixteen he was now man of the house.

4

York, 1879

One afternoon, Sadie Costello found a pair of Mr Abrahams's socks lost down the side of the copper boiler in the outhouse. 'Be a love, Greta, and see that he gets these, I've darned the hole in the heel. Check on him for me. I don't think the old gent is looking after himself in this cold weather.'

Greta needed no excuse to visit, curious to see him at his daily work. There was something about that workroom full of clocks and instruments that fascinated her. It was a wet day in late October and through the dusty window she could see the old man bent over the bench, his wispy hair tucked under his black skull cap. She tapped the glass and waved.

'Margareta, my dear, what brings you out on a cold day? Come in, come in,' he said in a breathless voice, beckoning her through the door.

The house was chilled and there was no fire in the grate, as Mother had feared. Greta produced the missing stockings, hand knitted in the finest wool, showing him the darning.

'I must pay your mother for her kindness.'

'No, no,' she repeated Mother's words. 'This is too fine to lose.'

'Adah, my wife, could knit as fine as a spider's web.' He sighed. 'She had such fingers for the needle. I miss her so. Would you like to see her lace work? Come, see in the living room. I have some things of hers about me for comfort.'

The old man showed Greta through to the little parlour which was crammed with heavy draperies and tall dark furniture. It smelt of tobacco and neglect and the dust made Greta sneeze. On the chair backs were lace cloths, yellowed with age. There was a photograph of a woman with a little boy in a tarnished silver frame.

'Ah, Benjamin.' Mr Abrahams shrugged his shoulders at the picture. 'He went to America on a ship. We never heard from him again. It broke his mother's heart. Adah was my helpmeet and my hand worker.' He sighed. 'She could string pearls, sort and grade stones with those long fingers of hers and had that special eye for quality, better than any apprentice. Now my fingers are stiff for such work.' The dust caught his chest and he coughed.

'Can I make you a drink while I am here?' Greta offered, not wanting to leave him in the damp chill. When he accepted she went through to the back room. The range was almost out so she banked it up high and put on the kettle. 'You sit down, sir.'

'I haven't time to be ill. I have a box full of repairs. It's the season for balls in the Assembly Rooms and everyone wants their finery on show. Why they leave it all to the last minute I'll never know, but business is business and Sol Landesmann is a good friend who sends work my way. I don't want to let him down.'

Soon the fire was rising. Mr Abrahams had a tap inside his scullery. She wished they had the same. 'You could do with some help, sir,' she offered, seeing the clutter and stale plates. 'We should wash your lace work.'

'No, no, leave things as they are,' he replied. 'But I see you have long fingers just like my wife. I wonder...' He paused. 'Would you be willing to learn to string beads of jet or stones? It's skilled work, you need a good eye and steady hands. I could do with some help and one day you could be a pearl stringer. I can't pay you much.' He looked down at his own swollen hands. 'Look at these clumsy stubs, how they shake and my thumbs go stiff ... old age is not for cowards, my dear, and it comes not alone, they say.' He coughed again.

'You must have some of my mother's elder-berry cordial. It's good for a chesty cough. I'll bring some next time.'

Greta heard the kettle rattling on the hob. She knew to give him tea with no milk. She saw how his hands shook when she passed over the chipped cup. 'I'd like to learn something but I have to ask my mother first.'

'She's a good woman. If you come to help here, I will pay extra for my laundry. What I can teach you might help you when I'm gone. It would certainly lighten my load but I understand if you don't think it is proper for a young girl.'

'Oh, it's not that, I'd like to come and help.'

'Your mother would not object to working for a Jew? You are Catholics.'

'Not exactly,' she replied blushing, knowing they were neither one thing nor another. 'My father was Irish born but Mother makes us go to the Mission Hall. They helped us when he died. I have a brother and sister to mind so I'll have to ask her permission.'

'You do right to respect your mother's wishes. If only Benny had done the same ... but there is no pain on earth like a thoughtless child. I will write a letter to your mother so that she knows the terms, Margareta.'

Mr Abrahams sat with his tea, nodding his head and smiling while Greta busied herself with chores. How strange that in the space of one wet afternoon she was beginning a strange apprent-iceship, all on account of a pair of lost socks. Now why didn't Nora Walsh see all this in her palm?

35

In the following weeks, Greta began her training in old Abrahams's workshop, first tidying his bench then watching how he cleaned and oiled each piece of a watch, standing back while he soldered on broken links and fixed loose clasps on bracelets and chains. In her spare moments she made sure his rooms were clean. She aired the dusty furniture and checked there was food in his cupboard.

One morning he sat her down with a box of beads and a tray, showing her how to sort its contents by size and shape and how to use a tiny needle to string the beads together with waxen thread.

'Always the best in the centre, the finest you have.' He showed her some Whitby jet beads. 'These stones came from the Yorkshire coast. Since our queen has been in mourning, everyone wants a brooch or a ring in black stones.' Then he demonstrated how slack strings would weaken the thread and catch on things. He was so busy with watches, cleaning, oiling, that it gave her time to practise all he was teaching her, sometimes scattering parts on the floor when her mind wasn't on the job. It was not as easy as it looked.

The jeweller who supplied Mr Abrahams with repairs looked in one lunchtime, surprised to see a girl by his side. 'What's this, Saul, and a *goy* too. Apprenticeships are for boys...'

'This is Margareta, my eyes and hands. She's going to make a good stringer. Her family have been very kind,' he replied, knowing she was listening. Greta could see Landesmann was not impressed, looking down at her threadbare dress and soiled apron with a sniff.

'Be careful or she might rob you blind,' he muttered in Yiddish. She needed no translation to sense what he was saying. She edged back out of the room.

'Take no notice of that old skinflint,' Abrahams said when the man had left. 'If I didn't need his work... Some people see only evil in this world, never the good in folk.' He could see that Greta was close to tears, embarrassed.

'By the way, I hope you won't be offended at this suggestion but I have some of Adah's garments, dresses and stuff, in a trunk. They will be turning to dust if I don't part with them soon. Do you think your mother might like to make something of them? The materials are good. She had a good eye for quality in everything.' He sighed. 'Please help yourself. Adah would love to know they were put to good use so, please, go, see upstairs.'

Greta climbed the steep stairs to the bedroom above the workshop. There were several large cupboards and a trunk which she opened, sneezing from the pungent stench of camphor balls in her nostrils. The box was crammed with clothes: woollen dresses, a cloak, black skirts and light cotton shirts, a silk two-piece, hand sewn and old fashioned, but she knew all of this could be transformed. Her heart leapt at such a wealth of choices. There would be clothes for all seasons for Kitty, for all of them. She clambered downstairs. 'Are you sure? There's a stall in the market that sells...'

The old man threw his hands up in horror. 'No!

Adah's clothes are not to be fought over by dealers. I just thought ... but if they are not suitable...'

'Please, sir, they are a gift to be treasured. You have no idea how welcome they'll be to us. You are too kind.' Greta's tears rolled down her cheeks. She had not wished him to think her ungrateful.

'Say no more then. It's a relief. I would hate to see vultures picking over our home when I am gone. Better to let things go now and have the pleasure of giving you warmth in these cold winters. Off you go. Tomorrow you will learn about pearls.'

5

Greta struggled home with a pillowcase full of Adah's cast offs. It felt like Christmas in the old days when there was money from the railways, meat on the table and little gifts for each of them. Working in the same old shirt and shabby skirt, shawl and bonnet day after day made her long for something smarter, something more suitable for an apprentice. She wanted a dark dress with a proper collar and a warm winter cloak like the girls who worked in the factories or shops. How could you work with pearls if you looked like a pig swiller?

'Kitty! Look what I've been given,' she shouted into the living room, spilling the garments onto the floor. 'What do you think?'

Kitty came rushing down the stair to see what Greta had brought. Seeing the pile of clothes she started ferreting through them, then jumped back putting her fingers over her nose. 'This is all old-fashioned stuff and it smells of mothballs.'

'Don't you be so ungrateful. Think what Mam can do with these.' Greta gathered the clothes up one by one, measuring the yards of useful material. 'Beggars can't be choosers and these will keep us warm all winter. There's tweed and wool and good cambric and crêpe.'

'Bagsy I have the cloak then.' Kitty grabbed the plaid waist-length cloak.

'No, I need that and it's too big for you.'

'There you go, you allus get first pickings.' Kitty threw it back at her in a strop.

'Cos I'm a working girl now,' Greta argued. 'When it's your turn...'

'I'll just get your shabby leftovers.' Kitty rooted through the dresses sniffing. 'I'm having this then. One day I'm going to wear the finest silks and satins, just you wait.'

'Wait and see what Mam says, she's the best sewer.' Greta wasn't going to let Kitty maul her bounty any more. She could be such a sulky little cow when thwarted.

Sadie came home tired after her laundry round, but her eyes lit up at the sight of Greta's unexpected present. 'Where did this lot come from?'

Greta told her about Adah's wardrobe stuffed with clothes.

'He can't bear to part with them and yet he gave you all these? I don't like the sound of that. What will folk think?'

'Why should they know once they are altered? We can help you do it. I want to wear summat decent for work.'

'I'm not sure.' Her mother hesitated. 'I was going to tell you that Ma Bellerby at the Goat and Feathers needs you to look after her bairns full time. You're so good with little ones.'

Greta looked up in honor. 'You can't make me go to that awful gin palace. She's that rough and there's always fighting. I like it with Mr Abrahams. He's promised to teach me threading and that's a respectable trade.'

'It's not proper you staying there all hours. I don't want you getting a bad name and wearing a dead woman's fancy dresses.'

'But, Mam, he's old and tired and this was a gift. He didn't want to sell her clothes. We can't afford to refuse, can we? How can I take all this and then up sticks and leave him?' Greta prayed her mother would see the sense of her pleading.

Greta and her mother worked by lamplight into the small hours, unpicking, ironing out the fabric, cutting a pattern then pinning the pieces into place until they'd fashioned one neat green skirt. Mam was careful to make sure the pieces of fabric that were shiny or faded were used in a side pocket where it would not be noticeable. She also turned the fabric inside out so the texture was brighter. Kitty sulked all evening. 'I'd look better in that than our Greta. My red hair shows the green off. She looks too plain.'

'Shut up and go to bed if you've nothing better to say,' Greta snapped knowing Kitty was indeed the prettier of the two of them. 'You'll get your turn.'

'I never get anything new. It's not fair.'

'Life's not fair, young lady, or why would we be stuck in this midden of a back yard?'

Mother's words silenced Kitty but Greta couldn't wait for first light to show off her new skirt to her employer. Over the next few weeks they could make her a whole working wardrobe of clothes but the skirt would do for now. Perhaps one day she could work anywhere in this neat ensemble, even among the pearls shops of Stonegate. To think she would be working with pearls. They were round like little moons, creamy as milk teeth. She couldn't wait to touch them.

'Now, young lady, show me your hands,' Abrahams ordered the next day. 'How rough they are from all that washing but they'll do. Oily hands are no good for my pearl repairs.' He lifted a clutch of pearls out of velvet cloth. 'Each one of these is a gift of nature, the tears of the gods. Good pearls are cold to the touch, here feel for yourself.'

Greta felt the cool round texture in her palm. 'Where do they come from?'

'They are from inside the shell of an oyster or mussel. When a bit of grit gets under its shell the oyster coats it with layer after layer of nacre, or mother-of-pearl. She grows the pearl like a baby in the womb. You could open a thousand shells and never find anything better than these.' He pointed to the pearls in Greta's cupped hand.

'But we sell mussels and oysters on the market to eat?' Greta was puzzled.

'Pearls in this country come from special mussels, *Margarita margaritifera,* they grow in freshwater riverbeds and in estuaries. All over the world there are different molluscs producing pearls in all the colours of the rainbow and most come out of the deep seas of the Orient. Divers swim down to collect them.'

He brought out a necklace for her to hold under the light. 'This necklace is weak and needs to be restrung and the clasp needs tightening. You must watch and work with other beads before I can let you loose on such a precious item but perhaps one day... It's delicate work for tired eyes but it must be done.'

Greta watched how he shed the pearls onto a tray, one by one in order of size, with such a tenderness of touch. 'We must not damage the pearl or bruise its surface.' He took off his glasses and smiled. 'I always think, without the grit there would be no pearl. Sorrows have a way of strengthening the heart, never forget that, child.'

She was concentrating on sorrows of her own as she polished the beads, ready to practise her own knotting. She tried not to think of her mother's threat about working for old Ma Bellerby instead of Mr Abrahams. How could she tell him this news when she was enjoying this so much? 'Mr Abrahams,' she blurted out, 'if I could come every day how long would it take to be trained up?'

He looked up, seeing the worry on her face. 'What's the trouble?'

She spilled out all her mother's words and the threat hanging over her. 'I don't want to spend my day scrubbing and cleaning. I want to do something like this, skilled work, a proper trade, but Mother thinks it's not proper ... for a girl like me.'

He peered over his steel-rimmed spectacles at her. 'Then we'll have to find a way for you to stay here. I will speak with your mother and explain. She has obviously misunderstood my intentions. Perhaps along with your little sister you could come and keep house here, live-in like a proper apprentice, and in the evenings we will conquer the art of pearl stringing. If I can make a good stringer out of you, you will never be out of work, believe me.'

Greta sank back in relief. This was perhaps as close as she'd ever get to the shops in Stonegate with their beautiful jewellery and shining gems, but to work with these delicate objects was wonderful. To touch the gold and the pearls made her forget the mud and chill bleakness of the Walmgate streets, transporting her into another life. Perhaps her hands were her fortune after all.

6

Perth, 1879

It was the week before Christmas when Eben Slinger made his last tramp round the villages, knocking on doors, showing them his card which read:

Ebenezer Slinger, Esq. of London

DEALER IN FINE PEARLS
AND OBJETS D'ART
Good prices given for the genuine article

No one was willing to open their latch to him in Glencorrin except when he came to a small lime-washed cottage at the end of a lane, set back from the road, little more than a but and ben. It looked faded and the garden ill kempt. He'd asked at the post office about the families who lived locally and the cheery wifie had told him that the woman down the lane had been recently bereaved. Her son was in the forest working for the laird. Their name was Baillie, which he'd recognized as a travelling family name. She'd told him they were keen pearl fishermen. Eben was well rehearsed by the time he reached the door. It was opened by a grey-haired widow in black with a white cap on her head.

'Mistress Baillie, I am sorry to interrupt your daily work but I wondered if I might have a word concerning your late husband.'

'Oh aye?' Her eyes were sharp but glassy.

'It has come to my notice that he was a keen fisherman, famed in the district for his collection of river pearls.'

'So what if he was? It's no any of yer business, young man.' She made to shut the door.

Eben held out his card. 'Madam, don't be alarmed. I am aware of many charlatans parading themselves as pearl dealers of repute but here are my references. I collect only the best and I give a good price for decent-sized gems. As you will see, here is a letter from the Laird of Kinloch himself recommending my services.' He thrust the letter under her nose trusting that her ability to read without spectacles was non-existent, if she could read at all. She glanced briefly at it, unsure now, and the door stayed ajar.

'I know, what with winters being harsh in these parts and the festive season upon us again, that many folk like a little extra siller to make ample provisions for Ne'r Day.' He tried to use the local dialect to reassure his customers.

'Aye, it comes gey pricey but it's my son who deals with all that. You'll have to speak to him.'

'Sadly I must leave for London to see my family. Today is my last day,' he lied, making to leave.

'Ach, come away in and I'll see what I can find. There's no much left now to my knowledge.' She left him standing in the kitchen next to the open hearth with its reek of peat smoke, the iron pot was simmering over the fire. There was a box bed cut into the wall and a shelf over the chimney. He had seen many such humble dwellings on his travels in the north but Scots were canny with their money, didn't splash out on fancy decorations.

'I cannae find much.' She was rooting in a wooden box. 'Just these wee things in the baccy tin.' They were the usual modest seed pearls he'd seen all season.

'Hmm,' he sighed, disappointed. 'I've got my fair share of these. I was looking for something bigger. Perhaps there's others down at the bottom?' He watched her pulling out smaller bags.

'I've not been in this kist since my poor husband passed away. You should ask Jemmy but he

45

works in the forest at the logging. I don't like to pry but you can see...'

'What's in there?' Eben's eyes latched onto a smooth leather pouch with a drawstring. 'Can you just have a peep in there?'

The widow opened the leather pouch and spilled out what looked like a white marble. Eben felt his heart racing at what he was seeing. His mouth went dry with excitement but he forced himself to stay calm.

'I think this is quite a nice one, Mistress Baillie. It would make a fine drop for a necklace. Can I hold it?'

He lifted it with tenderness and pulled out his tiny weighing scales. Almost the size of a paragon, a gem above all others, it weighed over 80 grams by the look of it, perfect in its roundness and shape, no surface blemishes. The lustre of it flickered in the firelight.

'I can offer you twenty guineas for this specimen,' he whispered, knowing such a sum was a year's wage for some in this district. He smiled. 'It's brightened my day to see such beauty. Where did your husband fish it out?'

'I dinnae ken, sir, pearls are no my concern but Jemmy will know it fine.'

'Unfortunately my train leaves this afternoon, mistress. I could stretch to twenty-five, if that would help things along.' He could see her hovering over the enormity of his offer, temptation fighting with caution. He rose to leave.

'Oh there you go.' She placed the pearl into his sweating palm. 'There'll be plenty more where that came from.' She sighed. 'A bird in the hand is worth more... Goodness knows we need the siller enough.'

'Precisely.' He smiled, holding his breath as he counted out twenty-five gold sovereigns from his inside pocket, placing each one into her hand. 'You'll have a fine Hogmanay with this,' he said with relief. There was nothing like the feel of gold in the palm to close a sale.

'Och, no, this is to give Jem his education like my Sam would want. He will be mighty pleased I found this.'

Eben swallowed the guilt, knowing what value this superb specimen might reach on the open market. 'That's very noble, Mistress Baillie. I wish you good day and the season's felicitations...'

She nodded, waving him from the door, no doubt bursting until her son returned home to tell him her good news. Eben walked away quickly through the village to the station halt clutching his prize close to his heart. This was the answer to all his prayers, with such a precious find his future would be secure. How close he'd come to missing such a bargain but his persistence had paid off. Now he must get south of the border and decide what to do next.

'You did what!' Jem screamed at his mother's news. 'You let a stranger into our house and sold him Pa's pearl? How could you be such a fool? How much did he give you for it?' Jem was shaking with fury, wiping the pleasure off his mother's face as she showed him the coins.

'I did it for you for your learning, so you could go to teaching college. It's what yer pa would want.' She threw the sovereigns on the table. 'I've bitten into them all. Twenty-five of these is better than yon bead in a bag,' she argued. 'I never knew it was there afore now. How was I tae know it was a good one when no one tells me?'

'A good one, a bead...' Jem spluttered, his face red with despair. 'Do you realize you sold some dealer the best thing that ever came out of this river; a queen among pearls, the very last thing my Pa fished out. He'd dreamt about it and you gave it away!'

Jem was beside himself, knowing it was worth much more than twenty-five guineas, at least fifty, a hundred maybe. Why oh why had he not taken it into the jeweller in Perth for a valuation? He cursed his idleness and guilt at not warning his mother of its true value. He would have to chase after the dealer and demand it back. He could go to the law and claim she was duped. 'What was his name, this pearl buyer?'

'I dinnae catch it, son. He showed me his card. He was a Sassenach from London, he said. He showed me a letter from a laird but without my spectacles... I'm sorry. You should have told me, son, not kept it all a secret.'

'What did he look like?' Jem was determined to glean every detail.

'Tall, thin, sandy haired with gingery whiskers, older than you. Not flashy and spoke like the laird. He looked like a gamekeeper but he's off hame now for Christmas.'

'Oh, Ma what have you done? There'll never be another Queenie,' he cried, pacing the floor with frustration.

'I'm sorry. How was I tae know if nobody told me?'

Jem softened his voice. 'It's not right to be cheated like this. I have to find out who he is. It was Pa's gift to me, my inheritance, and I was saving it for...' He paused. How could he tell her it was his future travels? 'And you gave it away for nothing, like Esau in the Bible story.'

'We have this siller, be thankful. It'll help you get trained. That'll do for me.'

'But not for me, can't you see? I don't want to be a teacher or a forester all my life. I have to find that wily scoundrel and get Queenie back. She belongs here by the river.'

'Now you talk nonsense. It's just a bead, a pretty bead, not a thing with a name.'

'No, no, you're wrong. Queenie was a living thing to Pa, a gift of nature to us. She was born out of a humble mussel, nurtured for years to get to that size and shape. There are some things money can't buy.'

'Oh, aye, and how do we feed and clothe ourselves? With thin air? Don't think I don't fancy a new bonnet or a new pair of boots, warm blankets of a night and plenty of food for our suppers. You can get mighty sick of oats and porridge, kale soup and scraps of mutton. We may not have much but I have my pride. If you go asking questions folk'll want to know our business. If you go blethering about how I sold too cheap, I'll be the talk of the district and how will I hold my head up in the kirk?'

'Is that all you think about?' Jem argued, sick at heart. 'What others think of us? No wonder Pa wanted to keep the pearl to ourselves for just the same reason. If people think you've come into luck, they would never be away from the door. I'll have to find that English man if it's the last thing I do. He's not to get away with this. On my pa's grave, I want my due.'

'Oh, son, don't go getting into trouble. It's only a pearl and it's not worth us having a row over it. Sit down and eat yer broth.'

'I'm not hungry,' he snapped, suddenly bone weary with disappointment. He sat down at the table, but in his heart he meant every word about finding the man who'd taken the pearl. Someday he would find Queenie and make things right, wherever it might lead him. Justice must be done. No man was going to steal his birthright.

Eben fought against the storm to catch the Perth Connector to Newport for the Dundee train to Edinburgh. He could hardly stand upright on the platform, huddled against the wind as the rain rippled along the track and the lanterns swayed. It was a slow creaking journey across the Tay Bridge, too dark to see much outside. It felt as if the very railway bridge beneath him was swaying and groaning. He thought of the raging torrent below and clutched his coat and his pearls to his chest. It was such a relief when the train reached the other side. It was almost New Year's Eve so he must do his business quickly in the city and move on south.

He sold most of his collection for a good sum but the big pearl, he couldn't part with. In London it would fetch a handsome price, enough to set himself up in premises. He didn't show it to anyone but kept it close to his heart in a pouch around his neck.

As he travelled through the Borders he began to wonder if it would be wiser to make his debut somewhere in the north country, in a prosperous industrial city perhaps. Leeds, Manchester or Liverpool were all well served by the jewellery trade.

But as the train drew close to the city of York, he noticed the Minster towers in the distance, those solid, grey stone bastions. It felt as if they were beckoning him. York, a historic city, its cobbled streets steeped in Roman history. Surely this was as good a place as any to set himself up?

He would rent premises. He'd visited once and knew that the streets near the Minster were cluttered with fine shops; the walls of the inner city enclosed gracious buildings.

No one knew him there. He still had some stock in store. He could do repairs, buy and sell silverware, but with his pearl of pearls he had collateral to take out a loan to acquire more precious gems. Suddenly a whole new future was opening out before him. He would follow his hunch as he had done in Perth. There would be rich pickings in this fertile city. He smiled, gathering his belongings and his great coat he let himself out onto the platform joining the bustle of passengers, hearing the newsvendors shouting in the station hall. 'Tay Bridge disaster! Read all about it, hundreds dead as train falls into the river...'

Eben grabbed a newspaper, his heart thumping as he read. *On Sunday 28 December, the evening mail train was derailed when the iron bridge collapsed in the storm.* He shivered with the thought that he was on that very bridge just before it collapsed into the River Tay. How close had he been to certain death? How lucky he was to have left when he did. Eben pulled his muffler firmly across his neck to protect him from the chill easterly wind. His hand touched the pearl tucked close to his heart, just to be sure. Was this beauty already changing his fortune by coming into his possession? Could it be true that some pearls brought good luck? Had it brought him to York to make his fortune?

7

York, 1880

As the weeks turned into months Greta learned how to work alongside the old jeweller. The threat of having to live there had receded. Kitty refused to leave home but promised to work harder at school. Mother got used to the idea of her daughter spending time alone in Mr Abrahams's house, repaying his lessons with chores. Sometimes Mrs Costello called in to see how Greta was getting on, bringing the old man some elderberry cordial. 'I don't like the look of you, Mr Abrahams. You should see a doctor,' she'd always say, noticing his face was grey and pinched, his lips mauve. Mr Abrahams shrugged his discomfort away. 'I'm fine, Mrs Costello, but busy, busy.'

Greta knew he was not, although he did have

some important repairs to do for private customers and the workbench was cluttered with watches to be reset and cleaned. One afternoon when the snow was frosting the pavements, Mr Abrahams stood up and, struggling to put on his coat, prepared to head out into the freezing streets to make a delivery to a customer. Greta could see he was in no state to go out into the cold.

'I'll take it for you. Tell me where to go,' she offered. Thanks to Mrs Abrahams's wardrobe, she had a thick dress, a warm long coat, a bonnet and good gloves.

'It's for a gentleman lawyer with offices in Lendal. Mr Blake's been a loyal customer of mine and this is overdue. I would hate him to think...' He sat back exhausted. 'This won't do. I would be grateful for your assistance.' He placed the gold watch he had mended in a chamois leather pouch. 'Do take care of it, my dear, put it in your apron pocket and don't linger, it's almost dark.' He sighed, shaking his head. 'I don't think you ought to be going so far.'

'I know where it is,' she replied, eager to please.

'Go round the back, of course, to the tradesman entrance and give my apologies. Hurry, Margareta. Please be careful for yourself.'

'I will, sir, I promise. It'll only take two shakes of a lamb's tail. I know all the back ways.'

'No! stay under the gas lamps. I really should go myself but this wretched chest is so tight.' He paused, looking out of the window. 'Perhaps it can wait until after the Sabbath.'

'Never put off what you can do today.' Greta smiled. 'You told me that, sir. I'll be back first

53

thing in the morning. You rest by the fire and promise me you will call on your doctor, or my mother will be round again with her awful mustard poultice for your chest.'

It was one of those frosty March days when lamps were lit mid-afternoon, shadows flickered on the busy street. Greta felt proud to be trusted with this errand. Working for Mr Abrahams had put good boots on her feet and brought them all winter clothes. She no longer felt like a street urchin. Each day she was learning more about stringing beads, how to tie a good knot and how to check for damage on any pearls.

She hesitated at the corner of Aldwark and, checking the lamps were lit, decided to take the familiar short cut that ran out onto the marketplace. She was halfway along the narrow lane when a shoulder jostled her, knocking her sideways. 'Mind where you're going!' she snapped.

'Hark at her, Maggie Costello. Been to see your fancy man then?'

A boy she didn't recognize pushed her. 'Jumped up little tart!'

'Let me pass,' she yelled, hoping someone would hear but she knew there were no passersby in the alleyway.

'A pretty lass like you should be selling your wares. Give us a bit of a taste then...'

'Gerrof me!' she yelled, kicking out. 'I know who you are,' she tried to bluff. 'Wait till my brother finds out, you're dead meat.'

'You and whose army? Got a tongue on her this one, Mickey. Let's have a feel...'

54

Greta was pinned against the wall roughly as the boy pulled her coat open to feel her breasts. She struggled as he pulled her skirt over her knees. Then his hand felt over her apron and he pulled out the pouch.

'So what have we here then?' He pulled out the gold watch with a laugh.

'Now here's turn up. This tart's no better than the rest of us, lifting stuff from that old Jew!' He was fingering the case. 'And gold too, takes one to know one, Mick.'

'Please give it back. It's not what you think. I am taking it back to the owner. Please, I'll be in so much trouble. It's not mine,' she cried.

They were too busy assessing the value of the timepiece to listen to Greta's pleas. 'We can say we found it in the street. Get a reward. Ta very much, slut...'

Suddenly her assailants vanished into the darkness leaving Greta frozen with horror at what had happened. Tears of fear and shame ran down her cheeks. She'd taken a short cut against instructions and now this, all for saving a bit of time. She'd been robbed. How could she face Mr Abrahams with such dreadful news? She had to do something. She made her tearful way to Silver Street to the police station to report the theft. She must explain what had happened. How could she repay her employer for this loss?

Greta was still shaking with fear as she mounted the steps of the station and pushed open the door. 'Please, I have to report a theft,' she cried, babbling about taking a short cut and being set upon by two boys. 'They stole my watch, not my watch but one belonging to Mr Abrahams... It belongs to Mr Blake of Lendal. I were just going to deliver it for him and then these lads—'

'Slow down, lass. Just whose watch is taken?'

She told them again about the repair and being sent to the lawyer's office.

'Aye, we know the lawyer Blake, and you say old Abrahams gave it to you? Sent you out on a dark night?'

'He's badly with his chest. He asked me.'

'Are you his maid?'

'No, I work for him, he's teaching me.'

'His apprentice, a slip of a girl like you?' The desk sergeant laughed. 'There's a good story.'

'Not exactly ... I do his cleaning and he's teaching me to string pearls.'

'So he sends you out with a gold watch at this time of night and now it's gone?'

Greta nodded. 'There were two of them, same age as me. They knew who I was, one of them called me Maggie Costello but I'm called Greta but Mr Abrahams calls me Margareta,' she tried to explain.

'Never mind your name, who was it who stole from you?'

'I don't know but one of them called the other Mickey. They pinned me against the wall and tried to do things,' she cried, blushing. 'He found the watch in my apron pocket. Mr Abrahams told me to keep it safe there and now it's gone.' She was crying so loud that other policeman gathered round.

'How do we know you aren't all in this together? That this isn't just a fall out among thieves, a pickpockets' spat over the spoils?' said another police-man.

Greta looked up at him in horror. 'But it wasn't like that. Mr Abrahams will tell you who I am. I live down Walmgate with my mother. I have never stealed in my life.'

'There's plenty down that end of town who have,' the tall policeman quipped. 'I shall have to make a report of all this and you can wait here until we get the truth of the matter. We'll speak to the Jew. Fancy sending a girl on such an errand, he ought to have had more sense.'

How could they be saying such things about her employer? 'But he's bad with his chest. What am I going to tell him? Mr Blake is one of his best customers.'

'You tell a good tale, lass, I grant you that but you'll go nowhere until this is sorted.'

'But the thieves, they will be still on the street. I could recognize them for you.'

'So you say, so you say, girl. Let's wait and see. Meanwhile, you will come and sit quietly in a cell, private and away from more trouble.'

Greta found herself sitting alone and shivering in a bare cubicle with tiled walls. 'My mother will be worried if I'm late. Sir, I don't tell fibs. I go to the Mission Hall. The pastor will speak for me. I'm a good girl and I can read and write. I have a job to go to, why would I steal from a kind man like Saul Abrahams?' She burst into more floods of tears, wiping her nose on her sleeve.

'Then you've nothing to fear from the truth, have you, lass?' said the policeman without sym-pathy before shutting the door and walking away.

It seemed like hours sitting on that bench, with the smell of carbolic and privy in her nose, listening to the clanging of locked doors, the shouts of drunks screaming curses. It would be really dark now and Greta knew her mother and Mr Abrahams would both be worried. She tried to distract herself by recalling every detail over and over. No one called her Maggie in the street, only at school in the playground. Those lads knew her, two boys, one called Mickey – but every other Irish boy had that name. If only it hadn't been so dark. She remembered the feel of those rough hands on her chest, the knee pressing into her groin. How dare they think her a street girl? She felt such shame.

Then the cell door opened and the constable with the ginger moustache gave her a look. 'You'd better come out now.'

'Have you found it? Did you catch them as did it? Did Mr Abrahams tell you he sent me?'

'Just come outside.' She walked down the passage relieved that the nightmare was over but then she saw her mother wrapped in her plaid shawl looking worried and puzzled.

'What's going on?' Greta asked.

They were both escorted into a wood-panelled office where a tall man in a black frock coat was standing by the fireplace.

'This is the lassie, Mr Blake, the girl that took the watch. Mr Blake has verified that it was given to Mr Abrahams for repair, a valuable gold timepiece belonging to his wife's grandfather.'

'I'm so sorry,' Greta croaked shaking. 'It was all my fault. I took a short cut to save my legs. Mr Abrahams was too sick to go out in the cold.' She turned to the police officer. 'Has Mr Abrahams told you the truth?'

'You can sit down there.' She was given a chair opposite a huge desk. 'Yes, we went to the house of the jeweller, knocked on his door. There was no reply so the officer went round the back and found the old man asleep in his chair.' He paused. 'In the sleep that has no waking. He's dead, peaceful but quite dead.'

Greta howled at the thought of him dying alone. 'I shouldn't have left him. I told him to fetch the doctor. I should have done it myself. Your watch could have waited, sir.' She flashed an angry look at the tall man with the whiskers down the sides of his cheeks. He had the decency to nod.

'Your concern does you proud, girl, but it alters nothing. There's no one to vouch for you.' The officer was unmoved by her sobbing.

'The girl is distressed. Let her home and I will vouch for her honesty. Take her home,' Mr Blake said to Greta's mother. 'I'm sure the watch will turn up somewhere in the city.' He spoke with authority.

'Sir, there's a report to be filled in first and she must come here every day until the matter is sorted one way or another.'

In the blur of signing papers and stiff lectures, Greta heard nothing. All she could think about was poor Mr Abrahams. They must inform his friend Landesmann and his lawyer friend, Mr Barnett. He should not be left alone all night.

'Who will see to his laying out?' Sadie Costello asked Mr Blake as she guided her daughter out of the door.

'It will be dealt with, Ma'am, by his own people. Just take your girl home. She's had enough of a shock tonight,' the lawyer replied.

Greta walked home in silence, sick at heart. Her employer, that dear old man, was dead, she had no work and she was in trouble with the police. All her dreams were shattered. It would mean she'd have to go back to skivvying, and all because she'd taken a short cut. There would be no more chances now that the old man was gone. How she would miss her daily trips to his home. She recalled one morning when she'd struggled to knot tightly enough and had had to keep starting over and over again, until she'd thrown down the necklace in frustration.

'My dear Margareta, patience, your mistakes are pearls to be cherished...'

Who would ever call her Margareta again? What pearls of wisdom were there to be learned from taking a short cut through a snicket at dusk? She sighed. How she'd shamed and embarrassed her mother and set a bad example for Kitty and Tom. Sick and weary, she clung onto her mother for dear life as they walked home in silence.

8

It was a bright spring morning and Eben Slinger peered out of his Pearl Emporium in Stonegate with a satisfied smile and smoothing of his whiskers. He still couldn't believe his luck in finding this shop right in the heart of the cobbled Minster streets. Competition was stiff in the city, there were several German clockmakers and many antique dealers, but he specialized in pearls and Whitby jet and he hoped he'd soon get a reputation for being the finest purveyor of these gems.

His pearl luck had held firm when he arrived in York on that chilly winter's day searching for modest lodgings. He spent a week meandering through the streets, sizing up just the right place to open his business. From a shop in Low Petergate he was directed to the Emporium of Handel Carswell in Stonegate just as the old man was thinking of selling up to retire. One look at Eben's prize paragon and the jeweller knew here was a young man who knew quality and might be able to buy him out soon.

To raise funds Eben scoured the country showrooms, building up a collection of fine pieces, buying mostly from auction houses and private sales. It was not easy working for another man's business, but after a few months he was able to take on the shop by himself. There were so many desperate debtors who had no idea of the value of their pieces and wanted a quick sale to keep them out of the debtors' courts.

As well as the shop, he'd acquired the three-storey town house and the workshop behind the premises. He set about rearranging the showroom to his taste, clearing away the dust and cheaper items out of sight. During his travels round the county, Eben collected some fine parures – sets of pearl necklaces, bracelets and ear drops designed to be worn together – and pretty pearl tiaras and

61

combs. He kept such items on permanent display in the well-lit window to lure in the touring visitors and gentry.

There was always a reason for pearls; a necklace for a young girl, a brooch for a wife, a ring for a betrothal, a present for an anniversary, a gift to assuage guilt or jet mourning jewels to offset grief when death came calling.

Arthur, the young apprentice who came with the business, was talented at fashioning popular mourning jewellery, winding horse hair into rings, cameos and brooches. This was much easier to work with than the locks of real hair customers wanted to use as mementoes and tokens of their grief. As long as the hair was dyed correctly, they wouldn't know the difference. Arthur could also drill pearls to perfection, knowing any mistakes would be docked from his wages.

No one could ever understand how Eben felt about his own private pearl collection. They were his beauties, kept in a mahogany display case, the drawers, lined with raw silk, tray upon tray in the cabinet assembled to his strict instructions. This was his secret hoard. Each pearl sat on its own little throne. Every night he would take out a chosen one to caress, marvelling at its special lustre. The selected gem slept under his pillow, or in a pocket sewn into his nightshirt, close to his heart.

He took delight in adding to this catalogue. Each of his beauties was named, weighed, measured and assigned their place in his harem. Although nothing matched his prized possession, the Scottish gem he now called Mary, Queen of Scots, paragon among paragons, there was a beautiful cluster of Abalone pearls from the Californian coast he called his stars of the sea, some Tahitian pearls, dusky as the night, which he called his Black Moons and a pair of pink twin baroques that he named his Blushing Roses.

Nothing gave him more pleasure than to dine above the shop premises using his cutlery with mother-of-pearl handles. He loved to cradle his tiepins and cufflinks, removing them from their mother-of-pearl trinket box. If Indian princes could adorn themselves with ropes of deep-sea pearls why shouldn't he do the same in private? He sat in front of the mirror, admiring himself in a silk shirt studded with seed pearls brought in from the Colonies. They shimmered in the candle-light giving him a frisson of delight.

What his house lacked was a woman's refined touch. The old housekeeper, Eliza Hunt came with the shop. She was cheap, an average cook, trustworthy, quiet and never found in drink – but was finding the stairs from the kitchen in the base-ment getting steeper as she was getting slower. He must have spotless premises and he followed her around making sure she cleaned in all the corners. Her eyesight was weak but she would do for now.

Eben headed out the door to inspect the pave-ment for dust and rubbish. It was time the boy came out with a bucket to spruce up the entrance and clean the step.

Let no one say his business wasn't up there with the more established York jewellers. His aim was to be the Pearl King of Stonegate. Some of his competitors were already asking his advice when certain items came their way and were noting Arthur's precision work with a covetous eye. He could be a sullen cuss when told to re-do his work. Eben wondered how long they would last together, but he didn't want Arthur setting up in competition with another jeweller down the street.

Eben stood out in the morning street to admire the freshly painted sign, sparkling in the sunshine as it hung above the bow-fronted window: The Pearl Emporium. Setting up in York was one of his better decisions, he thought, and today was going to be a good day.

Later, as the shadows crept across the cobbles and it was time to close the shutters, Eben noticed a furtive-looking boy lingering outside, eyes darting around to see if he was being followed, a look Eben recognized as shifty.

'Sir, I found this,' said the boy, his cap pulled low over his face. 'Found it in the back lane a week ago, put a notice in the shop window. Nobody's come.'

Oh yes? And my mother is Queen of England, Eben thought. 'Are you wanting to sell it or take it to the police station?'

'Nah, just wanted to know what it's worth first ... for the reward, like.' The boy was mumbling in a rough guttural accent.

'Come in then,' Eben ordered. 'I don't do business in the street.' He made sure there was no accomplice lurking across the road.

The boy put the watch down on the bench. Eben examined it with exaggerated care. 'It's got initials engraved, early last century, a fine timepiece in good working order. So are you wanting to sell or just a valuation?'

The boy looked at him surprised. 'Might as well sell. What's it worth?'

'Twenty guineas, may be more.' Eben made his paltry offer.

'Hang on, it's worth more than that, chap down the road offered me forty.' The boy had the sense to point down the street to a well-known clock-maker.

'Whatever I offer, I can't give you cash now. It's banked for the night and off the premises. You'll have to call back in the morning. Thirty-five is my highest offer. What's your name? I don't deal with strangers.'

'Bert Ryan, sir.' He added, 'It's a good one. I don't deal in rubbish. Found it back near Patricks Pool.'

'I see, and no sign of an owner then?'

'Not a soul around and my old man could do with some brass on account of him having no work, like.' Out came the sob story.

'Will you leave it here or call back tomorrow before I open shop? I will have my sovereigns ready. I might find a buyer but as you see I don't sell watches. Why did you come to me after you had seen old Muller? There are so many other shops.' Eben was curious.

'You're new to the street and I heard old Carswell as was here before, weren't fussy where some of his stuff came from, see. So tomorrow then?' He grabbed the watch and thrust it under his jacket. 'Thanks, mister.' Herbert Ryan darted out of the door into the street.

65

Eben smiled, found his coat and hat, locked up the shop carefully just in case and headed down towards Petergate in the lamplight. This deserved a pie and a pint in his favourite local while he decided how to play this intriguing turn of events.

Greta Costello hadn't been able to eat or sleep since the robbery. Then, one morning a fortnight after she'd been arrested, a man in a smart coat and black hat called at their door. She and her mother were elbow deep in suds and steamy washing and Greta felt embarrassed to bring him into their rough living space, cluttered with soggy underclothes.

'Miss Margaret Annie Costello? You were the late employee of Mr Saul Abrahams?'

'That's me, sir.' She bobbed a curtsey.

'This is for you.'

'It's the watch, oh thank God, it's been returned, Mam!'

'I know nothing about a watch, this is from the estate of the late Mr Abrahams. He left a gift for you in gratitude for all your hard work.' The man was shoving a blue leather box into her hand. 'My father, Mr Joshua Barnett, was given instructions that should anything happen to his client, this must come to you.'

Greta wiped her hands on her skirt to open the box. It was lined with pale blue silk and inside was a large single pearl set in a rose-gold claw on a thick chain.

'But this can't be for me, it's beautiful?' Inside was tucked a small note.

My dear Margareta,

My wife, Adah Joel wore this all her life, a gift from her father in better times. I could not wish for a kinder girl to wear it than you. Please never sell it. Pawn if you must and redeem when you can. When the time comes, pass this on with love but not for money and it will bring you joy in your life.

Your friend, Saul Abrahams.

'My goodness!' said her mother staring at the large pearl. 'You can't accept that. What will people think you did to earn it? Not after losing his watch, it wouldn't be right.'

'I can't accept because I don't deserve it.' Greta looked up at the young man. 'I lost his watch and betrayed his trust.' She closed the box to hand it back but he refused to take it.

'Not so hasty, miss. Don't refuse a gift from the dead. It's bad luck, especially with this being a pearl.'

'Is that so? I suppose the gentleman's right, Greta. I don't want you having more bad luck than you've got, losing the watch and losing yer job as well as the old man. What a kind gentleman he was taking you on. We must honour his memory then by accepting this. Thank you, sir.'

Greta's mother showed the young man out, leaving Greta staring at the single pear-shaped pearl which hung from its golden setting like a pendant or a holy cross. The gold claw was set with tiny diamonds.

'I can't wear this.' Greta shook her head weeping. 'He shouldn't have done this, and me in disgrace for losing his repair...'

'Maybe not now, love, but happen on your wedding day. To think he should be so generous. We'll put it away safe out of sight in the drawer. What a good bit of fortune, perhaps it will bring us luck, for heaven knows we need some with you out of work now.'

As if Providence had sprung into action at her pleas, a policeman called, asking them to return to Silver Street Police Station where there was good news. 'It seems you are in the clear, Miss Costello. We caught a young man red-handed yesterday morning trying to sell a fine gold watch to a jeweller in Stonegate. He came to warn us that someone was trying to palm off an item he believed stolen. We went to his premises and accosted young Bert Ryan with his brother, Michael, who we also caught in the chase that followed. They're a well-known family of pickpockets. Of course, they claimed they found it close to Patricks Pool, just as you told us. Your witness statement will be important in bringing them to justice. So, all's well that ends well, young lady. I have informed Erasmus Blake who is a Quaker friend of the Cocoa merchant, Mr Rowntree, and well respected. It will be returned to him forthwith.'

'We must thank the jeweller,' said Sadie Costello shaking her head with relief. 'It's good there's some honest folk around.'

'It is indeed but the gentleman in question wants to remain anonymous in this matter. He's new to the district and felt it was his duty to ensure that no one thought him an easy target for stolen property. If he remains anonymous he might help us again if the criminal fraternity call.'

'What a relief, lass, to have this burden off our backs. Two bits of good luck in as many days but they say it comes in threes.' Sadie smiled later as she was hanging out the sheets in the back yard. 'Perhaps things are looking up.'

Since Mr Abraham's death, Greta had been working at the market again, helping round the back at the greengrocer's stall. How she missed those evenings, sitting at the bench sorting out repairs, playing with Mr Abraham's little measuring scales, listening to his instructions. Peeling rotten spring greens was a thankless task. It was then that she had the bright idea of going to see Mr Blake in his chambers near to the river to ask if the repair was to his satisfaction. She could also ask if he knew anywhere suitable for her to find employment, even if it was a cleaning job.

In the morning she dressed with care in her Sunday outfit, a two-piece made from Adah's woollen dress. She also wore her straw bonnet trimmed with a bright ribbon and round her neck she wore her new necklace for luck. She might be from the bad end of Walmgate but she knew how to present herself.

'Miss Costello to see Mr Blake,' she announced to the clerk when she arrived at Mr Blake's imposing offices. When she explained why she was visiting without an appointment a clerk ushered her along a hallway lined with chairs and then through a door into a panelled room with a fine mantlepiece and warm fire in the grate.

69

'So, Mr Abrahams's young assistant, I'm glad we meet in better circumstances. How can I help?' Mr Blake smiled from behind his desk, indicating that she should sit in a leather chair opposite him.

'I came to enquire if the watch was still in a satisfactory condition. I am so relieved it has been recovered. It has been on my mind that it might be damaged.'

'It is fine and in good order and, as I recall, still only a watch. How are you?'

'Doing my best, sir, but I miss working for my late employer.' She paused, looking down at the floor, courage failing her. 'I wondered if ... but perhaps I'd better not...' She rose to leave. 'I've said what I came for. Pardon me for taking up your time.'

He rose from his chair to stop her. 'I don't think you walked all this way to inquire after my clock, are you still in trouble?'

'Not exactly, but I'm in want of steady work. Mother does what she can but the others are too young for real work. I need to find employment.'

'You want me to find you work?'

'No, no, it's just ... if you knew anyone who needs someone good with their hands. I was taught stitchery by nuns. I can goffer and iron and mend and I can read and write, oh and string pearls,' she added. 'Well, almost, Mr Abrahams hadn't quite finished teaching me.'

'I like your honesty, Margaret. As it happens my wife is in need of extra help in the house. I will speak to her and perhaps she might find a place for you... Would that help?'

'Thank you. I would be most grateful...'

'You would have to live within the household. My wife is most particular. She likes things done the old way but we will see what she says.' He showed her to the door and then paused. 'And a word to the wise before you leave, when you meet her don't bedeck yourself with any adornment such as the necklace you are wearing.' His eye went to the pendant. 'Fine as it is.'

'Mr Abrahams left this for me,' she replied proudly.

'That's as may be but my wife, Serenity, is of the old school. Quakers live in plain fashion as members of The Religious Society of Friends and follow a very simple way of dressing and speech. Serenity expects her household to do likewise. Uniform will be provided.'

'Thank you, I'll heed your warning... I mean suggestion, Sir.'

'Margaret Costello, you are a breath of fresh air. I wish you well.' Erasmus Blake smiled as she curtseyed. 'On your way home now.'

Greta almost skipped down Parliament Street and down Fossgate, pleased that she had taken a chance and it had paid off. This was a fresh start. Good luck had come in threes, she thought, touching the necklace and feeling the cold pearl. If only she could find out the name of the jeweller who had given back her reputation by catching those thieves. She hoped one day she might be able to thank him in person.

9

Greta made sure every article of clothing was sponged down and neatly pressed. Her wool coat and grey dress with its starched collar were spotless. Her boots were as shiny as glass, thanks to Tom's efforts, and her knitted gloves well darned. Her carpet bag was packed with stockings, shifts and a brush but she left her pearl behind as instructed. Satisfied she was presentable, she made her way through the familiar streets of York, crossing the river on foot and heading towards the tall houses on the Mount where the fine dwellings, with their sparkling polished doorsteps, rose in tiers above the town below.

The Blakes of Mount Vernon were prosperous, the front steps were for visitors not servants, so she made her way to the side entrance to ring the bell. A maid in a pinafore opened the door.

'You the new one?' she said, eyeing Greta up and down. 'You'd better come in.'

Greta followed the girl as they marched up the backstairs to the hall. 'Wait there. And it's first names here, not last. I'm told your name is Margaret.'

'Greta...'

'No, Margaret. I'm Patience, by the way.' Greta was ushered to the door of the morning room.

She hesitated to straighten her hair but there were no mirrors. She knocked with trembling knuckles and was summoned into the presence of the mistress of the house.

Serenity Blake was standing by the window, tall and poker-straight, wearing a light grey dress with a wide starched collar. Her head was covered in a plain cap which was tied under her chin. Her hair was scraped back from her face and coiled tightly into the nape of her neck making her beautiful features severe.

'Margaret Costello. My husband has recommended thee for an honest worker, loyal to thy former employer and being sole supporter to thy widowed mother. Is that correct?'

'Yes, ma'am,' Greta replied, bobbing a curtsey.

'We bow to no man but our Maker in this household. We speak plain. Our yay is yay and our nay is nay. As thee will learn we live in frugal fashion, not wasting on fripperies when money can be used to help others in need. We eat simple meals, dress plainly and observe First Day Worship. We are not Friends who have become worldly as they have grown in wealth. What I expect from thee is a practical skill for which we will give thee board and lodging, a half day to visit thy mother and a small recompense for thy labours.'

She moved closer to inspect Greta, her eyes dark as coals.

'We expect thee in return to be discreet in thy manner, work in silence, observe the First Day as we do, repair linen and laundry and support any charitable occasions that might arise here. Does thee understand?'

Greta swallowed and nodded, bowing her head. Why did she talk like the Bible?

'There are just the two of us in residence but my sons will return from their boarding schools, bringing with them, no doubt, much to be laundered, such items as vigorous boys manage to wear and tear. That will be thy responsibility too. What skills does thee have at thy fingertips?'

'I can darn and turn collars and cuffs, reshape garments, embroider, goffer lace... I was taught by the nuns and I can string pearls.'

'Enough, show me those hands.'

Greta removed her gloves, holding out her fingers for inspection.

'Good, thee's the rough palms of someone used to hard work and the fingers of a seamstress. There will be no fancy stitchery required in this house but sheets do wear and need turning, collars likewise. We prosper because we exercise frugality in all things.'

How could a face be so striking, with its arched eyebrows, thick lashes and bow lips, yet be so fierce and stern? Greta felt the power of those eyes peering into her as if to read her very mind. She daren't hold the woman's gaze.

'Thee will work alongside Cook and Patience and do whatever tasks they set you. No one sits idle. There is always something to be improved. That is all. Thy room is on the top floor with the other girl. And, Margaret, remember thee cometh without a character reference. Thee's here solely at my husband's recommendation so don't let him down.'

'I won't, thank you, ma'am.'

She climbed the stairs with Patience, she wasn't sure what she felt about the interview. It was done and dusted in minutes with no time to dare ask a question. Now she must find her place in this quiet household, with its white walls and bare rooms. There was none of the usual clutter of ornaments to be dusted, just rows of photographs on the walls. Everything looked of the best quality, to her untrained eye, but the emptiness was scary.

Her room in the eaves had a washstand, an iron bedstead with a firm mattress, a pull blind and a line of peg hooks along the wall next to a small chest of drawers. There were no pictures in the room, not even an embroidered Bible quotation for inspiration. She sat on the bed looking across at Patience's half of the room.

Mr Blake seemed so warm and open but his wife was cool and closed. Suddenly Greta felt homesick for all the noise and clutter of Walmgate. Although she was still in the same city she felt like a stranger in another country with a whole new language to be learned.

The following week it was the afternoon of the York Friends sewing meeting. The mistress was entertaining at home; tea, scones and fancy cakes were to be served in the drawing room to the gathering of ladies and their daughters who made 'benevolent objects'.

'What are they?' Greta asked her room-mate and Cook, who she dare not call Ethel.

'Useful garments they sew for the poor, like clothes for orphans and abandoned children and burial gowns for dead babies. They sew a fine seam. Not a scrap of cloth is wasted as long as it's black, white, grey or dark. Old clothes are cut down and remade.'

'Why is there no colour in this house?'

'It's our mistress's way. She likes to be colourful in her garden, as nature intended, but for herself there's no adornment, not that she needs it with such porcelain skin and her hair the colour of polished oak. The master is fair smitten with her beauty. Her sons take after her like that, handsome specimens. I've never seen a woman so taken with her children. They be her one indulgence, I reckon. But here's me gossiping.' Cook scuttled off to finish her duties.

'When will they be home?' Greta asked Patience.

'Any time now. Master Edmund is at college in Manchester, young Hamer boards at Ackworth. You'll soon know when they're back, the house fair rings with noise.'

Greta was getting used to the household's strict ways. She glimpsed Serenity, true to her name, gliding across the hall like a shadow, never rushing, greeting guests with a nod of the head while Greta and Patience received coats and gloves, dressed in their afternoon uniform of grey and white striped dresses with stiff collars and cuffs and starched caps that scratched.

No one wore their hair loose. Certainly the mistress kept her dark locks covered and Greta imagined it tumbling down past the mistress's waist when it was released from its tight bun. There was no crimping or curling with tongs. Hair must be as nature intended, but Greta's had the habit of coiling into tight corkscrews in the damp mist, much to her annoyance.

The Blakes' house seemed so far away from

Walmgate, from the foetid stench of the cesspits in the back courts, but Greta longed for the hurly-burly of the Saturday markets and Friday nights and as for Sunday, she sighed. How would she ever get used to them here?

When Erasmus Blake took morning prayers, they sat in silence. You spoke only if the spirit moved and none of them dared open their mouth. Greta tried not to grin, thinking about how the spirits moved the men in Walmgate, yelling and fighting on a Saturday night till the small hours. Here they listened to Bible readings and then sat still, trying not to fidget, until the master decided it was time to begin the day.

Everything changed a few days later when the silence was shattered by the arrival of Hamer Blake, home from school. There was a thunder of boots on the stairs, laughter in the kitchen as he pinched a biscuit. Cook made double portions of everything and Greta's mending basket was full of sporting shirts, torn britches and a mound of darning.

She heard the piano in the morning room being played for the very first time. It was as if a breeze of fresh air was blowing right through the house. Serenity smiled as she hustled her son into her bedroom to hear all his news.

The atmosphere erupted again when Edmund arrived home too and the household was complete for the summer. There were meetings for Young Friends in the garden, tennis parties to be arranged, outings to the seaside for the boys' friends and more washing and mending.

Edmund was introduced to Patience and Greta.

He was tall and dark like his mother, with the same penetrating eyes, but there was a sparkle in them. He was polite and asked after their families and then retreated to study for his examination. He had the beauty of his mother and warmth of his father, thought Greta. His mother hovered by his door and ordered them to tiptoe past his room.

'Thee must do the fires early and no noise to distract him, Margaret. He must be left to study,' Serenity told Greta. She noticed, however, that Edmund was never in his room and when she knocked on the door to tidy, the window sash was wide open. Somehow he'd scrambled down the pipes and away out of the house to goodness knows where. That was none of her business until a letter arrived in the post that sent the Blakes into a turmoil. Cook said Edmund had failed his law exams and was in disgrace.

The calm surface of the household rippled with a coming storm of arguments and doors slamming. Patience and Greta couldn't help overhearing the quarrelling from the top landing where they were polishing the banisters.

'Law is not for me, Mother. I don't have the qualities needed to concentrate.'

'But it is thy father's dearest wish for thee to continue in his practice.'

'I know, I'm sorry, but it won't do. I want to work with my hands like my Grandfather Blake before me. You should see some of the work that William Morris's Company are producing: tables, chairs of sturdy oak and natural woods. I've been attending carpentry classes. That's what I want to do, not sit at a desk all day listen-

78

ing to people's grievances.'

'Don't ever let thy father hear thee say such things.' For once the mistress was losing her composure. 'My family have never stooped to manual work but brought trade and prosperity to this district. Thou must do the same.'

'There's no shame in manual work, Mama. This is not cheap furniture cobbled together, it's part of a whole movement towards rediscovering those ancient skills we're in danger of losing: stained glass, fine jewellery, wonderful tapestries. It is uplifting work.'

'Thou was not brought up to value those worldly things, Edmund. It is not our way,' his mother argued, her voice raised again in despair.

'It may not be your way, Mother, but I see the hand of God in the artist's brush and pen and chisel.'

'Those are the devil's words, son. Who has lead thee astray to talk as the worldly do? Who has defiled thy mind with such ideas?'

'No one, I went to an art gallery and fell in love with what I saw. It touched something within me that has always been there. I was always the first to saw wood, to help the gardener or watch my father's father at his bench. I've attended lectures and seen the workshops of carpenters. This is what I want to do...'

'We do not mention that side of the family, as thou well know. Thy father saw the light of truth when he joined the Fellowship of Friends. He abandoned all those worldly pursuits when he married me.'

'You made him choose between his family and

you. How many times was I stopped from visiting grandfather before he died?'

'How dare thee talk to me like this? I won't have it. Go to thy room and pray for forgiveness for such disrespect. I won't have thee corrupting Hamer. Thy father will speak later.'

'Have you forgotten the Carpenter of Nazareth, Mama? Would you show Him the door too?' Edmund stormed out of the morning room with a face like thunder and left the house with a slam of the door that made the walls shudder. Patience stared at Greta. 'What do we do now?'

'Nowt, it's none of our business, is it?' Both of them heard the sobs coming from the other side of the door. The mistress mustn't know they had heard any of this or there would be trouble. Greta sensed this would not be the last upheaval. The peace of this gracious house was shattered. Poor Mr Blake would have to take sides, but she already knew whose side she was on.

One morning a few days later after yet another family argument, Greta went to put the laundry in the linen press. She saw Edmund standing on the landing, staring out at the garden where his mother was pacing along the path.

'I suppose you all know I am in disgrace. Voices echo up this hall.' He sighed.

Greta bowed her head not wanting to be involved in family matters.

'Such a lovely day out there.' He sighed again.

'It's a good day for a walk, sir,' she replied.

'No sirs here. I'm Edmund... A walk around the city ramparts would clear the air, before the next battle.' He was looking at her. 'It's such a beautiful city, isn't it?'

'It's an old city, I give you that.' She paused. 'But not so beautiful where I come from in Walmgate.'

'I suppose we're spoilt up here but on a day like this anywhere is better than–' he broke off. 'What do you do after a long day's work?' he asked, changing the subject.

'Visit home when I can, but it's the Gala soon in Bootham Field. I'm saving up for the fair and I'll take my sister Kitty. It's the best day of summer, isn't it?'

'I wouldn't know. I've never been.'

'Why ever not? Everyone goes,' she said, shaking her head in surprise.

'Friends don't attend things like that but I'm not sure why. Mama says you can catch diseases but it sounds fun.'

'Then you ought to go, just the once.' She hesitated knowing she shouldn't be giving such advice. 'To make your own mind up, like,' she added as more of a challenge, knowing the mood he was in now and wanting to encourage him to defy his mother.

'You're right, of course, but it's not that simple, not now.' He turned to look down at the garden. 'We are supposed to set an example and at the moment I'm...'

'But everyone needs time to be jolly, to sing and dance with all the fun of the fairground. You have to see it.'

'I'm supposed to be studying but–' She could see him glancing at her sideways. 'I'm making excuses, aren't I?'

81

'Yes, sir.'

'Edmund, please.'

'Perhaps you could go and take Master Hamer as a treat. He'd like to go on the coconut shy and the helter-skelter. It's only for a day, after all.'

'You know, Margaret, you're right. Just one day can't cause any more trouble than I'm in now.' He smiled and looked at her with those bright eyes. She didn't know where to look as her cheeks flushed. They were peering out of the window together as Serenity walked back, glancing upwards she had spied them deep in conversation. Her thunderous look said it all.

10

'Where shall we go next?' shouted Kitty as she jumped off the carousel, excited by the choices. 'How much have you got left?'

'Enough for an ice cream but we'll have to share.' Greta smiled at her sister as they caught up with Patience and her friend. 'Have you seen them yet?'

'Seen who? Oh yer not going on about Edmund bringing his brother. Is that why you're all dressed up like a dog's dinner?' teased Patience.

Kitty and Greta were dressed in starched cotton dresses cut down from Adah's precious materials and wearing battered straw boaters which sported crisp stripy ribbons. The sky was blue and crowds thronged the Gala field to the sound of the steam pipe organs and the hurdy-gurdy man. All the pennies in her purse were nearly gone but Greta still hoped that the Blake boys would come even though the atmosphere in the house was tense and gloomy. Would Edmund be forced back into his cage to do what he was told or would he stand up for himself?

How these people could deny themselves all the fun of the fair, the games and sports, on such a wonderful day, she just didn't understand.

It felt as if the whole city was crowded into the field in their finery, lace and silk dresses mingling with sailor suits, gingham skirt, striped blazers and straw boaters. Flags fluttered in the cooling breeze, kites flew overhead with balloons and children raced by waving paper flags and streamers. There were tents roped off for the dignitaries who sat together at tables. She recognized the ginger-haired policeman from Silver Street guiding the crowds, keeping an eye on any barefoot boys intent on pickpocketing. It cost nothing just to wander about so Greta, Patience and Kitty enjoyed looking at all the different stalls. There were Punch and Judy shows, marionettes, a shooting gallery and bands competing with the organ. Kitty had to be dragged off the seated swings. Little Tom and Mother were somewhere in the crowd too. It was in the queue for the helter-skelter that she spied the Blake boys and her heart leapt with relief. So Edmund had the guts to get out of the house and bring his brother for some sport after all.

'Margaret, Patience, over here,' he yelled, seeing them pause. 'Do you want a go?'

'Yes, please,' Kitty jumped up excited.

'No, Kitty, we're spent up. You've eaten your way round the whole field, you'll be sick.'

'You both look topping.' Edmund smiled. 'Kitty can have a ride with Hamer as my treat.'

So the children swung from side to side yelling and screaming. Edmund towered over Greta but whispered in her ear. 'Thank you for this. We're having a great time. Can't believe we've never been before. There's such colour and crowds. I'd like to take a picture of it all. I'm going to try and win something.'

After the swings the two youngsters charged for the shooting gallery with its scenes from the wild west. Edmund tried three shots but missed each time.

'Try again, squire?'

Patience, who had been open mouthed at the sight of the Blakes' arrival, jumped in. 'I'll show you, sir.' She took hold of the gun and cracked three potshots at the moving targets.

'Golly,' said Hamer shaking his head. 'How did you do that?'

'You don't grow up in a farm cottage and not know how to catch a rabbit for your supper.' She laughed, handing Greta a little stuffed elephant. 'Here's yer fairing.'

'Let's go and see the hot air balloon going up.' Edmund was shepherding them around. It was a hot day for wearing a dark suit, Greta thought, looking at Edmund and Hamer, but blazers and boaters were not Quaker style.

They lingered on for the dancing and Hamer and Kitty pranced about with other children.

84

Patience tried to teach her young master some steps.

'This is beyond me too,' Edmund apologized as he escorted Greta onto the wooden floor in a semblance of a waltz. As they clutched each other, Greta felt her heart racing. Here she was dancing with the son of the house. It shouldn't be proper but today was a special day of the year when all barriers came down. He looked down at her smiling. 'Thank you, Margaret, for making me seize the moment. We are only young the once and need to try out these sort of days for ourselves.'

'I hope there won't be trouble for coming here today,' she replied, not wanting the dance to end.

'Papa will be amused. I can always study tomorrow.'

'So you're going back to Manchester?'

'I'm not sure.' He sighed. 'Papa is torn, knowing I have found something I really want to do, something that links me to his humble family. I don't think I will ever pass the exams but I have to try for their sake. They are my parents after all and I owe them respect.'

The sun was setting when they all made their way to the exit. Mother and Tom waited to collect Kitty who stamped and sulked when it was time to leave. Greta introduced Edmund to her mother who curtseyed to him.

'Please don't, Mrs Costello. It is a pleasure to meet you and your family. It's been a lovely day for all of us, thanks to Margaret. She challenged me to come and enjoy myself.' He smiled. 'But all good things come to an end. We've stayed out a little longer than I intended.'

85

The four of them, tired and sun-kissed, made their way slowly across the Ouse Bridge and up the hill, carried along by the crowd that was returning to the city's public houses to finish off the day. There was a reception party waiting for their belated return.

'Where hast thou been?' Serenity Blake eyed the four of them with disdain, waiting on the steps, drawing herself to her full height. 'It is a burden to us to know that a good supper has been wasted because thee gave us no indication that thee were out of the house.'

'We've been to the Gala,' Hamer blurted. 'I won this coconut and we went on the swings and slides and the shooting stall with Margaret's sister Kitty.' He held out his prize as a peace offering. It was ignored.

There was no time for Greta or Patience to sidle off to the side entrance, their mistress had them in her sights. 'Is all this thy doing, Margaret Costello?'

Edmund was ready with an explanation. 'No, Mama, it was my decision to have some time away from my books, it being far too bright a day to stay indoors.' Edmund stood his ground.

'For a river walk, perhaps, but to the Gala Day. Thou knowest how thy mother feels about such excursions.' Mr Blake was hovering at the back of his wife, trying to intervene.

'I saw lots of Friend families enjoying themselves there,' said Edmund.

'Be that as it may, they must examine their consciences in encouraging intemperance and worldly pleasure. Haven't I taught thee anything?' Serenity's coal-black eyes were blazing.

'No harm done, dearest. It's only one day in the year. The boys need to let off steam and they've had a happy time coming to no harm. Let's go in and leave it at that,' Mr Blake ordered but his wife had other ideas.

'Margaret to the morning room, at once... I have not finished with thee.'

'Serenity, my dear, I don't think–' Mr Blake whispered but his wife swept past him.

'Am I not to govern my household in the light of our teachings? Come, girl.'

Greta followed her into the morning room and stood defiantly knowing she was in for a telling off, but she refused to bow her head and stared at the writing bureau with her chin lifted.

'This is where we come to the parting of the ways. I am sure it was thee who was behind today's disobedience. I have found thy work satisfactory enough but as for thy attitude... There is no humility in thy eyes. Thee encourages defiance in my son and this I will not have.' The mistress folded her arms. 'Pack thy bag and leave. There will be no disobedience. This is a house of truth and enlightenment and it's not to be contaminated by worldly values. My sons are destined for great futures and must not be misled by silly servant girls who don't know right from wrong or their place in society.'

'It was only a Gala outing. Your sons chose to come by themselves.'

'But who put the idea into their heads? I am not blind. I see the way Edmund confers with thee. Thou art a distraction, one he can well do without. Thee must go.'

'But what about my character references?' she pleaded.

'Thee came with none, as I recall, so nothing has been taken from thee. Patience is simple and easily lead but she has nowhere else to go. One of thee must be gone so everyone sees I brook no defiance in this house.'

Greta backed out of the door in shock but couldn't resist one last word. 'The defiance in this house, ma'am, was already in residence long before I crossed your threshold. You should look closer to home than your servant.'

She climbed the stairs slowly knowing she'd committed the fatal sin of getting involved in affairs above stairs but it wasn't fair to be dismissed without references. Who would employ her now? She would have to return to Walmgate in disgrace. What would her mother say?

It wouldn't be easy to return home after sharing a room in a gracious town house, having regular meals in the basement kitchen. The air in the Mount was fresher and less smoky. How could she return home with no wage to offer? The injustice of it all stung her pride. She could smell the chocolate factory on the wind. The smell was never far from the river and many in the city found work thanks to Mr Rowntree but, without a character, they wouldn't even look at her. Slowly she packed her bag, trying not to cry, swallowing back the bile of bitterness. She crept down the backstairs not wanting to see Patience or Cook or the scullery maid and made for the back gate.

Edmund was waiting, barring her path, full of apologies.

'Mama gets these fits. We will make her come round to see how unreasonable it is to blame you for my actions,' he replied, angry and embarrassed at her dismissal.

Greta was in no mood for apologies. 'I don't think that will happen. It's you she is getting at. She wants to rule your life.'

'Look, Margaret, ask your next employer to write to me for a reference,' he offered. 'I won't let her ruin your chances of work. Give them my address at Papa's office and I will respond. I am so sorry, Margaret.'

'Greta, I prefer Greta. At least I'll be called by my own name from now on.' Summoning every ounce of pride she could muster she continued, 'I don't understand why everything that's full of colour and fun is seen as sinful here. What sort of religion is that? You can't even create a stick of furniture without–' She wanted him to know she knew what was going on.

'I know. It's not my thinking either but my mother comes from a line of ancestors that she considers royalty within the fellowship here. She's descended from martyrs who died for their beliefs in the Time of the Sufferings two hundred years ago. They were the founding fathers of the True Light and she can't bear the thought of either of her boys leaving its confines for a broader church of beliefs or marrying a girl who doesn't belong to this Society of Friends. I'm sorry we let you down. Don't think badly of me. I have to find my own way out of this maze.' Edmund held out his hand

and Greta took it, bobbing a curtsey. 'Thank you, sir,' she said in defiance to his wishes.

'Please, Edmund.'

'No, sir, that's not how it works, is it?' She turned to leave, picking up her bag. He called after her. 'If ever you need any help. I am your friend.'

'Yes, sir, so you say ... but my friendship won't get you out of this cage.' She didn't turn back. Edmund Blake had much to learn about the real world outside of the sheltered confines of his Quaker community. If he wanted to plough his own furrow, he was going to have to grow a back-bone and quick.

'Look what the cat's dragged in!' Kitty called as Greta put her bag on the kitchen table. 'If you've got the sack you're not sharing my bed. I sleep with Mam now. You can sleep down here.'

'That suits me.' Greta shrugged her shoulders, she was in no mood for arguments. Kitty was at that awkward age, a little girl on the swings one day and then cocky and cheeky the next. 'Where's Mam?'

'Where do you think? At the laundry. She works all hours. Have you really got the sack?'

'It's not like that...'

'I bet you have...'

'Oh leave off, Kitty. I'm whacked lugging this thing from Mount Vernon.'

Sadie appeared in the door with a shawl over her head.

'Mam, our Greta's got the sack,' Kitty shouted so all the neighbours could hear.

Greta saw the weariness on her mother's face.

'Sorry, I'd nowhere else to go...'

'I'll hear about this later when missy here isn't flapping her elephant ears. Mash us some tea. It's good to see you, love. I never did hold with that starchy place.'

Trust Mam to say the right thing. It was such a relief to be back in this shabby room, back in the cobbled courtyard with all its squalid life. This was home and she was safe but she felt so guilty to be bringing home nothing but an empty purse. It had all been spent at the fair.

Later, when Kitty was out playing, Greta sat by the fire, spilling out her story. 'All I did was tell Edmund Blake about the Gala. I didn't make them go to the blessed thing.'

'But you put an idea in his head that wasn't hers. Best out of there, love, I saw the way the young man was admiring you. We don't want that sort of trouble.'

'What can I do?'

'You can join me at the laundry.'

Greta couldn't hide her dismay. 'I haven't a character to offer but I'd like to work in a shop.'

'You'll have to take what you can get, girl. The laundry's not that bad.'

'It's horrible and I want you out of it as soon as I get on my feet. Pa would turn in his grave to see what we've come to.'

'Don't go down that road. This is where we are and where we'll be staying.' Sadie looked round the kitchen with a sigh.

'Not if I've anything to do with it. I want to see you in a nice little cottage, in a decent street with a proper parlour and your own front door. I want to see Kitty set up in service and Tom in an apprenticeship. I want–'

'I want, I want, don't get. You have to accept what the Good Lord has given us.' Mother crossed herself.

'I don't think much of his choices so far.' Greta felt the bitterness rising in her throat.

'Margaret Costello. I'll not hear another word of blasphemy from your lips. Go wash out your mouth. Be careful what you wish for, it might come and bite you up the backside.' But there was a twinkle in her mother's eye as she spoke.

'Sorry, Mam.'

'I should think so, you gobby girl. Be grateful we're not in the workhouse and separated like some we know who can't make ends meet. We'll manage somehow if we pull together. So no more squabbling with Kitty, she sets such store by her big sister even if she doesn't show it. You'll find work if you don't go getting fancy ideas. There's always the market stalls.'

How could Greta settle for humping orange boxes and potato sacks or picking out rotten fruit after Mount Vernon? Being in service she'd seen another way of life, in the world across the river where homes had indoor water closets, fine furniture and beautiful gardens. How could she tell her mother she was past living hand to mouth in this terrible back court? How was she ever going to make her secret dreams come true?

11

Jem Baillie's dream of chasing the English pearl dealer faded over the months that turned into years. No one could recall the Sassenach's name or remember his address. Jem even went into Perth to complain to the police but no one was interested. The terrible tragedy of the Tay Bridge disaster and the loss of so many local people was on everyone's mind. His loss was nothing compared with that. School was now a far off memory, after his father's death, but he kept faith with his mother's wishes and turned from a log boy into one of the most trustworthy foresters employed on the laird's estate. Jem was now over six foot of hewn sinew and muscle, his shoulders had broadened, his hips were taut and his face had weathered into a nut-brown hue.

His sun-burnt face and jet black curls often brought taunts of being a gyppo. On one occasion Jem threw a punch, breaking his teaser's nose. No one roused him again. He kept himself apart in the logger's bothy preferring to smoke a pipe and read a book that his men thought gey queer for a woodsman but he didn't care.

Jem joined the library in Perth, devouring the tales of explorers such as Captain Cook, trappers in North America, Marco Polo and the pioneers of the wild west. There was a whole world out there waiting while he was chained by the ties that bound him to the district.

His mother Jeannie was failing in health with the same bad chest, wasted body and grey face that had taken his father to the grave. The doctor had done what he could for her and this time Jem made sure she took medicine. The pearls in his pouch were sold for treatment and comforts. He fished in the summer and found more but none to match Queenie. His inner restlessness never left him. 'You've got ants in yer pants just like yer pa,' his mother would tease. 'I had to chain him down with a stake...'

There were girls eager to make him stay but he had no eyes for the village lasses, the pretty young school teacher or even the minister's daughter, who took long walks into the forest on the off chance of meeting him.

'I'm collecting wild flowers to paint,' she simpered as an excuse when he met her on the path to the river.

'You'll no find many in these dark places,' he advised, impatient to be getting on with his work.

'Why, are there wolves lurking?' she replied coyly.

'Aye wolves enough, who'll take their chance with a silly lass wandering alone,' he snapped. How could he shake the silly bissom off? She held no attraction for him. 'Go down to the river and you'll find plenty o' weeds there.'

'Will you show me?' This girl was shameless.

'No I will not. I've an honest day's work to be doing, not pandering to some missy with too much time on her hands. Away and help your father, he'll find you some poor souls to visit.'

'Huh!' She turned heel and stomped away. 'No wonder they call you a soor docks.'

He laughed at her insult, knowing it was true. He was an acid drop, sharp to the tongue, but it suited him. Life was hard in this harsh climate, his mother was dying, his life was on hold until she passed away, but then it must change. He would not be staying here for the rest of his life.

Now it was the log rolling season. All the dams and sluices that regulated the flow of water were ready to be released when the weather turned and the water started rising, then they would float the timber down the river to the sawmill. Gangs of log floaters camped along the riverbank, men ready to guide the logs in a continuous train. It was always an exciting moment when the harvest from the forest was lined up ready to go. The laird liked to bring his shooting guests to see the spectacle.

Jem was given the task of making sure none of the laird's guests interfered with the progress of the log rolling. It must be done tactfully without causing offence to the visitors who often got in the way and asked too many questions.

That very morning the laird brought two guests, visitors from America: Jacob Allister and his son Jake Junior. They stood around in their tweed suits admiring the scene.

'Mr Allister has his own forests and lumber mills deep in the state of Iowa. He wants Jake to see the process for himself. Make sure he sees it all,' the laird ordered.

Jem tried not to grimace. He had enough work

without being nursemaid to a pampered boy who should be in school but he stepped forward to shake his hand, relieved that the lad seemed eager enough to observe everything with interest.

He escorted the boy down to the basin of water that held the pile of logs banked up to prevent them shooting down and spilling out too fast before there was time to control them. 'We wait for the opening of the sluices upstream. Then you will see how fast the logs can go,' Jem explained. 'But you must stand back.'

'What are those poles, the ones the guys are holding?' Jake asked.

'The log floaters have clips to hook the logs away from each other or from banging into the shore line if they start twisting and blocking the flow.'

'Can I hold one?' Jake seemed fascinated by the sight of men jumping from log to log as the water began to pour down at speed, sending the logs spinning. The loggers leapt to reset the flow like dancers jumping in a Highland reel. Suddenly Jake, in his curiosity, stepped onto a passing log and began to jump from one trunk to another. 'This is great!' he yelled.

'Come back at once!' Jem ordered, feeling responsible for the boy's safety. Then to his horror the boy missed his footing and fell into the fast-flowing stream, carried along at a furious pace.

Jem was sweating at the danger the boy was in. He could be crushed between the logs as they tumbled down a steep bank into the river. There was no time to think. Some of the log floaters had seen what had happened and were yelling to the men further down the river, trying to rescue the boy.

'Dam the bottom, stop the flow, jam the logs,' Jem ordered, racing to keep up with the boy in the water. The floaters quickly closed off the entrance to the river by hooking logs together to form a barrier. Now the logs would bank up and slow the flow.

Without thinking of his own danger, Jem leapt from the bank into the chilly stream, struggling against the force of the water. With a hook he grabbed at Jake's jacket and yanked him towards the bank, he climbed out of the water and pulled Jake out next to him.

The boy was lifeless and cold. Jem lifted him up and carried him to the nearest tent.

'Strip off his clothes, give me all your woollen plaids,' he shouted to the men. 'We have to rub the life back into him. He's so cold... He has to live!'

The men rubbed the boy all over and then wrapped him in dry blankets and jackets. To their relief Jake opened his eyes just as the laird and the boy's father, who had seen what had happened, raced into the tent. Everyone cheered at Jake's revival and Jem fed him whisky to revive him further.

'Who was the young man who brought my son back from the gates of heaven? How can I thank you for such quick thinking?' Jacob Allister shook Jem's hand.

'This is James Baillie,' said the laird. 'Like his father before him, a true forester.'

Jem, standing in his wet britches and shirt, was shivering with shock. He'd almost let a boy be killed. 'It all happened so quickly, sir. I did warn him but–'

'You've given this young buck of mine a lesson in the dangers of rapid water. We saw what he did. He'll not be doing that again, for sure. I am in your debt.'

What could Jem say or do but make his way home to change his clothes and sit exhausted by the peat fire until he fell asleep.

Much to his surprise a week later a servant from the big house arrived at the cottage carrying a basket. 'It's frae the laird's American.'

In the hamper was whisky, eggs, cold meats, cake and a parcel of clothes, which held a fine tweed suit, a woollen shirt and some thick socks. It was a complete winter's outfit. Jem read the card.

With thanks to James Baillie from grateful parents. If ever you need an introduction to our fine country, please contact us. We will be forever in your debt.

Jacob and Marcella Allister

How was he going to explain all this bounty to his mother without alarming her at the risk he'd taken to save the boy? Jeannie heard his tale with a smile on her face not a frown as she lay in her bed by the wall. 'There you go, one good deed begets another. When I'm away to my Maker that's the place to be heading, son, there's nothing to keep you here. Go and make your fortune in a new country.'

'But it costs to get myself across there on a ship.

It's too far to swim, Ma.' Jem smiled, relieved he had her blessing.

'Then get yourself back on the river next season and fish some more pearls. They'll see you across the ocean when I'm in ma box. You've got the knack just like yer pa. It's what he would want for you, son.'

If only it were that simple but there was no harm in making plans to travel one day.

First he must write a careful letter of appreciation to his benefactor and thank him for the offer. He would explain his present situation and, due to being under articles, he wasn't free to leave the laird's employ for a year or two. It would do no harm to express his desire to see America one day. Jem carefully put the note from Jacob Allister in his father's locked box along with the few pearls left. He smiled, thinking that if the river yielded up some more of its treasure perhaps one day he might just see those wild Iowa forests for himself.

Part 2

THE SHINY SHOP

Pearls around the neck, stones upon the heart.

Yiddish proverb

12

York, 1882

In the year that followed her dismissal, Greta tramped the busy streets of York looking for regular work. Respectable employment was hard to come by without a decent character reference in her hand and doors shut in her face. She'd heard nothing more from Edmund Blake. After another fruitless trip Greta arrived home ready to drop.

'Am I glad to see you. Shut the door.' Mama was standing by the table looking worried. 'Have you seen our Kitty on your way back?'

Greta was puzzled. Kitty didn't go out much; she was busy helping mother, delivering the washing and minding babies now she was out of school. She usually played in the yard but lately she'd been sneaking off further afield.

'I hear she's keeping bad company. I'm worried she's mixing with girls who are up to no good, and she shouldn't be out on such a cold night. But I don't want to bother you, with you being up to your eyes with job hunting. Any luck?'

Greta shook her head, disappointed not to be bringing in a proper wage. 'Kitty seems all right to me, she keeps wanting to borrow my things but that's only natural at her age.'

'You don't know the half of it, love. She's following an older crowd, hanging round the barracks

103

and such like. I gave her such a wallop for it. She just stood there and told me to boil my head and said that if she's old enough to be a skivvy, she's old enough to choose her own mates. Nellie Ryan and her gang are no better than they should be. I'm sick with worry that they'll get her in trouble.'

Greta sat down, winded by this news. How had little Kitty got to be a young girl and she'd never noticed? She shuddered at the thought of her sister getting caught up with street girls and flirting with soldiers. Surely she was too young for that caper? 'I'll go and look for her. You stay here with Tom. You look done in.'

'Oh, how I wish Brendan was here. He'd never stand for such doings. Ever since you came back from the Blakes, Kitty's been awkward. Happen you can knock some sense into that silly head of hers. All I get is a sneer of the lips and her flouncing out the door.'

'I'll go and fetch her for you,' Greta told her mother, heading out to find Kitty.

She'd been tramping all day and was ready for a sit down, but Kitty was only young and Nellie, a notorious little tart, wouldn't look after her. How had Kitty got in with them? Why hadn't she realized what was going on? Greta couldn't have her sister roaming the streets at all hours.

All the Walmgate women knew how to earn a few shillings if they were hard up and where better than outside the barracks gates? By the time she walked there Greta was in a steaming temper, seeing Kitty amongst the gaggle of girls hanging round a group of soldiers. To make matters worse, Kitty was wearing Greta's best three quarter coat made from one of Adah's. When Kitty caught sight of her big sister she tried to dart behind Nellie Ryan but Greta was in no mood for games.

'Kathleen Costello, you're wanted back home, right now!'

'She's with us,' sneered Nellie Ryan.

'Oh aye and a fat lot of good that will do her,' Greta yelled back. 'She'll end up like you, with her skirt up her belt and a dose of something nasty into the bargain.'

Nellie leapt to hit her but one soldier had the decency to stand in front of Greta. 'No scrapping, lasses, unless it's over us.'

Everyone laughed but Greta was in full fury, marching up to yank Kitty by the lapel of her coat. 'Come on, you. She's only fourteen and wasn't brought up to mess with soldiers.'

'Hark at her, she thinks she's above us but she's just a jumped-up skivvy.'

'I'd rather be a skivvy than a sixpenny tart. Home this minute, your mam has something to say to you.' It was then she saw something gleaming around Kitty's neck. 'That's my necklace! Who the hell gave you permission to take that outside?'

'You never wear it,' Kitty said in a sulk.

'That's because it's a gift and precious. How dare you root through my stuff. Take it off at once.'

Kitty unhooked it and Greta shoved it quickly into her pocket afraid someone might see its value and try to pinch it. 'What's got into you? Don't you know what can happen if you go with a soldier? Do you want to end up in the nun's home for fallen girls?'

'I don't care!'

Greta lost her temper and slapped her sister. 'Well I do. You're not to bring shame on our family by having a bairn and unwed, do you hear?'

Kitty rubbed her cheek, sobered by this outburst. 'There's nowt else to do round here. I was just having a bit of fun. Don't look like that. I haven't done nowt to be ashamed of.' Kitty started to whimper as Greta pulled her away and they headed home.

'Thank the Lord for small mercies. From now on you come with me. It would kill our mam if she were shamed, she's brought us up proper. We're not the sort to be whores. We are respectable and don't you ever forget it. Pride is all we've got left.'

They walked the rest of the way in silence. Kitty was trouble if she didn't find proper work. If only they could get out of the back court into a cleaner area with good neighbours. It wasn't right to leave Kitty to fend for herself, she was just a silly kid, bright, easily lead and too pretty for her own good, with her mop of red hair and tall, slim figure. If only Mam didn't have to work so hard to put food on the table. If only she'd found a job for herself. How was she ever going to find her work? How was she going to keep her sister safe?

Next morning Greta got her sister up early, determined to find them both a placement, however humble. Anything to avoid the drudgery of a laundry round again. She set off with Kitty by her side, scouring the shop windows for any openings, armed with a fierce determination to seize any chance that was offered, but there was nothing. By the end of the morning she was beginning to lose hope when a chance encounter in Low Petergate suddenly changed their fortunes.

Walking along after yet another rejection they almost tripped over an old woman who collapsed onto the cobbles right in front of them. Greta rushed to pick her up. Kitty knelt down not knowing what to do.

'I'm late,' the old lady kept repeating with what little breath she had left. Her lips were blue and her face ashen. 'He'll be wanting his supper.' She was not making much sense. A crowd gathered round, staring down at the woman in her cloak with bonnet awry as she moaned softly, unable to move. She peered up at Greta. 'Tell him I'm badly. I'll be in happen tomorrow, love.'

'Tell who and where?' Greta asked holding her hand.

'The Pearl Emporium in Stonegate, the master'll be expecting me. Tell Mr Slinger Eliza Hunt can't make nowt of herself today.' The effort of speaking was too much and she passed out again. Two men moved her into the doorway of a shop. Greta and Kitty kept fanning the woman's face with their aprons as they waited for an ambulance cart to arrive. The colour was leaching from Eliza's face.

'What can we do?' Kitty was panicking.

'Happen it's her heart,' said a policeman who had come upon the scene. 'Don't look long for this world to me.'

'Does anyone know this Eliza Hunt?' Greta asked round but the crowd was already drifting away. The policeman bent down and shook his head.

'You can move on, miss,' he offered. 'She's gone now.'

'Gone?' Kitty looked puzzled but then Greta saw the old woman was no longer breathing. 'Her name is Eliza, God rest her soul.'

'Aye, poor Eliza. A lifetime of service to end up in the gutter,' the policeman said, thinking she was a tramp.

'Oh no,' Greta said, quick to defend the woman. 'She said she was due at Mr Slinger's Pearl Emporium to make supper.'

'Then you'd better tell Mr Slinger that he'll be needing another maid of all work, if you don't mind, miss?'

Greta didn't need telling twice. There was nothing she could do for Eliza but perhaps there was something to be gained from the upsetting situation.

'Where're we going now?' Kitty complained as they rushed up the street. 'That was horrible seeing her dead. I want to go home.'

'Go back to Mam if you want.'

'No, I'll get lost. I'm staying with you.' They sped down towards the Minster, taking a short cut down an alleyway that brought them out behind the workshops and coach yards of Stonegate. The emporium was not hard to find. The back entrance was barred against thieves so they had to go round to the front of the shop. Greta didn't feel prepared for a proper interview but this was a chance worth taking.

'You stay outside and don't move,' Greta ordered. 'I'll deal with this myself.'

The bell clanged as she entered the shop, which was full of clocks and fine pieces of silver, but what caught her eye was the wall cabinet full of beautiful pearl jewellery.

A tall, youngish man stepped forward. He was sandy haired with bushy side whiskers and was wearing a black suit with a gold watch and chain across his waistcoat. 'Yes?' He eyed her up and down knowing she could not be a customer.

'Are you Mr Slinger?'

He nodded.

'Is Eliza Hunt in your employ?'

He nodded again.

'I'm afraid she won't be coming today.'

He raised his eyebrows. 'What excuse is it this time?'

Greta bowed her head. 'She died in the street, just now, on her way to make your supper. Her heart gave out and her last words were for you to be informed. I have just come from her. The policeman will be taking her body away.'

'Oh, I see and you are?' he towered over her, his eyes glinting like amber.

'Greta. I mean Miss Margaret Costello. I was just passing by when it all happened but I thought you'd want to know.' She drew herself up to her full height and stared back at him.

'Thank you.' He began to ferret into his pocket to give her a gratuity. She stepped back embarrassed. 'Oh no, sir, that's not necessary. I was on my way to find work but I have missed my appointment and who will want to employ a maid who cannot keep good time?' she lied.

He was examining her more closely. 'Margaret, did you say? Hmm, you know what your name means?'

'Yes, sir, a pearl. Mr Abrahams told me when I

109

worked for him.'

'Ah, Saul Abrahams... I recall that name.'

'Yes, sir, he showed me how to work some of his tools. I was his Saturday girl, in service there until he died.'

'And since then?' he quizzed.

'With the Blakes of Mount Vernon. They can give me a character,' she offered, hoping after all this time Edmund would be true to his word if she wrote to him.

The shop was empty so Mr Slinger showed her through the door into the back quarters. 'The kitchen is downstairs, the dining room on the first floor but I use that for private work. I don't have live-ins. I prefer to live alone.' He examined her more closely. 'You look sturdy enough for the stairs. Hunt found them a burden.' He paused. 'Dead in the street... Pity. Would you be interested then in taking her place, young lady? I would need references, of course. You would be on trial for a month and I have rules. You must never come in the shop, only to dust and polish under my supervision. Don't move anything. If there's a button out of place, I will know. You can have the half day and Sunday afternoons. Where do you lodge?'

'With my mother in Walmgate. Thank you. I am most grateful. I'm sure you'll find my work satisfactory. I learned a lot about jewellery from Mr Abrahams.'

'The watch!' he exclaimed. 'You were the girl who lost his watch.'

Greta flushed, sensing the offer of the job might be withdrawn. 'I went to deliver it and I was robbed of it. They thought I stole it but it was found.' She was ready to argue her case.

'Yes, I know. I was the man who received it and took it back to its lawful owner, Blake of Lendal. He's one of my customers now so all's well that ends well.'

'No,' she said. 'Poor Mr Abrahams died. The Blakes took me on for a while. They can vouchsafe for my honesty and I can provide a reference... Mr Blake of Lendal...'

'Ah, Blake. I will contact him today. Then we'll see how you shape up. In the future you come through the back door.'

'Of course but it was locked.'

'Locked and bolted. There's plenty who would like to get their hands on my stock. If you are on time the door will be open. If you are late then you will have no placement here.' He led her back through the shop to where Kitty was waiting, twisting her ringlets with boredom.

'Who is this?' the jeweller stared at Kitty with interest.

'Just my sister, Kathleen. She's looking for work too.'

'One is enough for now,' he said.

'Yes, sir, thank you. You have no idea how relieved my mother will be and to think it was you who saved me.' Greta bobbed a curtsey and sped out of the door, dragging Kitty behind her. She paused in Stonegate, stopping to look up at the elegant façade of the shop building.

'I've got a job, Kitty, a real job. He's given me the old lady's job. To think of all those Saturday afternoons I spent with my nose to the windows, staring at the beautiful rings and silver.' She was grinning from ear to ear in excitement. 'And now I get to work in one of these beautiful shiny shops!' Mr Slinger's Pearl Emporium was painted in gold letters over the door. 'Wait till I tell mam that he was the very man who had saved us from jail. Isn't it wonderful? He's making my childhood dream come true.'

'But what about me?' Kitty asked, trailing behind her in a sulk.

Eben watched the girls spring out into the street. This prospective new maid was sturdy with sapphire bright eyes but it was her sister, with the pearly bloom on her skin and that glorious mane of red hair, who took his eye. He was impressed that Greta had offered herself as an immediate replacement. It showed spirit and enterprise, just what he needed to replace Hunt. Now he was entrusting his household to this slip of a girl with no references as yet. Except she was not just any girl, she was the one who he'd rescued from injustice.

How close he'd come to keeping the watch, he could have easily removed the engraved initials and passed it on, but it was not good practice for a new face to be seen as a fence. Erasmus Blake had been grateful and had brought new custom to his shop. Now he had another reward for this good deed.

Margaret was a good omen for his business. Even the girl's full name was fitting. She would be grateful for work and her wage could be modest. Eliza had done him a favour in dying so conveniently. Later he smiled as he lifted Mary Queen of Scots from her velvet throne. 'I will always be grateful to you,' he whispered. 'You brought me such good fortune when you brought me to York.'

13

'Are you going to decorate your window for Christmas, sir?' Greta asked one December afternoon as she was clearing away his dishes.

'Whatever for?' he snapped back.

'It's just that I noticed the Manderfields and the Wehreleys have got pretty decorations in theirs. People like to window shop in this season, to get ideas for presents. I just wondered if...' Greta hesitated, knowing she had unsettled his morning routine.

'I don't see the point of cluttering up the window with cheap items. My pearls speak for themselves but if others are doing this to their advantage then perhaps...' He paused for thought, stroking his whiskers.

'I could help,' she offered. 'I've seen everyone's windows. We could do something different to catch the eye.' Greta drew a deep breath, not wanting to overdo her suggestion.

'I suppose it would do no harm. What had you in mind?'

'Something wintry and sparkling with loose twigs painted white, like branches. If you hang on bracelets and shiny trinkets, put a mirror flat on the windowsill underneath it would catch the sparkling gems and reflect them back. I've seen that done once before.'

'Where do you get all these fancy ideas?' Eben was looking up at her puzzled. Servants were not supposed to give their opinions but he supposed this girl was trying to be helpful.

'I'm always looking in shop windows. I may not be able to buy anything but it doesn't stop people like me from dreaming, does it? There are lots of visitors wanting gifts to take home. I've seen a little tree with bracelets and necklaces hung on it like Christmas decorations.' Greta could picture it all in her mind's eye and Mr Slinger had so many objects that were never displayed to their advantage, she thought.

'It will have to be done in your own time. I can't close the shop.'

'I could stay late one night, if that's convenient?'

'Under my supervision obviously.' He added, 'I hope all this effort will be worthwhile.'

'If you don't try, sir,' she blurted out without thinking of her place, 'you'll never know, will you?' She saw a brief flicker of a smile on his face at her boldness.

'I must say, Margaret Costello, you do surprise me with your ideas, especially for a girl from your...'

'Just because I come from the poor end of town, sir, doesn't mean I can't imagine. Mr Abrahams taught me how to look for good quality and workmanship, how to believe in going for what you want. I'll do my best not to disappoint, sir.' Greta bobbed a curtsey and turned round to leave with the tray.

'I didn't mean to insult you,' he called to her. She could see he was flustered. 'One evening, then, after the shop is closed, we'll put up the shutters so no one can see inside and you can make some exhibition. I can have a cold supper, a pork pie will suffice for once.'

'No, sir, I'll make a stew on the hob. It's too icy for cold food. Snow's coming, you can feel it on the air.' She gathered her coat and bonnet, making for the back door.

'Just this once, Margaret, go out the front entrance and see the other windows again before they put on their shutters.'

Greta lingered along Stonegate, turning down into Petergate then pausing at the shop doorway where poor Eliza Hunt had breathed her last. She said a quick prayer of thanks to the old woman for giving her this wonderful opportunity.

Mr Slinger was a tough man to please. Greta sighed as she scurried across the city against the cruel easterly wind. He wanted his fires lit, his breakfast cooked, errands made, house cleaned from top to bottom without so much as a please or thank you. He couldn't be more than thirty but he looked old before his time with his sandy hair greying at the temples.

Ned, the apprentice in the back, was a sullen creature. The workshop was out of bounds but Greta always made him a mug of tea, which had to be left outside the door with a shout. It was all so different from Mr Abrahams's little workshop where she had learned to sort beads and string pearls.

Stonegate was a bustling thoroughfare of shops. It had everything from dress shops and coach builders to bookshops and printworks. Greta never tired of watching people strutting by as she peered out of the living quarters above the shop, all the rooms stuffed full of books and silver to be polished to the master's exacting standards. Even his parlour was cluttered with bits of jewellery. From early morning to winter dusk she was polishing, mending and laundering but here was where she wanted to be.

Greta pulled her cloak tighter across her body. She had started walking home after work because she was saving her tram fares so she could buy presents for the family. She didn't mind the trek home but as winter gripped and the wind whipped her bonnet, she felt she needed more layers. She thought of how happy her Mam, Kitty and Tom would be when they opened their presents – they were going to have a good Christmas this year.

Slinger had no family, no visitors, no friends in the trade even. He kept himself to himself, always on the hunt for fine pearls, reading journals, taking walks around the city walls. Greta wondered how he filled the long evenings alone. He was a puzzle.

His shop was his life, especially when a customer came through the door. Nothing was too much trouble. He would sit them down, open cabinets, bring out selected items in a way that showed the sparkling gems to their best advantage so the customer soon forgot the cheaper brooch they'd seen in the window. He would explain the difference in quality and why the more expensive item would make the best investment. And sure enough, most times he would secure the more expensive sale and the cheaper item would remain in the window, ready to lure in another customer. She knew all this because one day when he was in a cheery mood he had explained his tactics to her.

'You have to let the piece sell itself.' He smiled. 'Quality always shouts the loudest and it is hard to resist.'

She felt sorry for the dealer. He might be a canny businessman but his home was just another showroom, everything in it was for sale – silver, pictures, clocks. He bought things, put them upstairs for a few weeks and then sold them. Nothing seemed destined to stay with him for long except a locked cabinet in his bedroom that she was not allowed to touch.

As she hurried along the cobbled streets, hearing the Minster chime the hour, a chill wind caught her skirts. Eben Slinger had everything and nothing, she reasoned. The Costellos had nothing when it came to money and possessions but they had everything that mattered. They had a roof over their heads, shabby and leaking as it was, and a family where there was love to temper their hardships.

Tomorrow night she was going to make her new employer the best Christmas window display she could give him as a thank you for trusting her with this position. She wanted to prove to him that deep inside Greta Costello was more than just a maid of all work and that she was capable of doing far more than black-leading the range and making broth. One day Mr Slinger would realise that she could be an asset to his business but she must learn to be patient for that time to come.

Kitty was in a foul temper when Greta came through the door. She thrust her hands in front of Greta's face. 'Just look at these paws. I've been scrubbing all day and you're late again! It's not fair you swanning around in your fancy shop and now I have to do your work.'

'We all have to do our bit to help Mam and it's nearly Christmas. I want us to have a good one so I'm doing some extra hours.'

'I want a new dress for the Mission party, I'm sick of that old thing.'

'Tom needs new boots first, but I'm sure we can find some material out of Adah's chest.'

'Why can't I have something new?'

'You know why... Tom's out collecting muck in all weathers. I'm doing my best. Look, you can come with me if you like. I've said I'll decorate the shop window and you can help. I'm sure Mr Slinger won't mind. It will be a change for you.'

Ever since the incident at the barracks, Greta was trying to keep her sister close to hand but it wasn't that easy.

'Can we have chips on the way home?' Kitty replied.

'Only if you stop moaning and make Mam her tea.'

Kitty slumped off in a sulk to do her bidding. Surely Mr Slinger wouldn't mind another pair of hands helping out? He'd have to lump it because Greta couldn't leave Kitty to her own devices. Not after last time with Nellie Ryan. Why did she keep worrying about her sister so much? Why did she feel it was her duty to keep her off the streets? Was it because she was wilful and easily lead or because she was growing into a real beauty? Could it be that she was jealous of her own sister's charms?

14

'You have to help me, Mr Slinger,' whispered a woman in a veiled hat from across the counter. Mrs Henry Claremont had been a regular customer until a decline in her husband's fortunes had prompted her to appear a few months ago clutching a rope of pearls with a look of desperation in her eyes.

'Can you sell these for me?' she'd pleaded and he had bought them for a fair price and sold them on to a London merchant for treble the price. Today she was looking anxious again.

'My husband is taking me to the Assembly Ball soon and will expect me to wear his pearls. I don't suppose you still have them?'

'I'm sorry, Mrs Claremont. I don't carry stock for long.' That wasn't true. He only sold when his buying was outstripping his profits.

She made to swoon and he rushed to find her a chair. 'I'm undone. What am I to do? I can't afford to replace them. He must never know.'

'I doubt if we would find a match for such quality. Your husband had good taste,' he offered, pausing to see the distress on her face. 'Perhaps it is better to tell him the truth.'

'That I couldn't manage the household budget during his lean times, that I panicked and sought to redress our income to keep up appearances but now things have improved...'

'May I offer a suggestion, madam?' He paused, seeing her eyes full of tears. 'It is possible to replace them with a replica.'

'You mean with fakes, oh, no!'

'Not fakes but costume pearls. They can be very convincing if well done. It's a matter of matching the size and length. You'd be surprised how many diamond pieces lie safely in the bank vaults while the lady wears paste.'

'Oh I couldn't, I mean, to deceive him... But if that is the only way. How quickly could it be done?' She looked up eager to hear more.

'For you, I will make an exception. I have the size and details of your purchase in my ledger somewhere. Leave it with me, but I might not have the exact diamond clasp.'

'I can hide it under my collar if necessary. They must look real.'

'Yes, they'll look real enough but I'd advise you not to leave them about.'

'How is it done?' She was curious now.

He tapped his nose. 'A trade secret, madam, but discretion is our byword. I shall have something ready in ten days' time for you to inspect.'

Mrs Claremont offered her gloved hand. 'Thank you, Mr Slinger. You have saved the day.'

Stupid woman, he thought, to sell such fine pearls just to keep up appearances. Faking pearls was easy enough as long as they were not tested on the teeth. In candlelight they would just about pass muster. After she'd left the shop, Eben went to his workbench to find some alabaster beads coated in a secret recipe of fish scales ground with mother-of-pearl, a stinking concoction to work with but they glistened on many theatrical costumes and cheap brooches and hairpieces. The long rope would be strung with silk and the fake pearls threaded through and graduated in size to look like the real article, but any jeweller would recognize them as costume pearls from the size of the drill holes alone.

This was not a task he liked doing but it was lucrative work and only he must do it so he could charge a premium for such a conspiracy. The saying in his trade that all that glittered was not gold was true enough. He looked at his timepiece and realized Miss Costello was tardy with his afternoon tea.

She arrived flustered, bringing his cup to the workbench. He could see that her eye was not on the task and she spilled some into the saucer.

'Sorry to be late, sir. The time just slipped by.' She paused, watching him sorting out pearl beads from a box. 'Are those real?' she asked curious at the rough way he was handling them.

'What do you think?' he replied, passing a pearl into her hand.

'They're warm not cold. Mr Abrahams loved his pearls and these look very dull, sorry.'

'Really? That's observant of you. What else did he teach you?' Eben was curious as to her knowledge.

'I used to sit by his side while he sorted and graded them into grain sizes. These are about twelve grains? But they don't shine right.' She made to leave.

'Wait, Margaret, you are absolutely correct. These are not real but imitations, good ones.'

'You sell fakes?'

'Not as such, but for insurance purposes or for pretty costume jewellery and bead work we can supply imitations. Some clients are too nervous to wear very valuable items in case of theft.'

'But surely people can tell they aren't real?' She stared at him with those intense blue eyes.

'Not in candlelight. And if you don't know real from fake, who is to know?'

'But it's not honest, is it?'

'Not everyone can afford the real thing. Why shouldn't any lady adorn herself with necklaces like these? There are moves afoot to grow pearls from oysters in oriental seabeds. Perhaps one day everyone will be able to have their own real pearls.' He smiled seeing the look of surprise on her face.

'But then your pearls won't be special any more,' she quipped.

Why hadn't he noticed how bright this maid was? 'What else did the old Jew teach you?'

'I was learning to string and knot beads before he passed away but he showed me how to measure and weigh pearls with his little scales and measuring tools.'

'Would you like to learn how to do this properly? A good pearl stringer will never be out of work.'

'But I have chores and duties here for the house,' she answered, flustered by such a suggestion.

'Maids are two a penny, a good pearl stringer and sorter is another matter, especially one who can do quality repair work. With each genuine sale, perhaps I could also offer an imitation copy for every day wear.' He was thinking aloud while sipping his tea and eyeing her intensely. 'I can find another maid to assist you.'

'I have my sister Kathleen, Kitty, who you met once. She's in need of work. I can train her up proper. She could help while I learn, but the apprentice, how would he take to a girl at the bench?'

'This would be a private arrangement between us. Since your reference from Blakes shows you have promise and I have found your work satisfactory, perhaps it is time to make use of your skill. The apprentice must do as I bid him.' He paused, another idea entering his head as he recalled how attractive he had found the young red head. 'If your sister is with you, there's no reason why you both can't live-in, you could have the room upstairs under the eaves. It's quite serviceable with a clean out, and then you'd both be on hand.'

'I'd have to ask my mam.' He could see the relief on her face at this unexpected arrangement. 'And when can we decorate that window, sir?'

'Tomorrow will be suitable, in the evening. And you can clean out your bedroom, that's if you...'

'Oh, yes, sir. We won't let you down.'

Greta almost skipped back home that night. How could one little thing change everything? Kitty would be under her eye, away from bad company, safely installed in Stonegate. Mother would have two less mouths to feed and she would have the chance to be a pearl stringer again. God was in his heaven the day he sent her to Mr Abrahams. She

123

would be able to work with pearls all day, help in the shop perhaps, and make sure Kitty did the work to everyone's satisfaction.

'I'm not being your skivvy!' Kitty sulked on hearing this news. 'Scrubbing floors, scouring pans at your beck and call. You tell her, Mam. My hands will be just as red raw.'

'Your backside will be raw, young madam, if you turn down such an opportunity.' Mother was banging the table in frustration. 'Stonegate is a respectable address. You will live under the Minster's watchful eye. Greta has done well for us so be grateful. I think it's God's purpose to have you both settled. One of these days there'll be enough coming in for us to rent rooms far from this midden of a backyard and it will be thanks to all our efforts. It'll do Tom's chest good to breathe far from these stinking fumes and damp walls.'

'You have to think of others, not just yourself,' Greta snapped, seeing the look on her sister's face. 'I promise you'll like it close to fine shops.'

'But not a penny to buy anything in them... I don't suppose you'll be getting a rise from that old skinflint.'

'Don't you ever talk about Mr Slinger like that. He's not old and he's doing us a good turn.'

'He's doing himself a good turn.' Kitty flounced round the table.

'Oh, Kitty, don't spoil everything. Tomorrow we'll help him decorate the shop window for Christmas. That will be something different and you can help.' Greta was looking forward to getting started, she had lots of ideas she wanted to try out.

'Huh!' Kitty stormed out the door. 'Remember you promised us chips on the way home.'

'Ungrateful little madam. I don't know what's got into her lately. You have no idea what a relief it will be to get her away from these streets. I fear for her, I really do, but at least she has you to guide her into better manners.' Her mother sighed with relief. 'You're a good girl, Greta. You deserve some success.'

'I just want to find a decent place for you and Tom and I don't care how hard we work to make that happen. Mr Slinger is kind enough in his own way.'

Mother stopped folding sheets to look at her. 'You don't think he's taken a fancy to you?'

Greta burst out laughing. 'What me? Goodness no. All he cares about are his pearls and his business. He's a strange man. I feel sorry for him. Don't get me wrong, he's very canny when it comes to buying and selling but as for anything else. I don't think he'd know what colour my hair is under my cap.'

'Well, most men stare at Kitty's copper locks. It turns heads and it's turning hers, I fear. She's at a silly age but she'll be safe under your wing.'

'Don't worry, I'll keep her on the straight and narrow. She'll be so busy, there'll be no time for shenanigans. She's only young and wants to have fun. At least this is a shop and not Serenity Blake's silent house with its thee and thou ways. Kitty wouldn't have managed there, that's for sure!'

'But the lad was kind to you, the son.'

'Oh, poor Edmund, look where it landed him

and me. I met Patience in the market the other week and she told me he's run away from his studies to be a joiner or something. It's Hamer I feel sorry for, left with his mother. At least I know she'll never darken the doors of the shop.' Greta laughed.

The following day, once the shop had closed, Greta and Kitty climbed the stairs to the attic to sweep out the bedroom where they'd be sleeping. Kitty moaned as they scrubbed the floor, made up the iron bed for two and dusted the cobwebs from the corners of the room. Greta found a guzunder pot, water jug and towels for them both. It was a cheerless room in need of a lick of paint but the advantage of living-in meant there would be no more traipsing through the snowy streets at dawn and dusk.

When they'd finished, Greta opened the window to let in some chill air. Spread out before her was a wonderful view of the Minster in the dusk. The city's rooftops sparkled with frost and smoke from the chimneys spiralled upwards into the still night air. There was a kind of magic about these ancient streets, where once the Roman legions had marched on their way north. Now the brass band played Christmas carols on the street corners and all the shops were festooned with decorations. Greta sensed it would be good to wake up to this view each morning, even if the Minster's chimes kept them awake all night.

Later she sat with Kitty by the range in the basement kitchen to sample the stew her sister had prepared earlier under her supervision. Greta showed her the cupboards and the larder and working table. Kitty would need watching but to-night was a night to relax under this new regime. 'You stay down here until the bell rings for you and he'll ring again to clear away.'

'Are you eating with him?'

'Of course not but I promised to help with the window. You can stand in the street and see how it looks when we're finished.'

'Ta very much and catch my death?'

'Kitty, this is your chance, don't ruin it before we've even begun. I know it's not what you want but give it a go for Mam's sake.' Greta tried to stay calm and not criticize again. 'Here's a list of duties in order, shall I read them out?'

'I can read just as well as you. Go and make a fool of yourself upstairs.'

Greta could feel her fury rising like bile in her throat. Take no notice, don't let her see she's got to you, she said to herself. Yet she was nervous going up those stairs, she felt as if she were entering a new phase of her life. Kitty was not going to spoil it for her by putting her in a bad mood. She'd dressed with care and, for once, put on the neck-lace that Mr Abrahams had left to her to bring her luck. Earlier that day she'd collected the broken branches of a Christmas fir tree that had been left for rubbish at the market then gathered them into a bunch to stick in a plant pot, which she'd covered with silvery paper. The branches were packed so tightly they stayed upright.

'I wondered if we could use this as a starting point, to hang bracelets and necklaces on,' she said to Mr Slinger, showing him what she'd done so far. 'Could we make a star out of brooches all clustered together?' she suggested.

'You have put some thought into this,' Slinger replied, ignoring Greta's creation and instead eyeing her necklace with interest. 'That's a fine piece you're wearing.'

Greta fingered the chain and smiled. 'Mr Abrahams left me this in his will. It was his wife's favourite pearl so I feel honoured to wear it.'

'It's a very fine pearl indeed. He had good taste.'

'It came from his wife's family. The Abrahams were together fifty years and very contented in marriage, I think. That's what matters, isn't it?'

'Yes, but you must take care of such a fine pearl. It will be valuable, too valuable for everyday use. What else did he give you?'

'Just this, and I've brought it here for safe keeping. I thought you'd like to see it. I'll wear it on my wedding day. I hope it will bring good fortune.' Greta made for the shop window. 'Do you want to start?'

'All this fuss over window dressing but you are right, Miss Costello, it's the little details that matter. We humans are always attracted to shiny things, just like jackdaws. Trinkets and pretty baubles will bring the customers into the shop then it will be worth this effort,' he said, turning to the task in hand.

'We all love brightness at Christmas. I love to look in the toyshop windows. It cheers you up on dark winter afternoons. How will you be spending your Christmas, sir?'

'What I do every day of the year. I shall be in the shop, filling in my inventory while drinking a

128

glass of fine port and maybe a visit to the Minster to hear the choir.'

'You have no family close by then?' Greta asked.

'I have no family. Now is that enough shiny bits?'

Greta smiled and nodded. 'Too much looks cheap, doesn't it? Getting the balance is what matters but I think it looks enticing, sir.'

'That's a big word for you to use.'

Greta bristled. 'I may be a servant but I was taught my letters.' She blushed at her forwardness.

'Of course, I made an assumption. Forgive me.'

'There's nothing to forgive. If that's all,' she paused, looking at her handiwork. 'I promised to let Kitty have a look before you lock the shop for the night. Please ring when supper is required.' When she went downstairs Kitty was fast asleep and the fire was almost out.

Greta had been so looking forward to decorating the window but the experience had been spoiled by Mr Slinger's superior comments. Why did men think they knew it all when they knew nowt? She was pleased at how the jewels sparkled on the branches through the window panes. The mirror looked like an icy pond. Even Kitty grudgingly admitted that it looked like fairyland as she shivered on the cobbles to give her judgement. Now they must remove the jewels for safe-keeping until the morning and close the shutters.

Lying in the hard bed, hearing Kitty snoring and the Minster clock chiming, Greta hoped she was doing the right thing in bringing her sister here. She only hoped Kitty wouldn't let the side down with sloppy work but she would watch her like a hawk. This was her big chance. All that mattered was that Mr Slinger taught her the art of pearl threading and knotting, gave her a lift up to a better position, then everything would be worthwhile.

15

In the weeks that followed Kitty's arrival and Christmas, Eben's quiet routine took a surprising upturn. It was the girl's hair that he found hard to ignore. It reminded him of the red-headed beauty in Burne-Jones's paintings. He caught glimpses of Kitty's burnished gold locks when she was off duty. Her skin was pearly white, her features sharp, and her hooded eyes questioning and insolent. He knew Margaret was covering for her sister's laxity but for some strange reason Eben didn't mind.

There was something about Kitty Costello that haunted his imagination, and he dreamt of her hair roped with pearls, the texture of those silky locks sliding through his fingers. He awoke aroused and ashamed, for the girl was too young to be the subject of such lust and she would be shocked at his longings.

The females filled the once quiet house with laughter and chatter. Margaret was reliable and steady, quick to learn with those delicate fingers and keen eye, while Kitty pranced around forgetting her chores. Ned, his apprentice, was smitten with Kitty too, blushing every time she appeared. Perhaps she would have to go.

In a bold move, he had decided to let Margaret assist in the shop on busy Saturdays in the run up to Christmas. She wore a black dress and her hair upswept under a cap. Her pleasant manner with the customers made her an asset to his business. Her Christmas window attracted much attention and brought in some new customers. Under his strict supervision she opened and closed the cabinet doors, rearranged the window displays and fetched and carried stock when required. A female shop assistant was a novelty and not a little daring. She was utterly dependable, not like her minx of a sister who was sloppy and uninterested in her duties. How could two girls be so different? Eben was curious enough to know more about their family and on an impulse suggested they invite their mother to afternoon tea one Sunday afternoon.

'That's kind of you, sir,' Margaret replied. 'But I'm not sure she would be comfortable. It's not usual for a master to—'

He interrupted her comment. 'I thought it proper for her to see your position here. After all these months, it might be a pleasant outing for her?'

And that was how he came to meet Sadie Costello, a faded little woman, quietly dressed in her shabby widow weeds. Sitting bolt upright in the drawing room she watched her daughters waiting on her with amusement. 'I hope my girls are doing their duty by you,' she offered.

'Certainly, Margaret is learning to string and sort pearls. Kathleen is young and full of spirit. She does her best,' was all he could say, trying not to blush. 'I am grateful you allowed them both to live-in.' It was an awkward meeting.

Mrs Costello sat nibbling on her macaroon while the girls hovered nearby. 'I'm so proud of them,' she added. 'They work hard so that Tom and I might find better rooms away from the river dampness and now with your employment... How can I thank you, Mr Slinger?'

'Not at all.' He looked away awkwardly. 'We must all help each other in life.'

'And I've not forgotten how you came to Greta's rescue over that gold watch business. I owe you an eternal gratitude for that. I know my girls are safe under your roof.'

When she left, he basked in the warm glow of her praise. It was not something he was used to in life. Perhaps there was something he could do to help this family achieve their goal, some little service that might also be to the benefit to his business. He would give this some thought.

'Don't you find old Slinger creepy?' Kitty was lying on her bed. 'He was so oily with Mother.'

Greta was folding away clothes into their pine chest. 'I thought he was most gracious and kindly to her, and don't be disrespectful of your employer. Besides, he's not old. We should be grateful to him for taking you on. You've not exactly covered yourself with glory these past weeks.'

'But he gets two for the price of one, I reckon.

He has you serving shop, cooking and working at the bench.' Kitty was unrepentant.

'I don't mind, I'm learning and you don't get wages for learning.' Greta felt her hackles rising at Kitty's lack of gratitude.

'So just when am I going to get out of that basement and do what I want to do? We've been here ages and I'm bored with being a skivvy.'

'Kitty! Why are you never satisfied? We have to get Mam and Tom into proper rooms, and I'll do anything to make that happen and so must you.'

'Oh, here comes the blessed Margaret of Walmgate on her high horse again,' Kitty snapped, pulling the counterpane over her head. 'I want to work at Madame Millicent's across the road. She says I have just the face for modelling her creations and my hair is perfect for this season's colours.'

'Hat trimmings, is that all you think about? You know that's not possible. I can't live here alone and I can't pay for your apprenticeship. Where do you get these ideas from?'

'Then get old Slinger to pay for me. He likes me, and you, of course. You could make him sweet on you and then we'd all be made up.'

Greta threw a shirt across the bed. 'Kitty! What a dreadful thing to say. He's my employer, nothing more. How can you think such things?'

'Easy. You want Mother settled and Tom to finish his schooling... You could make it happen if you set your mind to the job.'

'But I don't see Mr Slinger in that way at all,' she argued, sensing she was blushing.

'So? Why not look at him in that way and see

what happens.'

Greta was shocked and blew out the candle. 'I'm not listening to any more of this nonsense. Go to sleep.' She stared up at the darkness, her heart lurching with a fear. If Kitty carried on like this, they would both have to leave. Set her cap at Eben Slinger indeed, what a ridiculous notion and yet... There was both sense and madness in Kitty's reasoning.

He was a tradesman of note, a youngish bachelor in a secure position, but that was all. He wasn't handsome or attractive to her in any way. Besides she was his servant, his shop girl, inferior in class and education. The whole idea was both ungodly and wicked. But sleep wouldn't come that night as she tossed and turned unsettled by the troublesome thought that a decent marriage would see her family secure for life.

Eben woke sweating from his dream. They'd lain naked, wrapped together, a rope of pearls coiled over her breasts, her nipples pink like conch shells, erect to his touch, her legs open to receive him as his fingers nuzzled into her depths and her hands stroked him to ecstasy.

His cabinet of pearly queens was no match for the reality of Kitty Costello and it wouldn't do. But perhaps he could use them to work his way into her affections. A girl like Kitty wanted bright things: silks, hats to show off the colour of her hair, pearl-encrusted slippers... He sat up in bed, suddenly knowing such a girl must be wooed with pretty trinkets and gifts if he were ever to feel those tresses in his fingers. This would be a dangerous plan. She was too young and Margaret kept her on a tight rein, covering for her mistakes. Her very presence was temptation in the house. Perhaps it would be better to separate them in some way.

Yet if he replaced Kitty, Margaret might also feel she must leave too and she was by far the better asset of the two now she was almost trained up and used to his business dealings. How could he secure her services and achieve Kitty's continuing presence? Eben drew a deep breath. It was obvious there was only one way, even though it was unthinkable. He'd be the laughing stock of Stonegate but if he married his employee it would benefit everyone. Kitty could be sent across to the milliner, Madame Millicent, to work – goodness knows the girl spent most of her time there, trying on hats and admiring herself in the looking glass – while Margaret could continue helping with the business. Kitty would be close at hand just across the street and he could seduce her with gifts of pearls and gems.

He felt a rush of strange emotions. To give up his freedom for wedlock was ridiculous. But Margaret was a fine-looking servant, and eager to please. He could do far worse given his past failures with women, who never matched up to his exacting standards. Even her proper name was suitable: Margaret, the pearl.

Two weeks later, Eben made his way past a row of dilapidated old shop buildings, beer houses and ramshackle houses, searching out where the Costellos lived. He was shocked by the sight and

135

stench of poverty around him. He held a hand-kerchief over his nose. Men in shirtsleeves and caps stared at him when he asked for directions. He clung to his belongings and bent his head until he found their address. Sadie Costello, elbow deep in soapsuds and scrubbing on a board, was startled by this unexpected arrival. Eben took off his hat and smiled.

'Mrs Costello, may I have a word.'

She wiped her hands on her sacking apron, pushed back her hair and pointed at the one chair in the living room, looking anxious. 'What's up? My girls...'

'Margaret and Kathleen are at their duties. I just wanted a word in private.'

'Come in. Can I make a brew?' she asked with a look of relief flooding over her face.

'No, thank you. I can't stay long. It's just that I'd like your permission to address your daughter in a private matter of a personal nature.'

'I see.' She sat down. 'And which daughter is that? I know Kitty can be a handful. I hope she isn't causing bother.'

'No.' He held his hand up. 'Not at all, it's Margaret I'm talking about. I have grown fond of her over the past year. I know she's young but I would like to express my sincerest admiration to her with a view to her walking out with me.'

'You want to court our Greta? Well, I never. She's a grand lass, none better in the land. I don't know what I'd have done without her, sir.'

'Please call me Mr Slinger. She's such an eager pupil and a kind-hearted girl. I could do no better than to make her my wife in the fullness of time. Of course, if she is agreeable.'

Sadie looked shocked. 'What does my girl say to all this?'

'I have not declared myself, not without your permission as the head of the house. She may be my employee but I know she comes from a family with standards of propriety.'

'That's very kind of you to say so. It's no secret that some men do take advantage of the girls in their employ but I can see you are a true gentleman.'

Eben paused while his words sunk into her shocked mind. 'And please don't worry about your own situation. I would be honoured to make sure Margaret's wish to see you housed in a good district comes to fruition as soon as we're married. I'm sure we can find a better dwelling place at a reasonable rent and we would help, of course.'

The woman burst into tears. 'God bless you! What a blessing it was for us when you gave my darling girl her position. You have brought such happiness in so many ways. How could I refuse your kind offer but you will take good care of my Greta?'

'That is a given, Mrs Costello. I wouldn't ask if I did not think the two of us would make a good partnership in both business and private.'

'Then you have my blessing. I wish there were more in the world like you. It would be a far better place.'

Eben stood up to leave, having made his offer. He raised his hat as she led him to the door and waved him off. As he crossed the Foss and headed back towards the city he smiled, relieved to be out of such squalor and poverty. How had such a pearl of an assistant come out of such a rotten district? Now the first part of his campaign was all but accomplished, it was all clear to begin the second. The wooing of his assistant would pave the way to joining him into their family. It was time he took a wife. No one would suspect the real motive behind his choice and surely he was helping the whole family move away from those dreadful streets into a better life? Kitty would then be so grateful and it was for her alone that he was making this momentous step. He would wait as long as it took to make her his own.

16

Iowa, spring 1883

Jem Baillie clutched the letter of sponsorship from Jacob Allister close to his chest on the long journey from Glencorrin. The American lumber merchant had been true to his promise when Jem had written to him and asked if the offer of work still stood when Jem's mother passed away earlier in the year and there seemed no future for him on the laird's estate. He was restless for change. When the letter from Allister's lumber company arrived back, offering him a generous position, he'd sold his hoarded pearls to a jeweller in Perth and bought a passage on the *SS Circassia* from Glasgow to New York.

It was hard to leave everything he'd ever known behind but as he'd stood beside the mound that held his parents in the kirk-yard, he'd known in his heart that he had their blessing. His dream of distant travel had come about despite the loss of that precious pearl. *What's for ye'll no go past ye*, his mother used to quote and he knew there would be no better time than now if he was to make something of himself in a new country.

It was a rough crossing and his bed was a hard wooden bunk with a life preserver for a pillow. He leant over the rail as the steamship edged its way slowly into New York harbour; the outline of tall buildings in the distance, gulls screeching a welcome, hooters sounding from tugboats on the river. Once in New York he made his way by railroad to Chicago and then down to the city of Clinton where the Allisters had a great lumber mill.

To his embarrassment, on his arrival he was invited to meet Jake's mother and pretty sister Euphemia, and him still covered in dust and grime.

Marcella Allister plied him with sweet pie and thanked him profusely for saving Jake's life. Jem was mesmerized by the welcome. He had never been in such fancy surroundings. Or seen such a well-dressed family. He could not take his eyes off Jake's sister, who they called Effie for short. He'd never seen a girl with so many ringlets in her golden hair. They danced when she tossed her head and laughed.

The mansion stood outside the city with a porch full of pillars that went right round the house. The rooms seemed vast with white painted walls and drapes around the windows fringed with silk tassels. There were long blinds to keep the rooms cool and sofas and padded chairs of softest velvet. He was thankful that their gift of a tweed suit still fitted him for the season was chilly. The Allisters found him rooms in a lodging house close by and invited him to their vast church the size of a cathedral. They introduced him to their friends and neighbours as if he were an equal, which puzzled him. This would never have happened in Perth to a cottar's son.

It was just his luck he'd arrived at an important time in the new state as the demand for farmland was increasing so there was plenty of work for clearing forests and logging. What he hadn't expected was the vast enormity of the country, the depth of unchartered forests, the wideness of the rivers, but most of all the majesty of the mighty Mississippi that snaked down from the north.

He would be working upstream out of the little city of Muscatine, clearing vast acres of forest. He took the local train down there to inspect his new work station and caught his first glimpse of the huge lumber mills lining the shore, making the ones in Scotland seem so small and the River Tay little more than a mill stream. Yet they both had one good thing in common; their mussel shells also produced good pearls. Jem smiled at the thought that his pearl fishing days might not be over after all and that the skills Sam Baillie had taught him might just come in handy once more. Who knew what treasures lay hidden in the shallows waiting to be discovered? Suddenly he felt at home.

17

'Have you ever been inside the Great Exhibition Hall to see the paintings there? There's one portrait on the wall that looks just like your sister. You ought to see the likeness, Margaret.' Eben was standing next to the bench, hesitant, as if he wanted to say more.

Greta shook her head. When had she the time or the confidence to enter a fancy place like that?

He continued, 'I was talking to Millie Grocott, the milliner over the street and she is willing to let Kathleen model some of her hats. She also asked if I would make up a cap covered in costume pearls for some theatrical performance. Perhaps Kathleen would like to attend the dress rehearsal.'

Greta looked up from her threading and smiled. 'Kitty will love that. She is keen to work across the road one day, as you might have guessed from all the time she spends there, but I can't manage here without her.'

'Of course not, but I could hire a cook-cum-maid,' he suggested.

Greta felt herself go cold. 'But, sir, there'd not be a bed for another person to live-in unless she sleeps in the kitchen. I'd prefer not to share with a stranger.' She paused, waiting for his reply, her hands trembling at such news.

'I'm sure there's a way round this, don't worry. It's been on my mind lately to ask you something.' He hesitated again, as if summoning his courage, his cheeks flushed. 'Would you consider accompanying me to the Exhibition Hall in the Fine Art Institute to see those paintings?' he said. 'On your half day, of course. I'd like your opinion on these new artists they call the Pre-Raphaelites. Everyone is talking about them. I'm sure you will like their work.'

Greta couldn't believe what she was hearing. 'Thank you, sir.' He'd never asked anything of her before that wasn't to do with the shop. 'Kitty would love to see her double.'

'Hmm, I thought we'd go, just the two of us this time.'

'Sir, I'm not sure that would be–'

'I've spoken with your mother. She has no objections,' he interrupted her.

'When was that?'

'Oh, a while back and she was most pleased.'

Greta felt even more confused at this strange conspiracy. Mother had said nothing of such a visit when she'd called after church on Sunday. 'I'd like to check first. I don't want to be ungrateful but I'd feel most uncomfortable without a chaperone.'

'Have no fear, I'll explain later. Have you done that repair yet?'

'It's in the cupboard and labelled. I suppose everyone is getting ready for the Gala Day celebrations and wanting to look their best for the parades. Kitty says they are rushed off their feet with orders in the hat shop. I do love summer, don't you?'

'I prefer the Assembly Ball season myself. Summer's too quiet for business even when the trains of visitors arrive. My regular customers go off to the races and seaside or up to Scotland for the shooting season. They don't shop in the heat of the day. I shall look forward to our outing, Margaret.' He nodded and returned to his ledger.

Greta smiled, sensing they were like chalk and cheese in their opinions. What a surprise to be asked out to a special event in such a fancy building. Although if she were honest, she would enjoy a Gala day outing more. How things had changed between them over this past year.

'It's very kind of you, sir,' she replied. How strange he was paying her attention and taking the trouble to speak to her mother. Could it be that both of them were having the same idea?

Greta dressed with care for this unexpected outing, her hands shaking as she locked her necklace clasp into place. She wore a simple white cotton dress with pin-tucks on the bodice, reworked from Adah's old summer wardrobe. Greta's mother had refitted it without a bustle, and had braided the hemline with fresh ribbon. Washed and starched, it would have to do. Kitty had roared in disbelief at this sudden invitation.

'There you go, old skinflint's going to make a move on you. I've been watching him eyeing you when I bring you lunch in the back. He goes all pink when I catch his eye.'

'It's only a visit to see some paintings.'

'Better you than me. Why doesn't he splash out

on tickets to the Theatre Royal or take you boating down the river? You make sure you let the moths fly out of his purse when you're there. Make him spend. I would.'

'Don't spoil things, sis. I'm nervous as it is.'

'He should be proud to have you on his arm. I mean, he's no oil painting, is he?' Kitty giggled.

'I'm not listening to any more of your nonsense. Be useful and visit Mother for me and make sure Tom is doing his studies not out playing football.' She had to admit that Eben Slinger was not handsome, but he was well dressed, tall and presentable enough. Who was she to be choosy?

'There you go, bossy boots, always checking up like a mother hen. Go and enjoy yourself. You never know where it might lead. We might be calling you Mrs Slinger yet.' Kitty laughed and pulled a face. 'Greta Slinger, the pearl stringer...'

Greta threw a boot at her but Kitty was too quick and darted behind the door. 'Missed!'

Greta's jaw dropped as they entered the Institute building and Exhibition Hall with its vast vaulted roof. The hall was crushed with visitors all looking at the walls hung with paintings, nodding and smiling at some and rushing past others. It was like the inside of the Minster only noisy. She felt everyone must be staring at her in her homespun cotton with a boater perched on the top of her head.

Eben didn't notice her nervousness as he was staring at a large picture by Burne-Jones. He was obviously enraptured by the beautiful girl with the waist-length auburn hair.

144

'Isn't she splendid?' He turned to her.

Greta felt uncomfortable staring at her sister's double, and the woman was barely clothed. She smiled, nodded and walked on. This was a part of York life she knew nothing about until now: all these folk with nothing to do but walk round looking at paintings. Some of the exhibits she found brash and gaudy, others were tasteful landscapes of places she didn't know. Her eye was captured by some fine drawings and portraits in pen and ink. Some of the subjects of these Pre-Raphaelites were too personal for her taste but Holman Hunt's portrait of Christ holding a lantern entitled 'The Light of the World' moved her to tears.

'I thought it was you,' a voice whispered behind her ear and she spun round to face a tall young man with a thick black beard.

'I'm sorry?' She didn't recognize the owner of the voice and felt herself shaking her head until he smiled and then she knew him at once. 'Edmund Blake?' She could see he was with a group of brightly dressed young men. She turned to her escort, blushing as she introduced them.

'Sir, this is Mr Edmund Blake, the son of my previous employer. Mr Blake, this is Mr Slinger of the Pearl Emporium.' Had she done that the right way round?

Eben nodded, adding, 'Ah, Erasmus Blake's son. How is your father? We have not seen him in the shop of late.'

Edmund lifted his pipe. 'I'm not sure, to be honest. I've been studying in London. I'm afraid it didn't go down too well with Mama, but Margaret looks wonderful. I didn't know you were keen on this stuff.' He turned to address Margaret.

'I'm not, I mean… Mr Slinger encouraged me to come and see for myself. I work for him now.' What else could she say? Edmund looked so young and yet grown up, different from the studious scholar forced to stay in his room under his mother's control. 'Your parents are well though?'

'I'm afraid the black sheep is cast out from their Fellowship of Friends. Hamer is still at boarding school. We meet up when we can. How are you doing? I often wondered what happened after my mother threw her tantrum and released you for leading me astray… Only to the playfields on Gala Day,' he explained to Eben. 'This poor girl was blameless, of course, but Mother had to punish someone for my rebellion.'

Eben ignored this commentary. 'Miss Costello is training to be a pearl stringer. We are widening her experience of the art world. Come along now, Margaret. There's so much to see. It will soon be time for tea.'

There was no time to chat to Edmund, who raised his eyebrows, questioning her meekness as she was pulled away from his lively group. 'Good to see you again. Take care of yourself.'

'And you too,' she mouthed, wishing she didn't have to leave, but she was Eben's guest and beholden to him. How she wished she could spend more time with Edmund. What had happened to him since they last parted at Mount Vernon?

After viewing several more paintings Eben led them to the tea room, which was decorated with palms and pot plants. Greta sat bolt upright, uncomfortable in such lavish surroundings. 'Those artists are making a name for themselves but did you see that jewellery exhibit, soldered bits of metal with misshapen pearls, pebbles and stones of no value? I call it very primitive stuff. No wonder they are all as poor as church mice. Who will buy that chain mail design?'

'I'm afraid I didn't notice it, sir,' Greta replied, her mind unsettled by meeting Edmund. He had changed so much but he looked the happier for it.

'I suppose youngsters like to try something new, but such gaudy settings. It won't catch on. I hope you enjoyed our little jaunt?' he added, staring at her, demanding a reply.

'Thank you, it was most educational for someone like me,' she replied coyly, wanting to please.

'I wondered if for our next outing you would like to take a train to the seaside at Whitby. We can visit the jet factories and see their new stock. We have to keep up with the times, my dear.' He covered her gloved hand with his own and patted it.

'I've never seen the sea, sir,' she replied, letting his hand rest on hers. In an instant she knew that this was the crucial moment of choice. She could refuse this offer and squash his intentions for good and no offence would be taken. If she pushed his hand away and made no further comment, the message would be received and the matter ended right now. It felt as if her whole life hung in the balance, suspended, waiting for her response. If only she felt a little more excited by his obvious intentions, but try as she might, all she felt was gratitude. Was he really interested in being her suitor? For the life of her she couldn't think why, unless he wanted her services for free in the shop? She, on the other hand, had to do right by her family and they would want her to seize the chance of security once and for all. She let his hand rest on hers and smiled.

'I'd love to come. Thank you, Mr Slinger, you are too kind.'

'You must call me Eben on these outings, Miss Costello, and may I be permitted to call you Margaret?'

She nodded, relieved that a decision had been made and, as if to give her a sign, he added, 'Did I tell you they are building many new houses across the river, near the station? That might be just the district where your mother might prefer to live, don't you think?'

'But they would be beyond our means,' she whispered.

Eben smiled and patted her hand again. 'Not necessarily, where there's a will there's always a way to get what you want, I believe.'

Greta smiled back with relief. Perhaps they were two of a kind after all.

18

Their next excursion to Whitby was a great success. To view the great North Sea for the first time was such a thrill for Greta. She stared out over the shining silver expanses, feeling the salt spray on her cheeks, smiling at the boats bobbing on the choppy surface. Eben sensed he was making good progress with his plan. Work came first, of course, as they explored the jet factories along the harbour, examining the designs and wholesale prices of each little outlet while looking for something that would sell well in York.

He was looking for jet and pearl brooches, rings and pendants, which could be sold as mourning jewellery, but he suggested that Margaret choose something suitable for her mother to wear and a little gift for her sister too. 'Kathleen must have something in amber,' he said, pointing towards a cabinet of earrings. 'These will match her hair. She is too young for black.' Every time he thought of her, his heart raced with excitement.

'But they're very expensive, I don't have...' Margaret looked up at him aware that the gold settings cost more than her weekly wage.

'These are my gifts, my dear, and you must choose something for yourself too,' he offered, sensing she wouldn't dare to be too extravagant. Her choice of a bangle made up of a rainbow of coloured stones was not to his taste but she insisted on it.

'This is what I want. Aren't these pebbles pretty and so polished to look like jewels? It will always remind me of the seashore and this visit.'

They climbed the steep steps up to Whitby Abbey and a sudden gust of wind blew away Greta's boater. Eben chased after it and they both laughed. He had to admit she was good company.

They ate a fish dinner in a dining room by the harbour quay, as they looked out across the bay he told her of his ambition to have a chain of shops and be the most prestigious jeweller in York. 'I've got plans for bigger premises with such exclusive stock that all the gentry will come to our door.'

'But there are so many jewellery shops in the city already,' she cautioned, her blue eyes full of concern. 'And you have such a good position in Stonegate.'

'I want shops in Leeds, where there is money from industrialists, and Harrogate which is full of wealthy tourists going to the Pump Rooms to take the cure.' He could see her looking puzzled. 'You can be part of it, Margaret. You and I together will make a good partnership. I need someone to share my success with, and think what your mother would make of this arrangement?'

For a second he thought she winced at the idea and then she recovered. Perhaps it was shock at his hinted proposal but he knew she was as ambitious in her own way. If she consented to marry him, her family would be secure for the future. He could read her mind, weighing up the advantages and disadvantages of such an unexpected union.

He didn't love her any more than she loved him. One glimpse of how her eyes lit up at the sight of that penniless ex-Quaker, Blake, spoke volumes. A good marriage needn't be about romantic feelings, those might grow or not. He knew his first love would always be his pearls and his lust was for Kitty not Margaret. Thank goodness women didn't have those longings in their loins.

He would do his duty, provide her with his heir and enough children to keep her busy and then he would be free to follow his own secret pleasures.

Margaret was beyond reproach, pretty, sensible, loyal and hardworking. She was his cloak of respectability. His thoughts about young Kitty were not fit to admit even to himself. Margaret was the sensible choice, a sound business decision. Perhaps she would curb his lust for her sister. Inferior as she was, the girl would make a useful helpmeet, servant, shopkeeper, mother and hostess. Her manners for a working girl were impeccable, her accent was broad and coarse to the ear but with elocution lessons, it could be corrected. He would dress and groom her so that no one would slight him for his choice or recognize the Greta Costello in Mrs Ebenezer Slinger.

He noticed her staring out through the café window, deep in thought. She spun round. 'Why are you choosing someone like me to favour above others?' Those blue eyes latched onto his. 'I'm just your servant who happens to know something about pearls,' she challenged.

'That's not the point, my dear Margaret. You have other fine qualities I need: loyalty to your family's wishes, a keen eye for quality, and that can't be taught, an instinct for what is wholesome. I need your good counsel. I need you to keep my feet from leaving the pavement and jumping too high. You know I have admired you for a long time most sincerely. Besides, who can dress a window better than you?'

She smiled as he held his hand out and she clasped it tightly. 'And now we'll seal my offer and your acceptance with a glass of good wine.'

'Oh no, I can't. I've taken the pledge,' she replied, startled.

'There, see, you are already tempering my bad habits.' They both laughed. Eben smiled, relieved that everything was going to plan. They sealed their partnership over a cup of tea.

What am I doing? Greta thought as she stared out of the train window as they headed home, her stomach churning at their decision to become engaged. She hardly knew the man who employed her but he seemed to feel they were suited and would make a good partnership even though she was not of his class. There was a bit of her that was flattered by his interest but another part of her felt horrified at what she was committing to for the sake of her family.

She knew they would be pleased and relieved, their futures secured by this union. Surely it would work to everyone's advantage, but there was something missing. When she looked at Eben she felt no stirrings of desire. Perhaps such feelings were just a luxury for the rich folk to indulge in. Yet one glimpse of Edmund's dark looks had unsettled her more than she wanted to admit. He was out of her league in so many ways; he was educated and artistic whereas she'd finished her schooling years ago and she knew nothing about art. Better to settle for what was on offer. It would be a prudent choice that would lift them all away from the mire that was Walmgate. She must be grateful to Eben for giving her such an opportunity to better herself. In her head Greta was quite decided even though her heart was yearning for something more.

19

On a spring morning Kitty was helping Greta to dress for her wedding when she noticed her sister shivering at the sight of her shop-bought gown waiting on the bed.

'It's not too late to change your mind,' Kitty said as she pranced in front of the dressmaker's mirror they had borrowed, admiring her own bridesmaid outfit of apricot silk with a neat bustle edged with silver-grey fringing.

'I keep my word and I'm quite content with the arrangement,' Greta replied without conviction. Eben's sudden proposal had been unexpected and unwelcome but she had got used to the idea over the past months as they walked out together in public. He could be good company when he talked about the mystery and beauty of pearls and how they were found all over the world.

He had insisted on making most of the arrangements for the wedding. She was to be married from Stonegate in the Anglican church of St Helen's. She would have preferred the Mission Hall chapel but when Eben talked about marrying her in York Minster, they'd compromised on the ancient church not far from the shop. She sat with him each Sunday to hear the banns read out and warmed to the atmosphere of this most historic of churches. It was hard at first to find her way round the prayer book and she trembled at the vows they were about to make to each other.

True to his word, Eben had found a small house for Greta's mother and Tom closer to the railway station, across the river from Walmgate. Mother's eyes lit up with joy at its bright paintwork; it even had a cold water tap with a sink and its own lavatory in the back yard. So how could she have doubts when all her family were benefiting? Kitty was soon to join the milliner and a new live-in called Elsie was already engaged. It was as if all their lives were changing and Greta's qualms faded when she saw how much pleasure everyone was taking from this wedding. It was a sign of better things to come. Tom would escort her down the aisle in his new three-piece suit. He was no longer her little brother but a strapping lad of fifteen who had hopes of joining the army soon.

Greta's own outfit had been chosen with care. It must be serviceable. She decided on a navy and silver spotted silk skirt with matching fitted jacket braided with silver-grey trim. She was not going to waste Eben's gift on a white dress, much to Kitty's disgust. 'You'd look wonderful in oyster silk, dark is for widows.'

'This won't show the dirt,' she'd replied. It was a businesslike outfit for a businesslike arrangement that suited both parties. Eben was a good man who would look after them all. She would not waste his money.

As she placed her pearl pendant round her neck, she prayed they would find the happiness that Saul and Adah Abrahams once found in their marriage. She had saved its appearance for just this moment, hoping it would transfer a blessing on their union.

Her only extravagance was the hat, carefully designed to match the dress by Madame Millicent, or Millie as they now called her. It was a navy blue concoction with a mist of silver-grey netting to cover her face for luck as she entered the church. It perched on Greta's thick black hair, setting off her pale complexion and blue eyes. On her right finger she wore her engagement ring. It was a fine pearl surrounded by little diamonds. It was very unusual and made especially for her, Eben had announced proudly.

Nora Walsh had gasped at the sight of it. 'Pearls for tears, dearie,' she'd warned but Greta refused to believe in such nonsense, glad that mother would be living safely away from all that superstition. Pearls were pearls; some said they were an ill omen, some said they cured madness and despair but she still thought of Mr Abrahams's words – they were a gift of nature and you made your own luck in this world.

Hadn't they brought her good fortune already? She was soon to be mistress of one of the shops she had gazed into as a girl all those years ago. Now she would be living within the very street of her dreams. She had so many ideas to share with her husband: how to smarten up the premises, how to decorate their living quarters with pretty antiques and mirrors to add light and how to make the shop look even more enticing to passing customers.

As for the marriage bed, she knew what she must

endure on that first night. Girls around Walmgate heard all the gossip about how men had the right to mount their brides on their wedding night, causing pain and bruising for a while. Out of these couplings would come the children she would cherish so she intended to oblige Eben willingly in gratitude for all he was doing for her family.

There was some joy missing from all these thoughts, but it was easy enough to shove any concerns aside. How could she marry without feeling love for him? Perhaps these sorts of feelings would come in time when they were settled down together. Greta smiled as she arranged the net veiling over her face. 'You scrub up well for a skivvy,' she said to herself, knowing from today onwards she would be the respectable wife of a tradesman with a home in one of the best streets in the city. What more could she ask for when all her childhood dreams were coming true?

Eben was pleased with his wedding plans. It was a modest affair, just family and the vicar. Margaret looked charming in her tasteful gown and hat but he couldn't tear his eyes away from young Kitty in her apricot silk extravagance. If only it were she who he was marrying but that was out of the question. She was a useless maid, plain cook and no help at all in the repair shop. Kitty was for ornamental use and decoration. Her time would come but for now he must concentrate on making use of his new wife's assets.

They held a wedding breakfast in the Royal Station Hotel and he was relieved that Margaret's mother didn't shame them. He had made sure she was kitted out for public view in a new dress. He felt a deep satisfaction that everything was turning out so well. After the reception he planned to take his wife to Harrogate where they would stay in a fine hotel. They would peruse the shopping arcades in search of suitable premises; he was determined to open a shop in this wealthy town.

Once on the train he relaxed back in his seat opposite his wife. She really did look the part.

'Well, my dear, it's been a memorable day, has it not?'

'Thank you, it's been just wonderful. Mother was so thrilled and Kitty looked pretty. I can't believe how our Tom has shot up.' She sighed with contentment.

'I think you all looked charming. I am so glad you agreed to be my wife. I know our courtship was a little longer than I had hoped but those months gave us all time to find your family a proper home and to get to know each other. I have such plans for us.'

'It is grand to be on our own at last,' she replied. 'I've hardly seen you for weeks, it feels, and it's good to be away from the shop too.'

'Only for two days, I'm afraid. I daren't close for longer, not with the competition in the street. I think those new German jewellers are up to something. We must make sure their prices are higher than ours. We must go further out to country auction houses and see what gems can be found there.'

'But no business today, Eben, not on our wedding day, surely?' She sighed, knowing she must come second to his shop. 'We can plan all that when we return.'

'You're right, of course, Margaret. I forget myself sometimes. Forgive me.'

'Isn't it time you called me Greta?'

'I will always call you Margaret – my own pearl.'

'If you wish but I prefer Greta.'

Later they dined in silence, each aware that soon it would be time to retire for the evening and Eben must do what was expected of him. He knocked back another glass of wine to relax himself while Margaret sipped on her china tea with a little grimace. She did look ladylike, he thought, only her accent gave her background away.

He saw the pearl ring shimmering in the candlelight and he noticed how the pearl at her neck glistened against her cream skin. It was almost a paragon in size, set in a deep rose-gold claw. Everything about her looked perfect but his heart sank at the thought of making love to her. How could he explain that there was something offputting about her? A flicker of shame burned at how he had lured her into marriage knowing he could never really rouse to her. If only it was Kitty in his arms, wild, lively Kitty covered in pearls, her body at his disposal.

They retired up the grand staircase arm in arm. He undressed in the bathroom while she changed behind a silk screen into a long white nightdress, her black curls tumbling down to her waist. For a moment he wanted to flee from the sight of the girl waiting in the bed.

'Are you tired, my dear?' he ventured as he slipped in beside her.

'A little but it's been such a memorable day,' she whispered.

'Then let's just sleep on it all and tomorrow we can begin our new life together.' He kissed her cheek and sank back into the feather pillow with relief. After all there was plenty of time to consummate this marriage.

Greta also lay back with relief. Had Eben seen her fear, her distaste and anxiety? It was enough to be lying side by side as companions and partners in this sumptuous room with its velvet curtains and fine furniture. She wanted to savour every second of their stay in such luxurious surroundings. To be waited on as a lady was unnerving but she could get used to it in time. She smiled. Did they recognize her as just a humble servant or did they think they were not really married and she was his mistress?

There was plenty of time for them to come together physically. She was in no rush to be tied by children just yet. They would come, as God ordained, in the fullness of time. Marriage was not just about procreation, the vicar had explained, but for the *'mutual society, help and comfort that one ought to have of the other both in prosperity and adversity. In sickness and in health, until death do us part.'*

She'd breathed in those sacred vows by the altar where Ebenezer Alfred Slinger had plighted his troth to Margaret Annie Costello. How gracious were the words of the prayer book. When they returned she intended to worship again at St Helen's. It was considerate of Eben to make no demands on her tonight but when that time came, he would not find her wanting.

20

Jem Baillie watched the black women soaking the river clams in a barrel. He drew closer to watch the process as they lifted the clean shells, testing them, scooping out the flesh to reveal a rainbow sheen of shell within, precious mother-of-pearl, and then fingering through the flesh for any hidden pearls.

'Got one here, sir,' she yelled with a grin on her face, pulling out a sizable specimen from a curiously shaped shell. 'You can always count on dem elephant ears to give you good luck.' She promptly stuck the pearl into her mouth and tucked it in her cheek. 'Don't trust nobody here, sir.'

'Have a go yersel',' offered the bright-eyed beauty, looking at Jem with interest, but Jem was already backing away from the stench of rotting flesh piled ready for feeding hogs in the sun. He wasn't here to go clamming, fun though it was. His task was to survey the river and size up when it would be ripe to roll some logs down to the sawmill nearer to the town of Muscatine.

He stretched his arms over his head to loosen his muscles and looked back at the forest of white pines, breathing in the smoky air, the heat, smiling to himself as he watched the busy clammers lighting up stoves for their supper in their tented shanty town. Just as in Scotland, the summer camps along the river were full of amateurs, up to their old tricks so they could garner as many pearls as possible from the rich harvest in the riverbeds. It was this unexpected sight that made Jem feel at home and recall his outings with his pa all those years ago. Have I exchanged one forest for another? Not a bit of it, he thought.

This was no narrow-minded Scottish logging camp, full of his childhood tormentors, instead there were immigrants like himself from across Europe and beyond, all classes of working folk from blacks and soldiers to tough German loggers and Scandinavian giants. All of whom were risking everything to start a new life in the heartlands of Iowa. He was no longer just a forester but the gaffer in charge of the river logging team.

Even after a year he couldn't get used to the size of the trees, the variety of birds and the woodland creatures he couldn't yet name. The river was a vast jungle of vegetation, rocky outlets, islands and bluffs, a great highway for paddle steamers, fishing boats and barges dragging logs down to the south. He'd found a great camaraderie among the lumbermen as they'd worked side by side, cutting down virgin forest to stockpile and then float down the water in springtime to the waiting lumber mills. There was a willingness among the men to help build barns and log cabins, clear stubble, share suppers, and always someone was celebrating some event, be it a wedding or a wake, with hooch and dancing.

For the first time in his life Jem no longer felt alone or an outsider because everyone was an outsider here, different in language, colouring and

161

background. It was a melting pot of nations and faiths, bonded together by their desire to clear land and stake their claim. Good luck had given him a head start. *I'll not always be just a log master. Give me time and show me the way,* he prayed. Given his luck so far he sensed opportunities undreamed of in this strange new world. Perhaps a little pearl hunting might hurry the job along.

21

'And this young lady is my eldest daughter, Mrs Slinger of Slinger's Pearl Emporium, Stonegate.' Sadie introduced Greta to the neighbours sitting at the table of her new home.

'Greta, please.' Greta nodded, seeing them admiring her smart two-piece suit with tartan trim that Eben had bought for her in Harrogate.

'Are you well, love? You look a bit peaky.' Sadie winked and looked at her daughter's stomach. Greta blushed.

'Very well, thank you, Mother, but very busy and I can't stay long. We have new stock arriving.'

'She helps him in his business. He's such a good man to all of us and he's opening another store in Harrogate.' Everyone was looking impressed and Sadie glowed with pride.

Greta hated this gossiping so she smiled to the visitors and made her excuses to leave. 'I'll pop in later in the week. I don't want to disturb your gathering.' She backed out of the door disappointed not to find her mother alone. The house was always full of people from the street or Mother was out helping someone with their laundry. It was good to see her busy and happy in this new part of the city, but dropping hints in front of the neighbours that Greta might be in the family way was another matter.

Everyone in her family was happier because of her marriage to Eben. Kitty was thriving in the hat shop and now had her own circle of friends. Tom had taken the Queen's shilling at last and proudly turned up in his uniform. Eben was busy with his plans for a shop in Scarborough as well as Harrogate, travelling around by train, planning his new empire. So why did she feel so miserable? She ought to be on top of the world but all she felt was frustration and a failure as a wife. Something was wrong, something was missing, and she couldn't even speak to her own mother about it. How could there ever be a hint of a child growing in her belly when... Greta found she was weeping. 'I've been married for nine months and Eben has never touched me in that way,' she sobbed, kicking the autumn leaves in frustration.

He came to bed late but not before he'd checked on each of those wretched pearls by his bedside. He slipped under the covers and fell asleep while she lay awake yearning for some overture of love but there was nothing. The worst part was she couldn't share her sadness and puzzlement. What had she done wrong? Part of her was relieved that he did not try to consummate their marriage, because she had no real physical feelings for his body, but on the other hand she felt insulted that after nine months of marriage he was not inter-ested in her either. They might as well be brother and sister sharing a chaste bed and it wasn't natural.

She knew without the physical act there was no legal marriage. There'd been a couple in Walm-gate who'd had their wedding annulled by the priest because she was still a virgin after many years. It had been the talk of the street. Was this a game Eben was playing with her? Did he intend to separate from her when it suited him?

How could she not feel cheated and isolated by this shameful knowledge? Their marriage was a sham but she must play the part of a devoted wife knowing that in his eyes she was still just his pearl stringer.

What made it worse was that while she was suf-fering Kitty flourished in her new-found free-dom. She dashed in full of plans and visits to the theatre with her latest beau. She wore outrageous concoctions that came straight off the latest fash-ion plates, sallying forth like a ship in full sail, gathering admiring glances. Greta felt a terrible jealousy within her.

You rushed into this arrangement to please all of them, but what about you? her heart cried. Noth-ing had changed but the quality of the clothes on her back and the leather of her boots. From clogs to calfskin, serge to silk, is that all she had to look forward to? It was in this state of confusion that she wandered around the streets trying to look purposeful and prosperous, lingering along the market stalls where once she'd been content to help round the back. A strange longing came over her to revisit Mr Abrahams's old workshop in the Aldwark district. Once across the river she made her way through the town to the once familiar street.

Through the bow window she saw a silversmith beating out his metal in full view, making strange-shaped trinket boxes studded with polished pebbles. The designs were new and different. She paused in the doorway to take a closer look.

'Who designs these?' she asked, taking a professional interest in the metalwork.

'My wife draws them and I beat them out in silver or pewter. She collects the stones and polishes them.' A man of about forty stood up. He was wearing a linen smock over his shirt. 'Can I help you?'

'What attractive objects they become,' she replied. 'I once used to work here...'

'Irene!' he called and a woman drifted into the workshop from the living quarters, rubbing her hands on her apron. 'The lady is admiring your designs.'

Greta flushed, having no money on her to purchase anything, but she couldn't help noticing the beautiful pieces on display. 'This is in the new style, isn't it?'

'Yes, we use metal and stones together in harmony with each other. Have you heard of William Morris and his Arts and Crafts Movement?'

Greta smiled. 'I went to the Pre-Raphaelite exhibition last year.' Edmund Blake flashed into her mind. 'I knew a student who was keen on the new look when I was in service in Mount Vernon.'

'Not Edmund Blake, you know him? He's

doing some interesting designs out on the moors near Malton. There's a whole guild of craftsmen making furniture for the home using traditional methods. They often call in if they're passing. Who shall I say was asking?'

'Just Greta, I mean, I'm Mrs Slinger now,' she added, needing to make that clear. 'My husband is a pearl jeweller in Stonegate,' Greta said. 'But I love this work.'

'Oh, do come in, I'm Irene Patton and this is my husband, Norman. Do excuse the mess...' Irene bustled Greta through into the back room she'd known so well. Now it was a blaze of brightly coloured paint and tiles and the furniture was draped with fringed shawls and pretty cushions.

Irene took off her apron to reveal a flowing dress-cum-robe that hung loosely over her body. Greta was shocked to see that she was not wearing a corset nor was she pregnant. The woman's golden hair was flecked with silver grey and it flowed down her back in a loose braid just like the models in the paintings at the exhibition. Round her neck, she wore a thick Celtic cross decorated with glass-like stones.

Irene was quick to notice her interest. 'You like these? I'm experimenting with quartz and silver. I make bracelets to match.' The table was littered with sketches and paintboxes and little pouches of polished stones.

Greta looked round with longing for the old days. 'This was once Mr Abrahams's shop. I used to help him in the house and he taught me about pearls. I was very happy here.'

'It's got a good atmosphere. Norm and I love

this workshop. We reckon jewellers have worked here for centuries. If there's anything that interests you, we do take commissions.'

'I'm afraid I'm not in a position to buy. My husband chooses for me but I can think of someone who might like something like this as a present,' she offered.

'We've rented a stall at the market for a few weeks before Christmas, a group of us will be there, hoping to sell these for presents. Would you be interested in coming?'

Greta nodded, knowing the season would soon be upon then. 'I think my sister would love something like this. When is it?' Irene handed her a beautiful hand printed handbill with an exquisite scrolled edge.

'This is beautiful work, is it in the Arts and Crafts style too?'

Irene laughed. 'Everything you see is influenced by it: printing, bookplates, glass, jewellery and clothing. I have a friend who makes these robes too. They are so cool and easy to wear, with no restrictions and soft textures in warm colours of the heart. Do come if you can and tell your friends.'

Greta stared round the room, reluctant to leave. 'It's so lovely to be back here. I hope I haven't disturbed your work. I was just curious to see who'd taken over his house.' It was hard to keep the sigh out of her voice.

'Not at all and do come back and visit us again. You are a link to the little shop's past. Not everyone likes our work. I think they find our designs unsettling. As you see we don't exactly conform to Stonegate's standards.'

Greta made her way back home in a mist of excitement and unanswered questions about the couple who had just welcomed her so warmly. There was something different about them, not just the way they had transformed old Saul's workspace but the shared delight and pride they had in each other's work.

The Minster chimed three o'clock and a sudden realization made her pause. That was it! The Pattons' workshop was alive with new ideas and love, just as it must have been when Adah was alive and Saul was in his prime.

Now she was returning to a traditional shop displaying conventional designs. All the stock at the emporium was regimented in cabinets behind glass. You touched only by appointment or invitation. There was a place for everything and everything in its place, frozen in aspic like those jelly-like concoctions in shop windows. Greta walked home slowly, knowing now that she was trapped in a cage of her own making. You walked into the security of marriage with your eyes wide open. Did you do the wrong thing for the right reason? It was your dream come true but is it now?

She stopped and stood looking into a clock-maker's window, watching the ticking clocks, shaking her head in dismay. For better or worse, Greta, you made those vows before God. As she crept home along the cobbles, she felt a wild hope rising. Our bargain was never sealed. Perhaps there was some haggling to be done if this marriage was to survive. The door might be shut but it wasn't locked tight. But did she have the courage to release the catch before it was too late?

Eben couldn't understand how his wife had changed but something had taken place and it was unsettling his comfortable routine. He could tell she was not pining for physical union. She was cold that way and was content to lie alone in bed until he chose to retire. She worked on her pearl stringing and repairs, grading new purchases and putting them neatly in the purchase ledger, greeting customers with her usual civil manner.

There was no extravagance in her wardrobe but lately she had begun to change her appearance, experimenting with some handmade garments that Kitty laughed out of the room.

'Why are you wearing Romeo and Juliet costumes?' he had asked when she'd appeared in a particularly flowing gown.

'It's called rational clothing,' she'd argued. 'Why should we be always laced into unnatural shapes. It's not good for our bodies.'

Dear Kitty had sniffed. 'It makes you look fat.'

His wife took to loosening her hair into a coiled mass at the base of her neck and she started wearing the most gaudy paste necklace from some shop at the far end of town.

'Don't wear those in public,' he ordered. 'They are a poor advertisement for our shop, my dear, stick to our pearls.'

'But I like the bright colours and the metalwork settings are so different. Don't you think?'

'No I don't. It's cheap theatrical stuff. Wear it round the house if you must but not in the shop. What will our customers think?' She complied

169

for a few weeks and then started wearing it again but he had other things on his mind and this minor rebellion was the least of his worries.

He was on the brink of purchasing a fine shop in Harrogate. The business had failed and the owner was looking for a quick sale. There were staff only too willing to be kept on for a lesser wage. It was too good a bargain to be missed but it would need his full attention.

The stock was tired and the owners had been slack with repairs. The premises needed upgrading and the clientele needed wooing back from other rivals in the town. Once more his great pearl was held as a collateral in securing a good loan.

As for his other ambitious project, he was making progress with dear Kitty Costello, she of the Titian hair and skittish manner. Under Millie's wing she was blossoming into a knowing little tease, and establishing a reputation as an ambitious girl who was going places. She was photographed in studios with hats and costumes and he'd suggested she borrow some of his parures and other gems that could be used in catalogue advertisements. She was a vain little thing and when he'd given her a pair of pearl-encrusted slippers for her birthday she'd squealed with delight.

Margaret disapproved, thinking it such a silly gift for a silly girl, no doubt. But she had no idea of the fantastical garment he was creating late at night, something that would be for his eyes alone when the time was ripe. He'd purchased a satin corselet in deep cerise silk, to which he was adding row upon row of costume pearls until it was covered. He imagined it encircling Kitty's waist, glistening in the candlelight as they enjoyed their night-time tryst. It was all planned. Step by step he would draw his little minx into his arms. Not that it would be easy with his wife around but he would find a way to secure his obsession. He would know when his peach was ready for the plucking.

22

Greta dragged her sister to the Christmas arts and crafts stalls outside the market square. 'I'd love you to see their jewellery and I think you'd like some of the scarves and ornaments.'

'What do I want ornaments for? They'll only need dusting. It'll be so boring. You go on your own. I've got my own Christmas shopping to do.'

'Please, just for once, come because I'm asking you.'

Kitty huffed and puffed but the milliner allowed her to take a short break and accompany her sister on this trip. It was two weeks before Christmas and the shops were full of decorations and pretty candlelights. The market was crammed with craft stalls full of handmade greetings cards, stained glass panels in emerald, lapis and gold designs and wooden carved toys.

Greta spotted Irene and Norman's jewellery stand. While she went over to join them, Kitty drifted from one stall to another, catching the eye of a group of artists smoking pipes. The sisters eventually met up again at a stall displaying wooden racks, small tables, chairs and shelves. Edmund Blake was busy showing a customer some carved panelling.

'Isn't that...?' Kitty whispered, eyeing the young man with interest.

'Yes, Edmund Blake from Mount Vernon.'

'He's changed, gone all arty-farty... He used to be so handsome.' Kitty sighed.

Before Greta could reply, Edmund looked up in surprise, smiling at them both. 'Ah, the Costello sisters.' He laughed. 'Never thought I'd see you two at our humble show. I thought Stonegate shops were more to your taste these days,' he quipped.

'What's he on about?' Kitty turned to Greta. 'What's wrong with Stonegate?'

'Nothing, he's just teasing us. Have you made a sale yet?' she asked.

'I don't think York is quite ready for our designs but it will come. How are you, Miss Costello?' He bowed his head towards Greta in a mocking greeting.

'She's Missus Slinger now,' Kitty chipped in. 'But I'm still Miss Costello.'

'Not for long, Kitty. I can see some of those artists over there eyeing you for their model. So how is married life to the jeweller from Stonegate?' Edmund had heard about Greta's marriage.

Greta nodded, ignoring him. 'I love Irene Patton's designs and the hammered pewter trinket boxes. My mother would love something like that.'

'But not you, not quite up to Stonegate standards then? Norm sells to Liberty in London by the way.' Why was Edmund being so rude and curt?

'Her hubby has got two shops, one in Harrogate too, and I'm Madame Millicent's assistant,' Kitty added, sensing the tension between them. With a flounce she drifted off to the next stall.

'I hear you are working out on the moor?' Greta decided to stay. Edmund was once her ally. She didn't want him to think her above herself.

'Near Malton, I'm working on a new house up in the Wolds. The owner is a distant relative of William Morris. It's our best commission and it's called Tanglewood. We're doing the dining furniture and all the wall panelling.'

There was a brief silence as they took stock of each other. Greta forced a smile. She'd never heard of the place. 'I'm sure it's very splendid. I'm glad you found your vocation. Your family will be relieved.'

'Why do you say that?' he replied. 'You of all people know what they are like.'

This was too much. Greta gathered her paisley shawl around her shoulders and looked Edmund in the eye. 'I think family is the most important consideration in life. It's our duty to respect and support them before all else. My mother never had a moment's peace after my father died. Now she has a comfortable house and my brother has joined the army. Kitty is happy...' He had to know about her success. He had to understand her choices.

'But what about your wishes?' he interrupted, matching her gaze.

'I am content with where the Good Lord has placed me in life.' How could she be mouthing such pious nonsense?

'Oh well, each to his own. I wish you every happiness with your jeweller. You once told me you liked shiny things.' Edmund turned back to his stall to give out handbills to passing customers.

His rebuff felt like a kick in the stomach. Why had he said that to her and why had she felt the need to justify her actions? It sounded as if he were disappointed in her. How could she have the last word as she walked away? 'At least my family haven't cast me off.'

He glared back at her with a look of hurt that made her feel ashamed. He didn't deserve that riposte. It came from her own discomfort. If truth be told, she hadn't wanted him to know she had married her employer. She'd wanted him to see her as young, single with all her dreams ahead of her. If only he knew... She swallowed back her disappointment, wanting to walk back and apologize, but the moment had passed. The crush of people was too strong and Kitty was waving across to her.

'Greta, come here, you have to see these bracelets. Tell Eben I must have one of these for Christmas.' She was lifting up one of Irene's beautiful designs. Greta rushed over to join her.

'I told you it would be worth coming to see them.'

Later, they went to a tea room. Kitty was still going on about the bracelet while for Greta the crumbling cake felt like a stone in her throat. Seeing Edmund had stirred up a whole stew of feelings; shame because she'd insulted him, fury because he had belittled her. He had chosen to leave his wealthy family to pursue his artistic dream. He would never be rich but like Irene and

174

Norman he possessed other riches. Why did she resent him for this?

In her heart she knew the answer as they rushed back to the shops, their break over. This is what you settled for, Greta, she chided herself. A pleasant house, a good business, a grateful family and a husband who is considerate but cold. As they hurried up Petergate she felt tears blinding her eyes, hot salty tears of regret.

23

York, 1885

'You don't mind if I give Kitty a little surprise, do you, Margaret? I know it's her birthday while you are away.' Eben had asked Greta to do a spot check on the Harrogate shop and treat herself by staying over for the night in the flat above the shop.

'No, of course not, have you made something for her?'

'It's not quite ready yet but I thought I'd take her out somewhere...'

'If it's more jewellery, she'll be excited. You know how she likes showing it off, and now she's that painter's model, she just loves all the fuss,' his wife added.

'I'm not happy about her posing, it's not quite savoury. I'm surprised you agreed. Those artist types think such girls are their property. You

175

should chaperone her more carefully. We don't want her getting a reputation, do we? We have our position to think of.'

'You mean you have your position. Kitty's a sensible lass and Irene Patton promised to look in on the sessions. It's her hair they are after and she can't help that. It came from our Irish ancestors.'

Margaret always had a ready answer these days which was annoying. How was she to know how impatient he was to fit his pretty corselet onto his muse. He was going out of his way to please Kitty in every way, indulging her with that awful bracelet Margaret had produced for her Christmas gift and she had bought one for herself as well without consulting him. Over this last year he was sure she was softening to him.

When Margaret was busy in the Harrogate shop, he would take Kitty out for supper on the pretext that she didn't eat properly in her little room at Millie's and it was Elsie's half day. He would take her out to supper again knowing she would look splendid on his arm. He hoped strangers thought she was his young wife. The last time she drank copious amounts of wine, much to his delight, so that when they retired for the evening he was able to give her a more than brotherly kiss without any resistance.

She'd smelt of lily of the valley, which had made him so delirious with desire he'd taken his special pearl finger glove to bed to bring him some relief.

Margaret would be away for a night, which would give him time to complete his seduction. Kitty was old enough now to be wooed and won, and canny enough to know the rewards for whatever arrangement he could put in place. His attention would be a good introduction for her into the world of men's secret desires.

Margaret need never know of this liaison. He had no desire to use her in that way.

The next day, Eben waved Greta off, knowing she would be perfectly safe in the ladies' carriage of the train; he had instructed her to take a cab to the shop premises when she arrived in Harrogate.

On the way back from the station, he went to the barber to be shaved and have his whiskers trimmed. His hair was pomaded and he invested in a bright waistcoat with pearl buttons.

Returning home he checked he was alone. He unlocked his cabinet drawer in the workroom and brought out the pearl-encrusted waist corselet, now edged with a black lace trim and satin ribbon. His hands trembled at the touch of it. He busied himself in closing the shop, eyeing the ticking clock on the wall, barely able to wait until it was time for Kitty to dart across from the milliner to the emporium. She was expecting to have a birthday tea with them both tonight before she visited her mother but Eben had other plans for her on this special night.

The bell rang and he opened the door to Kitty as she scurried through the shop and up the stairs. 'I'm starving. Where's our Greta? Have I had a day with Moaning Millie! I couldn't do anything right for her this afternoon. I think she's jealous that customers choose me to serve them. I'm sick of wearing black all day. At least when I'm modelling

I get to wear bright robes. Where's Greta?'

'Margaret had to go to Harrogate. I would have gone myself but there's a dealer coming in tomorrow. It's Elsie's half day so we're going out to dine tonight.'

'Ooh, nice! Where is it this time, the Royal Station Hotel? I like it there but I'm not going dressed in this drab thing. Can we stop off and see my mam?'

'Margaret suggested you borrow her pretty frock as it's your birthday and you can choose anything from her jewellery box too. She's ordered a special cake for tomorrow.' Eben followed Kitty upstairs to their bedroom door and then hung back. Slowly, slowly, he must take his time.

Kitty shut the door behind her. He had spread the dress out on the bed, a turquoise grosgrain dress with frills at the sleeves, demure but very tasteful.

The door was flung open a few minutes later. 'Will I do, Your Highness? You are both so kind to me. You're sure she won't mind, only she doesn't like me rooting in her jewel box.'

'It will be our little secret. She won't know if we put it back safely.' Eben smiled contentedly, until he saw Kitty was sporting one of those chunky bracelets that Margaret insisted on buying for herself and Kitty for Christmas. She had also borrowed Greta's fur cape as the night was chilly and snow was in the air. 'Let's go, I'm starving!'

They called a horse-drawn cab to take them to the hotel by the railway station. Eben had reserved a table and they dined among the palm trees and jardinières on a mousseline of salmon followed by

178

Chantilly cream with strawberries washed down with champagne. Tonight he would spare no expense, knowing she was the finest-looking guest in the room. He touched her hand and they laughed at their little outing. He knew he must get her back to Stonegate before the effect of the champagne wore off. 'You'd better go back and change, dear. I know you want to visit your mother. There's one more gift I've got for you too.'

Kitty's eyes lit up. 'How exciting, poor Greta's missing all the fun.'

'Don't worry, you can have your family celebrations together when she returns. Tonight is our ... my special treat.'

On the way back over the cobbled streets, Eben felt his tension mounting, anticipating her delight when she saw his present. There would be a personal fitting that would lead to... He was hardening at the very thought. This scenario had been played out in his mind so many times. Kitty would lie back and his dream would be complete. They would be discreet, of course. He would find her rooms where all his fantasies would come true. Margaret would turn a blind eye to them, relieved that she would always be the proper wife. Tonight would be the beginning of it all.

Slowly they climbed the stairs. 'I hope you like my little creation. I've made it for you. It has taken me months to perfect the garment which will be for our eyes only, my dear.'

'Sounds mysterious.' Kitty giggled. 'Where is it?' She was quite tipsy and stumbled up the stairs. 'Oops, I'm tiddly, Greta will be cross. She never drinks liquor, does she?'

'That's her problem, she doesn't know what she's missing,' Eben replied. 'Come into the drawing room and I'll show you. There's no one in the house. I told Elsie she could stay at her home tonight.'

Slowly he opened the door, lit some candles and closed the blinds onto the street. The box was tied with a pink bow and was waiting on the sofa. Kitty grabbed it and pulled the ribbon to release the box, she pushed aside the tissue paper and lifted out the pearl corset. She looked at Eben in surprise. 'What's this?'

'It's for you to wear ... handmade with real pearls...'

'But what's it for?' Kitty was lifting the garment as if it were a duster.

'I made it for you to wear for me when we...'

'But it's underwear. I can't wear anything like that over my shift.'

Eben moved closer. 'It's for you to wear next to your skin, for me to touch when we are lying together.'

Kitty backed away with a strange look in her eyes. 'Don't say another word!'

Why was Kitty throwing his gift on the floor?

'It's disgusting.' She looked up at him in surprise. 'You made that thing for me to dress up in like a whore?'

Why was she acting like this? 'You will look like a goddess, with all your hair let down.' He picked up his creation and held it to the light. 'See how it glistens with pearls.'

'I'm letting down my hair for no man until I've got a ring on my finger. How could you even think

180

I would? And with my own sister's husband? You must be mad.'

'But she need never know. Why do you think I married her?' He sighed. 'Because of you, my darling girl. I've yearned for this night ever since I first saw you. Why don't you like it?'

Kitty was shaking her head as she backed towards the door. 'Because I hate pearls and I don't like you much either. And you thought I'd bare meself and wear that contraption to please you?' she whispered. 'Let me out of here, you dirty old man. I'm not staying here a minute longer. Wait till I tell my sister what you get up to in secret. If anyone should be wearing that thing it should be your wife.'

Kitty was afire with indignation as she made to leave but Eben barred her passage. This was not how it was meant to be. 'Stay, you have to understand how I feel about you. Don't tease me like this.' How could she deny him after all he had done for her family?

'Let me out,' she cried. 'I shall tell my mother too.'

'That wouldn't be wise. Who would believe your word against mine? I've seen the way you flaunt yourself with those artists, the way you thrust those breasts...' His nostrils flared with fury.

'Them boys have never laid a finger on me, and to think all this time you was planning this, sending our Greta away so you could pounce on me. I've heard about gents like you who can't do what they want with their wives and pay working girls to get it up. I'm from Walmgate. I know about dirty things like that. You should be ashamed of yourself. And we thought you was a decent cove. Wait till I tell them the truth.'

Eben went cold at her taunts, trembling as she threatened him. 'Now it wouldn't be wise to upset the apple cart, would it? You don't want your mother to lose her home. Who do you think pays her rent?'

'Why you dirty rotten... I'll not hear another word,' Kitty yelled as she pushed past him but he reached out to grab her.

'I thought you cared for me,' he pleaded. Why was she rejecting his advances? This was not how it happened in his dreams.

'Let go of me. I can't bear to be in the same room as you.' She spat in his face, making for the top of the stairs.

'No, no, we can't leave it like this.' He felt the panic rising. If she told everyone, he would be made a fool of. 'Let's come to some arrangement. Forget what I said.'

'I'm never coming here again. I'll tell the whole world what sort of man you are.'

'Don't be foolish. It's dark out there and you can't walk alone in the street. Stay here and talk about this. Just wear it the once for me and I'll never ask it of you again.' Surely she owed him something for all his lavish expense.

'Stop this. I'm off, and get your hands off me!' She turned her back on him to descend the stairs. Eben grabbed her, sensing danger if she ran into the night. To seduce his own sister-in-law, and Kitty being much younger, he'd be the laughing stock of Stonegate. She mustn't do that to him. He must not be humiliated. His hands lunged into her back and he thrust her from him in disappointed fury. 'Go home then, you stupid bitch!'

Then slowly, oh so slowly, he watched her lose her balance, tumbling, tumbling down the stairs, bouncing, hitting her head until she lay silent. There was no sound as she stared with her eyes wide open, piercing him with her glare in a look of terror and surprise. He found himself calmly walking down to where she lay, knowing she was dead, seeing that beauteous hair falling over her shoulders in a riot of curls.

It was as if he were in some nightmare as he lifted her limp body in that borrowed dress, staggering back to the bedroom where her shop clothes lay. He undressed her with tender care, eyeing her beauty with no emotion at all, closing her eyes and covering her face with a towel. He re-dressed her in her work uniform as if she were a rag doll then returned his wife's clothes to the wardrobe. He glimpsed himself in the mirror, he looked like some pale-faced ghost. He went in to the street and hailed a cab.

'My servant is unwell. Take us to Skeldergate,' he ordered, lifting Kitty inside and leaning her against him as if she were asleep on his shoulder.

They crossed over the Ouse and he knew what he must do next. He paid the man and carried her out as if taking her to the house nearby. When he was sure the cab was gone, he changed direction and walked down the steps to the edge of the River Ouse. The water looked deep. He filled Kitty's apron pockets with stones, the biggest he could find. Slowly he waded into the shallows, going as

183

far as he dared. He could see no lights flickering or any signs of movement among the boats as he rolled her from him like a heavy sack, throwing her as far as he could manage. He heard the splash and then silence as her body sank into the muddy deep.

Soaking wet, Eben walked back to Stonegate through the dark alleyways of the city as if taking a drunken midnight stroll. In a daze of disbelief at his terrible deed, all he could think of was that tomorrow it would be as if there had been no visit, no outing, no outrageous quarrel or terrible outcome. Tomorrow he must begin life afresh with his wife, but first there was the corset to strip of its pearls and destroy. Only then could he sleep in peace.

24

Greta was not happy with the running of their Harrogate store. The takings were down, just as Eben had predicted. Griffin and Squires were efficient but they'd treated her with disdain when she first arrived.

'We're doing nicely, Mrs Slinger, no need to worry your little head over the sales ledgers. They are in good order.' But she wasn't satisfied and demanded to see all the books. In the afternoon only two people came into browse. When it was obvious that they were about to leave without buying anything she stepped forward.

'Just a moment, we might have what you want in our York shop. I can have a tray brought over for you to see tomorrow,' she offered but the customers drifted out. She turned to the assistants. 'I notice you didn't offer to help them.'

'Oh they're just browsers, we get a lot of them, you can tell by the way they turn up their noses at our stock.' Mr Griffin rubbed his starched collar, not looking Greta in the face. She went back into the stockroom to examine the safe. It was crammed full of good necklaces and pearls.

'Who is buying all this? We can't keep all these valuable pieces out of sight,' she snapped.

'Your husband asked us to buy up anything that looks good.' Squires smiled. 'We're only following orders.' He was trying to make her look foolish but she knew better.

She lay in the tiny bedroom upstairs, unable to sleep. There was far too much stock here and not enough being sold. At this rate they would not cover the costs of this shop. Taking on Harrogate was a risk and if it drained the profit from their York business they would soon be in trouble. She couldn't wait to return early to Stonegate to report all her fears to Eben. He needed to see for himself the state of their profit and losses here. It would not be good news.

Greta arrived back late the same day to find Eben in bed shivering and feverish. 'How long has he been like this, Elsie?' she asked at the sight of his distress.

'I don't know, ma'am. He won't get out of bed.'

'Eben, what's the matter? Elsie, run for the doctor down the street.'

'It's just a chill. It was raining. I got wet.'

'Did Kitty like her present? She should have stayed to look after you.'

'I'm afraid she didn't arrive. I expect she was tired and went to your mother's,' he replied, his head buried in the pillow. 'You'll have to look after the shop today until I am recovered.'

'Of course, I hope Elsie has brought you beef tea and something to sweat the fever out of you.'

This was not the time to worry him about the Harrogate shop. It could wait. For once the shop was quiet so Greta got on with restringing a pearl necklace and checking over the books without Eben peering over her shoulder. Just as she thought, there was too much stock here too and it worried her.

Later, when he was sleeping, she took a walk across the river bridge to see her mother who was busy mending a torn sheet with a worried look on her face. 'I'm right glad you've come,' she said looking up with relief. 'It's our Kitty, she never come home to see me last night like she said and I've had a boy sent from the hat shop asking why she's not in work. Wait until I get my hands on her.'

'That's funny. She was supposed to come across to the shop after work. Eben had a present for her birthday. Now he's in bed with a chill and she never arrived.'

'It'll be them artist folk down Aldwark, she's allus hanging out there. You go and see if she's stopped over. I hope she's not back to her old tricks. I'm sorry to bother you, lass, when you

186

look so done in.'

There was just the possibility she'd gone to model for one of Irene's friends and they'd had a party. Oh, Kitty, you are so thoughtless. Greta sighed as she walked back towards the city, the chill easterly from the river cooling her frustration. I leave them all for five minutes and there's Bedlam.

When Greta arrived at Mr Abrahams's old workshop, Irene was busy in the backroom. She was surprised to see Greta but welcomed her in to sit by the fire. 'You look frozen through, girl.'

'Is Kitty around?' Greta asked, dreading the answer.

'We've not seen her for weeks, not since she did that sitting for Edmund's friend, the artist Jonnie Bairstow.'

'I'm worried. She seems to have disappeared. They wouldn't have run away?' Greta asked, blushing.

'Good Lord, no, Jonnie's not that sort of man. She'll be staying with friends.' Irene was trying to reassure her.

'But no one's seen her and she hasn't turned up for work. She may be a madam at times but she'd not risk her job. She was supposed to call in on Eben for a birthday present and you know Kitty and gifts but she didn't arrive.'

Greta returned puzzled and weary. Kitty wouldn't let people down without good reason. It was then a rush of fear seeped through her limbs and her heart thumped. Something had happened to her sister. 'Where are you?' she called out, but her cry was lost in the wind.

Two days later a feverish Eben was still in bed and in need of nursing. It was Greta who made her way to the police station on Silver Street to report her sister missing. 'I am that worried she never came home and we've had no word from any quarter. She's a respectable young girl. My husband is sick with worry.'

The desk sergeant took Kitty's particulars: age, colouring and occupation. 'Have you tried the infirmary, she may have had an accident and be waiting for you there?'

Greta was ready for this. 'I made inquiries and no one of her description has been admitted. Do you think something awful has happened in the street?' She began to shiver.

'Now don't you go getting upset, Mrs Slinger. Girls of her age, well they do silly things, run away and such like. Was she keeping company with a young man, a soldier?'

'Not to my knowledge. Kitty, Kathleen has lots of friends, shop girls and artists. She would've told me if there was anything going on.'

'You'd be surprised what youngsters keep from their families. We will make inquiries ourselves but I'm sure there is a perfectly good explanation for all this.' He paused, seeing the look on her face. 'If she's still not back by the end of the week, we'll take the matter further.'

His cautionary words brought no comfort at all as she made for the shop. It was a relief to see Eben sitting by the fire sipping broth. 'Any luck, my dear?'

Greta burst into tears. 'Something is wrong, I

188

feel it in my water.'

'Come and sit by me. We will face it together. I have been neglecting you of late, Margaret, letting you do my work for me.'

Greta seized the moment. 'I'm worried about Harrogate. It's losing money. You need to lose one of the staff. There's too much stock and not enough custom through the door.'

'Nonsense, it's early days yet. You worry too much.' He put his arms round her. 'I don't know what I'd do without my little helper.'

'What if Kitty is in danger? You hear about pretty girls being kidnapped and taken into slavery. She may be on a ship in the North Sea. You have to make the bobbies take notice, please, Eben.'

'When I'm on my feet, I'll go myself. I'm sure the constables are doing their best to search for her but girls do run away, you know.'

Greta clung to him. 'Not Kitty, she wouldn't let Mam down or you after all you've done for her.' She sobbed into his chest and he gathered her close.

'Let me console you for all this terrible worry. We'll face this together, Margaret.'

That night Eben reached out to her in bed, slowly making his intentions clear. It was only a swift act of love, and it hurt as well as comforted Greta as she lay in the darkness while he panted over her. Kitty's disappearance had brought them together at last. Tears flowed both of sadness and relief. They were one flesh now, properly wed. Husband and wife together whatever the future held.

25

In the months that followed Kitty's disappearance, life changed for the Slingers of Stonegate. The posted handbills asking for any sighting of Kitty faded in shop windows and on the police noticeboard. No one came forward with any news. Tom came back on leave to scour the streets to see if anyone had information about his sister.

Eben spent more of his time at Harrogate, coming home each night frustrated by the lacklustre performance of his business there. 'I don't understand why we are performing so poorly. There's money to be made and yet our shop seems to be losing it.'

'Have you got rid of all the stock in the safe?' Greta challenged him.

'Of course not! That's our insurance if ever our cash flow is tight. Don't you know anything after all this time?'

'Don't take it out on me. Our books don't balance. We have a safe full of quality pearls and gems here. Why hoard what we can't sell? I think we should close Harrogate. Right now. I don't trust those two, left to their own devices over there.'

Greta watched with concern as Eben pored over the books, wearing a permanent frown. He jumped when the shop bell rang and sometimes was snappy with customers who didn't buy. She put it down to the loss of profits and worry over

Kitty. She noticed creditors calling in for their unpaid bills and when she handed over money from the till, Eben was furious.

'Make them wait.'

'But they are our neighbours and word will get around that we are unreliable. We must sell on the most expensive stock and rely on the cheaper pieces for quick sales.' It was a reasonable solution to raise capital.

'I did not come into business to deal in cheap fripperies,' he snapped. 'We are a quality outlet. We'll just have to cut our overheads. Thank goodness the apprentice has left. Elsie will have to go. You can manage.'

Greta took to visiting her mother as much as she could. Sadie Costello had been distraught since the disappearance of Kitty and Greta tried to comfort her, but she'd noticed she was also being consoled by a new neighbour, a widower called Albert Langton, who worked in the railway sheds. Greta was so pleased to see her mother had found companionship at this terrible time and was relieved that she wasn't alone, especially now that Tom was stationed away in Colchester.

It tore Greta apart that Kitty wasn't there, squabbling, full of beans and plans, laughing and joking, sulking when she didn't get her way. How she missed all the things they used to fight over. Somehow her sister's absence heightened her own loneliness. She hated going home to Eben and seeing how he was losing confidence in his own judgment. He was letting things slip in the workshop too and was careless in putting stock away safely. There was no order in his repair work. He was letting her take over jobs he always did himself. It was as if he had lost heart in his business.

One morning she came downstairs to find him buying more pearls from a local rep.

'Mr Slinger, can I have a word,' she ordered. 'We can't afford to buy these,' she whispered, turning to the dealer with a smile. 'I'm sorry, Mr Bernstein, but we already have some of your lovely pearls but they have been slow to sell of late.' The dealer looked at her in surprise. 'Is that so? I thought we had an understanding, Eben,' he replied, looking over her shoulder. 'We were hoping you were trading out of your difficulties. Your wife seems to think you've not been straight with us.' He paused. 'Perhaps it's time you settled your outstanding bills with us. Better still, you can return some of your surplus stock to us at the end of the month. Trust works both ways.' He banged the door as he left.

'Now look what you've done. How dare you speak for me like that! This is my business and I will do things my way. I wear the trousers in this house and don't you forget it. I don't want him thinking we can't pay. It's bad for business.' There was a look of pure hatred in Eben's amber eyes that scared her for a moment.

She slept alone again that night. Something was going wrong and the hope she'd felt that there might be fruit from their recent loving wilted when her monthlies arrived on time. How could she make Eben face up to their mounting debts? It was now a matter of urgent concern and she felt sick in the stomach knowing things might only get worse.

Two weeks later Greta returned from the Harrogate shop with bad news. 'Griffin and Squires have been stealing from the till. I went to see the police with my suspicions and they told me to mark notes, which I did. When we closed the shop, the police were waiting outside to search the men. They had half our takings in marked notes. Can you believe it?'

'You had no right to do that without my knowledge,' Eben snapped, feeling foolish that she had taken such a risk.

'I was only trying to help,' she pleaded. 'To get to the bottom of why our shop was failing. Don't be angry. I did tell you that the eye of the master can't be in two places at once. They've taken advantage of us both. No wonder the books didn't add up. But it's not too late if we're careful.'

That night Eben opened his cabinet of precious gems knowing he would have to sell some of his beauties, but he would never part from his Mary Queen of Scots. He would never sell her no matter what and he hid her in a secret pocket far from his wife's knowledge. Stella Maris would fetch a good price in London and the others would have to go too. He sat clutching his girls, weeping. They were his life's work. How could he part with them?

Eben stood by the upper window, watching the waning moon ride slowly over the city rooftops, sensing that since Kitty's death, his days in York were numbered. In saving his own skin, in throwing her into the river's deep waters, he had brought down a terrible judgment on all his efforts, a failure in everything he touched. For that act of lust, the Furies were closing down on his future. He felt the presence of the great Minster looming over him and the wrath of God waiting to punish him. He was almost bankrupt, forced into selling his best stock. Now Elsie had left the basement kitchen, his wife was back working where she'd begun back in the scullery, lines of worry etched across her brow. Things were a mess, a terrible mess. He had to make provision to escape his creditors. How had it come to this? Surely the only solution was to pack up and leave before it all got worse?

Perhaps he should disappear alone and take his chances abroad? Perhaps it was time to leave his wife to face the wolves? But Margaret had her uses. She was his cover of respectability. He took a brisk stroll along the city walls at dawn to clear his fevered mind of panic, trying to regain his composure with the thought that, for better or worse, she'd vowed to support him.

He did not fancy public humiliation in the newspapers if they reported his bankruptcy. Better to leave before the bailiffs came to the door. Eben took heart from this decision. He must scour the trade journals to search for a solution that might just fit their dire predicament.

As he came down the steps to return back home he noticed a poster displayed on the ancient walls of Bootham Gate. He stared at the billboard, suddenly heartened. It was a drastic solution but this could be the answer.

'How would you like to go to America, my dear?'

Greta was busy dusting out the cabinet shelves in the shop. 'Why would I want to leave York?'

'Listen, come and sit down. You realize we are going to have to sell the business, let it go?' She looked up at him, shocked. He took her hand, quick to reassure her, smiling. 'But that doesn't mean the end of things. I've been reading about rivers full of pearls in the Americas. There would be work for a good pearl dealer. They had quite a pearl fever a few years back but now they've discovered unchartered rivers full of clams, as they call them. It could be an exciting adventure, a new beginning for us. After all you've been through lately, it would take our minds from–' He paused, not wanting to name her sister.

'But my family are here. How could I leave mother? We have to find out what happened to Kitty.' He knew she would resist at first but he persisted.

'Look, your mother has a new companion in Bert Langton. Tom is away in the army and soon to go to India. As for your sister, alas, we may never know. You can be free to travel without worrying about them. A new beginning is what we both need.' He knew he could persuade her given time.

'I still haven't given up on Kitty. She's out there somewhere. I'm sure she'll be found,' his wife protested.

'You have to face it, my dear, she's not coming back. Better to let her go. I think the New World is full of opportunities for people like us – hard-working, ambitious risk takers. I've seen a poster advertising passages in a steamer from Liverpool.'

'But it'll cost to cross the Atlantic and we have to live when we get there.'

'We still have a few assets left in the safe.' He was not going to tell her about his precious pearl. He would never deliver that up to pay for a debt. She was his lucky charm.

'Are things still bad, Eben? I thought we'd paid off most of our local debts.'

'You know they are. The Harrogate business has taken up all the slack. Why did I ever think it would work without good staff? You've seen how we are placed. I admit I've misjudged my purchases, been too trusting, but I'll never make the same mistake again. With you to guide me I won't go astray.' He smiled, holding her hand, eyeing her engagement ring. The gesture didn't go unnoticed.

'What if we didn't like it there?' She was softening to the idea and the possibilities.

'Then we'd come back. Think about it. Steamships go faster than sails. It need not be for ever.'

How could Greta concentrate on cleaning after his sudden idea of leaving the country? It was a shock to think Eben would give up on his business so easily but a relief that at last he was taking some responsibility for his mistakes. Why shouldn't they begin again as a couple who, having faced such sorrow, bravely carried on elsewhere? He was right, it would take her mind from the loss of poor Kitty. The knowledge that her sister might be dead sat like a stone in her heart. Greta had accepted that months ago, but a little candle of hope still flickered, hard to blow out. At least, in their terrible loss, Greta felt she and Eben were coming closer together as couple.

As she was sorting out the pearls they must sell, she thought again of those first words Mr Abrahams spoke all those years ago when he showed her his gems. *We are like pearls, Margareta. Without the grit there would be no pearls. Sorrows have a way of strengthening the heart.* Was the grit in her soul and the sorrow it was bringing all part of growing something good out of the bad?

When Eben returned he had brought her a cup of tea. Something he'd never done before. 'Here, drink this, dear. Please don't say anything to anyone else yet and especially not to your mother. It must be our secret. I have to make plans so we can leave without a fuss or morbid farewells. We'll just leave one morning.'

'But I can't do that. It's not fair on Mother. We can't just run away.'

'No fuss, Margaret. This is how it must be if we are to make a clean break. You can send a long letter from the ship. We will be travelling for ages and when we do settle you can give everyone our address. Promise me not to tell anyone?'

Greta nodded. It was all too much to take in. Now there would be boxes to pack, clothes to sort. But she just couldn't disappear like Kitty, it would be too painful for her mother. How could she warn her?

Later she stood on the shop doorstep, looking down the busy street. I love this place. *Why should I leave by the back door?* It didn't feel right to just flit off and not see their tenancy through.

197

She must trust her husband to do what was right but why did she feel so afraid?

Perhaps if she had been running things, this would never have happened. Eben was too generous, too trusting and extravagant. She had come a long way since those days as just his pearl stringer. Perhaps in the future she would be able to control some of his extravagances and steer him towards security and success again. Then they could return to take their rightful place once more in this most historic of cities.

26

'Where are you off to now?' Eben watched his wife rushing out of the back carrying a bag.

'I'm taking some of Kitty's things back to Mother's, I won't be long. We can't leave them here.'

'You're not to say a word. Tell her we going on a little holiday, if you must, but no one must know about our departure.'

He didn't trust her not to blab out the whole truth in a flood of tears now that everything was in place. He'd bought tickets in Leeds for a steamship to New York under their second names: Alfred and Annie Slinger. It was a second-class passage so at least they wouldn't have to share with strangers.

The more he thought about this plan, the more excited he became. The rivers of Ohio and Iowa were the ones to aim for. He had done some research in the library, asked dealers discreetly about the sort of pearls he could expect to find there, studying their shapes and properties in advance. Some beauties had sold for thousands of dollars in Paris and New York. Just one lucky break and his fortune would be made.

He thought of that purchase all those years ago, when his own special pearl came into his hand for twenty-five guineas. He recalled Perth and his lucky trip before the Tay Bridge collapsed. His pearl would bring him luck as long as he was faithful to her. He would not sell her to pay off his loans, but he needed money for their travelling. Margaret hadn't noticed her engagement ring was missing yet. A dealer took it off his hands for a decent sum. He was tempted to sell the old Jew's necklace but left it where it was sensing they would need more security when they arrived. In his eyes a wife's property was her husband's, no matter what the Married Women's Property Act said. His wife really was a trusting little soul and he felt mean in robbing her of the ring, but needs must. As long as she didn't give the game away, they would be safe for a bit longer.

'I've been having a bit of a tidy up.' Greta bustled into her mother's neat house, trying to look relaxed. She had been careful to pick off as many long red hairs from Kitty's shawl and bag as she could, weeping at the reminder of her sister's beautiful locks. She would save them to twist into a mourning locket once they were settled. 'There's a few bits of Kitty's stuff left. I want you to keep them here, and here's some of my clothes I thought you'd want to alter for yerself.' She tried to sound calm but her voice wavered with emotion.

'What's brought this on? You look done in, lass. I was saying to Albert, my Greta looks like a wraith these days. You've lost weight and those cheeks look pinched.'

'Don't worry, Eben's taking me on a little holiday soon so I've been tidying up a bit.'

'Who's minding the shop then?'

'We're closing, having a bit of a break away at Southport on the coast so don't worry, I'll soon get the bloom back in my cheeks. I thought you'd like these photographs of Kitty in her hats too.' It took every ounce of will not to cry and fling herself into her mother's arms. 'She looks so happy in them. I can't believe I'll never see her again.'

'Someone out there knows just what happened to her. I hope to God he suffers the horrors of hell fire for what he done.' Her mother banged on the table. 'As God is my witness, one day he'll pay for it.'

'We don't know something's happened for certain, Mam.'

'Who are you kiddin'? She's lying somewhere buried, I know it in my bones, my poor lost bairn out there in the cold.' They clung together until Greta found the strength to wipe her eyes and make for the door. 'Got to rush, things to do before we leave but I'll send you a postcard, I promise.'

'You do that, love, and have a good time. You deserve it.'

'Nothing will ever be the same without Kitty. I know me and her fought like cats and dogs at times but I'd give anything to see her bounce through that door.' Greta smiled through her tears. 'I'd better go. See you when I get back.'

Once out on the pavement she leant against a wall and sobbed. This farewell was the best she could do. She hated lying to her own mother but Eben had made her promise and he had enough troubles of his own. She walked slowly over the bridge back into the city, pausing outside a pawnbroker's shop on Coney Street hoping nobody recognized her going in. It was one of Saul Abrahams's old cronies Isaac Jerome and his son who ran the business. Would they know he had once given her this pearl? How could she be doing this? She set her face to the door knowing if they were to survive the journey then she must play her part.

Mr Jerome was sitting behind a counter with a grill in front. 'I know your face from the old days, don't I?' He smiled at her. 'How can I help?'

Greta pulled out the box and placed it on the counter. 'I promised Mr Abrahams I would never sell his gift but things are not easy at the moment.'

'Ah yes, you're the girl who used to help him and you married the pearl jeweller from Stonegate. I heard about Eben Slinger's business. Setting up in Harrogate is always a risk.' Greta handed him the box containing the pearl necklace, which he removed, putting his eyeglass to the pearl. He brought out his little measuring ruler to test the gem's size then weighed it on the pearl scales.

'It was his wife's pendant but I don't how else to help my husband.'

201

'It's a fine baroque pearl, good colour and no blemishes, I can give you fifty pounds on account and a ticket to redeem it later,' he offered.

'But if it goes in the window or on show, will you sell it?' Greta asked feeling sick at the thought of parting with his gift.

'Business is business, my dear. This is a fine pearl and good gold, but I will keep it in the safe for a while in honour of our dear friend or until such times as you can redeem it.'

She nodded in gratitude. 'Is that the very best you can do? I can't bear to part with it.' She felt the tears dripping again.

He could see her distress. 'Don't despair. Slinger will find a way out of his difficulties, I'm sure. He's a sharp dealer who overstretched himself. Charging London prices in Yorkshire won't do.' He closed the box, shaking his head. 'You'll be back, just you see. Abrahams had great faith in his little pearl stringer.'

Greta took the five-pound notes, shoving them into her reticule and out of sight, feeling sick with shame. She felt she had betrayed Saul but her only comfort was that it was pawned not sold and in a worthy cause. It could be redeemed one day and she had the precious ticket for proof but what use would that be when she was halfway across the world?

As she walked along Lendal she saw, to her horror, Edmund coming out of his father's office. She tried to dart out of his sight but he waved and crossed the road to greet her.

'Well, Mrs Slinger, what a surprise.' He raised his hat and smiled. 'Where are you off to in such a hurry, out shopping, spending your husband's well-earned takings?'

'Mr Slinger and I are taking a little holiday so the shop will be closed. Sorry to disappoint you but I've been to put the takings in the bank,' she lied as brightly as she could. 'And you have obviously made up with your father?'

'Yes, thank goodness, Papa has always been my supporter in good times and bad.' He paused, shaking his head. 'I was so sorry to hear about your sister. Irene told me the news. Nothing more has been discovered?' He grasped her hand with concern.

'Thank you but no, we haven't heard anything.' How could she play games with him when tears flowed at the very mention of her sister?

'Greta, please, let me take you for some tea. You look so sad.'

'No, no, I can't, Edmund. I wish I could. It hasn't been easy since Kitty... I must go.' She pulled her hand away. One more minute in his company and she would succumb and blurt out the whole sorry tale. Summoning every ounce of willpower and pride she gathered herself and smiled through her tears.

'Thank you for your concern but we're bearing up. A holiday will do us both good. I am glad things are going well for you and I would like to think we will always be friends.'

Edmund looked puzzled at her remark. 'I'll always be on your side.'

'Good afternoon.' She nodded, fleeing from him. Had circumstances been different she would have wanted more from him than friendship but her choices were made: for better or worse, only time would tell.

'Wake up, Margaret, it's time to leave!' Greta blinked at the lamplight in her face, woken from a dream of Kitty on the swings at the Gala Day fair, her hair flying in the wind.

'It's the middle of the night? What's going on?'

'Hurry, get dressed. I'll explain, pack a bag. There's no time to lose if we're to catch the milk train to Liverpool.'

'I don't understand. I've not packed our trunk yet.'

'We travel light, my dear, just hand luggage and outer clothes. It's the best way.'

'But I'm not ready. What's the rush?' She was suddenly wide awake and alarmed.

'Nothing to worry about, if we go now the debtors can have the furniture and what's left in the shop, fittings and furniture. I've sold the stock to Rushworth. Better to just go before...'

'But what will my mother do... I thought when I pawned my necklace it would help our debt and delay things. I noticed you sold my ring... I don't mind really but it would have been nice to have been asked. We must all make sacrifice but my little stone bracelet, the one you hated, did you really have to sell that too?'

She had been gathering up her costume jewellery that Irene had made for her and had noticed the turquoise bracelet had gone along with her pearl ring.

'Who would give me tuppence for that? And fifty pounds for that pearl is a drop in the ocean, I'm afraid. Never mind about all that now, just hurry. The bailiffs will want their due. I don't want to be here when they come knocking.'

'But we'll be disgraced. We have to stay and see things through. I just can't walk away.'

'Do you want to stay here to see our name in the *York Herald?* Doors will be shut to us. I want to protect you and your family from such a disgrace. This was all my doing and I don't want you involved.'

'But, Eben.' Greta was stumbling into her clothes, shoving her nightdress, her toiletries and little jewel box into her bag. Her gloves, bonnet, and thick coat were in the hallway. She filled every last space in the portmanteau with stockings and underwear.

Eben was fully dressed in his dark work suit and a long shabby coat she'd never seen before. He was waiting with impatience at the foot of the stairs. 'Come on, it's a long walk to the station,' he urged.

She was not prepared for the walk across Lendal toll bridge in such a dim light. It was as if she were sleepwalking yet awake enough to know they were leaving all their dreams behind, taking the back door out of the shop like thieves in the night. She heard the Minster toll out four of the clock and felt sick at this flitting.

Why had Eben given her so little warning? Had he not trusted in her silence? Thank goodness she had made that visit home to see her mother only two days ago. This was what their old neighbours in Walmgate did when they couldn't pay the rent. Were they committing a crime? Was it his plan all along to spring this exit on her? How could she be leaving her city, her home, her family to follow his whim? They must be in serious trouble. Was he protecting her or himself? Theirs was a strange marriage but she trusted he was doing this for both of them. If her mother didn't know the extent of their debts she could not be involved in any investigation, but for her to lose two daughters. It was too much to take in. Greta's mind was racing as they strode into the station and the booking office.

'You go for our tickets. I'll guard the bags.' Eben pulled his hat down and his collar up. She bought two single tickets to Liverpool via Leeds. They sat in the second class carriage with the blinds down until the train pulled slowly away from the platform and into the morning light.

Greta took one last peep at the grey Minster towers, choking back her fear that they were running like thieves in the night. Surely Eben must know what he was doing in taking this drastic action? It would be for the best of reasons. She had to trust and believe in this, and yet a niggle of doubt whined like a wasp in a bottle. Was there something more, something she didn't know about, that had forced this sudden flight?

The delay in boarding the ship in Liverpool docks, although normal, brought Eben out in a sweat. Boarding the ship wasn't as straightforward as he'd hoped. He had filled in the ship's manifest, declared their intentions and produced the tickets but they must await the arrival of their liner so were placed in decent-enough lodgings.

The port was a bustle of tugs and transatlantic

cargo ships. Eben was warned not to let porters steal their luggage but as they had only a bag each and the clothes they stood up in, it was unlikely to be a problem. While they waited to embark, Margaret insisted on visiting the shops to purchase clean shirts and feminine essentials.

Eben scoured the newspapers but their escape from bankruptcy hadn't reached any Yorkshire papers. A notice would appear soon enough in the *York Herald* but hopefully by then they would be halfway across the Atlantic ocean, out of jurisdiction. As a precaution he had allowed the clerk's misreading of Slinger to Stringer. He'd also knocked off a few years from their ages, insisting his wife's name was Annie Stringer. What she didn't know wouldn't harm her.

As the ship steamed slowly down the Mersey, heading out into the Irish Sea, Eben felt the tension seeping from his limbs, his breaths deepened with relief. He'd done it, escaped just in time. The old life was over and a new one beckoned. Somewhere on the journey he would offload all his responsibilities, including his wife, if need be. Better to travel alone, but not before he found himself far from prying eyes.

As the seagulls screeched overhead, his spirit soared in the salty air. He'd escaped – thanks to a customer in the shop who had left his newspaper on the counter where on the second page Eben had read to his horror: *The remains of a young female were dredged up from the River Ouse yesterday. The victim has yet to be identified but is thought to be a local girl reported missing months ago...*

How could he risk the police coming round

asking for identification? He didn't want the hangman's noose around his neck. Eben felt deep into the inner recesses of his waistcoat pocket. His fingers closed around the pearl he'd bought all those years ago and he sighed. His lucky talisman had done it again, kept him safe. Now she would protect him and open the way to a better life.

Part 3

THE LAST PEARL

Few European pearls were ever found that possessed the wonderful beauty and brilliancy of the pearls found in either the Miami or the Mississippi and its many tributaries.

Kunz and Stevenson,
The Book of the Pearl, 1908

27

Greta watched a crowd of children being herded onto the train just out of New York, and they were still there when they stopped at Cleveland. The children wore sailor suits and smocks, and were running amok along the gangways while their teachers seemed at a loss how to control them. Greta wondered where they were heading. Her curiosity got the better of her.

'You've got your hands full.' She smiled to a large woman holding a baby on her lap.

'You can say that again, ma'am. Twenty orphans between the two of us ain't funny, the poor wee devils.'

'Are they going on holiday?' Greta was curious.

'For a vacation? No, lady, they is all riding the rails to find new homes out west.'

'But some of them are so young,' Greta replied, eyeing the baby.

'The younger the better, I say. They won't know anything but the life they is reared to. It's those older ones that trouble me. Babes is easy to place, and the pretty girls, but some of these awkward inbetweeners...' She pointed to a boy with a squint who stared out of the window with an open mouth. 'He ain't going to find it easy. They just have to take their chance on the platform when we

211

stop. Word gets round there's a posse of little ones arriving in a township and the whole place turns up for the viewing.'

'You mean they're just handed round?' Greta was shocked.

'Not quite, some is already spoken for, like this baby here. A blue-eyed, golden-headed angel is Cornelius but those with mixed blood, that's another story. Farmers always like the tough boys for yard hands.'

Greta sighed as she watched the older boys racing up and down the aisles of the carriages. How she longed for a baby of her own to nurse but while they slept apart, there was no chance of one. She nudged Eben. 'Just look at those poor orphans. They're being shipped out of the city like parcels to be dropped off at stations.'

He shrugged his shoulders and yawned. 'Better than being cooped up in some orphanage.' He turned to his map, changing the subject. 'We must look for a halt called Muscatine. That's our stop.'

Trust her husband to be planning his campaign. They'd been travelling for weeks now, the little luggage they had was dirty and there was no prospect yet of a roof over their head. How could she not feel afraid? She smiled at the cross-eyed boy with his skinny knees. Here was another who had no idea of his fate or where he would lay his head. At least she had a man by her side. The child had no one and she wanted to gather him up for herself.

'Look at that little lad. He needs a good home. Why don't we take him with us? You could train him up to help you.'

Eben burst out laughing. 'What do I want with that runt of the litter? With eyes like that what use would he be to me?'

'Shush, he might hear you. He could wear spectacles.'

'Talk sense, woman. How can we burden ourselves with a child on our travels? It'll be months of travelling around for me. That's no life for a child or a respectable woman. Once I find a decent base, you will stay and make us a home.' He patted her hand as if she were a child. 'So no more talk of snivelling brats. Children cost and we've barely enough to keep ourselves.'

Greta hid her tears, gazing out of the window and swallowing hard not to answer back. When Eben spoke his mind there was no budging his opinion. If she wanted a child for herself she would have to bide her time.

They changed at Chicago for the Rock Island line, aiming for the stop by the Mississippi River but then Eben decided to change his plans and look elsewhere in Ohio. Both were feeling the stiffening effect of days and nights on the railway, only stretching their limbs when they stopped off at halts to buy food. Eben's hoard of dollars was thinning so he took back the ones hidden in Margaret's whalebone corset. She kept thinking about the orphans and how she wanted to adopt that cross-eyed boy but suddenly the children were all gone and the carriages were quiet till the next stop.

Crowds of tired families, babbling in foreign tongues, joined them, all crushed together smelling of damp wool and unwashed bodies. The porters were screaming instructions as people scrabbled over baggage in the rush to get on the train. Greta stared out of the window, wondering just where she would rest her weary head at the end of this exhausting journey into the unknown. What if they failed here and were trapped? Would she ever cross the Atlantic again?

28

Muscatine, Iowa

Greta sat in the shade of the veranda on the little wooden house they were renting off Front Street, Muscatine. It was one step back from the great rolling river and Greta felt a huge relief to be finally settled after all those months living out of travel bags. The journey down was punctuated with detours as Eben explored the best place to open his business. They'd spent a month by the Little Miami River but for her husband the grass was always greener somewhere else. Finally they pitched up in this busy river port with its fine buildings and steepled churches in time for the pearl fishing season. York it could never be, but at least it was a bustling town not the backwater she'd been dreading when they alighted from the train. Now she was defying Eben by writing at length to her mother, determined everyone should know they were safe at last with an address to write back.

The river is busy with paddle steamers, tugboats and river traffic day and night. The forests grow down to the shoreline, tall and thick. There will be such a lot to explore when I've found my bearings. My neighbour has welcomed me and I attend church but it's not a bit like St Helen's, more like our Mission Hall.

Our house is small, just one big room and a bedroom and one in the loft up a ladder. I spend many nights alone as Eben travels far and wide upriver in search of the pearling camps. I wish I could join him there but he won't let me near the camps as they can be rough places and the folks are suspicious of strangers.

I am aching for a big city's noise but I have the sound of the trains on the track, factory hooters and the bustle of the street vendors for company. It is not like York but, rough as it is, I feel glad to be among the people once more. I began to fear we'd never settle in one place.

Do write soon. You know I am desperate for news. I worry how you are and what has happened back home since we left. I expect Tom has now gone from Colchester out to India and there's no news of Kitty. We are all so scattered and can never be what we once were.

At least no one here knows our business or our shame for I fear Eben ran away from his debts and disgraced us all. He has no desire to return since he finds opportunity here to deal again. There are good prospects and already he has procured some good finds. There are fortunes to be made in the pearl business. Some of the pearls here are strange shapes and colours but I still prefer the creamy white ones that we are used to in our country.

Irene could make bracelets and pendants from some of the misshapes. Do let her know I was asking for her.

I miss my own bracelet to remind me of our friendship. It disappeared when we left but I fear Eben pawned it as I pawned my own precious necklace. I was saving up to send a money draft to redeem it from Isaac Jerome before it is too late but there is nothing left of my savings.

I feel so bad that I let down Mr Abrahams in parting with it. You know how much it meant to me but I didn't want to worry you with our troubles. I told you a fib, I'm sorry but I never expected to be dragged out of bed of a night and told to leave York.

Mam, I don't understand my husband these days. He acts as if I don't exist. I am his tagalong wife. Sorry for rambling on like this but I miss you so much but I mustn't sit here all day, it doesn't suit, but there's only so much dust you can shift in a day. Who would have thowt so much had changed in this past year?

By the way, please reply to this post box address. Eben doesn't want me to write to you or for you to know where we are. He has cut off all that part of his life and I fear that includes me. You know I am a stayer. For better or for worse I declared in church so I am staying put.

Life is not all chores. There was some excitement in the news last month when a boy was helping his gran in her garden by the river. He dug a clam shell out of the soil and when they opened it up, there was an enormous pearl that will secure his future life. His granny is so proud, she tells everyone in the street. If I hear it one more time, I shall scream!

Write to me soon,
Your loving Greta

The envelope was already addressed with a

stamp. Walking to the post office Greta smiled, content to know that there would be a reply sometime soon. Eben was not the only one with secrets.

Eben knew the great river, with its muddy sloughs that caught the biggest clam shells, was perfect for pearl fishing. There was a good long season and clams nestled in the shallows in the mud and sediment. The clams were easy enough to drag up from boats adapted for just the job. Thousands of dollars' worth of pearls were coming from rivers like this with others still to be discovered. It was like the gold rush of forty-nine when a fine pearl came out of the river. One, the size of a bullet, sold for four hundred dollars.

Eben had already collected several beauties and so far he had no complaints. His only frustration was that he had so much yet to learn about the different types of shells. Every colour of the rainbow came out of the shells, but so far nothing compared with Mary Queen of Scots who he carried in a small leather pouch around his chest, close to his heart. She was still his talisman for success.

It was a good move to settle his wife in Muscatine though he could see she was restless. He liked to find her by the iron stove or sewing in the lamplight. She was a good homemaker but he hoped she wouldn't send cards to all and sundry in York. Though he wasn't sure she would obey his order. There was a steely look in her eyes sometimes, a look of disappointment and regret and a questioning of his motive for leaving the country. He could see the words hovering on her lips unformed and then with a sigh they were sucked back.

Once he knew the layout of the land and camps, where the best rivers were, he would head up to greater sites where he'd heard there were even more clams full of pearls. Whether his wife went with him he was yet to decide.

29

It was weeks since posting that first letter from Muscatine and every time Greta passed the post office she looked in, just in case. Would she ever hear from her mother again? Then walking home one afternoon from the shops, as she passed the window, Mrs Schmidt waved her in. 'You've got a letter, Mrs Slinger, is this the one you've been waiting for?'

She hugged the envelope with relief. It was crushed and smeared with watermarks. She kissed the packet and made for the river path to read it alone. Eben mustn't see this precious link with home. Once at the river's edge she found her favourite bench. She tore the letter open, her heart beating fast as she read its contents.

Dear Greta,

Good to get a letter and an address at long last. I have had great fear for you. I wish I could give you happier news but I have to tell you that our dear Kitty was found in the river. What was left of my bonnie bairn was pulled out of the mud. It was her red hair what made them think of her and a bead bangle was caught in her clothes but not the one you give her for Christmas but the turquoise stone one as you had from your chum, Irene. They put a drawing of it in the Herald and she recognized it at once. It is a great mystery. They think she were dumped, bits of her apron had stones in the pocket and her neck were broke, my poor bonnie bairn.

We was gutted to the heart at this being her fate. Who would want to murder such a pretty girl? Some fella with lust in his heart, says Albert. Any road I thought as how you should know the truth of it for yourself. It being a long time past now and no witnesses, but the sergeant says they haven't given up hope of finding the devil what done it.

I wish you was here. Albert is being very kind but with Tom in India and you so far away, I've only me neighbours to cheer me up. Funny thing was she were found the day before you beggared off to Southport. I gather as how Mr Slinger were up to his eyes in debt and did a runner. The shop is now a dressmaker's. I don't ever go in that street.

I am sorry to give such hard words but better you know how things stand. Better to have an end on the matter but until the man as killed my girl is caught and hanged, how can I rest easy, nor I hope will you.

Your loving Mam

Write back soon and take care of yourself among them strangers.

Greta stared into the water, her eyes misty with shock. In her heart of hearts she'd known Kitty was dead but this was unspeakable. She felt the bile rising up and was sick, retching with horror at the sight of Kitty's broken body in her mind's eye. It was ten times worse to be so far away from her mam. She had not been there to comfort her at the burial. Here she was stuck in a strange town with a husband who didn't care for anything but his pearls and wouldn't even let her write home. What was her bracelet doing on Kitty's wrist? Had she been rooting in her little box of trinkets in her bedroom? It was all such a puzzle. Had Eben given it to her? Had she stolen it?

Suddenly her heart was thumping with fear. Did he know something about all this? Kitty had disappeared while she was in Harrogate. Did she come to the shop? No, it didn't make sense. Eben was sick in bed. The trees began to swirl around and the ground rose up as she fainted. She awoke with two fishermen staring down at her.

'You OK, ma'am?'

She nodded, rising slowly. 'I'm fine, just the heat,' she replied as she staggered slowly back home, clutching the letter. With relief she climbed the steps to her house and sat on the porch exhausted.

The door opened and Eben, home early for once, peered out. 'At last, where've you been?'

'Read that!' she snapped, throwing the letter in his direction.

He looked down at her, about to reply, but the ice in her eyes silenced him. He glanced through the letter, reading the news about Kitty with a sharp intake of breath. She stared at him. 'What do you know about this?'

Greta saw him hesitating.

'I wanted to spare you the pain. I thought it better for us to go before it all became public...'

'You knew she was found and you let me leave my mother to face everything alone?'

'Yes ... er ... no. I mean, I read something in the paper that a girl was found. I thought it was for the best.' She could see the flush on his cheeks and heard the stammer in his voice.

'The best for you, all right. You were in debt and it suited you to get us away so you could leave it all behind. How could you be so cruel, Eben? I trusted you,' she shouted, her whole body trembling in anger. 'I thought you cared for my family and me. We'll have to go back right now, back to England and do our duty.' She stood up as if to leave but he grabbed her as she swayed.

'No, my dear, it is too late now. It won't solve anything. Your place is here by my side. I need you here,' he pleaded, gripping her tightly.

'Why? I don't see why.' She stared at him.

'Because you're my wife and a wife's place is by her husband's side,' he said, shaking his head.

'A husband's place is by his wife in her bed so he can give her children and do his duty. You don't want me like that, do you?' Her anger was out in the open.

'It's not like that. Believe me, I'm very fond of you, Margaret. It's just nature has not given me the stamina to be that sort of husband. I know I'm a failure but I need you just the same. You made a vow.'

'Yes, I know, but I need more from you than just words. I have a life to live too. It has to have some purpose. The days are long here, too long

221

to be idle. You have to understand.'

He knelt down before her. 'I do understand. I have wronged you in being selfish. Let's begin again. We'll put this misunderstanding all behind us.'

She searched his face to see if he meant it. Eben was so hard to fathom out at times. 'Do you really mean that? Can we share a life like we did in the shop?'

He shook his head but smiled. 'Not in a shop again, my dear, but I promise you a better life right here.'

Greta stood up. 'Then I have to buy black cotton and make myself a mourning dress. I need time to mourn Kitty in my own way. No more running like thieves in the night, not this time, not ever again. To think Kitty was lying in the river all this time and you knew she was found...' She stormed into the house knowing there were other questions buzzing in her head. Did he know more about Kitty's death than he was letting on? Something in her heart whispered, *Tread carefully around these burning ashes, let them cool awhile before you rake over the past.*

Eben stared at Sadie's letter. Damn the old woman interfering like this. How could he have forgotten Margaret's flashy bracelet, the one Kitty borrowed with the turquoise stones. Why hadn't he seen it when he stripped and changed her clothes? How could he have been so stupid? Had Greta discovered its importance yet or was she too grief stricken to question its discovery?

One thing was certain, he must discourage any

more letters coming Greta's way. He needed to keep her busy and close to his side. If he ditched her she might become suspicious. It was time now to make a fuss of her, pander to her whims and give her reasons not to dwell on the past. York was far away. Surely they had been gone long enough for memories to fade about Kitty's disappearance? He picked up the envelope and shoved it in his pocket. It must be burnt and forgotten. He would indulge Greta's wish for a mourning outfit. He'd let it be known a relative had died in England and he would be the loving husband for a while and give her a gift to soothe her grief, a locket with a seed pearl frame or something. That would take her mind off the sorry affair.

30

1886

Jem sat on a bench overlooking the Mississippi as it curved slowly towards the setting sun. The sky was filled with crimson, orange and gold – it looked like a painting and was a reviving sight at the end of a long day. He could see the outline of the little city of Muscatine, stretching out on the bend of the river and rising up onto a bluff. He could smell wood smoke from a hundred chimney stacks and little camp fires dotted along the river. He smiled, knowing one of those columns of smoke marked his very own dwelling. Martha, his maid, would be preparing the evening pot pie.

He could see the silhouettes of lumber mills and factories lining the riverbank. The river was alive with barges toting logs and paddle steamers chugging closer to the shore to put down anchor for the night. There was talk of the company moving further away now that the stripping of the forests was almost complete. The industry was slowing down, the wood from the upper river almost vanished, but there were newer industries growing: canning factories, furniture makers and house builders all offered opportunities to a hard-working immigrant like him.

But rivers, forests and pearls were so much a part of his life that Jem couldn't imagine doing anything else. In his spare time he still bought pearls when he found good ones being offered for sale by the loggers. He often thought about his pa and the great pearl they'd found. If only his mother hadn't been cheated by that dealer. Would his life have been different if they had cashed it in, if he had bought an education and become a school teacher?

Jem stared around him, watching the men in the shallows fishing for clams. There was no point thinking about such things and he was making a good life for himself here. When the new century eventually came, he hoped he would have his own mansion house for Euphemia, who was now his darling Effie, and a quiver of bairns to pass on the Baillie name. The future was his alone to find and it was looking good.

He still couldn't believe how quickly everyone had settled to the idea that little Effie would make him the most suitable wife. He couldn't recall a moment when she hadn't been sitting next to him, and encouraged to escort him to church fairs and picnics. He was dazzled by her pretty manners and giggles, those blonde ringlets and exquisite features, but he'd also sensed there could only be an 'understanding' between them until he secured his position and found a stake holding in some successful venture in the area. He still had to prove himself to the Allisters.

His attention was suddenly caught by a woman walking along the shoreline. 'Watch out, ma'am,' he yelled as the woman, in a black bonnet, her face covered by a veil, almost tripped over some fishing nets and into the water. Like him she was gazing at the sunset as the last of the day's barges pulled logs down the Mississippi. He caught her arm to stop her falling into the murky river.

'Pardon me, lady, but you must take care down here,' he warned, guiding her back from the edge. 'The clammers don't like strangers around when they are about their business. You don't want to fall into that cesspit.' Jem pointed to a pile of rotting clams; the stench in the heat was fierce.

'Thank you,' she whispered not looking at him, lost in her own thoughts. He could hear the English accent and would have liked to make further conversation with the stranger but the veil and her distracted expression did not welcome any intrusion. He was curious to know how the young widow had landed up in this outpost but as she drifted slowly away, back towards the town in a world of her own, he wondered if she had even noticed he had just saved her life and honour.

225

Drunken fishermen thought any girl on the shoreline was fair game as they rolled off the boats and headed for one of the brothels. The girl who had just passed looked so lost and out of place that he wondered how she came to be shipwrecked on this stinking shore.

How Greta was ready for a feather bed and a hot tub to soak her aching feet after her long walk to clear her throbbing head. She had lost count of the time she'd been gone, and now her clothes stunk of fish, mud and sweat. Wearing black in this heat was not a good idea and she felt faint. Thanks to a stranger's warning she hadn't lost her balance and fallen into the water but the experience had given her a fright. The smoke from the factories was choking and her eyes were stinging. Would she ever get used to the fumes assaulting her? The stranger was right, she must head away from the river stench where wild-looking men stripped to the waist were going about their business dredging up clam shells.

The brick buildings behind Front Street were more prosperous, and the streets buzzed with buggies and horses pulling trams. She noticed how the town seemed to lean out into the river and then draw back in a curve. The reason she'd headed out was to find a private spot to write her letter home but it was so hard to reply with comforting words.

I'm coming home one day, I promise you, she'd begun, hoping to add something cheery to lighten them both. How could she tell her mother how she really was feeling?

I am so lonely here. I long for normal married relations that would produce a child to distract me but Eben's love making is over in a second and leaves me cold. He prefers to sleep on the sofa in the living room studying his new clam shells and purchases.

My monthly curses give me great pain. We lived like gypsies and carpetbaggers for weeks before we found this place. I have to pare the postage from the house-keeping purse. Letters are my necessity, my lifeblood link to home and to you.

She'd torn the letter up into shreds and scattered the pieces over the water in disgust. No one wants to hear your moaning when they have troubles of their own. She would write a cheerier one later that disguised all her anxieties.

Everything she had done in Stonegate had been for her family. She sighed as she strolled back towards their house. She'd married Eben to secure her mother a home and keep Kitty safe, she'd pawned Abrahams's necklace to help her husband with his debt. Had it all come to nothing in the end?

To be trapped in this new country was not of her doing but perhaps here she might make a better life for herself despite all that had happened. Life had to go on without Kitty. Perhaps she was brought here for a purpose, but just what that was, was beyond her at the moment.

Surrounded by the noise of sawmills and furnaces and the smelly fumes of fish and dust in the air, Greta kept on walking. Yet hope still surged at the thought of a stranger's kindness just now in guiding her from the abyss. If a stranger could look

227

out for her then she must look out for herself. If Eben was busy and successful and she found herself an occupation here, they might at last find some measure of happiness together. As she paused to watch the glorious sunset slide down as if into the water she prayed that it all might be so.

When she returned home Eben was waiting expectantly, holding a package for her. 'Here, something for you to wear round your neck.'

She unfolded the paper to find a small box and inside was a locket with a black cameo surrounded by tiny seed pearls. She looked up for an explanation.

'I know you haven't a likeness of Kitty to put inside but I just thought...'

'It's lovely. Thank you.' She was touched by this unexpected gesture. 'Does it open at the back?'

'They usually do. Why?'

'Oh nothing, just an idea,' she replied, and when he had left for his evening at the saloon bar she rooted into her little jewellery pouch, pulling out a tiny packet. Inside were the carefully preserved strands of hair she had picked from Kitty's clothes all those months ago.

By lamplight she sat coiling and twisting them to fit, opening the back of the locket to place inside all that remained to remind her of her sister. Tomorrow she would buy a satin ribbon for this memento to hold Kitty close to her heart.

31

It was like pearl hunting in Scotland all over again, Eben smiled, only more dangerous.

He felt the old thrill of the chase in the smoky camps as he stalked clammers and persuaded them to show him their finds. They trusted no one and he'd discovered that they hid their best finds in the pockets of their cheeks like squirrels. He'd become used to men spitting out their finds and then polishing them with dirty rags.

An old man with a leathery face shuffled up to him. 'How much?' He sat down with his gaunt-looking wife opposite Eben and pulled a pouch from his cap. There were some small pearls and some pinkies.

'Is this all?' Eben asked, seeing the look of desperation on the couple's faces.

'They told us the river was full of pearls. We saw in the paper, so we tramped from up country to find if it were true. But here clammers stake their patch with guns, spit on strangers if you go near their stake-outs. We've had to keep moving on...'

'It's a young man's game,' Eben replied, examining the pearls. 'They work in gangs and families.'

'Then we go to one camp and our neighbour makes a find. He says it is my turn next but my feet are raw with trailing in the mud.'

'Now we haven't the railroad fare home,' his wife added, clutching a ragged bag to her chest.

Eben looked up. 'Don't believe what they write in the papers. Luck is luck and some have it and some don't. Hard slog is what delivers. You are too old for this caper. I can give you two dollars for this lot.'

'Have a heart, they are worth more than that.'

'It's more than they are worth. The grey slug is big but dull.'

'Give us five so we can go home.'

'Three is my best offer. I have to make a living too, some days I can buy nothing so I can't sell nothing.' He fished into his deep pockets for the money. 'Three is my best offer.'

The man grabbed it, scowling, and his wife led him away. 'Calm down, Caleb. Tomorrow's another day. Our luck will turn.'

You fools, thought Eben, risking everything on the chance of fishing out a gem worth hundreds of dollars. The papers loved a story about instant wealth: a widow finding riches in her goose's gizzard, a pearl found in pig swill or a fortune made by a black boy who opens his dinner to find a beauty. It brought the hordes of hopefuls descending on rivers and lakes, dropping jobs, harvest and security in search of wealth. Only when they arrived at the river they found themselves shooed away by drunken, violent men, intent on keeping their stake-outs.

The river here was not paved with gold but with broken dreams, slime and empty shells, exhausted, ruined families fighting over the leftovers once their supplies were used up. How many men like Caleb had he seen on his travels, arriving too late at the feast? If they kept up this mad race to clear the shell beds, soon even this site would be fished out. He had arrived just in time in this peculiar area of the river. The current slowed down as it coursed east to west and curved down southwards, a perfect place for clams. It wouldn't last for ever but now was the time to go about his business and not waste a moment worrying about old timers. He looked again at the small pink slug-shaped pearls. They were worth at least five dollars apiece. If a man didn't know the value of his pickings then he shouldn't be down here.

Now he could trade back in town and send the best stuff up north. As long as these fools were ignorant of the true value of their find, he would make a comfortable living. So far nothing of real note had come his way but he had the summer fishing season ahead of him and he was in no rush.

32

'I hear you're buying into property, young James. That's what I like to hear, enterprise at work. You Scots are pioneers for striking out on your own. Have you set a date yet?' He turned to his daughter. Effie smiled across the dining table at her father who was puffing cigar smoke over the orchid flower arrangement.

'Papa, we've only just got engaged,' said Effie, admiring her diamond engagement ring. 'I want the best wedding in Clinton. There'll be so much to prepare but Jem is hardly ever here.' She

231

pouted in his direction.

Jem shrugged his shoulders smiling back. 'Only the best for the best, *mo ghoil.*' They had decided to make their understanding official on her birthday in August after he had asked her father's permission one evening.

'I want to build us a house first, sir.'

'Euphemia needs a firm hand. She's been a little spoilt but I see so much of myself in your drive and enthusiasm. I know you will take care of her and cherish her. If you don't, you'll have me to answer to, young man.' They had shaken hands as if it was a business deal.

Effie had her own opinion on this decision too. 'Please don't make me live down by the river's edge with flies and the smells or the noise from the factories,' she said, wrinkling her snub nose. 'We have to live high on the hill with fresh air and beautiful views.'

'All in good time, lady,' said her mother as she dabbed her lips with her napkin. Ever the Southern lady, Marcella turned to her daughter shaking her head. 'We have spoilt you, Euphemia... Poor James has to make his business decisions before you start talking about mansions in the hills but we will help, of course.' Everyone laughed.

Jem nodded, relieved that Effie's parents were so understanding about the delay in marrying. He still couldn't believe how the Allisters had gathered him to their side when he first arrived in the States, championing his ideas, promoting him to manager of the sawmill and now they were trusting him with their precious daughter too. He would not let them down.

Perhaps it would be better to build close to their home in Clinton but Jem sensed Muscatine had a good future even if the logging industry moved on. His mind was always full of imaginative ideas to create a lucrative income. He wanted to repay Jacob for rescuing him from the drudgery of a life in the Scottish forests and promoting him. He must strike out on his own sometime with a new venture. He didn't want to live beholden to the Allisters for ever. Besides Jake was the natural heir to their business. Surely success on his own account was the only way to earn their respect?

He had been so lucky finding his place within this society. He knew others were not so fortunate and he thought briefly of the young widow in black who had nearly drowned in her distraction. Her coming must have been a bad choice judging by the state of her grief. There was a story there, no doubt, of loss and penury. He had not seen her since that day but the image of her forlorn figure had stayed in his mind and he wondered who she was.

33

1887

'The orphan train's coming through the station depot next week. Are you going?'

Greta was in the dry goods store on East Street when she overheard two smart women in front of her eyeing a poster with interest.

'You don't want one of them. They bring disease and vermin in their cases from New York.'

'No, Betty, the Children's Aid clean them up ready for inspection. My sister out west got a real cute baby in place of the one that died last fall.'

'But, Lottie, you don't know what you're getting, do you? They might have mixed blood and bad habits. I wouldn't want my Mary-Lou mixing with such heathens.'

'I'm sure the orphanages train them up real good. A strong boy is what my Hiram is after, a yard boy and good with horses. We'll be going to see what's left after the folks on Davenport's station had first pickings.'

'On yer own head be it, Lottie, but don't say I didn't warn you.' The women moved away leaving Greta to stare at the poster. She had not forgotten the faces of those children on the train, or the boy with the bony knocked knees and squint. She remembered their scrubbed faces, with not a ribbon or badge to brighten their pinched features. She knew she must go and see for herself and if she saw a child that needed a home then this time she'd bring them back, no matter what Eben said. This was going to be her decision. Besides, him being away so much, they might as well be separated and she was in need of company. It would be good to train up a young girl to keep house and sew. They had a spare room in the loft with a mattress and chest of drawers that could be quickly tidied up in readiness but to Eben she was not going to say a word. It would be her big surprise.

She set about sweeping the dust and dead bugs

from the little attic window. She borrowed her neighbour's sewing machine to run up some curtains with gingham stripes, then found a faded second-hand quilt cover from a church thrift sale to cheer up the camp bed. Eben didn't notice any of this activity or the look of determination on her face.

On the morning of the train's arrival the depot was packed with townsfolk and farmers' wives all pushing for a better viewing point. Those holding papers proving they had pre-ordered children were set aside to greet the first arrivals.

There would be no shortage of people wanting the babes in arms, then the strong lads followed by the pretty little girls would be the next to find homes, Greta reckoned. As the train hooted and chugged to a halt there was a flurry of boots shuffling along the platform for a closer view. It was like a cattle auction and Greta felt ashamed to be part of this crowd but she was here to give a child a good home.

The children were marched off the train in a line then herded onto a makeshift platform. Smart in their sailor suits and pinafores with brushed hair and scrubbed faces, the children stared out into the crowd, their eyes darting around in fear. As she feared, off went the babies, the first graders, then the older boys and girls. One girl of about thirteen caught her eye, a gangling child with long limbs and a plait of unmistakable red hair disguised under an ill-fitting tammy. She was pushed forward towards a rough-looking couple. Waving a ticket, they eyed her up and down and shook their heads. 'That's not what we ordered.'

'One girl for dairy work,' said the organizer. 'That's what it says, Mrs Deitweiler.'

'Well, sir, you can send her right back. I'm not having no red head on my farm. They's bad luck and they bleed too much. She's all skin and bone. How can I get work out of that drink of water?'

Greta couldn't bear to hear any more; the poor girl was blushing, her shoulders hunched with embarrassment at being singled out and rejected.

'She can come with me then.' Greta stepped forward. 'She looks fine to me and I like red heads. My sister was one.'

'Rhodabel Bacchus, over here,' said the woman in charge. 'This one'll give you no trouble and she's good with babies. Been a right help to me on the train has our Rhoda...'

The girl crept across to Greta, she was hesitant and nervous. Greta shook her by the hand and the girl bobbed a curtsey. 'I'm Mrs Slinger, you are coming home with me.'

'Yes, ma'am.' Rhodabel bobbed again not looking at her. Greta and the girl went over to a man with a clipboard who asked for signatures and gave her the child's history, such as it was. 'She's been brought up by nuns, found on the doorstep and given the name pinned on her person, we suspect by her own mother. You can always change this mouthful. It's a bit fancy for a plain Jane like her,' he added as an afterthought. 'Changing names is a good idea. Makes 'em yours good and proper.'

Greta smiled. 'But I like her name, it's all she has left of herself. I wouldn't dream of making her change it.'

'Suit yerself, ma'am but a name like that sort of

sticks out.'

'Oh, I don't mind,' the girl butted in, her eyes pleading to be removed from this cattle market. 'I get called Rhoda or Bel.'

'Well, I think it is a beautiful and unusual name. Welcome to Muscatine, Rhodabel. I hope you will be happy with us.' They walked back from the station in silence at first but Rhodabel couldn't take her eyes off the river.

'I've never seen such a big river. It's wonderful but it sure smells.' She pulled off the tammy with relief. 'They made me wear it to hide my hair but it never stays put. No one likes red hair, do they?'

'Well, I do and it reminds me of my sister Kitty. I think it is beautiful hair.' Although with her scraped back hair and sticking out ears no one could call the child handsome.

Greta showed her the stair ladder to the attic bedroom. Once in the little room the girl stared in shock. 'Is this for me?' Rhodabel whispered. 'All by myself?'

Greta smiled and nodded, recalling how she had felt all those years ago when she went to the Blakes' house on Mount Vernon. 'I'm glad you like it.'

'It is fit for a princess. Miss, what do I have to do?'

'Just chores at first. Mr Slinger works away.' She hoped the girl would be easy to train so she would keep house while she found work for herself.

'You will call me Miss Greta. I am Mrs Slinger and I was once in service in England so I know what it is like to live among strangers.' Greta hoped she could do what Mr Abrahams had done for her and give the girl a chance to better herself.

'Were you put on a train and sent round the railroads?'

'No, but I've travelled on one of them with children like you. What did they tell you at the home?' She was curious as to how much preparation these children had for the changes in their lives.

'Nothing much but to say I was good with laundry and babies and brought up a good Christian.'

'Then I think we'll get along fine. There'll be just the two of us most of the time.'

'I never met anyone from England before, you talk different.'

'I'm from a county called Yorkshire and we talk even more different there. Now you go and unpack your case and come down for tea. Have a nap if you need it, it must have been a long day.'

Rhodabel bobbed again. 'I sure am going to like it here… I thought I'd end up down some farm track in the middle of nowhere. I hate animals. I won't let you down, Miss Greta.'

It was said with such feeling that, just for a second, Greta saw that same spark of pleasure that used to flash over Kitty's face when she was excited. Remember, though, she's not Kitty, she thought, fingering the locket of hair in the cameo tied round her neck. No one will ever be Kitty again but there was a faint resemblance with those freckles and green eyes, a likeness that had touched her heart. Perhaps Eben would notice it too?

Eben was horrified when he saw the red head

standing in the kitchen. She looked up and smiled and for a second he thought he was seeing a ghost. 'Who is this?' he snapped throwing his travelling coat across a chair.

'This is Miss Rhodabel Bacchus, our new helper. I went to the station office and we picked each other out. This is Mr Slinger, my husband. Welcome back, I wasn't expecting you today...'

'So I see.' Eben was furious. How dare she go to the expense of hiring a maid, especially one who looked so like the very girl he wanted to erase from his mind. 'Can I have a word outside, Margaret?' He pushed Greta through the door to the outside porch. 'How dare you take on that thing without my permission,' he said, grabbing her arm and slamming the door behind them.

'I didn't think I needed permission to find help. The girl needs a home and we can give her one here.'

He didn't like her tone of defiance. 'And who's to pay for her?'

'We'll keep her and clothe her. She'll work for us in return. I thought I could teach her house-work and perhaps we can both do piecework, sewing and threading. You are away so much she will be company for me in the evenings. Do you begrudge me even this?'

When Greta had that glint in her eye he knew he must tread carefully. 'She looks just like your sister with that frizzy mop. I'm surprised you wanted a reminder,' he sneered. This was not the homecoming he was expecting. 'You don't know anything about her background.'

'I know enough to know the girl has no family

239

and is at the mercy of the orphanage. She is not Kitty and never will be. Kitty lives in my heart and can never be replaced. You should be pleased that we are in a position to give charity to one less fortunate. She'll make our lives easier. I do intend to resume work of some sort or another, perhaps as an assistant in a jewellery shop.'

'We're not going over that again. I don't want you going outside the house to work. I am dis-appointed yet again that you show me no respect. I see only defiance. Don't think I don't know about your correspondence. You go behind my back at every opportunity. Where will it end? And now this.' Eben spat the words out into her face like venom.

'Lots of women work to help their families,' she argued staring up at him with such boldness he wanted to hit her.

'Not my wife and we have no family.'

'And whose fault is that, pray?' she snapped back, knowing he hated the topic.

Eben stared out onto the street, furious. Did she not understand she was here under sufferance, only because it suited him? Perhaps it was time to leave her to stew in her own juice with her new-found companion but he had rented the house for a year and paid in advance so he took a deep breath and turned to her. 'Yes, well, you don't encourage a man to be loving when you defy him at every turn. Working-class women should know their place.' As soon as he said this he knew it was a mistake.

'In this country every woman has her place and value whatever her class. We're the ones making the homesteads and townships fine places with our bare hands, we are equals among the men. This isn't England. The rules are different here.'

'Is that what you think?' He smirked. 'Scratch under the surface and they are not. It's the men who make the fortunes that you spend so quickly, men like Allister, Hershey and all the lumber barons. There's a pecking order in this town. You only have to look at the mansions on the hill and how the houses on Cherry Street rise above the shanties on the shore. And where do you see the women? Hanging on their men's arms showing off his jewellery and fine furs!'

'Muscatine is different, I'm sure. Women run their stores and teach school. There's no shame in work.'

There was no point in arguing with her when she was in this mood. He picked up his hat and stormed out. 'I shall eat in the hotel tonight and be gone in the morning. You do what you want.'

'I intend to,' she replied, staring at him again.

What had happened to his Margaret of old, the quiet pleasing helper who had done his bidding without question? Now she was hard and coarse. He had never loved her as a wife but he'd enjoyed her company. Now he couldn't wait to be out of her sight. He felt rage surging through his body, the very rage that he'd felt once before when Kitty had stared back in horror at his lustful suggestions. Now he was being punished all over again. He must leave before this violent fury got the better of him.

'Calm down,' he muttered, his face like thunder as he sipped his beer in the billiard bar on Front

241

Street. He stroked the pearl hidden round his neck under his shirt to soothe himself. *Bide your time, find those big pearls and then you can vanish like smoke.*

'I ain't caused you trouble, have I?' Rhodabel scurried around trying to make herself useful. 'The master don't like me much.'

'No, dear, this is a private matter of long standing. He's gone to meet his friends in a hotel. He gets these turns when he's tired. He'll be back when it suits him.' Greta was trying to reassure both the girl and herself. There had been such a look of hatred on Eben's face that it troubled her.

Once she and the girl had found paid work, he would change his mind, surely. The two of them could brighten up the wooden house a little more by making fabric cushions and pretty covers. This place would never be as fine as the one in Stonegate, with its antiques and fancy silver, but they could make it homey.

Eben's pearl hunting was not bringing in the fortune he'd hoped to make. She stared at his old travelling coat. It was threadbare, patched and muddy. Wasn't it time he bought himself a new one? He looked such a tramp in it and surely that didn't inspire confidence in him as a dealer? It smelt of wood smoke, stale clam flesh and sweat. Everything in the house smelt of stale fish. Rhodabel had been quick to notice the scents of industry when she left the station. The least Greta could do was to put the coat out to air on the back porch. Why did he keep wearing that old thing? Suddenly she felt so weary and tearful, she sat down to hide her distress.

Rhodabel was quick to see her tears. 'Missy, what's up? Have I done something wrong?'

'No, no.' Greta looked up. 'It's just I miss my old home and it's a while since I heard from my mother in York. She might be badly for all I know.'

'This York, is it like New York?'

Greta sighed. 'It was there a thousand years before your city. Roman legions came and made a camp, then the Vikings set up a town and kings and queens came to the Minster. Look...' She brought out her little wallet of precious postcards to show the girl.

'Wowee, it looks old, like out of a fairy tale book, and you lived there? Why ever did you leave?'

'That's a long story but one day when we are rich, we'll go back by ship and see it all again. I will take you down Stonegate to see the shops and the hat shop where my sister Kitty worked.' She paused. 'Kitty died but you look a little like her with your red hair.'

'No one likes it. I stand out and I'm not pretty so I was told to put that hat on and stand at the back so no one would see my bony legs. I had to have my hair shaved off once. I hoped it would come back fair but it came back worse than ever.' Rhodabel tugged at her plaits. 'I hide it most times.'

'The Good Lord graced you with your colouring. Never be ashamed of it, so come on, this won't butter no parsnips,' Greta said, wiping her eyes on her pinny. 'Let's get this old coat out in the fresh air. The wind is in the right direction. One day, we will go back to York.'

'To the old York not the new, that's neat.'

Why am I moping when this girl has nothing and no one in her life? Greta chided herself for her selfish thoughts. *I have a family back there. I've had adventures here and a skill I can sell in this pearl-struck city.* She smiled, wondering just what they might do to earn their passage home.

34

It had been one of those days at the saw mill. His best foreman had been off sick, there had been a new delivery of logs for sawing, a machine that had needed fixing and there was a back log of wood on the wharf. There was a brief lunch with another man wanting to set up a canning factory and who was looking for premises and a letter from Effie complaining he was neglecting her.

Surrounded by heat, fumes, dust and the drunken chatter of river men, Jem was ready for some peace and quiet and time to think. He made his way to Hogey's billiard room where he caught sight of the new Englishman who had been dealing round the camps – a tall willowy man with a sandy moustache who always seemed preoccupied with his own thoughts. Tonight he was hugging his glass, looking fed up and as if he had all the troubles of the world on his shoulders.

'Mind if I sit?' Jem asked as he plonked his rangy frame onto the padded bench covered in fake tartan. The man looked up surprised and shrugged his shoulders. 'New in town?' he continued, curious. He didn't look like the usual dealers he met on his travels. The man nodded.

'Eben Slinger, late of England.'

'James Baillie, late of Scotland. Funny how many of us Brits are landing this side of the pond. You in the pearl business?'

'That obvious?' Eben smiled. 'You go where the rivers are ripe at this time of year and you see what you can find.'

'How long have you been in town?' Jem noticed the acquisitive glint in the man's eye, appraising the value of everything it saw, looking him up and down assessing him.

'Too long. We arrived in eighty-six... I don't fancy another winter like the last but it's a good base. You're a dealer too?'

'Ach, no, not since I got regular work in lumber but I'm interested in the new industry here. You aren't camping then?'

'No, my wife and I have a house up the road. I prefer to travel around. She prefers to stay put. Camp life is not suitable for the likes of women, is it?'

'Clammers are good folk if you treat them right but I wouldn't walk through a camp on a Saturday night in the season. There's some wild coves with dogs and cudgels who don't like visitors. Does your wife like it here? There's plenty of work for women in the town and on the farms if you need it.'

'My wife doesn't work.'

Jem saw he had touched a raw nerve by the look on the man's face.

'You work hard to give them what they want and they go behind your back. She's just taken on one of those orphan brats from the train. Goodness knows why...'

'I've just had a letter from my fiancée complaining I don't give her enough time but a chap has to make his mark in the world while he's young, don't you think?' Jem knew he shouldn't be talking to a stranger like this but it had been such a frustrating day.

'Precisely.' The dealer nodded. 'Don't get lumbered with appendages until you have to, sir. That's my advice. They come dragging baggage behind then, family problems, ambitions of their own. Another whisky?' he offered, rising with his empty glass.

Jem smiled but refused. 'Thanks, but I must get back to my house or Martha will holler that I've ruined her supper. Nice to meet you, Slinger, it's a small town, see you around.'

The Englishman nodded and turned back to stare into the fire. What a miserable chap, Jem thought, so ground down by his harridan wife that he had to stay out at night. They were a couple to avoid.

Some people have all the luck, Eben thought, as he staggered down East Street before turning off towards his house. That Baillie chap, judging by the cut of his cloth had everything going for him. He no doubt had a well-paid position in some big lumber mill with a house and housekeeper. Baillie's life here was mapped for success while he was still wandering about in search of some luck.

It wasn't fair that the Scotsman should have it so easy. How had he got on so fast? He had made the right connections, but how could he do the same?

As he clambered up the steps to the porch, Eben saw his old coat hanging on the line. He pulled it down. Anyone could have lifted it off the rope and stolen it along with all his instruments, his best pipe and his secret stash hidden in the lining. Didn't that woman realize his coat was his office, his storeroom, his disguise? But if he told her she might start searching through it and picking off his pearls for her own use.

Hold fire, he cautioned. Draw attention to it and she will be curious, pretend indifference and your secret will be safe. Eben opened the door to darkness. They had both gone to bed, thank goodness. Tomorrow he would go further up the river and see what he could find. Two women in his house again was more than he could stand.

Greta was determined to earn some extra dollars. She heard that there was laundry work for hotels. Sheets could be delivered and collected from home so she applied to the hotels and boarding houses asking to be part of their round. The pay was poor but between the two of them she and Rhodabel could boil, scrub and iron just as she and her mother had done. She also made inquiries to three jewellers to see if they needed a pearl stringer, quoting her experience in York and put a small advertisement in the local paper for private work. There was polite interest but no offers. They would not trust an out-of-towner with their precious pearls unless she was in the shop and they had no vacancies. If only there was something she could do for herself using her skills.

To Greta's delight, Rhodabel was a good little worker and eager to please. It was a blessed day when she came into the house. She told such stories about her life in the orphanage and how one day she was told to pack a bag with new clothes and climb aboard the steam train to find herself a new home. Eben ignored her but Rhodabel was used to being invisible and didn't seem to mind when he shooed her out of the room when he was drinking heavily.

Eben complained there was damp washing everywhere and he hated the sheets blowing on the line or the piles of ironing laid out neatly in baskets to be collected. He never congratulated them on their industry but instead moaned about the mess in the room.

Greta's hands were raw and she thought of how her mother had done all this for years without a murmur. She took particular pride in doing baby linen and starching shirts, taking care over the pin-tucking and soft cottons. It made her think of her pretty wedding suit and Kitty's dress. Would she ever wear anything like that again?

How eager she'd been to secure Eben for the family, but it was too late now for regret. This was her strange life now. 'Come on, let's finish this basket and then we can go down town to see if anyone has replied to my advertisement in the *Journal*.'

There was a sale in Batterson's window and Greta and Rhodabel stopped to look.

'You'd suit that shirt, miss.' Rhodabel was pointing to a pretty checked work shirt but Greta's eyes went to the other side of the display where stuck at the back was a large man's coat in bold check wool at a knockdown price. It would be perfect for Eben to wear on his travels, smart and yet serviceable. She hated seeing him dressed as a tramp when he left home. If she could afford the price, it might cheer his mood and show she did care for him.

Fishing in her purse to see what spare money she could safely spend, still thinking in pounds not dollars, she knew she would have about enough.

'Stay here,' she ordered Rhodabel and darted inside to inspect the coat. She returned with a brown paper parcel under her arm and a big smile on her face. It was such a bargain and Eben would be so pleased.

Now they would have to double their efforts to repair the hole in their savings but when she called in again at Swann's Jewellers on the off chance, to her delight, they offered her the repair of a small bracelet as a trial. This successful visit into town demanded a celebration so they stopped off at the Soda Fountain for ice cream floaters. Then it was back home to the ironing to make up for lost time.

'Will you wear your new shirt to make your visit?' asked Rhodabel.

'I can make my own shirts for half the price so I bought Mr Slinger a coat in the sale. I'll be glad to see the back of that old thing. It stinks out the house.'

'I thought you were going to buy something for yourself.' The girl sighed.

'Don't worry, I have bought a little something for you.' She fished in the package for a length of bright green tartan ribbon. Rhodabel fingered it as if it were silk. 'Is this for me? It's not my birthday yet.'

'I thought it would make a bow to show off your lovely hair now it's pinned up like a young lady.'

Rhodabel was wide-eyed with surprise. 'No one has ever bought me anything before. We got Christmas presents under the tree but they was never labelled with your name on. You had to take pot luck. One year I got a boy's cap.'

'Well, this is for you. If Mr Slinger has a gift so must you.'

'Can I try it on?'

'When we've finished the mending. Time's money and we're short of it today,' Greta replied. How little it cost to make this girl smile.

There'd been a fight in the camp over a find; a large baroque-shaped pearl had been discovered when the pearl fishers steamed open some clams in the boiler. Three men had claimed they were the finders and had begun to argue. Shove became push and then fisticuffs. One man received a broken nose and busted head. Eben was called in to examine the pearl, a fine-enough specimen worth at least a hundred dollars in the trade so he offered sixty and gave each man twenty dollars. They muttered and grumbled but it was a good day's work for them, and for Eben. He rode home, ready for a bath and a beer, hoping to catch up with that Scots man in the bar and show him just how good he was at spotting a bargain.

He made it his business to find out more about James Baillie. He was well connected in the district with a fiancée in Clinton and a future father-in-law who owned one of the big mills in town. Before Baillie became manager of the saw-mill he had been a humble logger and he apparently knew the best of the pearling sites. If Eben stayed close to him he might find out better places to visit. The upper Mississippi was rich with pearl finds. He made sure he sat close to him whenever he turned up in Hogey's Bar.

He'd even thought of asking him to supper but he wasn't sure he wanted him to meet his wife. Baillie would soon see she wasn't the finer English sort who would match his fiancée but a Yorkshire woman of lower class. Over the years since their arrival her skin was coarsened by the sun and her clothes were tired, her cooking adequate but plain. No, he would keep his new friend to himself.

On his return to Muscatine, he demanded a bath and change of clothes. That was when he found the coat in chequered wool cloth waiting for his approval. It was long enough but it made him look like a cheap travelling huckster. He took one look at it and nearly choked. 'You spent good money on this for me?'

'Don't you like it?'

He saw Margaret's face crumple and felt mean. 'Well, it's bright enough to glow in the dark, smart in a loud way.'

'I thought it would replace that old thing and keep you warm,' she offered.

'Oh, it's too bright for campsites. Someone saw you coming, my dear, to foist this on you.'

'What do you mean?' she said. 'I thought you'd like it.'

'Oh, I do,' he lied. 'But you shouldn't spend your dollars on me.' How could she think he'd ever be seen in that?

'I had a bit put by. It was a bargain in the men's department, an end of a line.'

I'm not surprised if that was the sum of their styles, he thought. 'I shall wear it for church.'

'You hardly ever go to church.'

'It's too good for everyday. I'll save it for best.'

The girl was staring at him all the time with a puzzled look. 'Miss Greta's got a pearl repair job so she bought me this ribbon and there was a shirt she liked but she wanted this for you instead.' Then he saw that familiar look of shock and disapproval on her face, a look he hated in a woman.

'Speak when you're spoken to,' he shouted in her direction. 'When I need your opinion–'

'Eben!' Margaret interrupted him. 'She means well.'

'I don't like that tone in a serving maid.' All he wanted to do was get as far away from that parcel, out of this house of females with their silly notions. His wife meant well enough but she'd be better to smarten herself up instead of this awful garment. The red head was going to have to go back to the Children's Aid. He would demand her return as he was never party to Margaret's impulsive action. He would suggest she was totally unsuitable for them.

Now he needed to drown his frustrations in whisky in a room full of men. He was touched that his wife had tried to please him but why did she get it so wrong? If she really wanted to gain his favour she must get rid of that girl and soon.

Greta sewed by lamplight with a heavy heart. Her gift was rejected, the surprise gesture found wanting. He hated the coat and she had seen the disdain and weariness at her perceived lack of taste in his eyes. They were becoming strangers to each other and bringing Rhodabel into their lives was making matters worse. The girl was witness to all their disagreements and, bless her, by trying to put in a good word for her mistress, she was only making things worse. Now the girl sat at her sewing, her young brow furrowed with concern.

'Don't worry, Rhodabel, it'll be fine in the morning. Mr Slinger works hard and gets tired and fretful.' She sighed. 'But I don't think they'll take back the coat as it was in their sale. Any road he's gotten two coats now and we can always patch up the other one again.'

'But there's old folk down by the shore who need a coat on a cold night when the wind roars down the river. Folks only need one coat,' the girl replied, not looking up.

'My husband likes things to be as he sees them. We have to respect his decisions.'

'Why?' The girl paused.

'He's the man of the house, and some would say our master.'

'He ain't mine,' Rhodabel said. 'I don't belong to no one.'

'Yes, you do, young lady, you belong here with us,' Greta answered in a stern voice. 'We signed papers, remember. Don't forget my husband pays rent for us to stay here.'

'But you work hard too... Why should men have it all their own way? I'm never going to marry.'

Greta looked up from her mending, smiling. 'One day you'll change your tune and marry, share a life with someone, bring up a family and support each other in times of trouble.' Yet as she spoke these words she realized just how empty they sounded as they rolled off her tongue. There was none of this in her life. The marriage she'd hoped for all those years ago was all but dead and buried.

35

September 1888

At the beginning of the fall there was a welcome letter from England but it was addressed to her in writing she didn't recognize at first. Fear gripped her that it was bad news about mother but then with relief she saw it was from Irene Patton.

My dear Greta,

I was so relieved to find you are settling down at last and have found work and some companionship with your orphan girl. I wish I could write with better news. Your mother is in health and will be writing but she is much mithered by some startling news which she asked if I would relay to you first.

After all this time a belated witness came forward on

seeing a public likeness of poor Kitty in her pretty millinery model portrait. He is a cab driver who thought he saw her in the hotel by the station in the company of an older gentleman who he recognized as being formerly in business in the city. He noticed her because of her pretty dress and the colour of her hair. He waited for months before telling the police as he was uncertain that it was indeed the same girl who had been found in the river. His information puzzled the police because Kitty was not wearing an evening dress but normal shop girl wear when they found her. Someone must have changed her out of the evening dress and put her back in her workwear if he is to be believed. How could this be done out of eyesight unless it was in a private room?

This means whoever killed her changed her from the pretty dress to her own outfit but left your bracelet on her wrist. I am thinking such dreadful thoughts now. Could it possibly be that she was wearing something else of yours ... if so I will name no names on paper but make a warning to you. Are you sure that your husband has been telling the truth that he didn't see her that evening? Be careful, my friend. Such knowledge may not be safe for you to know.

Come home. Norman and I are uneasy. I have taken the liberty of speaking to Edmund Blake and his father, Erasmus, who also advises you leave. Destroy this letter at once and come home.

Your dear friend,

Irene

Greta dropped the letter in shock. Surely not, surely they didn't think that her own husband was involved in Kitty's murder? Her heart thumped with fear. It was utter nonsense. He had been ill in bed when she returned from Harrogate. He said he'd not seen Kitty but he had said he might take her sister out for her birthday. Was he lying when he said she never arrived? But the bracelet, her own bracelet from Irene's workshop with its turquoise stones that went with her turquoise dress, that bracelet was missing when she left England. But the dress? Had Kitty borrowed her dress and put it back or had it been taken off her ... and put back carefully. Surely not? There'd been no time to pack and she'd left that dress in the wardrobe. Had Kitty been in his company? Had she been wearing that evening dress? Had he lied to everyone? What could this possibly mean? Suddenly she was afraid.

Her throat went dry as she saw Eben walking up the street in that old coat and looking like a tramp. She shoved the letter out of sight and gave him a weak smile but his mood was grim judging by the tight line of his lips and the crease in his brow.

'No luck today?' she asked. 'You look tired.'

'I'm beginning to think this place will be fished out of shells before long and we must move on.'

'But we've only just settled down in the town. I'm beginning to get to know folks. Sit down and I'll fix supper.' She rose to go indoors.

'Rhodabel can do that. Let's go for a walk.'

'Not in that old coat, please, Eben. Why don't you wear your new one for me? The nights are getting chilly. Winter is coming.'

'Suit yourself, so what have you been up to all day?' He threw his coat through the door. It landed on a chair.

'Mending and darning socks, but I think I've got

another repair coming from Swann's the jewellers, their normal repairer is off sick. Isn't that good news? It's just a link of seed pearls but it's a start. They liked the quality of my last one. Perhaps they will give me regular work so the laundry deliveries can stop.'

Smile, look normal, act natural. Don't let him know the effect of the letter smouldering in your pocket, she thought. He must never suspect the terrible doubts surging through her mind. They must walk arm in arm like any old married couple in the town.

Before heading out she dashed into the kitchen to give Rhodabel instructions. 'Heat some beef and dripping for the Yorkshire puddings. Do them like I showed you in the skillet under the meat, keep the range hot and tidy up. We won't be long.'

'Yes, miss, I'll try.'

There was a chill wind blowing as they walked down to the levee to see the new bridge under construction. There was no flaming sunset today. The greying sky reflected Greta's dour mood. She found no pleasure in this unexpected togetherness for the terrible suggestions in the letter filled her limbs with dread. She began to choke and cough. She was fishing out her hanky when, to her horror, out fell Irene's letter. Eben saw the envelope and stiffened. 'Who is it from this time?'

'Just the usual news from Irene. Mother is well and Tom may be coming home soon from India. The business in Aldwark is doing well enough.'

He lifted it from her trembling fingers and she tried to stay calm and not snatch it back but to her relief he just glanced at the envelope then handed

257

it to her. He never took an interest in letters from home. On the route home she dropped it into the nearest rubbish bin without him seeing. Only then did Greta feel safe enough to relax and take up his arm again.

Eben was sitting in his usual bench in the Hogey's Bar supping his whisky with relish and trying to work out why he sensed his wife was plotting behind his back. During their walk he'd felt the tension radiating from her. He'd caught her eyeing him with shifty glances. Had she been offered employment? Was she planning to leave him? That stupid girl was still in the house spying on him. He wouldn't put it past them to be stealing behind his back.

He must be master in his own household. The atmosphere in the house was reminding him of York when Margaret and Kitty ruled the roost and it unnerved him. He felt limp at the danger he was in. It was the women's fault he had had to flee his country. Now it was happening all over again. Margaret and the girl were ganging up on him, telling him what he should and shouldn't wear, working together, defying his orders and still the letters from York kept coming.

If only he was achieving his goals. The place was now full of dealers, wealthier and better connected than him. Had he lost his touch? Perhaps Margaret had her uses. He might return to the jewellery trade and use his wife as his repairer, but without capital it wasn't possible. He must not be defeated.

He staggered home in the darkness and fell into

a drunken slumber on the sofa, waking the next morning with a rusty tongue and a hammering headache. It was time to go about his business but he was still in last night's shirt and trousers. Margaret had taken the boots off his feet and left him to sleep alone.

'Where's she now?' he asked the girl as she offered him coffee.

'Gone to the store early,' came the reply.

'That should be your duty,' he snapped. The very sight of the red head set his teeth on edge.

'I know, sir, but she insisted she needed fresh air,' Rhodabel replied giving him one of her sullen looks. Eben swallowed the bitter coffee to clear his head and made for his coat but it wasn't on the hook at the back of the door. 'Where's my coat?'

'The checked one is there.' She pointed to the new one.

'Not that one, stupid, my work coat!'

'That old thing ... it's gone.' He saw her blush and drop her eyes to the floor.

'What do you mean?' He could feel his blood rising.

'When Miss Greta buyed you that fine coat with her savings and you said as how you'd gotten one already, I didn't think it right with winter round the corner so I reckons if you have only one coat then you'd wear it and Miss Greta would be happy so I took it down to the shanty store where they give poor folks clothes.'

'You did what!' he yelled.

'It's OK. I checked the pockets. Here's your scales and calculator for sizing up your pearls and your baccy tin.'

Eben leapt up and struck her on the face. 'You stupid bastard, you took my coat and gave it to some tramp without my say so. How dare you go into my pockets. What else did you steal?'

She jumped back with indignation. 'No one needs two coats when others have none, I reckons.' She rubbed her cheek.

Eben grabbed her by the arm and pulled her towards him. 'Why you little thief, you've been stealing my pearls and cheating my wife...'

'No, I ain't no thief. There were no pearls, sir, in yer pockets, honest.'

'How dare you take it upon yourself to give away my property!'

'I did it for Miss Greta, let go o' me...'

He was shaking her so hard and with such fury that her flame hair flew into his face as he pushed her into the wall and banged her head against it. Fury was swirling like a rip tide, all these months of anger were building up into one surge of rage. 'No one gets the better of me,' he muttered as his fingers found her throat. 'I've done this once, I'll do it again. I know who you are. You're Kitty come back to haunt me.' He watched the girl's face turn red with fear, her eyes bulged and her body lost its strength. He felt the power, the exhilaration, the stirring in his loins as he took her breath away but then a crashing blow to the back of his head loosened his grip and the girl slipped from his grasp and fell limp to the floor.

'Get out of this house, you murderer! Now I know all about you and what you did in York to my sister!' Greta was holding the heavy skillet, ready to strike again, her face puce with anger. 'I

260

should kill you right now.'

'She stole my coat and my pearls.' It was all he could say, stunned into silence by his wife's sudden attack. 'If you kill me, you'll hang.'

'Get out! Get out, I want you out of this house and out of my life!' Greta was going mad, wielding the skillet like a weapon.

'Gladly, do you think I've enjoyed these last few years? Do you think it was you I ever wanted in my bed? Do you think I married you for your charms, Margaret?' he blurted out with a sneer, feeling the room spinning and his eyes losing focus. 'It was your sister I wanted, not you, but she led me on and made a fool of me...'

'Don't you Margaret me. Get out or I'll call the police right now!'

Eben staggered to the door, his eyes seeing two of everything. He saw her lifting the pan to attack again and knew he must flee. He felt sick with fear at the sight of those eyes, which were as hard and sharp as flints. He guessed Margaret knew everything, catching him now in the very act of throttling the girl. He must flee from her fury before she hit him again.

36

Greta rushed to Rhodabel's side, fearful that she was too late, but to her relief she stirred, coughing and clutching her chest. Greta saw with horror the red marks around the girl's throat as she stared up at her in fear, unable to speak.

'You're safe now, he's gone. I'm so sorry.' Greta rushed to the pump for a glass of water. 'Take some sips, slowly,' she whispered lifting Rhodabel's head up to help her swallow. 'Thank the Lord I got here in time. I am so sorry...' How could she explain how she'd been halfway to the store when suddenly she'd felt the locket on her chest burning, heavy, and her heart thumping. Danger! She'd just known she had to turn round and run home. Something bad was happening there. She'd feared it was a fire and had expected to see smoke but then she'd opened the door to see Eben throttling the child. Kitty had saved the girl when she couldn't save herself.

'He kept calling me Kitty, miss. I gave his old coat to the charity and he went crazy, calling me a liar and accusing me of stealing his pearls.' She was coughing but her face and lips were pinking up.

'Don't speak, just rest. We'll talk later.'

'Call the cops. He may come back and get you too.'

Greta could see the fear on the girl's face. He had nearly killed her in rage. *My husband is a killer and tried to kill again because a girl gave his coat to a beggar. What monster did I marry?* Suddenly all became clear, as if her mind were rinsed clean of all doubt by his words. Here was a monster who had only married her as a means to seduce her own sister. Was that the truth of it? *No wonder he had no desire for me*, she wept as she rushed into the yard and was sick, shaken to her very core by what she had witnessed. They had never known the wicked nature of this man. How could she have been so stupid to think he married her for herself, when he was only serving his own needs? Was she also to blame in marrying him to help her family? What a disaster this had caused for all of them. He had taken her sister out and when things did not go to plan had he throttled her too?

She sat on the step, wounded by the knowledge there was no one here who she could go to with this awful truth. Rhodabel could bear witness but would they be believed? How could they link this attack to the murder in York? One thing was certain, they must leave and soon. What if he came back to threaten them, told the police she'd attacked him? They were no longer safe.

That evening she shuttered and bolted every door into the house but even then she didn't feel secure. Unable to sleep she spent a restless night planning what to do next. She kept the skillet close by just in case he returned.

Jem found the English dealer slumped over his usual bench as if he were asleep. He must be drunk again. 'Better get you home,' he offered, but the man didn't respond. When he touched him he fell and then Jem saw the gash on the back of his head. The poor chap had been in an accident and knocked himself out. He would be in no fit state to walk back to his digs, wherever they were, so Jem lifted him bodily and took him out into the fresh air where he was promptly sick. He lifted him up onto his buggy. He needed the services of the doctor in Walnut Street. Eben hardly stirred as Jem helped him up the stairs to the room where the doctor examined his wound. 'He's been out for the count and in the wars,' Jem explained.

'Quite a gash there but not deep. How did it happen?'

'No idea. He keeps a bench warm in the Billiard Bar. He's English, a pearl dealer. There's a wife somewhere.'

'Better he's watched overnight. Would you take him home, James?'

That was how he came to put up an unexpected guest in his house and how he noticed the leather pouch on a chain round Eben's neck and the money belt tied to his waist. These dealers trusted no one and rightly so in this wild midwest frontier land. Keeping cash close to your chest in a dog-eat-dog world made sense. The wealth of this town was built on those lucky enough to make valuable finds in the mud. He'd not done so bad over the years himself. This poor man had yet to strike it lucky. Had he been in a fight with a clammer? Jem left him to sleep, perhaps he'd find out more in the morning.

The next day, Jem found his guest looking startled, no doubt shocked to find himself in a strange bed.

'What happened to you, Slinger? The doc says you must rest. Martha can run and tell your wife where you are...'

'No thanks, it was that vixen who did this to me.'

'Some quarrel.' Jem whistled.

'Believe me, don't ever marry. You don't know what you're getting till it's too late. The maid took my coat and gave it to some beggar – a coat full of

264

pearls. You know how we dealers hide our pearls in deep pockets or hidden seams, the tricks of the trade? Now I've lost all my trading pearls. I have to find the guy who is walking around with my pearls, got to get it back.' He rose as if to be on his way and staggered. 'My head is still spinning.'

'You were sick. The doc says you must go back and check with him first.'

Eben shook his head and closed his eyes. 'I'll be fine, thanks to you for being the Good Samaritan.'

'Better let your wife know though. She'll be feeling guilty. Why the head bashing?' Jem was curious. 'Quite a temper, has she?'

'You can say that again. I'm not going back there. She cares more for that sassy orphan maid she foisted on me than her own husband so when I went to punish her, I got this ... but thank you, James, for taking me in. I have to find that coat.'

'Call me, Jem. No bother, can't have you stuck out on the street. Do you know where the girl left the coat?'

'On some shack by the wharf where they give charity, I think.'

'Leave it with me. I can find out who took it. Just you rest. Tell me your wife's name and I'll make sure I don't bump into her on a dark night. She English too?'

'Margaret's from Yorkshire, with a tongue on her like a fishwife, don't know what got into her...'

'Say no more.' Jem laughed, making a note never to cross the woman's path, but he would send his housekeeper Martha to Eben's house so this fishwife knew exactly what she had done to her husband.

Greta tried to restring the pearls but her hands were shaking with fear and anger and she kept slipping the thread, unable to fit the needle into the drill hole. This was her first large repair for Swann's and she was making a hash of it all.

Late in the morning a maid arrived at the door to say Mr Slinger was being attended to at Mr James Baillie's house in Cherry Street and that he was recovering from a blow to the head. She was giving them both very suspicious looks. Rhodabel stood listening by Greta's side.

'You tell her what that man did,' she whispered, stepping forward pulling her collar down to reveal the purple bruising on her neck. 'He's one crazy horse. Tell her.'

Greta pushed her back out of earshot. 'No, we say nothing for the moment. This is private business, Rhodabel.'

Greta thanked Martha, the maid for her information and sent her on her way.

The maid stared back, uncertain what to do next. 'All I knows, they's gone upriver looking for his coat. Won't be back for a few days, I reckon.'

'We'll be gone by then. Tell Mr Slinger I want nothing more to do with him,' Greta added.

'Yes, ma'am.' The girl fled leaving Greta and Rhodabel standing on the porch.

'Where're we goin', Miss Greta?'

'Anywhere but here but I'll have to finish this repair and we'll need to wash all the townsfolk's linen to pay our fare.' There wasn't much left in savings since she'd spent the spare on that cursed coat.

'You won't leave me here, will you?' Rhodabel sniffed.

'Of course not, wherever we go, we'll go together but it's not going to be easy.'

True to his word, Jem Baillie traced the coat to the hut by the wharf where the good ladies of the town gave out clothing and food to some of the old clammers and river rats. These worthies of the Blue Ribbon Temperance Movement were always on the lookout for converts, strong drink being the curse of the old timers. Many of the men signed the pledge in return for warm boots and clothing and one man who'd done just that was Caleb Blackwell who, with his wife, was heading upriver for one last chance to fish a fortune before the season came to an end. It was fortunate that one of the women recalled the old couple who were down on their luck and glad of the coat.

Jem had business close to Davenport, the next city upstream, and he offered to give Eben a ride in his buggy to the nearest camp within walking distance. Eben felt sick and dizzy but he didn't want to miss this opportunity so he climbed aboard, trying to focus his eyes on the track ahead.

How could he have gone for the girl as if she were Kitty Costello? It must have been that red hair. Now the whole of his life was turned upside down by Margaret catching him and forcing the truth out of his lips. He'd seen the look on her face when he'd told her that he'd only married her for her sister. How could he have been so stupid?

267

Now he couldn't go back to Muscatine. They would go to the police and show them the marks on the maid's neck. He would be a wanted man yet again.

Perhaps it was better just to move on alone. Did he really need this coat when he had his coins and his pearl? At least this lift would get him far away from his wife's clutches. He would make sure Baillie steered clear of her, blackening her name at every turn in the road, making her out to be an ugly witch who had dazzled him with a spell.

The two old clammers could not have gone far and sure enough at the first camp, he asked if there had been any new arrivals and someone pointed out a meagre tent in the backwoods where he recognized the same old woman he'd seen earlier in the summer. He would have to be canny to avoid suspicion. He must gain their trust. Thankfully Jem stepped in to help him.

'Anyone here just back from Muscatine?' A few onlookers stepped forward including the man wearing his overcoat. 'Anyone call in the temperance store and sign the pledge? You know the score, pies and the pledge,' he added. They laughed. 'My friend here has good news for one of you.'

This was Eben's chance to step forward. 'There was an old timer who received an old coat. I'm afraid it was given away by mistake, it belonged to one of the lady's husbands who was out fishing at the time. You can imagine his surprise when he found his favourite fishing jacket had gone.' He paused to hold out his checked coat so everyone could see. 'This new coat was the one she should have distributed, a special gift from Batterson's store. I don't suppose the lucky man is here in person?'

All the men rushed forward. Who wouldn't want a new coat?

'Now, I have specific details about this item of clothing so if you step forward one at a time and show me your coat, I will be able to recognize the right one.'

One by one the men showed Eben their jackets and ragged old coats until Caleb came forward.

'I think this might be the very one. It had a patch on the elbow right here.' Eben smiled, swallowing his relief. 'In return here is your brand new wool coat.'

'It's mighty bright.' The old man lifted it. 'But it's sure better than that old thing, it was too heavy for me. Look, Minnie, I got me a new winter coat.' His wife raised her pipe in approval.

Eben could hardly believe his luck. The couple didn't recognize him. He could have tramped for weeks to find it. Were his hidden seams still intact? It stank of rough baccy and the old man's sweat but his familiar travelling companion was back in his arms, his trusty protection, and all thanks to Jem Baillie. He owed him a drink and a decent meal, if only he could see straight. His head was still throbbing from the blow.

Baillie went on to do his business and they arranged to meet up at an old shack where they served the best crab cakes and chowder. Eben waited by the shore, watching the last clammers out on their boats raking up the shells. He knew some of the families by name now but he was

269

here only to find his overcoat not to deal so he waited for Baillie to return, trying to steady the thump in his head with whisky and rough beer.

Reunited with his trusty coat, he wanted to head north, far away from any trouble waiting back in Muscatine. Once Baillie knew the truth he would not be so accommodating but he owed the man a meal. Without him he might be lying in a ditch somewhere or, worst still, behind bars in the jailhouse, if his wife had anything to do with it. What a relief to be a free man again. She could go hang for all he cared. He'd done his duty by her. He couldn't wait to strike out on his own and keep his fortune to himself.

37

When Jem returned he saw Eben slumped over his tankard and unsteady on his feet. They sat by the shore watching the sun go down, purple, pink and orange sliding into the river until the water rippled like molten gold. The dealer was looking pleased with himself.

'You saved my skin, old chap, first in Muscatine and now here. This coat may look old but I wouldn't be parted from it. It brings me luck. Let me tell you what secret it holds.' Jem watched as Eben delved into the lining through a hidden slit in the seam and went deep into the coat before bringing out a piece of cloth into which pearls were stitched. 'Just a few sprats to catch a mackerel.' He smiled and Jem noticed the glint in his eye as he fingered each one.

'I noticed you have a pouch around your neck too.'

'Ah, you must have seen that when I slept. That's my beauty. Shall I tell you a secret? She's my talisman, my Queen of Scots. I've never shown her to anyone. She's the security I need when things get tough.' He tapped his nose and bent forward.

'Then tell me more,' Jem said. 'I'd like to see this beauty for myself.'

'All in good time.' Slinger was slurring his words. 'I've travelled all over but the freshwater pearls of Scotland are the best, as well you know. One year I stayed on at the end of the pearl fishing season. I have a nose for a paragon and I heard there were rich pickings near Perth.'

Jem smiled as they drew closer and Eben spoke in whispers.

'I called on one of those cottar wifies, a poor ignorant biddy who had no notion of her late husband's fine dealings. She pulled out this beauteous pearl that he'd fished out the Tay or thereabouts. When I saw such a perfect gem, I nearly wet myself with excitement. You wait all your life for a pearl of such worth. She had no idea of its value, of course, but she was content with the price I gave her. It was like snatching sweets from a baby,' he laughed.

Eben pulled the pouch over his head to open it. 'As thanks for your good offices, I will show her to you, my Mary Queen of Scots.' He lifted the pearl out of the soft wool protection that surrounded it and placed it in Jem's hand. 'Have you ever seen such a thing in your life? Of course, I will never part with her. She is my guiding light.'

Jem stared at the pearl and went cold at the feel of her. 'Could I ask one thing? What year, pray, did you pay yon cottar wifie for her gem?' He strained to keep the tremble out of his voice.

'Ah, that's easy to recall. I was on the very last train to cross the Tay Bridge before it collapsed in December 1879. Why do you ask?'

'I just wondered if you found this pearl of great price close to the village of Glencorrin?'

Slinger shrugged his shoulders. 'Scottish names are all the same to me. Why, what's it to you if I did?'

'And did you pay the princely sum of twenty-five guineas for such a treasure?' Jem's hard words could split steel and Slinger sensed tension now.

'How did you guess that? Amazing! You gave a good estimate there. I could have sold her for twenty times more in Edinburgh and even more in London. Of course, no one will ever pierce her beauty with a drill hole. She is my virgin pearl.' He was looking to take back the pearl now but Jem's fingers had closed around it and there was a hard look on his face as he spoke.

'My father and I fished this out in the summer of that year. It was the last pearl he ever found. It was his dying wish that it buy my education. He caught a chill in the fishing of it and here you stand boasting of its value, delighting in how you cheated my own mother because of her ignorance.'

Slinger tried to snatch the pearl back but Jem was too quick for him. He dangled it above his head.

'Hang on, Baillie. How can you say it's your pearl? One pearl is the same as another. Give it back to me!' The atmosphere was changing from jovial to threatening as they shouted at one another. Jem felt his mouth tighten, his eyes flashed with fury as he lifted the pearl high, far out of reach, as the dealer began to shout and swear. A crowd, excited by the noise, circled them.

'Do you not think I don't know the queen of all river pearls when I see her? How many eighty-five grainers do you find in a lifetime in a small tributary of the Tay? It's perfect in form, not a blemish and the colour of a silken moon. I would ken this anywhere.' Jem's accent broadened as he clutched the gem tight in his palm. 'It was my pa's last pearl and you cheated my ma out of it.'

'He's lying!' Slinger looked round for support. 'Give her back to me. What low-down trick is this? I showed you her in good faith. Give her back to me at once,' the dealer screamed, jumping up to take her back but the pearl was out of his reach.

Jem laughed but there was menace in his voice. 'Come on, boys, gather round and see the trickster who stole my mother's treasure. When I found out she was cheated I vowed to destroy that villain. I would get even with him if it took a lifetime. Little did I realize that heaven heard my plea and brought him right to my door. We know how to deal with thieves, am I right, boys?'

Eben suddenly felt the threat all round him, like a chill wind from the river. It was time to bargain, to make a deal, but the man opposite was crazy with anger and still holding his pearl high. 'Look, we can come to some arrangement. I can share it

273

with you. How was I to know it was your mother? Nah, it's too much of a coincidence. You are stealing my pearl. It's a trick.'

'How can I steal what was my own in the first place? It was my own feet that found her.' The man stood like granite rock with a fearsome sneer on his face.

'Come along, be sensible. I didn't know it was your family,' Eben pleaded, his stomach churning, but Baillie wouldn't budge.

'Here's the sort of dealer who doesn't care who he cheats as long as he gets a bargain. I've seen so many of your kind stalking along this river, weighing your scales short, fobbing off clammers with low prices. I'm sick of your sort. You are the scum of the earth. That's right, guys?'

Eben stood his ground. 'You can't just take this off me. I bought it fair and square. I didn't steal it. A price was agreed. We must go to the law to settle this.' He was desperate now.

'No, I have a better idea. I'll leave it to these guys to sort you out.'

Eben saw the men barring his path. They had sticks in their hands, and panic rose through his body.

Before he could decide what to do, Jem spoke again. 'But I think there's another way to find justice. From the water she came, to the river she will return...' Jem made to throw the pearl as far as he could into the water.

'No, no, are you mad?' Eben jumped up to grab Jem's hand. 'Give her to me, she's mine.'

'A pearl is a gift from the gods of the sea, so go and fish her out again.' Jem swung his hand towards the river and Eben raced towards the water's edge with the clammers chasing behind him. Dizzy and disorientated he leapt into the cold water towards the direction of a splash, screaming, 'You damned blaggard, may you rot in hell!'

The water was cold and his swimming was poor, and he was weighed down by his clothing and his boots. It was madness to be chasing it but he had to find that pearl, his own beauty, but his eyes weren't focusing in the dusk. He stood up feeling dizzy. He was about to stagger back to safety but then he saw the men with sticks edging ever closer to him in the water. There was nothing for it but to swim out away from them to a safer landing spot. He could feel the chill water, the mud sucking at his feet as he dragged himself ever deeper into the river's silent depths.

He had to find where the pearl had settled but his body was tired. Then with a rush of knowledge he heard that splash again. How stupid, a pearl wouldn't splash it would float, bobbing on the ripples. If he could see her floating on the surface he could swim to her and bring her back. Slowly, against his will, he felt himself being carried along by the mighty river, far from his beauty. This was not how it should be, this was not how it should end, but he was powerless against the current now.

Never fight the current, he'd been told, go with it, but he also knew this river never let go of a man with clothes on. It was too late and he was too tired, too cold. He felt himself weakening as he struggled helplessly against the power of the rushing water. He panicked, trying to find a footing as his lungs filled, and then he struggled no more.

Jem watched as if in a dream while the men walked back up the shingle. It was too late now. The current would carry the man along to his death. He had been given his revenge but Jem stared into the gunmetal water feeling nothing.

If Slinger had shown one jot of remorse, one iota of shame for his dealings, there would have been a chance that Jem's fury would have abated, but all he saw in the eyes of that man was greed and obsession.

I didn't kill him, he thought. He killed himself with his own greed, chasing after an illusion. Eben had been too drunk to realize that Jem had slipped the pearl in his pocket and substituted it with a pebble. This he flung into the water. Jem felt the cold pearl in his hand, the last link to his folks and his far-off country. Revenge was a dish best served cold, they said, and he felt a flint of ice enter his heart at the thought of Slinger's needless death. He put the pearl back in its pouch. This majestic globe, he mused, his father's very last pearl, did it bring only death and deceit? Was it now a cursed and bitter legacy?

Better it had lain unfound on the bed of the river than to have wreaked havoc. Why did he feel no remorse or guilt? The dead man had a wife, as bad as he was, no doubt. She would have to be told the news. He looked down at the old coat lying lifeless on the shingle and shivered. Whatever was hidden in the linings belonged to her now.

38

October

Greta and her young assistant were up to their armpits in soapsuds with a pile of ironing to finish but, despite all their hard work, they still didn't have the money to buy their passage to York and wouldn't for months to come. Eben had not returned and wasn't missed. For the first time in ages, Greta felt at peace. It was up to her now to make their future. If she could do extra shifts somewhere they could take a train back east but for now it was enough to know Eben's welfare was no longer her concern.

There was a knock on the door and when she went to answer it she saw the outline of a tall man with Eben's coat in his hand, the shabby one she'd recognize anywhere. 'Oh, you found it, sir, thank you. My husband has been searching for this. Did the ladies on the shore find the owner? I'm sorry he's not here to thank you in person. Please excuse the mess but it's wash day.'

The man in a smart suit took off his hat. 'Mrs Slinger?' There was something about the way he was staring at her that stopped her chatter. His dark eyes were searching her face hesitantly and it felt as if a dark shadow had fallen across the room.

'Please, come in. I'm Greta Slinger and this is Rhodabel my helper. Mr Slinger will be most obliged. He's away at the moment in search of this very coat.'

The man didn't move or speak at first then stepped inside and placed the coat on the chair back as if it were made of silk. 'Mrs Slinger, I have something to tell you. Please sit down. There's bad news...'

She heard the soft Scottish lilt in his voice and couldn't help staring at his handsome face as he gazed around the room. 'Your husband met with an accident two days ago.'

Greta stood very still. The room began to spin but she gripped the chair for support. 'Go on.'

'We met at a camp where he was searching for his coat. There was a quarrel and some hard words exchanged. He had stolen a pearl and the clammers chased him into the water. He got out of his depth and the river carried him away. No one could get to him in time.'

'Was he searching for pearls?' she heard herself speak.

'Yes.' The man nodded, relieved she was taking in the news.

'Then he died as he lived. They were the true love of his life. Thank you for taking the trouble to bring this back,' Greta replied, feeling her legs begin to shake.

'Can I be of assistance?' The man hesitated, reluctant to move.

'Thank you but no, I prefer to be alone. I didn't catch your name, sir.'

'I'm sorry, how rude of me. James Baillie from the Allister lumber mill.'

'You are our landlord, if I am correct.' She

278

nodded in recognition of the name. 'I would be grateful for some leeway on our rent until we are in a position to leave.'

'Of course, don't worry about such things...' He paused. 'I knew your husband here in Muscatine. I was with him on the night that he died... I'm sorry.'

'Then thank you for taking the time to tell me in person.' She closed her eyes as Rhodabel ushered the man to the door. When she opened them he had gone but his presence still filled the room. Eben was dead. Why did she feel empty and cold as if his death didn't matter? Then she began to shake.

Jem backed out of the doorway. He wasn't wanted. He sensed her dismissal of him. Had she guessed his part in her husband's death? Why hadn't he told her the whole truth? Why hadn't he explained his part in the man's death?

Eben's wife wasn't what he'd been expecting, she wasn't a hysterical fishwife. Instead, he'd found a young woman and her maid busy at the sort of chores he knew brought in a pittance. The room was clean and neat. Her quiet dignity had disarmed him. How could he burden her with the truth of their sordid quarrel that had ended so badly? He had teased the man to distraction, a man already dizzy and drunk. How was he to know Slinger would dash into the water like that? He had killed that man as sure as if he had felled him with a blow.

Now the wife would be destitute and he felt a surge of guilt and confusion. What made things

279

worse was she was his tenant.

He had not expected her to be so young or to have such striking blue eyes and black hair. Had the English voice he had heard once before on the shore belonged to her or was he just imagining it? How did a man like Slinger claim a woman of such presence and beauty? There must be a story there. Even in homespun clothes she stood out. If only she had cried out and made a show of emotion, blamed him for not saving her husband, but all he had seen was a calm acceptance and courage. He felt ashamed.

As he drove down to the lumber mill he knew he couldn't leave her to struggle. He would have to help her out. He had to ease his own troubled conscience, but then he recalled Slinger's head injury. Perhaps there was more to know about this strange couple before he decided what to do next.

Greta sat down to write home.

Dear Irene,

I lift my pen but such a weariness has overcome me of late, everything has been an effort of will since we received bad news.

Eben is dead in an accident that no one seems able to explain to my satisfaction. They say he jumped into the freezing river chasing after pearls and got into difficulty. This is according to a witness, our landlord James Baillie, a Scotsman of good reputation who was present at the scene. It's a long story how they came to be together that night.

Mr Baillie is being most generous in letting us stay on in our house. Since discovering I can string pearls from his friend Mr Swann, he has promised to put some private repair work my way. It will make such a change from sewing and taking in laundry for pennies. Rhodabel is really efficient now so we are saving like mad.

You must have guessed years ago that my marriage was not the happiest of unions especially after you hinted things about my husband that troubled me. I caught him in the very act of assault on my maid and know that my sister died by his evil hand. He has gone from us now and our aim is to return to York as soon as we can raise the tickets for home and wipe the dust of this cursed place from our feet.

I am being harsh. I do like Muscatine, wild as it is at times, and our neighbours have been most kind and generous over the years. I'll be sad to leave them when the time comes but when we return I intend to start my own little business so I will never be beholden to any man ever again for my future happiness. I will write to Mother that I shall be bringing my little helper with me. Rhodabel is so curious now to know what England will be like, thinking it's all lords and ladies in castles, but one trip round the city will cure her of that notion.

Thank Edmund Blake for asking after me. I imagine his furniture business flourishes. I was glad to see he is reconciled with his father before I left. Mr Blake was the kindest of employers. Mother told me his mother had died but I will not speak ill of the dead though I am sorely tempted.

I would like to think this is my last letter before we leave for home and I shall see you all in person but I don't want to tempt fate.

Your dear friend,
Greta

There was so much else she could say but didn't. Had she mentioned her landlord too much? Her feelings were confused and it wasn't wise to put them on paper for it made them real. How she wished Irene was by her side to guide her and explain the strange discomfort she felt whenever he called at the house. Over the past weeks his maid had brought gifts of cookies and pastries from his own kitchen and he had offered to escort them to the very place where they had found Eben's body, a place the locals called Dead Man's Corner. Here the current slowed at the bend in the river and bodies often came to rest there. Mr Baillie had formally identified Eben's body, sparing her the sight of her husband's bloated corpse. It made her think of Kitty, lying in the river for so long. Would her sister rest in peace because in some strange way justice had been done? The river had taken Eben as he had taken Kitty to the Ouse?

There would be an inquest and funeral. Baillie offered to help her in this but she refused. There was guilt written all over his face, as if he wanted to share something with her but couldn't bring himself to reveal the truth. What had really happened on that fatal evening when Eben died? Was there more to his dying than she was being told? Her feelings were complicated further by her lack of grief for a man she had come to hate, a man who had robbed her of so much hope. Greta would play the part expected of her, she'd wear her widow's weeds, but she would not be standing like the mourning widow folks expected around here, watching from the upper window of the house for those never to return. He was gone from them. There would be no more sorrowing on her part but the very effort of it all was tearing her apart.

39

November

The inquest in the court house was a formal affair. Several witnesses came forward who knew Eben Stringer as a dealer. The quarrel with Mr Baillie was aired. He stood up to say he challenged the dealer for his false estimates and under weighing pearls. He told how they exchanged his travelling coat because it contained pearls. This was news to Greta. No wonder Eben was furious and had attacked Rhodabel in his rage.

Baillie confessed how in anger he pretended to throw one such pearl into the water as a rebuke never thinking Eben would chase after it. The clammers were angry and followed after him but, when the river had carried him away, they tried to rescue him. He deeply regretted his action. At this point he glanced at Greta.

So that was what he was hiding. Then he added something that made her tremble. 'I have to add in fairness to the deceased that Mr Stringer was not himself having had a recent gash on his head. I took him to the doctor myself as he was dazed and unsteady. The doctor gave him something to ease the headache but I fear he drank too much and his judgement was impaired. The doctor will confirm this.' Then he sat down not looking in her direction. So he knew all about their quarrel? Had he spared her embarrassment at this revelation?

As was expected, the verdict on Ebenezer Alfred Slinger was one of accidental death while under the influence of alcohol. His body was to be released for burial. Sympathies were extended to the widow but as she walked out into the chill wind she felt numb. She went to the church and asked for a simple service of interment, nothing more. The coffin would be closed and there would be no headstone over his grave. Her husband didn't deserve the expense of such a memorial. She felt her heart harden. Why should she beggar herself to be a hypocrite? Back at home, after Rhodabel retired up the stairs, she lifted up the old coat, taking her scissors to its seams, pulling and tearing it apart in anger, knowing she would find secrets within. Lo and behold, there they were, hidden in carefully concealed pockets, pearl upon pearl. Greta wept in fury as she threw the coat down in disgust. This lot could all pay for Eben's funeral expenses since pearls were his first love, not her. His beloved coat was now nothing but a torn-up rag to be burned.

Two days later Baillie came to her door with his own pouch of pearls. 'I hear from Swann that you are a good pearl stringer so I wondered if you would consider making these up for a gift.' He spread each one out for her to view. 'It's for Euphemia, my fiancée, for her wedding day. I have collected them over the years.'

She fingered them in silence. They were fine freshwater pearls with rainbows of light on the surface. 'What was your quarrel with my husband? What really happened?' She spoke quietly, not looking at him.

'I found that years back in Scotland, he had cheated my widowed mother of a great pearl, the very one he had hidden on his person. If he had shown one ounce of regret...' Jem paused. 'I'm not proud of what I did so I pretended to throw it away, the rest you know.' Then he fell silent.

'Can I see this pearl of great price that my husband was willing to die for?' Her voice was cold.

'I don't carry it on my person but I will bring it later for the centre piece of the necklace once it has been drilled. But while we are being honest, can I ask you how Eben came to have the wound on his head? Why did he curse his wife to high heaven?'

She caught his eye and held it firm.

'I hit him with this.' She walked across to the stove and picked up the skillet. 'I stopped him from throttling my maid and killing her as he did my own sister back in York. Eben was attacking my maid because she gave away his old coat.' She saw him step back in shock at her words. 'That is why I shed no tears for him. You did us all a favour.'

'Hang on, lassie, I did not kill him. I'm sorry if you think that. I had no idea he was such a man. You must be so shocked.'

'I don't think anything any more only about leaving for home. I'm a widow and I am free to go where I choose.' Her lips trembled at the power of those words.

He nodded, pointing to the pouch. 'These pearls will give you work. I will make sure you don't have to take in washing. I can give you dollars in advance...'

'No! We will accept no charity. I will not be beholden to anyone. This is work I will accept as a commission but as soon as I have our fare, we will leave. Thank you, Mr Baillie.' She dismissed him with a cool glance towards the door.

Later Jem paced his bedroom floor. *You have to stop going to visit her. You have to stop thinking about her. She is your tenant, the wife of the man you let die. You have a fiancée who loves you. Don't make a fool of yourself. She'll be gone soon. You have given her work and you have the great pearl that will finish off the necklace to perfection for your bride. The widow will leave and you will be free of this madness, free from the spell she casts over you.*

Every time he visited the little house with some excuse or other, he vowed he wouldn't go again but somehow his feet found their way to her door. He must be strong. Seeing her in mourning reminded him of that first time he had helped her on the shoreline. How strange they should be meeting again under these circumstances, drawn together by tragedy.

Why was it when he thought of Greta, all thoughts of Effie faded? This strange fever filled his waking hours. All he wanted was to catch a glimpse of those dazzling blue eyes. When he saw that quiet, serious look on her face he was lost. Why did she remind him of his new found pearl?

He clasped it in his hand, that beauteous

Queenie who came out of his home river, a perfect centre gem to set off the rest of Effie's necklace except now he didn't want to pierce her or part with her. She was a reminder of those forests and lochs of Scotland, his parents and all that was lost when she disappeared. Strange how fate had returned her to him. So why couldn't he let her go?

In the light of day, he made his excuse. He wasn't sure her rainbow of reflected colours complimented the other American pearls. Beside her they seemed dense and almost opaque. Why was he hesitating about this bridal gift of love then? Did his feelings for Effie really fade before Greta Slinger's presence? He felt himself sweating at such thoughts. Why didn't he want to give her that last pearl?

When Queenie was drilled and threaded and Greta placed this last pearl in the centre, the necklace would be finished. She would leave Muscatine and he was torn, wanting her gone and wanting her to stay. This was ridiculous. Time to visit Clinton and make it up to Effie for all this disloyalty but how could he leave when the mill was busy? He would write with loving promises excusing his absence from their coming Thanksgiving. But in his heart he knew the true reason he didn't want to leave town just yet.

40

There was a bitter chill coming off the river but excitement in the town for the coming Thanksgiving celebrations. Greta was hoping for an invitation to celebrate with her kind neighbours next door but instead an invite came from an unexpected direction when Baillie turned up on her doorstep with yet another request for a repair from the wife of one of his friends.

'We are inviting some of our employees and their wives for a Thanksgiving supper this year and I wondered if you would like to join us. You can't go back to England without sampling a true Iowan Thanksgiving supper with all the trimmings and Rhodabel might like to help Martha with the dishes.'

Rhodabel jumped up and down at this news. Greta tried to look calm. 'To be honest, I am curious. Mr Slinger was not one for that celebration. I've never been to a Thanksgiving supper before. I'd be pleased to attend but I am in mourning. People might think it unseemly...' She paused, not looking at him in case he saw her cheeks flushing with pleasure at such an invitation.

'I guess many of the first pilgrims were bereaved when they celebrated their survival. It's a time for family and friends to join together for a holiday. Martha assures me her pumpkin pie has no equal.'

Greta smiled. 'Then we look forward to meeting Miss Euphemia and sharing it with you all.'

'I'm afraid Miss Allister won't be attending. She wants to stay with her own family but when we are married, of course,' he replied.

'Of course,' Greta nodded. 'Please come in. I'll show you how far I have got with grading the pearls for Euphemia's necklace but don't forget to bring the centre pearl. I do need to start with that first. Rhodabel will make us some coffee,' she offered.

'No, I can't stay, much as I would like to. But you will come to the supper then?' Jem seemed anxious to leave, backing from the doorstep, raising his hat with a smile. When he left Rhodabel was bursting with excitement. 'What can I wear?'

'We'll think of something. I can wear my black Sunday best.' She sighed, already sick of being drained by the dark colour but proprieties must be kept. 'If we add bright ribbon trimmings to your Sunday grey, it will cheer it up. There's no money for new, I'm afraid, but when we get to York I will make you the prettiest dress.'

How she yearned for something new for herself. She was still young and full of life. Black made her feel old and worn. Perhaps she could dress her hair in a different way and put on her special necklace. Then she remembered it was sitting in the pawnbroker's office or sold by now, but she had Kitty's locket and she could hang it from a purple ribbon. She might not have Mr Abrahams's necklace any more but Kitty's cameo would brighten her drabness. It kept her sister close to her heart.

Jem gave Martha such a string of orders she had to laugh. 'Lordy, master, I shall need four pairs o' hands to get fixed in time.'

He wanted his new mahogany table to sparkle with polish, his silver candlesticks to gleam and the linen to be starched. He had twelve guests plus Greta's girl who would help Martha in the kitchen.

Effie wrote, telling him she was peeved that he wasn't returning to her family but that his excuses had been accepted. He didn't tell her how keen he was for the English widow to have a farewell Thanksgiving supper. No one should be alone on that special day when families gathered from far and wide to celebrate.

He knew Greta was waiting to finish off the threading but he still hadn't given her his last pearl. He sensed her thoughts were turning east and to her home in York. He knew all about that ancient city and had once passed through it on a train south. How different it was from Iowa which was still a young state full of farmers and loggers, but they were making history in their own way.

Thanksgiving always made folks think of home and yearn to see families left behind. How he longed to see Perthshire again, but he had no one back there now, he must learn to belong here and grow roots with his new-found family in Clinton.

Greta was rootless too after all these years travelling. Greta... Greta, always his thoughts turned in her direction and it troubled him. Why had he singled her out, asking her to dine? Why was he inviting her to meet with employees? Would it be misconstrued? Effie should be the one by his side, especially as Muscatine would be her own home one day.

He knew she would want a large home high on the hill among the grand mansions, three storeys high with towers and fine views over the river and a large yard full of roses. She would need a cook and maids and the sort of society she was used to. He wasn't sure Muscatine was ready for Euphemia Allister yet. It would be better to build her a home and let her arrive as his bride. That would take time and Greta Slinger would be long gone.

Yield not to temptation, for yielding is sin, went the revivalist hymn. He had done nothing to be ashamed of. All he was doing was extending Christian charity to a grieving widow before she left for good. Surely there was nothing wrong in that?

Greta put on her black dress and Rhodabel fixed her hair in a shapely bun. The girl coiled Greta's dark curls in the latest fashion before pinning the strands in place with little pearl-studded pins, her one piece of ornamentation.

'You will sit in the kitchen with the other servants and don't gossip if they ask questions about us,' Greta ordered, fixing her bonnet and veil carefully over her hair.

'No, ma'am.' Rhodabel was wearing new pretty pink braid on her skirt to disguise how the hem frill had been let down. They would go to church for a special service before walking to Mr Baillie's house mid-way up Cherry Street, accompanied by one of his office assistants called Mr Cochrane and his wife, Mabel.

The streets behind the river were emptied, the whole town silenced as families gathered together on their porches to greet each other.

As they left the church and walked slowly up the street holding onto their bonnets, Greta felt the first winds of winter beating at her chest as it used to do in York on a winter's evening. She thought of Mam and Tom and Kitty and her friends in Aldwark and felt sick with sadness. There was nothing better than a loving family and close friends but she had only Rhodabel now. They were strangers in a foreign land and must endure a dinner with more strangers, however kindly meant. Greta paused, wanting to turn back for their house. 'I can't do this.' Then she saw the excitement on Rhodabel's face and knew she must make an effort.

The thought of seeing Baillie in his own home stirred up a deep feeling of unease in her belly. It didn't feel right to see him in this way. Better to meet formally in the street or when he brought work to the door. She was shivering and not from the chill.

'We're here.' Mrs Cochrane pointed to a large house halfway up Cherry Street. 'The young man started out with nothing but look how well he's done for himself. He deserves his success, he works that hard for the mill.'

They were ushered up steps and into a tiled hall where a maid took their coats and led Rhodabel into the back of the house. Greta found herself in a parlour with padded chairs and dark furnishings. Tall windows were netted with lace curtains so the street was hidden from view. 'Come in, ladies, sit down.' The room fell silent as she and Mrs Cochrane entered and Greta tried not to shake as she was introduced. She felt the eyes of the other women on her.

'Well, I'd be fried for an oyster, if that ain't the prettiest way to decorate your hair,' said one of the wives, fingering the pearls securing Greta's bun. 'I'd never think to use them for any way but round my neck.'

Greta smiled, relieved that their attention was on her hair and that her modest idea was approved of. 'I don't possess many pearls so I just thought...'

'And your husband a pearl dealer...' said Mrs Cochrane. 'Oh, my dear, I forget myself and him not cold in his grave. I am so sorry.'

It was a small town and they all knew her story. She nodded, backing herself into the corner of the room. James Baillie was nowhere to be seen so she smiled and accepted condolences from all the visitors. Then, to her embarrassment, they were called into supper and she found herself placed next to Mr Baillie as the honoured guest. He stood by her chair wearing a frock coat and a fancy tie, his hair for once combed back, untamed strands curling round the nape of his neck.

'We'll have to talk Mrs Slinger through all the different trimmings that go with our splendid turkey roast. They don't do this in England. Here is cornbread, greens, sauces – all representing something from that first year when the pilgrims celebrated their harvest. Or so we are told. I'm not sure they ate turkey, just whatever they caught in the forest.'

Everyone was chattering and asking her question and she felt her host watching her as she tried to tackle the enormous plate of food. How her brother would have wolfed this all down. Her stomach was tight and she could hardly breathe.

Then came pumpkin pie and pastries. She struggled to do justice to Martha's cooking. 'This is the sort of feast they call a belt loosener in Yorkshire,' she offered and everyone laughed. The cordials packed a punch, going to her head and making her feel dizzy.

Baillie stood up and lifted his glass. 'In the whirlwind that is our life we all realize a longing for home and far-off kin but first we give thanks to God's bounty for guiding us to safety on this special day. To absent friends and family.'

They all stood and toasted in silence. The Cochranes came from Ireland, the Schindlers from Germany, the Causses had family in France. Greta took comfort that all of them must be thinking of another place called home. *I shall remember this next year, God willing, when I'm back home with my own kin,* back home where she belonged.

They retired to the parlour where there was a piano and Mrs Schindler sat down to play. The piano was a little out of tune and tinny but they sang the old favourites: 'Home Sweet Home', 'Loch Lomond', 'Sweet and Low' and 'Danny Boy' which Mabel Cochrane sang with tears in her eyes.

Was this a life she could love, if she were safe and sheltered by a good man, secure from harm?

When she looked up at Baillie, he was staring at her again with those dark deep eyes and her stomach lurched with longing. She felt as if she were being drawn to the very heart of him like a magnet clung to metal. She knew her cheeks were pink.

It was time to leave before she disgraced herself. 'I must say thank you for such a wonderful feast and such pleasant company,' she said to him quietly as she made her way to the door, not wanting to break up the party.

'I will walk you back, it's dark out there. Or better still get you a cab.'

'I wouldn't hear of it. The fresh air will do Rhodabel and I good. Thank you, Mr Baillie, for your kind invitation.'

'No, I insist, the party will go on, knowing my staff. I will walk you home.'

She stood in the hall while a maid brought her cloak and bonnet. Then Rhodabel appeared ready for the off as Baillie wrapped the cloak around Greta's shoulders. 'Thank you for coming.'

She could smell the pomade in his hair, the tobacco on his breath and something she couldn't name, something manly and mysterious. It was a heady mix.

The three of them walked downhill, through the silent streets. Candles flickered in the windows as revellers enjoyed their parties but as they got nearer to the shore she heard all the raucous singing and shouting rising up from the riverside bars. Down there was another world of wild men and women. The sky had cleared and now was full of stars, the moon almost full. When they reached their porch, Rhodabel dashed ahead to open up and light the lamps.

Greta paused and turned, looking up into his face to thank him again. He smiled, disarming her. For a second she sensed something was about to happen but then, stepping back, she slipped on the ice. He reached out to steady her, his face shadowy, intense, and her breathing quickened.

When he kissed her she made no protest. His lips covered hers and she shuddered as he pressed his body against hers. No, No! Her body was responding, telling her what her mind didn't want to hear. She wanted this to go on for ever. A wildness she didn't recognize took hold of her as she revelled in his touch. They were kissing with such passion, her limbs melted. In that moment all she wanted was to be crushed under him, drowning in deep water, but yet she struggled to breathe, to surface, fighting all her senses to reach some sort of sanity.

She pulled away just as Rhodabel stood in the open door. Greta could hardly stand. 'Good night, Mr Baillie, and thank you.' She held onto the porch rail as she climbed the stairs in confusion.

Later she lay sleepless, going over and over their embrace, the ecstasy of his body close to hers. Never had she had such feelings with Eben. This was something far beyond her experience, a wild torrent, the most exciting sensation she'd ever known.

If this was how she felt with just a kiss, where would it lead? Her limbs wanted to know more of him. How would her body respond to ... if they...?

She stopped herself going further. Baillie was

engaged to another girl. He shouldn't be doing this when he was attached elsewhere. Was he taking advantage of her because she was poor, widowed, lonely and at his mercy? Was this invitation merely a ruse to get her to succumb to his lust?

Had he planned this assault all along? Did he want her for his mistress? How could she have been silly enough to think he wanted her for herself? Suddenly her desire turned to fury. How dare he do this when her defences were so battered? Did he think her so cheap as to fall for this false friendship? Greta Costello was no sixpenny whore, not then, not now. He could go hang!

41

When the last of his guests had gone, Jem paced the floor, reluctant to turn in. What had he just done? Was it the punch, the wine, the evening or the holiday that had gone to his head? Was he just sorry for the widow with the sad eyes and the look of longing on her face when they were singing the songs of home? He had seized a moment of weakness in both of them, taken his chance to taste her lips, to feel her response to his and now he felt nothing but shame.

Effie was beautiful and full of poise and feminine charm. Yet there was something about Greta that had captured his attention in a way Effie's charms never had. Greta was careworn, her face pinched by sorrow and her accent broad and yet there was a beauty of a different hue in her features. Was it that he felt he owed her attention and help because of Slinger's fate? Had she in turn cast a lustful spell over him? Was she luring him into an entanglement that would end in tears?

One thing he did know was that it must not happen again. He would never spend time alone in her company and he'd make sure he was in Clinton for Christmas. He must apologize for this lapse in behaviour. He'd write Greta a contrite letter and make sure he stayed away.

Jem always prided himself on his sense of honour. He was a fair employer, a fair judge of men and he tried to hear both sides of any dispute. He was respected in Muscatine. What on earth was he thinking of, kissing a frail woman, giving her ideas that there was a future in this relationship with him? In the eyes of many, what he had done was tantamount to a proposal. What if she made overtures? What if Effie got to hear of this behaviour? She didn't deserve this betrayal. It had to stop, right here, right now.

Damn those Slingers, first the husband and now the wife, unsettling his ordered regime. He would distance himself from their house. He'd send any pearls with Martha and that would mean he didn't have to see her again. Once she received his letter she would understand how things were. Perhaps he could help her leave Muscatine, ease her and the maid's passages home but how could he arrange it without it looking as if he were buying them off?

'You look pale, Miss Greta,' Rhodabel said as she

298

spat on the iron to test its heat.

'I'm fine, just get on with your sheets,' Greta snapped, knowing she was being unfair to the girl but unable to stop herself.

The weeks between Thanksgiving and Christmas were a blur of laundry. All the rooms in the house were full of steam and damp washing. There had been no more jewellery repairs. At this rate it would take months before they could leave for home and she could no longer settle in the river town.

In those first days after that dinner she was relieved that Baillie did not return to press his attentions on her but then, to her surprise, she felt the icy draft of his absence and missed his casual visits. She wondered if Rhodabel had witnessed them kissing. Had she seen their loss of self-control? Now Greta felt ashamed of her weakness. It was Martha who brought things to a head when she arrived on the doorstep with a letter.

Dear Mrs Slinger,

Please forgive my abominable behaviour last week. I have no excuse other than too much wine and the merriment of the occasion. I am sure you will agree that it is better not to be seen in company together. People are closely observed in this town. I would hate to compromise your reputation.

As I cannot find that last pearl to complete the necklace which you have so carefully worked on, I intend to leave the rest in your hands as payment for all your time on my behalf. Please feel free to dispose of them as you see fit.

I know how eager you are to return to your family.
I hope they will help you on your journey.

Yours sincerely,
James Baillie

Greta's first instinct was to throw the paper into the stove. How dare he? she thought, indignation burning in her throat. Yes, it was a breach of bad manners to take advantage of the moon and starlight but she hadn't kissed him, he'd kissed her first and now he was paying her off for her silence with a tray of pearls, to hell with that!

'Martha, just a moment,' she called out. 'Please take these back to Mr Baillie.' She rushed to find her toolbox and the package of pearls and the half-threaded necklace, putting them all together into the servant's hands. 'Thank him for his note. I shan't be needing these and they are far too valuable for me to keep.'

The coward hadn't the nerve to say all this to her face. What did he fear? That she might compromise his standing if she made a fuss? Perhaps he thought she would write to Miss Euphemia and spoil his chances? How dare he think so little of her? How many times had she rehearsed what to say when they met again? How dare he get in first and spoil her own dramatic lines of reproof? How dare he back away from that kiss, the power of which still lingered on her lips?

His letter stung her confidence. With his help she had overcome the horror of Eben's deeds and the relief at his death but she was surviving independently, without a man, and had given an orphan a home. Her pride now withered.

For one brief moment she had found comfort in his arms and then he'd sent this cowardly letter.

Those pearls would see them home safely but to keep them would mean she was being bought off, that her presence must be banished from his sight because he felt foolish. Stuff and nonsense, she was worth more than that. When they returned to York it would be on her terms and without the help of any false friend. Even if it took a year she would stay the course and defy him. If he felt uneasy around her living in Muscatine, so be it. That would be his burden not hers. Here she was staying until she was good and ready to go.

42

January 1889

It was just after their quiet Christmas and New Year when Rhodabel suddenly doubled up in pain. 'My guts is aching,' she complained and then she fainted onto the floor. Greta felt her forehead and it was burning up. 'Bed for you, my lass.' She was up half the night with a bucket and mop as the girl retched up everything. She called her neighbour Clarrie in to check Rhodabel over and the woman looked worried. 'That girl ain't right, Greta. I'll sit with her while you fetch the doc, the good one in Walnut Street.'

The wind was blowing hard and Greta had to battle through the winter snow on foot. She reached the doctor's house and called for his help. He got his bag and accompanied her back to the house. Greta took him straight upstairs to examine the girl.

'Looks like she's poisoned herself with something, so starve her and see she drinks plenty of water.' He eyed Rhodabel with interest. 'She's not one I delivered, where's she from?'

'Rhodabel came on the orphan train from New York.'

'Oh, she'll be a tough one, up in no time. Don't worry, young lady. She'll be fine. Give her plenty of water.' He set off and she felt she'd troubled him for nothing.

Only Rhodabel didn't get better and her fever rose even higher. Greta noticed a rash over the girl's body when she bathed her with cold water to cool her down. Her breathing was laboured too. This was not good and every instinct told her the girl needed help.

This time when the doc came there was no small talk. 'The kid's got enteric fever. Be careful now. Boil your water, burn her clothes. I'll send the ambulance cart for her.'

Greta stood in shock. 'Where are you taking her?'

'To the fever ward, they know what to do there, but I'm warning you now. It's not looking good. She's gotten very weak. We have tests we can do to confirm this but I've seen this rash before. Don't worry, she'll be in safe hands.'

Greta sat in a daze waiting for the ambulance

cart to plough through the frozen streets.

'Where am I going?' Rhodabel was thrashing so hard, trying to resist the men as they lifted her onto a stretcher board. 'I'm not going back to the orphanage, am I?' Her eyes were rolling with terror.

'You're going to the hospital to make you better.' Greta was trying to calm her.

'Don't leave me, I'll die. They won't bring me back!' The girl was screaming and Greta was crying as they slid the stretcher onto a shelf in the small ambulance cart.

'I'll be right behind you. I'm here. I won't leave you,' Greta called out, flinging on her cloak and muffler ready to walk behind them to the hospital. She could hear the girl shouting in delirium. 'He's going to kill me again. I can see the master coming to get me. Don't let him kill me.'

Greta was numb with cold and fear as she slithered over the ice, trying to keep up with the cart. If only they would let her sit with Rhodabel in the cart to ease her panic but when they reached the isolation ward, nurses wearing masks came out to escort the patient through the door.

'I'm sorry, you must leave,' one of the nurses ordered.

'But the girl needs me.'

'I'm afraid this is no place for you.'

Rhodabel turned to her, helpless with fear. 'Miss Greta, please, save me, the master is coming to get me.'

'Don't worry, it's only fever talk. We will sedate her. You must go now.'

Greta stood by the railings, weeping at this sudden turn of events. How could she leave Rhodabel alone and in pain? There was nothing to do but pray and wait.

Word soon got round. It was Martha who called at the house first. Seeing the state of panic Greta was in she offered to help her strip Rhodabel's room and burn the bedding and her clothes. They opened the windows to air the room. 'Let's hope the wind changes and we get some fresh air. You must boil your water. Don't worry, she'll be fine up there.'

Greta swallowed the urge to snap. If anyone else said 'she'll be fine' she'd hit them. How could she bear another loss? The doc had mentioned the dreaded word typhoid – a deadly curse. It was a poor man's disease caught from dirty water and bad food. How had Rhodabel picked up such a thing? Then came news from the town that two other people had come down with the fever and they were testing a drinking fountain in town. Perhaps something had fouled the tap – a carcass or worse. At least they'd found the source but that was no help to Rhodabel who must have drunk from it on one of her trips to the stores.

Every day she walked up the hill to visit the hospital but each time she was turned away. All she knew was that Rhodabel and the two others were fighting for their lives. Greta had to walk back in a daze of despair. Nothing was going right in her life this past year and now her little friend was at death's door and there was nothing she could do to help her recover.

The house felt cold and silent without Rhodabel's chatter and companionship. Greta sat by the stove willing Rhodabel to fight on and live. It was hard trying to sew and mend the torn laundry sheets but their livelihood depended on it now. Her hands were shaking and all her food tasted like metal in her mouth. When the doorbell rang she feared the worst and crept to open it in dread.

Baillie was standing on the porch. 'What do you want?' she snapped.

'I've just heard the news from Martha. I'm so sorry. How's the lassie doing?' Baillie walked inside without invitation. Greta closed the door behind him, too numb to care what anyone might think.

'She's battling on, no thanks to me. I can't even see her and this is all my fault. We should have left when we had the chance...' She could not look him in the face.

'If onlys, if onlys, it's nobody's fault. Just one of those things that anyone can get if they drink from the wrong place. You don't expect it in winter. Bad luck all round.' He paused to stare at her. 'Sit down, you look wabbit out, as my old ma used to say. Fit to drop.'

She was too exhausted to protest. 'They won't let me visit. How's she to know I'm there if she can't see me? If she dies she'll be all alone and afraid. I can't bear such a thought.'

The sobs poured out of her whole body as he gathered her into his arms. 'Let it all out, Greta, let it out. She'll be fine, such a strong lassie. They know what they're doing these days.'

'No, she won't be fine.' She was beating her arms against his chest. 'The doctor told me she's skin and bone and they've had to shave off all her beautiful hair.'

'It'll grow back, just as red and curly. You really have taken to her.' He spoke as if to a wounded child.

'She so reminds me of my sister who Eben murdered in York. Kitty was so full of life, too, and now this. I'm sorry to burden you.' She pulled back, aware of his closeness, the scent of cigar smoke on his lapel.

'What for? It's me who's sorry for staying away, leaving you, running away. It's just that being with you...' He stopped himself and sighed, stepping back to hold her at arm's length. 'What is it between you and me? I can't stay away from your troubles. I feel responsible.' She looked up puzzled, seeing him pull away from her.

'When he showed me the pearl, the one I told you about, I knew it was the very one I'd fished out with my father. It was my father's last pearl.' Jem stared into the fire not looking at her. 'Pa had such hopes for my future. For his sake I vowed to get even with the scoundrel if ever I found him. I dreamed of finding the man who stole it from us. I recognized the pearl straight away as the very one we lost. I had to get even with him,' he paused, bowing his head. 'I teased him and taunted him, pretending to throw it into the river. I knew he'd go after it but it was only a pebble I threw in not the pearl. It was still in my hand. The rest you know. I'm sorry...' He turned to face her, flushed with shame and regret.

'What's done is done, James Baillie. Thank you for coming. I know it's not where you want to be.'

'Ach, I don't know what I want any more, Greta.'

'But the letter...'

'When I am here with you, there's nowhere else I want to be but I know I should be in Clinton with Effie. When I was there, I was thinking only of you alone here at Christmas. I hoped you were being looked after by your neighbours. I didn't want them talking about me visiting you. I'm so confused. I don't know what I want any more.' He bowed his head with a sigh. 'And please call me Jem.'

'Oh, Jem, if only we had met under different stars. I can't help you, not now,' she replied. 'I'm bad news. Everyone I've cared about is the worse for knowing me. Edmund, my friend, fell out with his family because of me. I married Eben to help my mother, but look what happened to Kitty. She died because of his desire for her, not me. Now Rhodabel is dying.' She looked up at him. 'Even you, I've caused a rift with your intended. I can't seem to get anything right.' There was nothing else to say.

As they sat in silence, Greta noticed his broad shoulders and the way his black hair ruffled over his coal black eyes. He was lost in his own troubled thoughts. Then he glanced up at her. 'What are you thinking? How can I help right here, right now?'

'I'm just glad you're here to comfort me. If you could stay awhile longer, I don't think I can face this night alone.' She matched his stare with her own. 'I have no shame, Jem. I just need someone by my side. I am so very lonely and sick at heart.

I've reached the end of my road.' The tears were rolling down her cheeks, dripping off the end of her nose.

Then he was kneeling before her. 'Are you sure about this? I can fetch Martha to sit with you?'

She shook her head. 'Martha can't give me what I need right now. I am cold and afraid and for so long have known no proper comfort. I need a body's warmth.'

He lifted her and took her to the bedroom. He lay her down on the patchwork quilt, stroking her hair, unpinning it so it fell like a shawl around her shoulders. 'You are a brave woman. The moment I first saw you I knew you were special. It was on the shoreline, you tripped over the nets and I caught you. I wanted you then. It was as if I'd been waiting for you to arrive in my life but now it's too late since neither of us are free. Are you sure this is what you want from me? I can offer no promises for the future.'

'I don't care about the future. Just for tonight I need a body close to mine, a voice in my ear, lips to touch. I need your warmth. It's been so long. Eben would never touch me...'

She was weeping again and he stopped her tears with a kiss, a kiss that made her body dance with pleasure, a touch that when it came was all she had ever imagined it would be. He filled her senses, flooding her limbs with desire so they relaxed and melted, opening to his own passion until they were one body. They drank of each other until sleep overtook them.

In the dim light of dawn when she woke, he was gone and she wondered if it had all been a dream.

43

No one witnessed his early morning exit from Greta's house. The heat of the night was soon chilled by the winter outside. He must call in at the mill, carry on as if nothing had happened, but he had crossed the Rubicon by giving into her desire and his own. He couldn't wait to return to the warmth of her loving and to give Greta the support she so badly needed.

Jem had made himself stay away because it was the right and honourable way, however hard it was. His attraction to her, he argued, was mere lust but what happened last night, those intense feelings she raised in him, brought him to his knees. He struggled through the day in a fevered daze.

She'd asked only for his comfort and he had given it willingly but now he had fallen into that silken web of desire that he'd read of in poetry books. Now he knew why the laird's daughter would run away with the gypsy boy or the princess with the pauper. Why passion triumphed over duty and honour. He ought not to return to her but he knew that he would.

Greta waited for his knock. Under cover of darkness he walked to her door, not wanting to announce his presence with his buggy. Martha must know the score but she was loyal, however much she would disapprove.

Earlier that day she'd battled through the snow to see how Rhodabel was surviving. She'd arrived filled with dread but then, as if all her prayers were answered, the nurse had told her that the girl was over the worst but needed nursing care before she could return home. Suddenly it was as if a great burden had lifted from her back and she'd hurried back home to tell everyone the good news. Soon she would be allowed a brief visit.

That night she prepared supper for Jem with a grateful heart, knowing he would be relieved for her. They were drawing so close during these long nights when the outside world disappeared and he lay with her until dawn. This was no time to think about what would happen when Rhodabel returned. She mustn't expose the girl to these secret trysts and they would have to end.

In these past weeks, in the darkest of times, she had secured Jem's heart, his body and his company. But Jem was not a free man. He had an obligation to his fiancée in Clinton, whose name was never spoken but whose presence hovered over them like a dark shadow.

A man couldn't keep faith with two lovers, not a good man like Jem. There would come a time when he had to make his choice but not yet, please God, not yet. She didn't want to think about that. It was enough to live in the present, waiting for his next visit.

In her daydreams she imagined herself living high on the hill as Mrs James Baillie. There would be plenty of room for both Rhodabel and Martha, a baby or two in time. She would be a respected citizen of Muscatine. They would return to York on their honeymoon trip to visit her mother and Albert and call on all her dear friends. Then they would travel north to Perth and stay in a fine hotel for old time's sake so she would know where Jem lived as a boy. She wrapped these warm imaginings around herself like a blanket to ward off the chill of what might happen next.

Two weeks later Jem returned from the lumber mill where they'd had a great delivery of logs. He'd torn off his jacket and mucked in like old times. When he'd finished for the day he was tired and aching, he needed a bath before setting out for Greta's home. Martha heated up the zinc tub, seeing his impatience. In his new home they would have a tiled bathroom for every bedroom, he decided, with hot and cold running water.

'Mercy me, I forgot to give you the letter. It's from Clinton,' Martha announced with pursed lips. 'From Miss Euphemia, no doubt.'

'Thank you, Martha. I'll read it in the bath.'

'You are out again tonight?' she snapped.

'Yes,' he replied, sensing her disapproval. Closing the door to the bathroom he opened the envelope with a sinking heart.

Darling Jemmy,

Mama and I will be coming down on the train tomorrow to see this wonderful view you've promised me for our homestead. Mama says she wants to see if it is in the right direction for the sun and where the yard will go. I can't wait to see how your plans are

311

forming. It's been so long since your last visit, I am beginning to feel you are avoiding us in favour of all your businesses.

What plans? I've only just bought the plot, he argued to himself, knowing the house was the last thing on his mind lately. Though why shouldn't his fiancée come down to inspect the plot? Why shouldn't Marcella care where her daughter would be living? They would prefer Effie to be closer at hand. He knew he'd been neglecting the family and it had been noticed. This was more than a viewing, it was a closer inspection of Jem's life away from their luxury and scrutiny. He was their protégée and now he was under review.

He threw Effie's letter into the hearth in frustration. Why must they come now? It wasn't that long since Christmas. Travelling was a dreary business in the winter. Was Jacob wondering about his loyalty?

He dried himself off roughly. They would have to stay at the best hotel and this house must be prepared. Martha would want to make preparations for this royal visit. He must absent himself from his work to escort them. Oh damn and blast! How could he go to Greta tonight?

She waited with supper on the table, waited until the lights flickered, sensing he would not come tonight. He called in most evenings. He lay with her until dawn and left quietly so as not to disturb her. Tonight she ached for his news, for his kiss, his throaty laughter. Perhaps something at work had delayed him or was something wrong?

312

How dependent she was growing on his visits. Only the ticking of the clock gave her company and it was reminding her only of absences. She recalled all the clanging of the clocks in Mr Abrahams's house, how they'd all chimed at different times. That was how he filled the silence after Adah's death. Now she knew how that felt. Suddenly she felt a shudder of fear in her chest. Why didn't he come to her?

She picked up the quilt she was sewing for Rhodabel's return, piecing together different shapes and sizes to make a crazy quilt edged with blanket stitch. She'd cut up some old dresses Clarrie had given her. It would be good to have her little companion home again to fill the gap, for she sensed her time with Jem would soon be over. When her eyes began to droop, she blew out the lamp and made her way to bed knowing tonight she would be sleeping alone.

It was the following week when she was walking down East Street towards Swann's to return with a pearl choker repair when she caught sight of a familiar figure striding towards her. He stood head and shoulders above the shoppers on the pavement and was wearing his now familiar bowler hat. She quickened her pace to greet him. Then she saw the two women at either side of him, one clinging to his arm, a beautiful young girl with fair ringlets bobbing under a plum velvet hat which matched her velvet three-quarter-length coat edged with fur. She was carrying a matching muff.

If only she could have fled from the sight of them but there was no time to dart across the busy street. 'Mr Baillie.' She dropped a curtsey as did most employees in this situation.

'Ah, Mrs Slinger. May I introduce you to Mrs Allister of Clinton and her daughter Miss Allister, my fiancée.'

The two women nodded to Greta, seeing a widow in black but no more.

'I hope you are enjoying your visit to Muscatine,' she offered, not daring to catch Jem's eye.

'Oh yes,' said the girl. 'James is building a house for me right up on that bluff.'

'Then you will have a beautiful view of the river. Pardon me, but I have a pressing appointment. Mr Baillie is well respected in this town. I'm sure you will find the townsfolk very welcoming.' She bobbed again, not waiting for any reply.

So they were the reason for his absence. He was otherwise engaged. Greta felt a stab of pain in her chest, knowing she couldn't compete with that paragon of wealth and beauty. Miss Allister belonged in a world she knew nothing about, among the rich mansion owners of the city whose daughters never dirtied their hands with trade or housework.

Jem had dragged himself up from humble beginnings to a position where he could marry into such a world. How could she have ever thought that theirs was anything other than a fleeting passion? He had given her what she asked for with no promises for the future. At least he'd been honest.

The girl in the velvet coat was his future. He had made that plain enough, but why hadn't he warned Greta that his fiancée would be in town? Would there be another letter of apology waiting on her doorstep? Greta fled down the street, clutching her parcel. You don't need this. You're not going through all this again, she cried. All that was left for her now was to collect Rhodabel as soon as she was allowed and bring her home. Then they must head back to York.

Effie stood on the high rise of the bluff looking out across the river as it curved on its way south. 'I want windows right here,' she said and then paced out the size with her dainty bootees.

'Your wish is my command.' Jem raised his hat with a smile but his heart was heavy. Meeting Greta in the street had unnerved him. He should have warned her but he'd thought it better not to make any contact. He was not proud of this. Once the Allisters were settled in the hotel, he hadn't wanted anyone to see him in Greta's company.

It cheered him that Effie was thrilled and full of plans. Her mother stood by, observing him as if she sensed his hesitation. 'Is everything going to plan, James? You look strained. I know Effie will have expensive ideas. We've spoiled her, but I think you've got the measure of how things should be. How long will these building works take?'

'We can start early in the spring. It will be ready for summer.'

'Shall we say July then for the wedding day?'

'Sounds perfect,' he replied.

'Good, then that's settled. I was beginning to wonder...' She paused to eye him closer. He could see her hesitate.

'To wonder?' he replied.

'Oh, nothing, just a little niggle of doubt about

your intentions but I see you work so hard here. You're a young man with ambition. Jacob recognizes himself in you, as he was years ago, rough round the edges. He's trusting you with his greatest possession. I know you won't let him down.' Her face was inscrutable. Was there a hidden warning in such mild words? *Betray my husband and daughter and you will never work in this country again.*

Later they took the carriage back to the station. 'I wanted to see where we are going to live, Jemmy, and it's going to be perfect. Write to me with all the plans and photographs. I have to know every detail. It's going to be heavenly.'

He escorted them along the platform into the first-class carriage. 'Write soon,' Effie pleaded, lifting her cheek to be kissed. 'I worry when you are silent.'

He waved them away with regret and relief. It had gone to plan. Marcella was satisfied, a date was now fixed for the wedding and he had his orders. They saw how successful he was at the mill, how busy his work kept him, but he felt uneasy. Was he trapped by ambition and the desire to fulfil all the promise that Jacob had seen in him? He strode back along the shore to clear his mind.

It wasn't Greta Slinger who had trapped him with her wild passion, rather he had ensnared himself in a net of his own making. He'd walked into a gilded cage, proud and delighted to be the chosen one. Now the door was shutting slowly on his freedom. How could he let them down?

But there was Greta to consider. Would she understand that he felt he must always oblige the

Allister family and keep his promises? Greta was strong. Effie was still almost a child, in need of his protection. Greta would survive but the thought of not being with her again stung him. He wanted both women but that was not in his Scottish nature. There must be another solution. He could always disappear, leave them all behind and start again. He stared at the wide grey river. He could take a boat upriver to Minnesota, lose himself in the forests there, but in his ear rang his father's warning: *'Nothing is got without pains, laddie, but an ill name... I didnae bring a coward into the world. You made this trouble all by yersel' so sort it one way or another or yer nae son o mine.*

44

Greta was in a mood for clearing out all that remained of her husband's belongings. Considering how little they had brought to this country there were still bits to dispose of if they were to travel light. She would take back nothing of him, not even his name. From now on she would be Greta Costello again. Her heart hardened at his fate. That part of her life was over, but she still didn't have enough to secure their passages home. How she regretted not keeping those pearls. No wonder Jem Baillie wanted rid of her.

She was done with men and it felt good to be throwing all Eben's clothes into a sack but not before they cut off all his fancy pearl buttons.

The Blue Ribbon Ladies Charity stall were not having those.

Eben always took trouble with his shirts and clothes and was so particular about how they were laundered that he did them himself, hanging them out to dry, never letting her iron them, which was fine by her. 'You cut off the buttons first,' she ordered Rhodabel, glad to see she was almost back to her old self again.

It was while Greta was fingering one of Eben's best shirts that she felt a familiar fullness along the seams. Could it be? She reached for her scissors and began to unpick the stitches until pearl after pearl slipped out and onto the table.

'Well, what have we here?' she cried and Rhodabel stared down at the find.

'Jesus, Mary and Joseph! Are them real?'

Greta lifted one and felt its coldness, inspected its size and colour and took her teeth to its surface. It felt gritty. 'Oh, yes, his freshwater beauties. He must have been carrying these around for months. This shirt was on his back when we left England. No wonder he was particular about washing it by himself. To think I nearly chucked this in with the others. Do you think there could be more?'

This sent them into a frenzy, unpicking the seams of his trouser pockets and underwear, even his nightshirt, and sure enough there were pearls hidden all over the place, sewn into the seams closest to his skin. Greta was furious to think the old skinflint had carried this wealth around when so often she had gone without. She put their finds down on a piece of cotton cloth to sort and size them and to stare at this unexpected bounty. 'You

318

know what this means.' Greta grinned. 'There's hundreds of dollars' worth, I reckon, if we can find a good buyer. Eben knew his pearls and these pink ones are rare.'

'Are we rich?'

'Not really, but when I think how I scrimped and saved to keep us fed and clothed, taking in dirty linen for a pittance, when all the time Eben had these hidden away, it makes my blood boil. These will get us home,' she said, shaking her head in disbelief.

'Wait until I tell Martha and Mister James what we found.' Rhodabel was jumping up and down with excitement.

'No, you tell no one. This is our secret. Promise me you'll say nowt or I shall be leaving you here,' she threatened.

Greta searched in her box for the brass pearl measure and scales. Each one would be itemized, its value estimated, any poorer quality ones separated. There were always visiting dealers from New York in town and she would be no pushover for cheap deals. She would go to the top for the very best price. She shuddered to think she'd nearly chucked all this away. Thank goodness Eben trusted no one, not even his wife, with his booty. How many folks had he cheated for these gems?

They are mine now to do with as I please. Something good must come out of this treasure. Suddenly she felt such relief that there was now a way out of Muscatine. Eben would be paying for their return. She slid the pearls into a pouch and set to clearing out the rest of her husband's belongings with renewed vigour. Just knowing they could afford a passage home put a spring in her step. The last few weeks had been exhausting, her whole system was out of kilter and she felt tired and jaded. It hurt that Jem hadn't come to say goodbye or discuss his decision face to face. But she would think far worse of him if he tried to dally with two lovers. Those weeks together she would never forget. He had helped her through a difficult time, given her the comfort she needed, but now it was over.

Jem couldn't settle to his work, his heart was not on the job. He'd attended meetings with his architect, taken a trip to Davenport to see a banker about funding for his mansion. He had hardly given a thought to these plans because all he could think of was how to tell Greta that their affair must be over. He wouldn't shame her any more by making her his mistress. Many of his colleagues led two lives but it was not in his nature to dissemble. Loyalty and duty must come before his desire for the Yorkshire woman.

He wanted her to know that giving her up was not an easy choice. Letter after letter he had composed and crushed, trying to explain his actions. But he felt such a coward. This had to be done face to face but how and when as Greta was no longer alone in her house.

'Martha, would you invite the Bacchus girl to supper?' he asked. 'I'd like to speak with her mistress alone.'

'I thought that canoodlin' was all over, sir?' Martha looked at him with pursed lips and a scowl.

'Of course it is and it's none of your business. I

just want to be sure Mrs Slinger knows it too.'

'The sooner you is married to that sweet angel of yours, the better. You've had a devil in you these past weeks and that's for sure.'

'Martha, that's enough!' he snapped.

'Lordy, someone has to reign you in. You can't have your cake and yer cookie in this town.'

He shook his head and walked away knowing she meant well, telling him off as if he were a naughty child, but his heart was heavy when, later that week, he made his way to Greta's house.

Greta was on the porch, swinging on the rocker. She watched him as he half stumbled up the steps, tripping over a mess of boxes and clutter.

'You spring cleaning?' He raised his hat.

'No, just getting rid. Come in, I was expecting you.'

'You were?'

'Why else would Martha ask my girl for tea unless you prompted her?' She walked inside and beckoned him in.

'I just wanted to explain about Effie and her mother,' he stuttered, unsure what to say next.

'She's pretty and I can see how much she loves you.'

'I know but I feel torn between–'

She didn't let him finish. 'Enough, she's your intended and wears your ring. How could there be any other doubting?' Greta pierced him with those flinty blue eyes. 'And how could you carry on with me when I am on the other side of the ocean?' She was pointing to the boxes. 'We leave in a few days.'

'So soon?' He was shocked.

321

She smiled and nodded. 'So soon, there's no reason for us to stay, is there? Not now. Thank you for all you've done, giving me work, staying when I needed you. There were no promises made to me for you to break, remember?'

This was not what he was expecting, this matter-of-fact, cool appraisal of their relationship. Greta seemed different.

'Don't look so shocked,' she continued. 'I was always going to head back to York. This place has only bad memories now, much as I've loved the kindness of folks around us.'

'Can I help you in any ways? Do you have your fare?'

Greta held up her hand to stop him. 'We're fine. I have what I need. Rhodabel will be coming too. She's part of my family now.'

'But what will you do to live?'

'Oh, I've got ideas. Travelling has taught me much about myself. I'm tougher for knowing in this life you must rely on yourself not others to sort out your problems. I will never be dependent on anyone else.' She was looking him straight in the eye. 'Ever again...'

What else could he say? 'I wish you well if that is what you want for yourself. I wish things were different. If I were free, you wouldn't escape so easily.' He sighed.

'But you're not free, are you, Jem, and never were?'

'I'll never be free of you.' He felt his resolve weakening, wanting to hold her to him.

'Oh, yes, you will, when your bride comes and your house is built and you have beautiful children round your hearth. Time will ease all our desires in the end. Some things are just not meant to be.'

'How can you be so calm? I was not expecting you to be...'

'Oh, I see, you came to see me fall on my knees to beg you to stay. To beg you to choose me above all this.' She gestured down the street. 'I'm sorry but I'll bow to no man again. I'm free of all that and I set you free to go home and forget about me.'

'Greta, what's got into you? You've gotten so hard.'

'Tough as a clam shell, do you mean? A dear old man once told me without grit there'd be no pearl and that sorrows when they come can make the heart stronger. I didn't understand his warning then but I do now, Jem, I do now. You came to us at a bad time. You filled an empty space and gave me hope and trust. I'll not be greedy. That time is over. I will not do to Effie what was done to me. Trust once lost is hard to grow again. I guess we both know what might have been but we have to live with what is and help make our futures what they will be. Off you go, I think everything has been said.'

She waved her hand as if to dismiss him. Jem backed out the door in a daze of disbelief.

How could she be so cool about the passion they had known between them? He'd gone to let her down gently but she just jumped in and pulled the proverbial rug from under his feet with her infuriating dignity. It was that dignity that first caught his attention. Why was he letting someone precious drift out of his life like a boat drifting into the river mist? She was being strong and realistic while he was weak willed. He must find that strength in himself somehow, but first he needed a drink.

Greta collapsed on her bed after he left, prostrate on the little love bed where she had discovered such intimate desires. Now she lay cold and stiff, protected at first from the pain of their parting until the numbness wore away. At the thought of never seeing his handsome face again, she began to weep. They could have been such a team, husband and wife, a force to be reckoned with in the district but now Effie must take that rightful place by his side. How could she bear to be in the same town once Effie was his wife? How cruel and cold she'd been to him in letting him walk away humbled, confusion written all over his face, but what else could she do?

There was a new life waiting across the water and the sooner they found it the better. Greta jumped up, suddenly full of resolve. No time like the present. When Rhodabel returned she would see no tears or hysterics. The first cut is the hardest, she sighed as she began to pack.

45

Jem slept off his hangover. Martha tutted around, waking him to bring his shaving water. 'You is late for the office. Old Mr Allister will be hearing about this. Shift yer ass, sonny Jim.'

He had to laugh at her rudeness. 'We'll see about that, woman.'

He was waking from a wonderful dream where everything was clear in his mind. All was not lost. It was a mistake to think he had to marry Effie. The house wasn't finished yet. He was not married, no vows had been exchanged. Could he still extricate himself from their understanding? There was one solution. He could resign from the company, pack his bags and start a new life with Greta out west. They would travel overland to the new territories. Man and wife together, opening a farm, making a homestead, logging. Together everything was possible. They were young and strong. And he had his pearl of great price in his pocket to make it all happen.

He sloshed cold water over his face, smiling in the mirror, suddenly wide awake with hope. There was always a solution if you wanted a thing badly enough. His choice was made, pity he hadn't realized it last night. Was it that determined look of resignation on Greta's face that had shocked him into this change of heart?

How could you lose a woman like that, a woman

who had come halfway across the world married to that villain and survived? Greta would travel as his equal to the other side of the States. She would bear him sons and teach them right from wrong just like his own mother. Jeannie would have loved Greta as a daughter-in-law.

He couldn't wait to tell her of his decision. The mill would wait another hour as he made his detour. He'd find her busy at her chores, pegging washing out on the line. She would look up and see him smiling and she'd know he had made his choice once and for all.

At Greta's house, he kept knocking on the door but there was no reply. It was the woman next door who came out, rubbing her hands on her apron at the sight of her landlord.

'They's gone, Mr Baillie. I got the key for you.'

'Gone where?' This news did not register at first.

'To catch the early morning train east. Going home she told me when I seed her leaving.' The woman paused. 'I reckon she done had enough without her husband so she packed her bags in the night and left as the sun was rising, took the orphan girl with her.'

Jem raised his hat and nodded, making his way back towards the mill. His hand felt the pearl in his pocket, the pearl he would have sold for their future together. It was as cold as river ice.

Part 4

A LITTLE SHOP OF PEARLS

To love or have loved that is enough.
Ask nothing further.
There is no other pearl to be found
in the dark folds of life.

Victor Hugo, *Les Misérables,* 1862

46

As the Minster came into view from the carriage window, Greta's heart leapt, seeing it towering into the ink-blue sky. There was early blossom in the streets and spring in the air, a familiar waft of cocoa from the factories and the stench from the river. She stood in the station forecourt with a smile of triumph, knowing the girl who had fled the city all those years ago was not the same person as the elegant lady who was waiting for a cab.

Rhoda stood in awe at the sight of the ancient walls. 'It's like a picture book just like those postcards you kept. When are we going to see your folks?'

'Not just yet. There's things I must do first so let's find a porter to take our luggage to the hotel.' Determined not to arrive like a whipped pup she was learning to let others do the fetching and carrying, tipping them, taking pleasure in watching them doff their caps, treating her as a lady of means. 'We must rest and unpack. It's been a long journey.'

'Are you still feeling sick?' Rhoda asked.

'Not at all, not since I got off the ship in Liverpool,' she lied. 'This York air will clear my lungs... Why do you ask?' She bristled a little at Rhodabel's remark.

329

'You don't eat much. I thought it was because you–'

'Don't fuss, I'm fine.' It was true that she had suffered bouts of sickness on the ship. Perhaps she had eaten something that had disagreed with her, but enough of such worries. There were urgent affairs to attend to, private stuff, not for Rhodabel's flapping ears. Everything must be in order before she gave her mother the biggest of surprises.

They entered the Royal Station Hotel and took a room. Rhodabel unpacked their cases and Greta changed from her tired travelling clothes into the outfit she had purchased on Fifth Avenue, New York when she had sold some of Eben's secret pearls for a good price. They had stayed there so Rhodabel could revisit old haunts and Greta could see the great city before she left. This time she spared no expense in treating them both to new outfits.

Over her dress she wore a short velvet cape while her perky new hat was softened with black net veiling her face. She hoped she looked mysterious and important. A cab took her to Lendal to the offices of Erasmus Blake. Her heart was thudding at this boldness but she wanted to be sure she was safe in the city.

'May I see Mr Blake on urgent business?' she inquired and a tall young man with hair parted down the middle ushered her into a waiting hall and then into a familiar wood-panelled room that she had last entered as a girl all those years ago. Now she glided in knowing she would not be recognized. 'Mr Blake, thank you for seeing me so promptly and without an appointment. I have just arrived from abroad but need to make inquiries before I proceed further in the city.' She could not disguise the American twang she had cultivated over the years.

'Please be seated,' said the old man, who was stooped and white haired; time had not been kind to the Quaker. 'May I ask your name. Miss...?' He hesitated.

'I'm a widow as you can see but before I tell you more, sir, I would like to ask you some questions that may affect my visit here. I've lived in the States for many years but I was born in York. My husband who also lived in York died recently. He left here under unfortunate circumstances and in considerable debt. I would like to know, since he is deceased, if I am now responsible for these debts about which I knew nothing then?' There was no time to let him reply, she wanted all the facts spilled onto the table. 'If so, what is to be done? Furthermore, I have become aware that while living in the city he committed the most terrible crime against a person which he confessed to before he died. How must this be dealt with? Should I say nothing about any of this to anyone?'

'Please, stop right there...' Blake held his hand up in protest. 'You must tell me your name and more of your circumstances before we go any further.'

Greta lifted her veil. 'You knew me as Margaret Costello, wife of the late Ebenezer Slinger of Stonegate.'

'Greta?' He peered down his spectacles in surprise.

She nodded. 'The girl from Walmgate who you

331

rescued from certain jail when you believed my story of Mr Abrahams's watch and gave me work in your home.'

'Goodness me! I would hardly recognize you...'

'It was many years ago, sir. A lot of water has flowed down the Ouse since then, for both of us. I made a bad choice of husband and I've every reason to believe he killed my sister Kitty. Her body was dredged from the river the week we left for America. It was only later I discovered what a mean and violent man Eben Slinger was. He attacked my maid when she crossed his wishes. He later drowned in the Mississippi as a result of his own greed and obsession.'

'Write all this down, write everything down and sign an oath so this tragic situation can be cleared. You had nothing to do with this crime, I trust.'

'Only that I married him to help my family, which then brought my sister to his attention. Her death broke my mother's heart and then he made me leave her without telling her where we'd gone.'

'So why have you returned?'

'This is my home. I have not seen my mother for years. I would like to start afresh. I don't use my married name any more, but once people recognize me as his wife...' She sighed, shaking her head. 'How can I deal with his reputation and his creditors? Who will want to trade with me?'

'Memories are long here but I can suggest there might be one way. I once heard about a gentleman who got into financial difficulty and could not pay his bills, but with hard work his fortune changed and although his debts had long been written off by others, he returned every penny he owed to them. He said he wanted to look every one of them in the eye. Slinger's debts were not yours but I suppose as his wife they could be seen by some to be so. Are you in a position to pay them back?'

Greta nodded. 'It depends. Given time I would try my best to wipe the slate clean.'

'I'm afraid word will get around about your return. A woman in business is an easy target. It's not the usual way of things except I suppose you being a widow might help...' he cautioned.

'Believe me, the life I have lived has taught me how to defend myself. I will survive. I have good friends.'

'Then you are rich indeed and I wish you well. It is best that we write to the police to inform of them of the confession so they can close that mystery. I am so sorry for your loss. My own wife passed to Glory. She was well respected and has left a gap in our lives so I know how you must feel.' He peered out of the window with a sigh.

'I had a letter from a friend who informed me of your loss. And Edmund, is he well?'

'Busy in his workshop out in the hills and much in demand from architects who build in the new Arts and Crafts style.'

'And Hamer?' she added.

'See for yourself.' He pressed a buzzer and the young man who had showed her in entered.

'Yes, Father?'

'Do you remember Margaret Costello, the maid?'

Hamer laughed. 'She took me to my first Gala and then lost her position.'

Blake turned in Greta's direction. 'Well, here

333

she is returned from America to start up a business and with her trunk full of stories, which one day I'd like to hear. I imagine it was an exciting life out there.'

'That's one way of putting it,' Greta replied, rising up to leave. 'Thank you for putting my mind at rest. It is the least I can do for Kitty, to see that she gets some justice even if it is a little late in the day.'

'Write the fullest account of your affairs and we will take it from there. You must call in at the bank and set things straight with your husband's creditors. Please feel free to call in and keep us informed. I wish you well in whatever you decide to do. You're a brave warrior...'

'I've been a foolish one in the past but not any longer, you've been most helpful. Give my good wishes to your other son.'

As they left the room Hamer asked, 'May I ask what line of trading you will take up now you've returned?'

She paused on the step. 'I've thought long and hard about that, young man, and it has to be something I know best. Pearls and all things shiny.' She smiled at him. 'I intend to open a little shop of pearls.'

47

Muscatine, May

Jem was so busy he had no time to brood on the past month's events, caught up as he was in completing his new mansion at the very top of Cherry Street, the best address in town high up on the bluff. Things were slack at the lumber mill so he'd taken the time to work on the house, supervising the final stages of landscaping the yard and making sure Effie's new home was a delight to the eye.

Jacob Allister had insisted that his daughter's house had the best of everything. It sported the latest Roach and Musser's sash windows, the best money could buy, a massive wraparound porch, the latest sanitary ware in each bathroom, walk-in closets and polished oak floors. There were fine kitchen quarters for Martha and her maid. On the third floor was a viewing tower overlooking the river complete with a balcony walkway. Effie would be queen of all she surveyed and the envy of the matrons of Muscatine.

'So how's it going, young James?' asked his future father-in-law as he surveyed the house with an eagle eye for detail. 'I hear you've been sniffing round some button-making process. Am I not working you hard enough at the lumber mill?'

'It's in the early stages of development at the moment. Johan Boepple has got his machine up and running. You know, I can see its possibilities. Logging here won't last for ever and another new industry will ease us into another line. Never have your eggs in one basket, you once told me, sir.' Jem threw the challenge back to Jacob. 'It makes sense, don't you think?'

Jem knew he had to impress his sponsor with big talk about the future. He was excited by the prospect of getting in at the start of a new business. Money talked and appearances mattered, he reckoned. Allister would expect him to keep Effie in silks and furs and fine pearls. Successful as Jem now was, managing the sawmill, there was still a long way to go if he was going to be able to keep his new wife in the manner to which she'd become accustomed. This new idea of a buttoning industry was worth exploring further. He would have to think how to make the best of any opportunity should it arise.

'There's a great future in buttons, Johan Boepple is the man to watch. A button may be the poor man's pearl but once the technique is sorted they will sell in millions. You know the river and how the mud sloughs can hold great piles of clams. Well Clammers look for pearls so now we can have them collecting the shells. There's money to be made here, I'm sure.'

Jem sensed the way the winds of change were blowing down the river, logging was on the wane, but this new venture looked promising and it would give him distance from the Allister family.

'I hate to bore you, sir, but have you seen the size

of some of the clam shells? They have a toughness I never saw before,' Jem shared his enthusiasm with Jacob. 'Boepple found this river on a map long before he left his old country and saw how it meandered from east to west before it turned south. He's already experimenting in the evening, splitting the shells by hand to release the mother-of-pearl and stamp out the blank shapes ready for making pearl buttons. You know he's even made his own machinery out of wood. I think he's got something and I want to be part of it.'

'That's what America is all about, young man, it always offers you the chance to better your lot. Keep me posted. It sounds interesting.'

Jem nodded, glad of this approval. The process Boepple was working on was still top secret and guarded from all but a few friends. If things took off, Jem could make his home here a permanent fixture and transfer his energies into this industry. Then there might be work making pearl buttons for everyone in the town. Pearls ... suddenly he was thinking of Greta.

Sometimes when he passed the little shack at the end of East Street, he'd pause to see if there was washing flapping in the breeze and then he'd curse himself for such idle thoughts. Greta was out of his life, and if Martha knew anything of her whereabouts she was tight-lipped. Once he'd caught sight of a postcard from York so he knew they had arrived back safely in England.

In July he would be a married man with the prettiest and sweetest of wives on his arm. He ought to feel excited and proud of himself but try as he could he felt only a leaden weight on his shoulders at the thought of being obliged to the Allisters for life. That's why a new venture that was all his own idea was so important.

To think he had almost ditched his fiancée in favour of a murderer's wife. He was ashamed of the power that woman still held over him but the past was the past and there would be no more temptation now she had fled. Instead he had a beautiful home to give to his new wife and the family he hoped one day would be theirs. He turned to see Effie running towards him. Thank God she couldn't read his thoughts.

'Oh, Jemmy, it's so beautiful, and the view, you made my dream come true. Look, Mama and Papa. Look at my yard and the view from my own little morning room. Isn't Jemmy wonderful? I can't wait for our wedding day.'

'It's not quite finished but by the time we return from our honeymoon to Washington it will be.' Jem smiled at them all, relieved to have this approval.

Effie's mother eyed everything and nodded. 'You have done it well. Effie will be happy here. She's such a special girl and you are a very lucky man. Treat her well.' Marcella's eyes never left his face and he felt his cheeks flush.

'I will be proud to make her my wife, Mrs Allister.'

'We have put our trust in you. Don't let us down – again.' The last word was spoken so only Jem could hear.

It was then that Jem realized Marcella knew about his affair with Greta. How she knew was of no matter now but he knew she would watch over him like a hawk once he and Effie were married. He felt trapped by this unspoken but implied accusation.

'Have I shown you my little surprise for Effie? Come and see,' he whispered, changing the subject. 'It's a secret so while she is with Mr Allister in the garden, I'll show you. Come to my makeshift office.'

His desk was already sitting in the bare room with its empty bookshelves. He opened a locked drawer and brought out a blue leather box. 'I had these made up by Swann's in town. It's for her to wear with her wedding gown.' He opened the box to reveal a string of milky white river pearls, with a diamond heart-shaped clasp. They were the ones he had offered to Greta but she'd returned half strung. 'Aren't they beautiful? The finest I've collected. I thought they would be perfect against her skin.'

'Did you now?' Marcella examined them for defects with a seasoned eye. 'Hmm, perfectly matched, but no daughter of mine will wear pearls on her wedding day.'

Jem stared, not understanding.

'Surely you know pearls on a bride means sorrow and ill fortune for the wearer? Put them away and give them to her for her birthday.' She snapped the box shut. 'My nanny from the South once told me that pearls belong in the sea and will want to return underwater. "They'll take you with them down into the deep," she told me. Pearls are unlucky. You of all people should know that.' She scowled, but he held his ground.

'That was not what I was told. I don't believe

such superstition,' he argued. 'They are a gift of nature, even savages have worn them as decoration.'

'Good enough for savages who know no better perhaps.'

'Queen Victoria and all the great ladies in the English court wear them by the hundred.'

'And look what happened to Victoria's husband. Now she wears them for tears and mourning. Put them away, James.'

'I would never do anything to harm Effie.' He sighed, shutting them in the drawer and turning the key, trying not to show his frustration, knowing his mother-in-law would interfere at every turn if he went against her. She wanted revenge for his mistake.

Thank God Effie would be here by his side. Once they were settled she would not have her mother at her shoulder. Marcella was his enemy now; he would defy her and send the box with Martha to Effie on their wedding day. If Marcella wanted a battle then she would get one. Effie must wear those pearls, to please him not her mother. He did not believe that superstitious nonsense. A pearl was a pearl, nothing less, nothing more. He thought of his Queenie hidden in the safe, waiting for another day to make her appearance. Once Marcella saw the size of that beauty round Effie's neck she would not be so quick to complain.

48

York, May 1889

Five days after their arrival in York Greta and Rhodabel left their hotel and headed towards Micklegate before walking down the cobbled Priory Street to her mother's house. Greta had imagined so many times how her Mam would open the door, delighted by the sight of them bearing gifts of spring flowers. It was a crisp morning, all the leaves on the trees were a sparkling green. Greta was ready to face her mother with all her news. It was going to be such a reunion.

How could she explain her delay in not coming straight home or her urgency to first seek out advice about her predicament? She wanted it all out of the way before their reunion as Mam would only worry about any debts being paid. Mr Blake had helped her secure a meeting with the bank where she'd opened an account and deposited the last of her money and pearls. It was here she secured information about Eben's creditors and discussed a means of reimbursing them. After that she sought a list of empty retail properties with living accommodation. She had wanted all of this in place before seeing to family matters. Business must come first from now on.

To the outside world she looked like a prosperous young widow returned from the States, but it

341

was all an act. She would be living off her wits from now on, hiding secret fears under a cover of brash confidence, hoping her mother wouldn't dig too deep under this shaky surface. Finally they reached her mother's house and Greta, with a grin on her face, rapped the shiny brass knocker on the familiar front door. An unshaven man in his shirtsleeves opened the door. 'Yes?'

'Is Mrs Costello at home?' she asked, puzzled by this stranger.

'I'm the lodger, she don't live here no more.'

'But I'm Greta ... her daughter. I sent a letter to here. I don't understand.'

'Oh, she and Bert went down south on a visit. He works on the railways. Sadie went with him, but don't fret, lass, they're back now and you've saved me a job with all this post. She'll be at Bert's place down the street. She lets this place out to railway men.' He was eyeing them with interest. 'So you're the one from away? Oh yes, your letters are here with the post on the dresser. You can give it her all together.' He shouted inside. 'Harry! You know where them other letters is?'

Another man shuffled from the back holding Greta's most recent letters and postcards. Greta shoved them in her bag with relief. If her mother hadn't got the news she'd sent then she wouldn't be aware how long it was since Eben died. She nodded and backed away from the door uncertain where to go next.

'See that house down there, you'll find her there, if she's not at the market.' He was pointing down the street. 'She won't half be surprised to see you.'

'Thank you,' Greta said.

'Any time, love.' He nodded, closing the door.

'What was he sayin'? I couldn't understand a word of it,' Rhodabel whispered.

'My mam's moved to Mr Langton's house but she's been living away so she doesn't know about Eben yet so leave all that to me. You don't have to say anything but nod when I ask you? Right?'

'Sure, I got the message, Miss Greta.'

How flat she felt. This was not turning out the way she'd planned but they marched down the street to the next address and knocked again.

This time it was opened and her mother looked her up and down, unsmiling. 'You took yer time.'

'Mam!' Greta moved to fling her arms around her mother but Sadie stepped back. 'You'd better come in, and your lady friend.'

Greta was stunned by her coolness. 'I thought you'd be surprised to see me. I sent a letter from Liverpool. We're home for good!'

'Happen I would've if Nora Walsh hadn't stopped me in the market to tell me her Mary saw you days ago trotting round Monkgate in a cab with this girl on your arm.' The hurt on Sadie's face was clear to see.

'I'm so sorry but I thought it best to set my affairs in order. A lot's changed for me since I last wrote but I gather you never got any of my letters.' She plonked all but the last one into her mother's hand.

'What affairs might they be then? I see by your widow's weeds that that devil must be out of this world at long last.'

'You don't know the half of it, Mam. Please

don't be cross with me. I had my reasons.'

'And who might this be?' Her mother eyed the stranger with suspicion.

'I'm Rhodabel Bacchus. Miss Greta took me off the orphan train and gave me a home. She didn't want to leave me behind so I'm going to be her assistant.'

'Are you now? Assistant in what, may I ask?'

Greta had had enough and stormed through into the house. 'Don't we get a cup of tea or shall I leave now?' She was close to tears at this cool welcome. It had all gone wrong.

'I was disappointed someone else saw you first but I've made my point.' Sadie unfolded her arms as if to relent. 'It's grand to have you back and no mistake. I never did trust that husband of yours after he left me having to find the rental when you flitted in the night. It were Bert Langton who saved the day with his lodgers when Slinger did a bunk from all his money mess. He blackened our name. Tom wanted to kill him.'

'Pity he didn't but I will see everyone right.'

'What with?'

'Don't worry, I didn't return empty-handed but there's so much you need to know about Eben. It was no bed of roses with him and he betrayed us all.'

'He tried to kill me,' blurted Rhodabel. 'Like he did Miss Kitty...'

Greta saw her mother blanch at those words and tried to check the girl but it was too late. 'I was coming to that. I wrote you a long letter but never mind... Let's calm down and take this slowly. We brought you some flowers. Rhodabel will fix them for you. Are you living over the brush with Mr Langton?' It was Greta's turn to be nosey.

'None of that, girl, we did things proper.' She shoved her wedding finger under her daughter's nose to make the point. 'He works over the tracks and got sent south so I went with him. I wrote you... You didn't get it, did you?'

'No, Eben didn't like me getting news from family, but we now know why.' Greta sat stiffly in the dark front room with its lace curtains and hard chairs, the picture of Kitty on the mantlepiece. It smelt of love and polish, of home, but at that moment she felt like a visitor. Her mother had aged but she had filled out. Married life must be suiting her.

'That friend of yours, Irene, seems to know stuff I didn't. She kept me up to date when I met her but they've flitted out on the moors. She's left an address for me to send on to you.'

'Oh no, I was hoping to see her. Where've they gone?' Why was everything changed in York? No one was where she had dreamt they would be.

'See for yerself, the name don't mean a thing to me but I'm the last to know anything.'

'Please don't keep going on about things, it's not like you to get so upset,' Greta accused.

'How do you expect me to be? I lose my hubby and bairns, then our Kitty and you do a runner with a crook. Tom's out East and hardly writes. Bert works away a lot. What have I done to deserve all that?'

Greta took a deep breath and smiled. 'I'm home now and I won't be going anywhere. Tom will come back one day and we can be a family again.

We brought you some things from Muscatine.' She needed to change the subject, knowing that this was not the time to talk about her own situation.

'First what I want to know is how that devil was taken?' said her mother, taking off her apron.

'It's a long story and not very uplifting, I'm afraid. He drowned chasing a rare pearl; he jumped in the river to find it and was swept away. Before that he'd attacked Rhodabel for giving his old coat to charity so I whacked him on the head with a skillet and he disappeared. We never saw him again.'

She paused knowing what came next would upset her mother. 'I know now he murdered our Kitty. He as good as told us when he attacked Rhodabel. Rhodabel can bear witness to the truth of it, can't you?' She turned to the girl who nodded her assent. 'He wanted Kitty not me, Mam, so he married me to get to her but I guess she saw him off sharpish so he did what he did.' She could hardly mouth the words, crying softly. 'You know the rest. She must have been wearing my best dress for some reason and my stone bangle; the one they found on her. How could I stay over there knowing all his wickedness and cheating? What a fool I made of myself thinking he loved me when I knew in my heart he was cold as ice. Then when he died we could finally come home and I was sick every day on the crossing and now you treat me like a stranger.'

'Hey up, lass, no more tears. It's been a long time for both of us. We've all had to survive as best we could. So you married a wrong'un with my blessing. We was both fooled by his fancy manners. I'll put the kettle on. My Bert will get a shock when he comes through the back door. Come along, Miss Rhodabel. I hope you don't mind but yer name's a bit of a mouthful.'

'Mr James told my friend Martha that it means "beautiful rose".'

'Very nice, I'm sure, but we shall call you just Rhoda. There's one or two with that name in York. Let me show you how to make a decent cup of tea. We don't hold with coffee in this house and we're teetotal.'

Greta felt the tension in the room lifting, and was grateful to see her mother softening by the minute. There was still so much to say and share but the biggest surprise she feared was still to come. *Sufficient unto the day is the evil thereof* said the Good Book. It was enough to know that the broken bridge to her mother was being repaired.

49

'Pass the brush,' Greta ordered as they swept out the old shop floor. Rhodabel was sneezing with the dust and grime of years that had accumulated on the steps to the upper floor. How they were ever going to live in here she'd never know but Miss Greta had that look on her face that meant business. She'd been up and down stepladders, distempering the walls and painting woodwork. It was all very strange but exciting. The rooms were beginning to look presentable but there was no furniture to make a home of the upstairs. It was all very bare and not a bit like Muscatine, but Bert Langton had offered to find a horse and cart to shift any furniture they might buy and he said he'd help carry it upstairs.

The empty shop was in Goodramgate, squashed between Todds the grocer on one side and the timber archway into St William's College on the other, not far from the Cross Keys public house. Behind the row of shops and houses the east corner of the Minster loomed over them like a mighty stone giant. The windows of their shopfront would not be troubled by sun spoiling their goods. There was a cold tap and sink in the back and a privy outside. Above the shop were two floors of living space with room for storage. Everything was going well and Greta was pleased with the shop's location – it wasn't the best end of the city but it was situated on a busy-enough thoroughfare to attract custom. Then her mother arrived to help and it was clear she was not too taken with her daughter's scheme.

'I don't understand the rush. You've not been back five minutes and here you are taking on this dusty thing. Where's the brass to set this all up? Think on, don't be rushing into debt.'

'Don't fret, Mother, we'll be fine if you give us a hand. I know what I'm doing,' Greta snapped, shoving a kettle into her mother's hand. 'Keep us topped up, it's thirsty work.' Then she disappeared up the stairs again.

'Why all the rush? You've been like a whirling dervish since you got off that ship. Was she like this out there, Rhoda?'

Rhodabel didn't want to be disloyal or speak out of turn. 'She likes to be busy and you should've seen how she got good prices for the pearls in New York,' she offered diplomatically.

'Busy, you call this? I call it summat else, a madness, jumping at the first premises she can find, flashing brass as if there's no tomorrow. You need to calm her down before she makes herself ill. A puff of wind would blow her over, she's that thin and pale.'

'Don't worry, Mrs Langton, I'll keep an eye on her. I'll be helping in the shop and this was the best shop we could find. I think it's very exciting.' Rhoda smiled, hoping to soothe the old lady.

'You're young, love, and don't see the dangers.' Greta's mother sighed. 'I'd have thought after all that Stonegate funny business with him, she'd have had enough of pearls but who am I to know owt about owt?' she muttered as she put the kettle on the range. 'It'll all end in tears.'

On fine evenings after work in the shop Rhoda was marched around the city to see just where Miss Greta had worked in the market and in the little house in Aldwark. They travelled across the river to see Mount Vernon where she'd been a servant. They paused to throw some wild flowers into the river in memory of Kitty. One Sunday afternoon they went to the churchyard where Kitty was buried and laid flowers by her headstone.

Bit by bit Rhoda was getting to know her way around the walled city, but her favourite visit was into the Minster itself with its statues and magnificent coloured windows. How could there be so

349

much history in just one place? Even the name of their street went back a thousand years to the time of the Viking raiders who settled in York. It's like living in a history book, she wrote to Martha, who wrote back a few weeks later with all the details of Mr James's new home – its bathrooms and elegant drawing room and the views of the mighty river. Rhoda told her mistress all the news from Muscatine but Greta just sighed and carried on with her painting.

That was the thing with her mistress, Greta could be chatty one minute and then silent and cool another. There was no reading which way she woke up. Sometimes it felt as if she wasn't listening, that she was lost in her own world. They had been shopping in Coney Street when she'd made for a doorway but then suddenly stopped. 'Where's Jerome's gone?' she asked a passer-by. The woman paused to look up.

'The pawnbroker,' Greta added.

'Not been here for years, love. The old man died and his son moved on,' came the reply. Miss Greta looked as if she was going to faint so they took refuge in a tea room while she composed herself.

'What's a pawnbroker?' Rhodabel asked in all innocence.

'It's just a place where you can take things and get money on account. Then when you can, you take your ticket and buy back the item you sold. They must have those in Muscatine too?'

'Oh, you mean the hock store.' Was Miss Greta in trouble? 'Did you have something in there?'

Greta sighed. 'Yes, I pawned a necklace to get money to travel to America. It'll be long gone now, I'm afraid. I kept the ticket. I just hoped ... never mind. Come on, things to do and no time to do it in.'

Rhoda was trying to keep pace with her as they left the tea room and raced through alleyways back to their new home. 'You've never said what we'll be selling in our store,' Rhoda said.

'Haven't I? I'm still thinking about it, bits and pieces, probably,' Greta replied vaguely. 'I'm not sure my first idea will work.'

'Bits of what then?' This was a funny way to go about doing things, she thought.

'Oh, wait and see ... plenty of time before we open our doors. Don't dawdle!'

It was with a heavy heart Greta returned to Mr Blake's office to report her progress the next day, trying to hide her uncertainty behind lists of what she had achieved so far. She hoped he would be impressed by her industry.

'You've acquired premises in Goodramgate. Have you bought in stock yet? What will you be selling?' he asked.

'I'm not sure,' she admitted with a sigh. 'I thought I'd be going into the pearl jewellery trade but I fear it's a step too far. Who will buy pearls from the widow of a bankrupt? I can't support us by just threading pearls all day. Buying good pearls from dealers is expensive.'

Blake leaned back on his chair, stroking his whiskers. 'Hmm, wise caution, young lady. So what is it that's driving you to go back into the retail trade, especially when it went so wrong before? I thought it would be the last thing you'd want to be doing.

351

What is it that drives you to take such a risk?'

This was something she found easier to answer. 'I love being in a shop, working behind the counter and meeting new customers, finding gifts that give them pleasure and hearing their stories. I like the new modern jewellery too, with its simple designs made out of less precious stones, but I will always love pearls best of all.' She dipped into her bag for a pouch and showed him the misshapes. 'They call these "slugs". I know these can be used to make pretty pieces or earrings. I think even misshapes can be beautiful in the right setting.'

He smiled at this answer. 'I couldn't have put it better myself in a sermon. Who is perfect in this world or without blemish? It's what we do with our blemishes that counts, and you're right. Given the right setting everyone can shine. If that's what interests you, perhaps it's time to think who would help you in this venture. There are plenty of artisans and silversmiths with no outlet for their craft or you could order from the catalogues of the big jewellery factories in Birmingham. I'm afraid this is not within my sphere of interests, I have just heard Edmund talking about it, but you must know others who can help.'

'I do, I do, there's Irene and her husband and their friends. It was her stone bracelet that helped identify Kitty.' Suddenly Greta felt excited and full of ideas.

'There you go, already you can see a door opening, but I would caution you. Don't start your business without a clear idea of what you want to achieve. Put everything in place before you open and keep to your budget. You will have to let people know just what you are selling. Perhaps invite people to an official opening. I have Friends who always encourage creative enterprises. I can help you there.'

'Thank you so much,' said Greta gratefully and stood to leave.

'I wish thee every success, Margaret Costello. You've come a long way and suffered much so if you invite me along I shall be honoured to attend.'

Greta sprang out onto the pavement inspired by his kind words of encouragement. She knew she couldn't compete with all the fine jewellery shops in Stonegate but she could make her shop quite different and attractive to all sorts of customers not just the wealthy.

She patted the slugs in her bag. They might seem ugly to some folks, and Eben would have cashed them in without a second thought, but he wasn't here to criticize. For the first time she passed their old shop without shuddering with shame. *I am not him. I will succeed and I know just the person to help me. Together we'll make something beautiful out of these misshapen pearls.*

Later that night Greta eyed herself in the long mirror with dismay. How could she ignore what was happening to her body? First came the sickness and now the thickening around her waist and the tender breasts. There was a feeling of fullness in her belly that she sensed meant only one thing. *I am carrying a child, Jem's child.*

She'd tried to fool herself into thinking it was the turmoil of the journey home, the excitement of her return, that had stopped her monthly courses but who was she fooling? That niggling doubt was now flesh and blood within her. She was sure no one suspected but once she began to show, what then?

All those years, she sighed, when I longed for my own baby and now I must carry my burden unsupported, but what was new about that? Hadn't she always been alone? Now she was making a huge decision in setting up this new venture. How would a child change all her plans? Just at this moment it was the last thing she wanted, yet something was flickering into life inside her and how could she deny it space in her future? She pulled in her stomach with a sigh, knowing that for the moment this unexpected news must be hidden.

At least Rhodabel would be able to help, and her mother, who would think the baby was her late husband's offspring. To the outside world she would be just one of those unfortunate widows left to rear her child. No one need know the true facts of this private matter. If she tightened her stays for now and then took to wearing loose-fitting dresses like Irene, it would be months before they guessed her little secret.

50

Two days later, on a bright summery morning, Greta and Rhoda rose early to catch the milk train out into the North Riding moors and towards a village just beyond Kirbymoorside. Greta had sent a postcard to Irene telling her to expect their visit and she hoped there'd be someone at the station to meet them. It was good for them both to be out of the city smoke and fumes and they enjoyed the fresh cool air and the scent of blossom as their train headed into the rolling hills of the countryside.

The last time Greta had been in this direction she'd been on a train to the coast on that first fateful trip to Whitby with Eben. She felt a lifetime away from the innocent woman she was then. She couldn't wait to see Irene and Norman again in their new home. When they arrived at their halt it was a relief to find a carter waiting for them. They were driven through narrow lanes banked by high stone walls, while the scent of elderflowers hanging in white snowy clusters filled the air. As they passed a grand house with black-and-white-timbered gables and mullioned windows, the cart began to slow.

'Your friend lives in this castle?' Rhoda pointed to the house in awe.

Greta smiled. 'I don't think so. The address is Hall Farm Cottage. It will be a smaller house round the back somewhere.' Dogs barked at their arrival. A woman with a plait of black hair and wearing a smock smudged with paint emerged from one of the outbuildings to see who had arrived. 'You're Irene's friend. Welcome, you'll find them over there.' But suddenly Greta saw Irene rushing out to meet them.

'Is this a school?' Rhoda asked the woman with the plait.

'You could call it such, more of a college for

working people to learn crafts. Elliot Grainger who owns the big house is a follower of the Arts and Crafts principles of William Morris so he lets the outbuildings to families to pursue their work. Come and see my studio when you've time,' she offered.

'At last, Greta!' Irene was hugging her. 'It's been such a long time but now you are here. Let me look at you ... just the same?' she paused, seeing Greta nodding. Then she turned to the girl. 'I guess you must be Rhodabel. Greta wrote to me about you.'

Rhoda bobbed a curtsey out of habit.

'Hey, none of that here,' Irene teased. 'We are all equals here. There is no rank among the workers, and I can't wait to show our newest member.'

They entered a cottage and followed Irene into a large but cluttered living room to see a little child sitting in a wooden high chair, a gold-haired toddler of about a year or so.

'This is Rafe, our little guest. Just when we thought that no child would be ours along he comes to bring us new life and hope.' Irene had filled out, her hair was now white and coiled around her head, her cheeks brown with the outdoor life. 'I'm glad your mother passed on my address to you when we moved. I was so worried that we would lose contact. I got your letter about Eben. I knew you'd return to us.'

'Did I send you a letter? I don't remember. It was all a blur but you were right to warn me about him. Oh, there's so much to tell you.' She recalled all those torn-up attempts before she finally wrote with her news.

'We've plenty of time. Come and have some breakfast. We have fresh eggs from our chickens, jam from our strawberries and lovely fresh bread baked this morning. You both look starved. Norm has taken an early morning class in the house. We have lecture rooms there. The Graingers are our patrons. I can't tell you how lucky we were to come upon this place.' The child banged his horn spoon on the tray in front of him and grinned.

'Little Rafe's not ours by blood but a son of a dear artist friend who died a few months after giving birth to him. Her parents wanted him brought up here among his mother's friends. This is a safe place to bring up a boy, away from disease and the busy city. We are all his family here.'

Greta shivered at her words, knowing her own baby would have to live above a shop and grow up as she did within the confines of York. She had hoped to share her news with Irene but now was not the time.

After breakfast they made a tour of the community of artists; the blacksmith's forge and metal workshop, the carver's barn, the stained-glass workshop and the room where a group of women were embroidering and weaving. There was such an air of industry and some of the work was wonderful but Greta was impatient to see the jewellery workshop. 'How do you sell your work?'

'You mean how can we survive?' Irene was carrying Rafe around. 'I'll be glad when he is walking. He's a hefty little chap. The Graingers are true patrons of the arts. The house was designed by George Walton, the famous Scottish architect, in the Arts and Crafts style. The family charges us a

low rental and we eat what we can grow, vege-
tables mainly, and we keep chickens. The locals
think we are a peculiar sect, fearing we live in sin.
The only rule is that we are teetotal on the premises and share what we can. It's a good place for
families, if a little unconventional, but some of the
children attend the village school.'

They walked to the big house and once inside
Greta was stunned by the polished oak panelling,
intricate tapestries and the magnificent tiled fire-
places. There was so much to admire, and walls
were as full as an art gallery. It smelt of lavender
and beeswax.

'The Graingers use this for their holiday home in
the country. As you can see many of the artifacts
are made by us and everything we create is guided
by the principle that you should have nothing in
your house that you do not know to be useful, or
believe to be beautiful. Norman and I do supply to
Liberty and Company in London and William
Morris's company in Manchester. The whole of
the North Riding is scattered with artists and craft
workshops like this. The churches round here are
filled with fine glass and ornaments. You can feast
your eyes on such wonderful objects.'

Greta loved everything that she was seeing here,
not just the work of the talented artists but also the
peace and beauty of their environment. How she
would love to live somewhere like this, but she
must press on with her quest.

'Now I'm home, I'm back for good and I want
to open my own shop. I don't want to compete
with the established jewellery shops in York and I
want to sell something a bit different. I was

hoping to buy some of your silverware and jewellery for my new shop,' she explained.

As they walked back to Irene's cottage Greta shared with her friend all that had happened since her arrival home. 'I have to earn my living now and Eben's pearls give me an option to rent something modest. As for Rhoda, I couldn't leave the girl behind.'

'I see what you mean about her likeness to Kitty. Doesn't that upset you? And who is this Jem you mentioned in your letter?'

'Did I? He was our landlord but he's not important now,' Greta dismissed her curiosity.

Rhoda, who was carrying Rafe, chipped in.

'He's getting married soon, my friend Martha told me.'

'So he is, I forgot,' Greta replied and went quiet. She wanted no reminders of him.

Irene changed the subject. 'Guess who lives not ten miles away? He will want to know you are back, I'm sure.'

'Oh, yes, Mr Blake mentioned Edmund was working out here.' He was the last person she wanted to meet at this moment. She saw the expression on Irene's face. 'Don't look like that. I have no time for any of that in my life. I have a business to run.'

Rafe started to cry and Irene gathered him up. She looked down lovingly at the small boy. 'You would have liked Rafe's mother, Celia. She was a beautiful embroiderer. But she wasn't strong. It was her heart...' her voice tailed off.

'And Rafe's father, why did he not take him?'

Irene shook her head. 'He's an artist, a famous

359

one who took advantage of her naivety. Not all artists live like puritans, as you may know.'

'That's not fair. He should help support the child.'

'Celia didn't want him in Rafe's life. She was not without means. We're not young but we manage and it's better the boy has two parents, don't you agree?'

Greta sighed knowing how hard her own mother had worked to be both parents to them and it hadn't been easy, but when life dealt her blows, Sadie just got on with things and so must she when the time came. First though there was too much to do. When they got back to the cottage and Rafe was settled upstairs, she brought out the pearl slugs. 'What could you do with these? Could you make me some pieces to sell?'

Irene shook her head. 'I don't have as much time as I did but I do have some unsold pieces ready.' She looked up and saw Greta's dismay. 'Don't fret. You look like you've lost a guinea and found a sixpence. I'm sure I could make some things for you. They are interesting shapes, a bit like maggots.'

Greta told her all about finding Eben's secret hoard. 'These are from the Mississippi,' she said, spreading a few of them out on the table. Irene fingered them with interest. 'They'd be perfect for pendants and earrings. I've seen some work done using misshapes. There's a whole style for making brooches and pendants with animal motifs. These could be set in gold–' she picked out some tooth-shaped slugs and arranged them like a flower – 'there! But surely you can't open a shop with just these few things?'

'I know. I have ordered some regular pieces from the manufacturers. The brooches that spell out a name are popular, they're the sort of thing that can be bought for sweethearts and girls. I'll also stock some unusual hatpins and hair combs but they have to be affordable – why shouldn't working people have pretty things to wear on their scarves and lace jabots? I want some special items made for discerning customers too.'

'Then you should concentrate on insects, butterflies and bees – they are all the rage. The enamellers can't make enough of them to sell. I could make some butterflies up with pretty stones.' Irene paused to hug her friend again. 'Oh, it's so good to see you back. You must come and stay and meet all the artists here when we have a meal together. Take your time to see if anything they make might be suitable. There is always a way to fill your shelves, you know, by buying things on sale or return, for example, but it's a risk. We couldn't make it work in Aldwark. We feel very blessed to have found this haven, especially now we have Rafe.'

It was hard not to feel envious of her friend as she kissed her goodbye. There were two of them devoted to their little ward. How would they react to Greta's secret news? Rhodabel was reluctant to leave, she was entranced with the whole place. 'Wait till I write to Martha. She'll never believe me.'

'All in good time, missy, first we have to find our way back to the station.'

Norman, who'd arrived belatedly, said that he'd drive them himself all the way back to the village halt.

'I shall work on these and give you some prices,' Irene promised, waving to them from the gate. 'See you soon and good luck. I think you are very brave,' were her last words to her friend.

As they rode back to York on the train, it was enough to know her friendship with Irene was renewed and that she had found a source for quality items. These were the first trembling steps towards her new future. Next she must find a suitable name for her shop and find some proper fittings for inside. Greta took out her tiny notepad and began to make a list: so much to do and so little time.

51

One Sunday afternoon Greta walked up to the church cemetery with her mother to change the flowers on Kitty's grave.

'Once she were found, all the street clubbed together to give her this headstone, folks as I never knew chipped in.' Sadie sighed, pointing to the little stone angel. 'It gives me comfort to know she's only up the street in Holy Trinity. I still can't believe she's gone. I keep thinking she'll just walk through the door, large as life and twice as noisy. And to think you married her murderer... What a family we are. Tom across the ocean in India and you so busy, I never see you.'

'I have such a lot going on with the grand opening soon.' There were so many details to see to now.

'Why did you have to jump in so soon?'

'You know why. Once the stock is ordered, I need to start trading. Irene has made some lovely brooches and pendants. Wait until you see them.'

'I'd rather be spending time with you but when I call in you're allus out.'

'Running a business is my dream. It has to come first for the moment and besides...' Greta took a deep breath knowing it was time to tell her mother about the baby and to plead for her support. She looked at the little angel and the words stuck in her throat. Plenty of time yet to keep her secret. Once the shop was running smoothly, then she could let them know about the child. She was still slender. Once her mother knew she would fuss and fret. It was better they kept their distance from each other.

'You've never told me what you're going to be selling,' Sadie asked.

'Just pretty things and some pearls and modern stuff. Kitty would have loved all the bangles and trinkets I've ordered. I shall always keep the turquoise bracelet they found on her as a memento with my locket.'

'Aye, she loved her shiny stuff.'

'I'm going to name the shop after her so she won't ever be forgotten,' Greta said quietly.

'You're a good lass. It's a pity you haven't settled down again.'

'One marriage is enough for me,' Greta snapped. It was the last thing on her mind at the moment.

'Don't be so sure. Don't go filling all your time with shop work. Make time to meet new folk.

You're still young. You never know what's round the corner waiting for you.'

Oh, but I do, thought Greta as they walked back down the path. You won't be so pleased when you know the truth about why everything has had to be done in such a rush.

52

'Is everything ready?' Greta was pacing the shop floor, checking that the cabinets and shop counter bought in a closing-down sale were polished and that everything looked perfect. There was a selection of Irene's lovely pendants and bracelets made from linked bloodstones, carnelians and agates. A pincushion was covered with silver hatpins topped with rock crystals, golden cairngorms and purple amethysts. In the window was a display of butterfly-shaped shawl pins and bar-shaped brooches in enamelled jewel colours alongside tortoiseshell hair combs and pretty hair slides. Her own favourites were Irene's bees, butterflies and frogs each decorated with seed pearl eyes but she also loved the flower brooches made from drop pearls; each brooch had a special clasp that meant it could be fitted onto a chain and also used as a pendant.

Greta had taken Mr Blake's advice to advertise in the *York Herald* and she'd invited as many people as they could to the grand opening, sending invitations to the neighbouring shopkeepers and their wives. Bert and Sadie were stalwarts in the back room laying out trays of refreshments to hand out to guests.

'What if no one comes?' Greta asked anxiously.

'Of course they'll come,' her mother snapped. 'People are nosy and they'll want to see what's hidden behind them curtains in the window all week. And you've set tongues wagging with what's on the door.'

'But it only says "Kitty Costello" over the front.'

'Aye, that's a nice thought, but it's the gold lettering that's different. *All things bright and beautiful within...* I've never seen owt like that afore. Now sit down. You look done in, my girl.'

'What if they don't like my bright and beautifuls?' Greta perched on the seat by her mother.

'Stop mithering and go and get changed.'

'But I am changed. Don't you like my dress? It's new for the occasion. Rational dress, they call it, with no bones and curves.' Greta was proud of the outfit she'd had made up. It was in crushed lilac velvet with a corded green ribbon trim. She was wearing a large enamelled peacock brooch.

'You suit the colour better than the black. Surely he's been dead long enough to get shut of mourning. Especially after what he...' Her mother paused. 'It makes you look fat. There's no shape to the robe. I thought it was a fancy dressing gown. After all that running round you should be skin and bone.'

Trust her mother to tell it how it was. Over the past months she knew she was filling out but these outfits were proving a good disguise. At nearly seven months, she had done well to hide the swelling but the last few days had taken its toll on her feet and back. Greta pushed herself up from the chair knowing she must stand and smile all evening even though her body was aching for rest. Once this night was over and the shop established then it would be time to prepare for the birth.

How could she not be excited standing outside on the cobbles to admire the window display once it was drawn back. *K & M COSTELLO of Goodramgate: Purveyor of pearls and other fine adornments* ... was etched into a stained glass panel by one of Irene's friends. She'd set the benchmark high for an Irish lass from the back streets of York. Not that she was that girl any more but a woman who had dipped her toes in one of the mighty rivers of America, survived ruin and disgrace and made her lifelong dream come true.

Rhodabel couldn't believe how many visitors had crushed themselves into the shop as she handed round cordials in little gasses loaned from the Cross Keys up the street. Mrs Todd the grocer's wife, resplendent in her best hat, was eyeing up the goods with the help of the butcher's daughter and Mrs Webster from next door. The three women were equally intrigued by Irene and her friends from the Grainger place who had come especially to support Miss Greta. It was a hot and sticky night for September and Rhoda almost dropped the tray of glasses but luckily a tall young man with a dark moustache came to her aid.

'Let me hold these for you, Miss Bacchus.' He had a pleasant face and a friendly smile. 'You're the girl from America?'

She nodded, shy to be singled out, but glad she

was wearing her best striped dress and that her hair was pinned up in a padded coil.

'I'm Mr Blake's son, Hamer, and pleased to make your acquaintance. Can I help distribute these?'

'Oh, no, you're a guest,' she replied, blushing.

'Then at least let me clear a path for you,' he offered.

'Thank you, sir.' He parted the sea of coats and jackets allowing Rhoda a clear passage until they came to a crowd gathered round the window display. Some were shaking their heads.

'She's used the line of a hymn to advertise her wares ... that's not proper, surely?' said a woman in a large bonnet pointing a walking cane at the lettering on the door.

Hamer was quick to Greta's defence. 'Madam, I think it describes exactly what she's put in her shop, all sorts of bright and beautiful gifts. The words bright and beautiful belong to no one, hymn or no,' he added.

Rhodabel smiled at this riposte, seeing the look on their faces. 'That was brave,' she whispered.

'You're the brave one coming all this way to York, and to hear such small minds at work as these,' he replied.

'I had no choice when Miss Greta left. Besides, I wanted to see what England was like for myself.'

'And do you like what you see?' he asked, staring down at her with interest.

What could she say? 'It's not as big as I expected. I once lived in New York but I prefer the old York and Miss Greta is kind.'

'I know. She once worked for us a long time ago.

I'm glad you like York and I'm glad you came here.'

'I'd better go in and help,' Rhoda stammered.

'By the way your name means beautiful rose. Did you know?' he added.

She nodded. 'But everyone here calls me Rhoda now.'

'Will you be working in the shop?'

'Spec so or working in the back.'

'I work in my father's office in Lendal so I'll come and see how the shop's getting along, if you like?'

'Sure, that'll be neat, Mr Blake.'

'Hamer, please...'

Rhoda smiled and pushed her way back indoors. Greta was behind the counter as some customers were choosing little pins and asking questions. She looked flushed and exhausted. 'Find me a chair,' she mouthed, so Rhoda rushed into the back where a man she didn't recognize was presenting a high-backed carved stool to Irene.

'I thought this might come in handy for customers, if there is a queue.'

'How thoughtful,' said Irene. 'Rhoda, come and meet Mr Blake, he's made this for the shop.'

'How many Blakes have we here tonight? I've met one already,' she asked.

'My brother's out there somewhere and my father too. It was lucky I was up from London and staying with them. This is just something I made for the house but it will be of more use here.'

He was older than Hamer with the same kind face. He was the furniture maker she'd heard them all talk about, a friend of Greta's from the past.

'Do you mind if I take it now, sir. She's asking for a chair. We've been up since dawn to get ready and she's hardly slept for days.'

'I'll take it then,' Edmund offered and pushed his way towards Greta.

'He's a grand chap with no side on him. She'd do far worse than set her cap at him,' Sadie whispered in her ear. 'But don't say owt. You tell her one thing and she'll do the other. A mother can tell it how it is. Not that she'd listen.'

'I never had a mother,' Rhoda replied.

'I know, love, but you're part of our family now so chop, chop and clear away the empty glasses before we break any.'

It was another hour before the shop finally emptied. Greta returned the remaining gold and pearls and precious items to the big steel safe they had secured from another shop. Sales had been brisk, especially the enamel brooches and pretty hatpins.

Greta sat back on the carved stool, shaking her head but smiling. 'Didn't it go well? I can't believe how many people left cards and gave us compliments. I have two orders for Irene's gold-and-pearl pendants.'

'Are you all right? You look done in, lass.'

'I'll be fine once I hit the hay.' Greta yawned. 'My back is giving me jip. Had it all day and it won't shift.'

Sadie returned with a mug of hot tea. 'Get that down you. Bed for you now, my girl.'

'Don't fuss, mother!'

'I'm not. I've seen you wincing. Up them stairs before we drag you there. You just never know when to give in.'

Suddenly Greta bent double with pain as she felt something seeping from her onto the floor. 'Mam, get me out of here before I mess my stock.'

In a flash her mother rushed over to her. Rhoda was made to stay downstairs as Sadie helped her daughter upstairs. She used a mop and bucket to clear up the mess as best she could. There were noises in the living room above. Something wasn't right. Was Miss Greta ill? What if she died and she was left an orphan again? Why was she crying out in pain like that? All the excitement of the evening's grand opening was forgotten in the fear of what was happening to her mistress.

53

'It can't be coming yet,' Greta screamed as she felt the tight band across her stomach. Even she knew it was too soon, weeks too soon. There was nothing prepared, no layette, no cradle. That was all waiting until the shop was underway. Why was this happening so fast?

Her mother was boiling a kettle on the range and grabbing clean linen. 'Why am I allus the last to know? It all makes sense now, that loose dress and all the rush to get the shop going. You didn't want folks knowing your business, carrying the bairn of a killer? I understand, but why in God's name couldn't you tell yer own mother?'

This was no time for a confession. It was a relief

to have her mother by the bedside for she was afraid of what was to come. They'd all heard the screams and tales of bad birthings in Walmgate. They said a woman in labour had one foot in the graveyard. Was she going to die? Who would see to Rhoda or the shop?

It wasn't fair, not after the success of the opening tonight. The force was on her so strong she felt as if the baby was in a hurry to escape the confines of her tired body, impatient to be out. Not surprising since she had not let up for weeks or given the child within any rest. Now the poor mite was being born far too soon. This wasn't in the plan.

'I don't want to die,' she cried out.

'Who said anything about dying?' Sadie snapped back. 'It'll not be long now judging by your pains. You'll have to grip the towel on the bedpost and bear down when you feel it pushing. This is what comes from being so headstrong. Still, the Lord gives and the Lord takes and perhaps it's as well...'

'It's all my fault,' Greta whimpered.

'Shush, just go with yer pains, you'll be tough enough to see it through. Does the girl know about these doings?'

Greta shook her head.

'Well, time she did, I need her to give me a hand. The sooner she sees how the world is the better. There's too many lasses as doesn't realize that babies come out where they went in. Rhoda!' she yelled. 'Come and give us a hand. I hope she doesn't mind the sight of blood.'

The girl hovered in the bedroom doorway. 'Is she going to die?'

'Not if I have anything to do wi' it. She's only

371

having a bairn so stop gawping and find me the wash bowl, warm some towels on the rail to wrap the thing in. Fill a stone hot water bottle and find some cotton rags. Keep the fire up. Mind and send Bert out of the way for more coal.'

Greta was lying back in a haze of pain and confusion. 'I've nothing ready. I just didn't want to think about it yet. I'm sorry.'

'It's a reminder of him, I know, but poor mite can't help who its pa is. Life is a life and this one won't last long, girl, so be prepared.'

Then the urge to push got stronger. There was so much pain, a burning and a rush as a tiny body slid out onto the old sheet, purple but oh so perfectly formed and mewing like a skinned rabbit.

'My holy aunt, that's not a proper size.' Sadie wrapped the baby in a warm hand towel and lifted the bundle up for her to see. 'It's a girl.'

'Let me hold her.'

'No not yet, there's the cord to be tied. Rhoda fetch a carving knife and some string. Better not to get yer hopes up. Lassie's too small.'

'But she's breathing and pink and beautiful.' Rhodabel was smiling. 'Look at her tiny fingers.'

'You'll never feed her. We'll keep her warm and let the Good Lord take her to the angels. I can christen her. Have you got a name?'

'Stop it, give her to me now. She can lie on my chest and I'll keep her warm.' Greta sat up, bringing the bundle onto her breast. Then the rest of the birthing came away.

Sadie examined it with care. 'My mam delivered more babies than hot dinners and she said a clean afterbirth means a healthy mother. Yours looks fine so let's have some sweet tea.'

All Greta would think of was the tiny creature resting in the warmth of her body, mewling like a kitten but fighting for life and breath. How could she let her go now she had touched her and felt her so close? Tiredness overwhelmed her into a deep sleep.

The next morning she woke in a panic, fearing the worst. The baby wasn't there but then she saw the enamel wash bowl by the fireplace and in it the baby, wrapped in towels and cotton wool padding. She was draped in a long cotton gown edged with broderie anglaise lace.

'What's this? It's far too big.'

'It's her burial gown,' her mother replied, not looking in her direction. 'I've been out to the Irish linen shop. I didn't want to waste yer money, lass, in buying a layette that didn't fit. She's too little to feed, she'll not last the day. See how quiet she lies.'

'Over my dead body. My daughter isn't going to die. I will feed her somehow. There must be a way, with a sponge? Call the doctor in so he can give us advice. Rhoda can sew up some nightdresses in warm flannel and tear up towels for napkins. It's time to open the shop. Make me a pad.'

'You're not getting up already. Don't be a crackpot.' Sadie stood back in horror.

'I have to get up and doing.' Greta eased herself out of bed, wincing but determined. 'Rhoda can see to the baby and keep everything spotless around her. If you could just change the bedding and see to some laundry, we can manage. Thanks for being with me. You saved the baby's life.' She looked at her mother's drawn face, shaking her head. 'I know you're tired so go home and rest. I'll never forget what you've done for us, Mam.' She hugged her mother. 'But now I have to attend to my customers. Then the two of us can swop turns for a while but I will close early and rest, I promise. I can be a shopkeeper and a mother but no one need know for a while until we're ready to take her into fresh clean air. I'll not risk her tiny lungs in the smoke and grime of these streets.'

'You're not right in the head, girl. What if you bleed and then we'll have two to bury?'

'Tell that to the factory girls who daren't lose a day's wage by giving birth and resting up. I will be careful. Please tell no one about this night's business just yet. Go to the drug store and ask for advice. When my milk comes in I want to make sure she gets it fresh from the dairy.'

'She won't suck yet.'

'We'll see. I'll find a way to keep her alive. And by the way, her name is Kathleen Pearl Costello but we shall call her Pearl.'

54

Muscatine, 1890

When Jem Baillie held his firstborn son in his arms in the spring of 1890, he felt such a surge of pride that life could give him no better gift. The baby was born with a shock of black hair and a lusty set of lungs. Effie lay exhausted after a long and difficult birth, anxious her offspring was perfect in every way. There was a nursemaid and Marcella in attendance, and they confined her to bed rest for at least two weeks to recover from the shock of it all.

Jem was banished to the local hotel where he wet the boy's head many times over, naming him the Gaelic form of James: Hamish. His middle name was Allister to please Effie's family.

'So here comes the next generation in the family, Jem. You'll be after taking him hame to Scotland and dipping his toes in the Tay. That's where it all began, don't forget?' laughed Jake in a mock Scots accent as he sipped his bourbon.

'One day perhaps but first we must make sure there's a business for him to inherit from me. Are you going to join me in this new button-making outfit?'

'You bet, if old Boepple will let us in on his secrets. He's not very forthcoming but I see the possibilities of making use of spent clam shells.'

'He's got his little workshop but has his eye on making it into a factory. Great oaks from little acorns.' Jem added. 'Better to be in at the beginning of a venture.' Jem was sure this was the way forward for the city after the logging industry moved elsewhere. Muscatine was changing. There were rumours that the Heinz canning factory was going to open on the riverfront. There were so many fine vegetable farms springing up around Muscatine's river island due to its rich soil. The paddle steamers still ploughed their way up the river bringing visitors on tour, and the railway connections were firmly in place now. The civic buildings springing up gave an air of prosperity to the area. They were all set for a great boom.

Later he stood admiring his son cocooned within a lace-covered cradle. Now his family was complete. His wife had been shocked to find herself with child so quickly after the honeymoon. It had been a splendid time in Washington. They'd stayed at The Willard on Pennsylvania Avenue, wandered around all the wonderful Capitol buildings and taken a trip to the coast. It was the first time they had been alone as a couple and he'd enjoyed her prattle and her excitement at buying gifts to bring home.

Once he'd caught himself wondering how Greta was surviving in her home city but he'd quickly pushed this curiosity aside. Martha must know, being still in correspondence with the orphan girl, but he never asked for information and none was volunteered. He stared across at the silver-framed wedding portrait on the bedside table, hardly recognizing himself in his black frock coat and silk top hat. Effie was a princess in her wedding gown. It was a little fussy for his taste with those waxy looking flowers edging the lace trim. Even her shoes were studded with silver beads. Around her neck was the rope of pearls that Martha had slipped into her wedding trousseau as she helped her dress. Marcella was tight-lipped and angry at this defiance of her wishes but no one noticed the coolness between them and nothing was spoken.

Sometimes he had to pinch himself at just how far his fortunes had risen since he stepped off the ship from Glasgow but there were times when he longed to return to see the old country, walk through the fir trees that lined the River Tay. Who lived in their but and ben cottage now in Glencorrin?

Dear sweet Effie was creating a beautiful yard full of paths with a summer house overlooking the curve in the river. She was quite the little gardener, with catalogues of plants and shrubs, and the yardman was kept busy following her instructions to the letter. She had spent the weeks before her confinement drawing up lists and planning her borders. It was good to see her so engaged. It made him feel less guilty about the hours he spent in his office and down in Muscatine at meetings.

Now she would have baby and help at hand, which meant that Marcella could go home at last. He could sense her always checking up on him. It was strange how his feelings had changed towards his benefactors. They were once such an inspiration but now he saw his mother-in-law as cloying and interfering, hovering over their marriage like a shadow.

One day he would take his son back home, when he was old enough to appreciate just how beautiful Scotland was. Until then it was business and duty. *You came from nothing, James Baillie, and one day to nothing you will return so make the most of your opportunities. Count your blessings and be content.* How could he have ever doubted his choice to stay put, now that he had a son and heir?

55

1890

It was one of the quieter mornings when Greta could get on with her bookkeeping while rocking the baby in the cradle with her foot until Rhoda came back from the shops. She still checked on Pearl's breathing, cocooned as she was in her knitted shawl and bonnet. Against the odds, the baby had survived, first on a sponge soaked in sugar water and then by drinking from a tiny feeding cup with a lip until finally she'd latched onto Greta's breasts with a strength that sent her mother's spirit soaring with hope. Pearl was a survivor, of that there was no doubt. They kept her warm, swaddled and in a wicker cradle. The burial gown was shoved at the back of a drawer, an ever-present reminder that the sooty foetid air of York streets brought death to many tiny babies.

How glad she was of her mother's regular visits to mind the baby, leaving Greta free to see to any customers, but her forthright comments were not so welcome. 'That lass doesn't get her looks from either of you, her eyes are like jet buttons and she's got a shock of black hair. You should have called her Onyx not Pearl.'

Greta waved away Sadie's comments. 'Who knows where Eben came from? We never really knew his background,' she replied. It was hard to lie when she knew the baby had Jem's dark looks.

She was also grateful for Rhoda's help. How could she have managed to keep going in the shop without Rhoda by her side? The girl worshipped the tiny mite and gave her a special nickname. 'Can I take Persie out for a walk? It is such a crisp morning.'

'Not until the spring comes,' Greta said. 'Baby mustn't catch cold.' In their living quarters, Persie was safe, protected from the bustling dusty street. She was six months old before she dared take her out of the door.

It was her mother who insisted Greta went to be churched as was the custom in the Church of England and make an appointment for the baby to be christened. 'She'll thrive better once she's been done, they tell me.' A week later they carried Pearl into the other ancient church of Holy Trinity Goodramgate behind the shop to be baptized Kathleen Pearl Costello with just Rhoda standing as a godmother. They had told no one outside the family about the baby, fearing she might not survive those first dangerous months of life. How many nights did Greta lie awake listening for the snuffles and gurgles of her tiny daughter? She felt such guilt that the baby was nearly lost by her carelessness. Pearl was the one precious reminder of Jem's lovemaking, the baby who was now giving her such hope for the future.

When Rhoda received a letter from Martha full of news about Jem's wedding that included a cutting from the local paper describing it in great detail, Greta didn't want to know how the bride wore a taffeta ecru gown with a silk chiffon over dress edged with lilac silk flowers and trimmed with point de Venise lace.

'It sounds very fussy,' said Rhoda. 'When I get married I shall wear something plain and simple. Hamer says simplicity is often more striking than fancy.'

'He should know coming from a Quaker family. His mother wore grey to great effect. I don't suppose they wear wedding day dresses much.'

'I know,' Rhoda sighed.

How could Greta resist teasing the girl knowing Hamer Blake was taking a lot of interest in her welfare? One lunchtime when he called, Persie was bellowing to be fed so they had to tell him that Greta's child was not to be noised abroad as she was still sickly and they wanted no visitors. Irene was informed by letter, knowing she would be a true friend, and sure enough by return came a beautiful handmade nightgown and a bonnet several sizes too big as another sign of hope. Irene must have realized just when Eben died but made no mention of the discrepancy on dates.

After that first rush of curiosity, the little shop weathered leaner times but the Christmas gift season brought new customers to purchase trinkets. Now she was facing the coming summer season and Greta's first test came when a couple brought in a rope of pearls for valuation with a view to sell. Apparently they were inherited from some aunt and were not wanted. Outwardly they looked expensive but she wasn't in a position to buy.

'I can give you a valuation for a small fee,' she offered noting they were eyeing her closed cabinets with interest and she wondered if they were here as spies.

'You could do with something like this in your window to attract quality customers,' offered the man with beady eyes and a lisp.

'Rhoda!' she shouted, ringing the bell. 'Just one moment, my assistant will hold the shop while I get my glass and weighing instruments.' She wanted to be professional about this valuation but she didn't trust them to be left alone.

First she held the pearls and found them warm not cold. She weighed them and, out of sight, checked them with her teeth to be sure. The pearls were smooth not gritty. The string was of poor quality, not fine silk thread, and too tightly knotted.

'I'm sorry, I can't help you,' she said placing them on the counter.

'What do you mean? Them's fine pearls all matched.'

'I agree, a fine set of costume pearls made from beads covered in mother-of-pearl paste. There's not a genuine pearl among them.'

'How dare you, they're the finest river pearls.'

'If you say so, madam, but no decent jeweller will agree. They've never seen the sea or the river. You might sell them to a theatrical company for costumes, but feel free to go to shops in Stonegate if you don't believe me. They will tell you the same.' She recalled how Eben had had to deal with fakes.

The woman grabbed the rope and stormed out of the shop. 'You're making a big mistake, lassie.'

'And you made a bigger one thinking I don't know my business. Get out and go and find another sucker to trick. I've seen your sort before!'

she yelled.

Greta was shaking. 'Just because I'm a woman, a sole trader, they think I am easy meat. Let that be a lesson, Rhodabel. If in doubt, always double check and trust your instinct. Come on and let's see if Miss Persie is awake.'

Some you win, some you lose. There would always be charlatans wanting to pull the cash from her till. The business world was like a jungle where only the tough survive and you had to be on guard for scavengers and the smile on the tiger's face. Woe betide anyone who thought Greta Costello was an easy target. She had claws and wouldn't hesitate to use them.

But there were winners too. One market afternoon Mr Broadhurst, an old customer of Eben's, called in to see if it was really Mrs Slinger behind the counter. He was a farmer from outside Wigginton selling his cheeses at market and he wanted her to make up a pearl necklace for his daughter's twenty-first birthday.

'It's a few years off yet but I know you'll have an eye for a good pearl and you're a good threader, I'm told. I'll pay up front if you'll be so kind as lay them aside in your safe, three at a time, until we have enough for a little string.' It was the way many bought good pearls as heirlooms and she was honoured he was trusting her with this task.

'He must love his daughter,' Rhoda replied with a tinge of envy after he'd gone.

'Yorkshire men like to part with their brass carefully. It's not easy to find matching pearls and he's right to plan ahead. If things get tight for him, he can delay until he's flush again. It means he's a

382

regular, and who knows, he might buy other things for her too.'

'There was a guy in the other day, top hat and big moustache, he bought three identical bracelets. How many daughters does he have?'

Greta coughed. 'You mean Ernie Pickering? Oh, it's not daughters he buys for but his lady friends ... little trinkets to keep them happy. We used to have men like him in the other shop buying expensive jewellery for their wives when they went astray.'

Rhoda laughed, realizing her meaning.

'Not all men are as keen and faithful as your young Quaker friend. Believe me, given half a chance, most men will always find another tree once the cherries have been picked from yours.'

'But you like his brother. Why will you not let him visit?'

Edmund had called once but she refused to see him and stayed upstairs telling Rhoda to explain she was busy. 'I don't want anyone knowing my business just yet.'

'But he made the stool for us. He's kind.'

'Yes, I know but I don't want to talk to him.' She knew she was being unreasonable and Rhodabel was confused. But it was hard to explain how she was feeling.

'Hamer has asked me to show the Society of Friends girls' evening class how we do patchwork. What do you think?'

Greta looked up from her pearl threading. 'What a good idea. You'll do it well. It's about time you got out of the house more. When?'

'Not sure yet but only one evening a week, you

don't mind?'

'The only thing I will mind is if that young man of yours doesn't escort you back home afterwards. The streets are badly lit and unsafe at night. A word to the wise, you do know the Society of Friends isn't like Holy Trinity. They do things in a different way.'

'Sure, but we're all Christians?'

'Of course, good lass. I didn't bring you with me to sit in the shadows. You enjoy yourself. Now fetch us a brew.'

56

Autumn 1892

Despite the terrible flooding in the city, Greta was one of the lucky shopkeepers whose cellars didn't fill up and the River Foss was far enough away not to interfere with trade. Persie was now a sturdy toddler, small for her age but the darling of all the neighbours and dressed like a doll in handmade dresses and bonnets. No one had commented on her sudden appearance, understanding the widow's premature baby had needed to remain cosseted carefully indoors. They spent a few days holiday that summer with Irene, Norman and Rafe on the Grainger estate where Persie had the freedom to roam after Rafe in the orchard, getting muddy and rosy cheeks.

Edmund now called regularly to see them. He

was busy preparing samples for a national exhibition in London but he still found the time to take them all out to see his workshop. It was a stone barn smelling of sawdust and polish, full of his unusual designs. His furniture was angular made from dark woods which he enriched with intricate carving. He was commissioned to make some church memorial panels decorated with figures from the Bible, angels and swirling patterns. Greta was in awe of his talent.

He never asked her much about their life in America. He sensed her reluctance to talk and presumed her memories were too painful to share. She relaxed in his company but if he gazed in her direction, she ignored those meaningful looks, despite Irene's encouragement. 'You could do far worse than Edmund. He's talented and a good friend.'

'I'm not in the market for anything other than friendship. I've had one husband. I'll never have another...'

'Never say never, Greta, don't be so hard on yourself. You made one bad choice. Not all men are like Eben.' It was the first time Irene had ever challenged her.

'I won't be taken advantage of ... by anyone ever again.'

'Who said anything about taking advantage? What's got into you? Are you worried about business?'

Edmund drew close, overhearing Irene's question. 'What's happened?'

'Last week got off to a bad start. There's this wretched woman from church, the wife of a city bigwig, who collared me and wondered if she could borrow a pearl-encrusted necklace to show her husband who is too busy to come to the shop to see for himself. She brought it back saying it wasn't suitable but she was seen wearing it to a posh wedding in the Minster. I'm that livid. Would you believe the cheek, she's asked if she could take it to show her friend. What am I to do?'

'Just say no. You can be tough when you want to,' Irene offered.

'I know, but I have to face her each Sunday. I would like to make a sale.'

'Do you know what she might want it for?' Edmund added.

'There's a charity ball in the Assembly Rooms next week in aid of the flood victims, I think that's the occasion she'll be wearing it.'

'Then you don't need me to tell you what to do, do you?' Edmund smiled. 'You must go and check things out.'

'What, me go alone to a ball?'

'No, we'll go together and see for ourselves.' There was no refusing this kind offer.

It was one of those glittering York assemblies when the great and the good from the clergy and city gathered in their finery for a worthy cause. For the first time in years, Greta allowed herself to wear a long evening gown. It was made out of purple satin and had the puffed sleeves and a wide neck around which she would put one of Irene's fabulous insect pendants decorated with garnets, amethysts and pearls. Determined not to miss an opportunity to show off her wares, she even had her dark hair professionally dressed in Stonegate, upswept to emphasize her décolletage and studded with pearl headed pins. She borrowed Irene's long evening gloves and carried a pieced reticule made up from leftover bits of the satin material covered with coloured glass beads.

Rhoda's eye popped at the sight of Greta in her finery. 'Cinderella shall go to the ball. Be sure to be back by midnight.'

'Cheek!' For once in her life she felt like a queen or at least one of York's successful businesswomen, but she was on a mission. If Prudence Seddon was there wearing the pearl-encrusted necklace then she would be getting her comeuppance tonight.

'I work hard for my success. No one will put one over me.' She looked into the mirror. Part of her wished it was Adah's pearl round her neck. It had been her lucky talisman but it was gone. Tonight she would be eyeing up the other ladies' necklaces with interest just in case... The guilt she felt for pawning it never went away and it was on occasions like this she felt the loss keenly.

Edmund looked dashing in his borrowed evening dress. He would be a most attentive part-ner and she was looking forward to spending the evening with him, but then she thought of Jem and her heart flipped. He would never be Jem and at the moment she had no desire for a sub-stitute but Edmund's friendship and company were welcome tonight.

The candles flickered, giving the mirrored walls a magical glow. There were silks and taffetas in every hue, bustles, puffed sleeves, lace and hair adorned with roses and shining combs. But it was not the glamour she was seeking as she scanned the crowds for one particular couple but so far they were not in view. She hoped she hadn't gone to all this effort for nothing.

'Come on, let's dance.' Edmund put one hand on her waist guiding her onto the ballroom floor and they edged around in a circular shuffle. Neither of them were expert in waltzing but they tried their best before starting to giggle, recalling those first attempts all those years ago at the Gala.

'Can you see her yet?' he whispered. 'Sorry, am I treading on your toes? Quaker boys don't take dancing lessons.'

'So I've noticed, but neither do girls from the backstreets of Walmgate. I hope they've come after us going to all this expense.' She winked at him as they made their way towards the elegant supper table, taking a glass of strong punch and examining the array of ornate pies and cold meats on a table strewn with petals and garlands.

It was then that Greta spotted her prey standing amongst a group of clergymen from the Minster in their black frock coats and gaiters. Mrs Seddon had her back to them but Greta recognized her stoop and mousey hair. There was no time to waste as she pulled Edmund towards the woman. 'Ah, Mistress Seddon, I thought it might be you.'

At the sound of her name Prudence Seddon whipped round to reveal the borrowed pearl necklace on her décolletage. 'Oh, Mrs Costello, I didn't expect to see you here.'

'No, I don't suppose you did,' Greta replied with the sweetest of smiles as she turned to the woman's husband. 'Mr Seddon, I'm so glad you decided to buy your wife my necklace at long last. I'm sure she will find it useful for weddings and balls. It's such a delicate piece. One of the finest in my stock... Your wife has been hovering over it for months but I'm glad you've chosen it for her.' She nodded to the listening guests. 'We do take commissions but tonight is not the place to talk business, is it? Enjoy your suppers.'

Prudence's face was pink with fury and her husband looked flummoxed. 'What's she on about, Pru?' It was time to beat a hasty retreat.

'That'll teach her to borrow, use and bring back. I shall be sending them an invoice first thing on Monday morning.'

'Greta, how could you embarrass them like that in front of their friends?' Edmund pushed her away, seeing the grin on her face. 'You're incorrigible.'

'Hang on, it was your idea to come here. What did you expect me to do? It's the only way I know to get payment. You have to shame it out of them sometimes.'

'She'll never darken your door again. Word gets around...'

'Do I want her sort of custom? She won't try it on with others after that. I think I've just done all the jewellers of York a service. Good, now that's sorted we can enjoy ourselves. I'm starving.'

Later they took a cab home and she could see Edmund was eager to come in. She let him kiss her cheek but no more. Rhoda would be waiting to hear all about the ball. 'You know how I feel about you, Greta,' he whispered, kissing her gloved hand.

She smiled but held back. 'You're a lovely man and a great artist but I'm not the woman for you, not with my cold heart.'

'Oh Greta, you say the strangest things!' he protested but she held firm.

'Good night and thank you for giving me the chance to right things. You are a dear friend,' she said waving him off. 'Good luck with the exhibition,' she added. 'When I build my country mansion all my furniture will come from your studio and that's a promise.'

How strange to be saying such a thing, she sighed to herself. How could such a dream ever come true?

57

Muscatine, 1893

Effie couldn't wait to be out in her yard, picking flowers to arrange on the dining table and hallway. She loved big showy blooms that grew best in her glasshouse. It was good to be out in the fresh air, her face hidden by a wide-brimmed sun bonnet. There must be no taint of darkness on her skin.

Hamish was toddling after her in his silly long gown and boots, his black ringlets shining like jet. Jem was dying to take him to the barbers and put him in a sailor suit but the women wouldn't hear of it. Cutting hair on infants was bad luck. Only poor children had shorn locks. There was always Nurse and Marcella hovering in sight, much to his annoyance. He liked to spend time alone with his wife and son after a busy week in town but Marcella needed no excuse to visit and check on them all.

'I don't want another child,' Effie had told him months ago. 'You have your heir. He's enough. I'm not going through all that again. Mamma says it would be the death of me. Hamish is enough.'

'Wouldn't you like a little girl one day?' He was trying to be patient with her refusal to sleep in the same bed as him. He had his needs but she turned her back on him, spending every hour in the garden, playing with the boy, making a pet of him, fussing over his dresses and worrying about his motions. Marcella didn't help his cause, suggesting the air was too foul here and that Effie and Hamish would be better in Clinton. Jem was boiling with frustration. Damn it, Effie was his wife not his sister and they were making a sissy out of the wee lad.

Who'd blame him if he discreetly frequented the whorehouse hidden behind Front Street? That would give Marcella something to chew over if she knew but he resisted temptation for fear of gossip and put his energies into civic duties and his business interests, anything to keep his mind from the cloying atmosphere at Rosemount.

Sometimes he no longer felt master in his own household. Martha was his only ally but she was getting older and slower, a fact noticed by his mother-in-law. 'I don't know why you keep that mulatto around the place.'

'Don't speak of her like that again. She's been

my loyal housekeeper. She goes nowhere,' he snarled with venom, showing Marcella she had gone too far. She shrugged her shoulders but never questioned him, instead she whined to Effie about the dust on the skirting boards.

Like mother, like daughter, he worried. Was this their future? Bickering over trifles? No wonder Jacob Allister took so many business trips. Perhaps he should do the same? How had it gone so sour, so flat between them?

Perhaps if Hamish had not come along so soon after their wedding, Effie might not feel this way. The long difficult birth had left her low in spirit for months afterwards.

As he sat observing them all, trying to read the newspaper, he wondered why he had been so grateful to the Allister family? Would it have been better to have forged his own path without their help? Hindsight was a pointless exercise. This was his life and he had to make the best of it. Effie was a delight to the eye, with her neat waist restored and her outward beauty, but he wanted more than porcelain skin. Where was her curiosity and lively mind? If it wasn't in a raised border, a rose or a shrub, she wasn't interested. She spent hours in the winter making paintings of flowers. They hardly entertained because Effie couldn't stand their neighbours or his committee friends. His wife was not the sort to fit into this busy community at all. She lived in her own little world and would never want for anything in the way of comforts.

Part of him felt sorry for the limitations of her mind and class. He had wanted her and she had given him a precious son and he must respect that this was all there would ever be. It left him feeling cheated, restless and angry at himself for not seeing all this before they married.

Were other marriages similar? Was it only when you lived with someone for a while that you found out whether you were suited or not? If so, they were mismatched in every way and it was all his doing.

How then could he not recall Greta and their passionate coming together, those blissful weeks in her arms had never faded from his memory. He thought of her courage and ambition and what might have been if only he had spoken sooner? He knew he should stop hankering after the past, after a lost lover. He sighed, wondering how she was faring. Did she know he had a son who needed him now? The boy was strong and healthy. He had plans for his future education if he could prise the child from his mother's clutches. He intended to make Hamish his future project and a good businessman some day.

There were plans to expand the button-making industry from back room to factory. Clammers were bringing tons of shells to the city shoreline, stockpiling them to be stamped from blanks into buttons. Machinery was being developed to speed up the process and Jem was investing in the finishing process. There was so much to think about. He felt his eyelids closing in the heat when he heard Effie cry out.

'I've been stung,' she yelled, dropping her basket of cut flowers to touch her lip. 'Where did that come from?'

'Vinegar and bicarb of soda,' Marcella suggested. 'It'll take the sting out.' Effie's lip was swelling up fast.

Jem rushed to her side, ordering the nurse to remove Hamish in case there was a swarm. With Marcella's help they moved Effie to the cool veranda, shouting to Martha to bring the remedies. Now Effie's whole face was swelling and she couldn't open her eyes. Jem was alarmed. 'Send the yard boy on the bike for the doctor.' He carried his wife upstairs to their bedroom. She was limp in his arms and not responding to his voice.

'You must keep her cool, sir,' Martha suggested. 'Can she speak?'

Effie was trying to open her mouth and speak but she was struggling for breath, gasping as if choking. Jem began to panic.

'It's the throat swelling, I seed it once before. Open the windows to let in some air.'

It took ten minutes before the doc rode up with his bag. He came in looking bright and efficient but Jem was paralysed with fear at the sight of Effie's suffering. She was fading away before his eyes. 'Will she be all right, doc?' he asked but the doctor was urgently pumping something into Effie's arm with a syringe.

Only minutes ago she was beautiful and smiling and now she lay inert, bloated with swelling and not breathing. 'I'm afraid it's too late, James. She's gone.'

Jem refused to hear him, trying to shake her back into life. 'For God's sake, wake her up. Do something!'

Marcella screamed, beating the doctor with her

fists. 'You can't just let her die! I won't have this!'

'I'm sorry, I was too late. Has she been stung before?' the doctor asked.

'How should I know?' Marcella screamed. 'She loved being outdoors but she was always covered. The bee came out of a flower. How could it kill my daughter?'

'It's mighty rare to have such a reaction but the venom in the bee sting entered into her blood and caused this. She was very unlucky but her body just swelled up, blocking her airway. It was so quick she didn't suffer.' He was doing his best to comfort them but Jem had seen his wife struggling for breath surrounded by fear and panic. How could the doctor tell them such a lie, and what could he say to Hamish?

'I've been stung lots of times,' Jem cried. 'Why her, why now? It's so damned unfair.'

'It's all your fault,' Marcella screamed, punching him in fury. 'It's this wretched place, too near the water, too many trees, too many bugs. You should never have built this house. It's your fault.'

'It's nobody's fault, Mrs Allister. Let me give you something to calm your distress...' His words faded away as he led Marcella from the room.

Jem stayed by Effie's side all night, unable to close his eyes, staring at the candles and the black drape over the mirror in disbelief. Then a terrible thought surged through his mind. Was this his fault for insisting she wore her wedding pearls? Marcella had warned him. Was the superstition true that pearls meant tears for a bride on her wedding day? Had he tempted fate? How could a simple necklace bring down such ill fortune? It was given in love and it would be buried with her.

Jem neither ate nor slept until after the funeral. He stared at the walls, racked with guilt that on the very day of her death he was moaning to himself about her shortcomings as a wife. He'd been critical, impatient and almost ready to betray their marriage by finding relief with other women. Had the Fates heard his grumbles and decided to snatch her cruelly away?

Thank God Hamish was too little to understand her absence. 'Mama has gone to Heaven,' he said to anyone who met them offering their condolence.

Marcella was mad with grief and Jacob silent and withdrawn. 'What harm did she do to anyone?' her mother cried. Effie overnight became a saintly wife and mother, tragic heroine of the hour. There were flowers from people she had never known or cared for. He didn't feel worthy of all the letters of condolence. His mind seethed with anger and it boiled over when Marcella arrived ready to take Hamish back to Clinton. 'He's better off away from all this sadness.'

'You will do no such thing,' he growled, unable to contain his resentment. 'I won't have you interfering in his life. He stays here with me.'

'But he needs a mother.'

'He has his nurse and Martha. I will be father and mother. He will want for nothing.'

'That's not the point. You gave my daughter everything except your attention. Don't you think she didn't know how you ignored her?'

'That's not true! How dare you say such a thing?'

'Marcella, my dear,' Jacob intervened. 'Now is neither the time nor place. Come away.'

'No, he should know how unhappy she was.' She turned to Jem. 'Why do you think she spent so much time in the garden? You were never at home,' she said accusingly.

'Why are you saying all this?' Jem felt battered by her words. 'Hamish is my son, our son. He needs a father. I did love my wife. You are wrong as you have always been, interfering in our marriage. You never gave her the chance to be the woman she could be.'

'That's enough, Jem.' Jacob stepped in trying to cool their fury. 'Grief is making you both want someone to blame. The child, of course, is under your care but give us the chance to see him. Let him not lose a mother and grandparents. That isn't fair on him, now, is it? We will leave you to your thoughts.'

'How can you say I never loved her?' Jem was weeping, Marcella's cruel words stinging in his ears. Had he made Effie so unhappy? He had never meant to hurt her. How could he live with such knowledge?

He sat in the summer house until the sun went down, sobbing out his pain until exhaustion overtook him. Had he only thought of things from his point of view? Had he never seen hers? Had he made the worst decision of his life when he chose to stay here to make her his wife and put those pearls around her neck? Had he condemned her to death?

58

Greta sat in the York meeting house waiting for the wedding ceremony to begin. There was no organ or bridal procession, just a table set before the benches around which sat black-suited elders and guests waiting for the union of Rhodabel with Hamer Blake, who sat together looking so young and earnest.

She was glad Serenity Blake wasn't there glowering over the proceedings, knowing her son was marrying 'out'. They had convened the clearing committee to assess the young couple's suitability as partners for life which was the custom within the fellowship. Rhoda was now part of their assembly each week. How Greta would miss her cheerful company now she was leaving home. How proud she was of the skinny red head from New York as she sat tall and slender in her lilac silk dress and bonnet beside her intended as they solemnly repeated their marriage vows.

'Joining in marriage is the work of the Lord only and not a priest's or magistrate's for it is God's ordinance not man's.' Rhoda had quoted.

Edmund sat with his father looking across at Greta's family with a smile. Persie was dressed in her best organza dress and was sitting on Greta's knee. Bert and Sadie sat by their side bemused by the whole service, or lack of it. The elder had explained that everyone was to sit in silence and observe the simple ceremony. In the quiet, Greta's mind wandered far and wide from the room. She touched the locket around her neck, wishing Kitty was here to share the day with them too.

Now she must run the shop alone or take an assistant. It was hard to let Rhoda go. She knew their stock, was good with customers and was like an aunty to Persie. But Greta couldn't begrudge her a new life and family. After the wedding Hamer and Rhoda were going across to see Friends in Pennsylvania, taking greetings from the Friends in York. They planned to stay for at least three weeks. Would Rhoda make a detour to see Martha in Muscatine? Greta wondered. The two women had kept up their strange correspondence over the years and Rhoda often shared some of the news Martha's letters contained.

Did Rhoda ever wonder if Jem Baillie was Persie's real father? If so she never said a word. Was she so innocent of the ways of the world not to realize how close they had become? One thing Rhoda had passed on was that Jem was married with a son born not long after Persie. It was hard to think Persie had a half-brother called Hamish across the ocean, a brother she would never know.

Did Jem ever think of her or those months when they'd lain in each other's arms until dawn, but how could he do that and not betray his wife? They met still in her dreams, where she felt the touch of his fingers along her body and woke with such a yearning.

'Please come and sign the marriage certificate.'

The words jolted Greta from her daydreaming. Row upon row stood up to put their name down as witnesses. Even Persie was allowed to sign her name and wrote Pearl in wobbly baby lettering.

Edmund escorted them to the wedding breakfast at Mount Vernon. 'Do you mind coming back here?' he asked with concern. 'I know my mother made life difficult for you.'

'Not at all, that's all in the past. We're different people now,' she replied. How could she forget her own days there as a maid under orders? The house looked more cluttered and brighter. Erasmus Blake had definitely loosened his late wife's hold over the décor and there were several of Edmund's carvings on show around the house. The garden was a riot of flower borders with tables set around in the shade. Looking around at the guests in their plain outfits, she knew there would be no customers for her shop here. The simple pearl brooch she had given Rhoda to wear was one of only a few jewels on display.

She thought about Mr Broadhurst and his daughter's necklace lying in the safe just waiting for the last matching pearl. You could wait years to find that last pearl, the perfect match to set off the whole string and so far none had turned up that would do. She thought about the pearl necklace she had threaded for Jem's wife all those years ago. She enjoyed Sam Broadhurst's visits. They'd become good friends over recent months and he always called in on market day with a hunk of good cheese and a lollipop for Persie.

'Little'un reminds me of our Letty wi' them corkscrew curls, curly kisses we call them.'

They would look over another pearl to put away and discuss the news. 'Nowt but the best for our lass, I just wish her mam had lived to see the day.'

Letty must be a great girl to inspire such pride and devotion. She would be proud to thread them up when the time came and find a good clasp. *That's the joy of my little shop.* She never knew who might come through the door, whether it was a factory girl from Rowntree's Cocoa Works who collected silver charms or tourists who like to buy jet and amber designs.

Her heart went out to old Miss Fielden who had once lived a better life in a country house, a rector's daughter who ended up a governess, frail now and living in rooms near Bedern. Every locket and ring she possessed was sold and her future was looking grim. So many lost dreams and stories in life. 'There but for the grace of God go I,' she heard herself sigh and then Persie wriggled and brought her back to the moment.

Poor bairn, you didn't choose your birthing but I'll give you the very best to compensate. Education will be your key to independence. Hidden by the shrubbery out of sight from the chattering wedding guests, it was good to sit and dream of such things.

There have to be dreams and love in your heart. What's life about but drudgery and pain without them? Persie's birth had opened the tough membrane around her heart. Her customers brought their tales of joy and woe through the door, softening her once-frozen spirit. They relied on her to give good service and valuations. Many of those transactions were more than a mere passing over of silver and notes. They were an act

401

of trust. All things bright and beautiful, she might stock but it was dreams she was selling.

'What are you doing skulking in the bushes?' Edmund stood over her as she was daydreaming.

'Just thinking about Persie's future, how different it will be from my own.'

'You're not planning her wedding already?' He laughed.

'I can't bear to think of her growing up and leaving one day. Is that selfish?'

Edmund sat down beside her. 'But she will go, that's the way of things. We move on to different lives. Look how you went away and came back. You don't regret coming home, do you?' He stared into her eyes and she found herself blushing.

'I'm going to miss Rhodabel while she's away. I've got used to her company.'

'You don't have to live alone. Persie might like to have a new father.' He leaned forward in hope.

'No, Edmund, please. I'm content the way things are. It's just that weddings remind me of how I made a mess of my own.' She jumped up, not sure how to go on. 'I'd better find Persie. It's time to be away.'

'Let me escort you back,' he offered as she knew he would.

'No, thanks, you must stay with your family and friends.' Why was she always shoving him away? What did she fear in allowing him closer in her life?

59

'I can't believe we're coming into Muscatine.' Rhoda was hanging over the rail, pointing to the shoreline as the paddle steamer chugged its way down the Mississippi. 'So much has happened since I was last here. Thank you for letting me come back. I can't wait to see Martha again.' The crossing from Liverpool gave them plenty of time to adjust to this new life together – the fun of making love and being alone. Rhodabel recalled her last journey and how nervous she was to be leaving her home country. 'We must send a postcard to Greta and Persie as soon as we arrive here.'

It would be a short visit only, a couple of nights in Muscatine itself. Martha had suggested they stay in the best hotel in town but that was not their style so they chose a more modest one. As they walked down the gangway Rhoda sniffed the fishy air, thinking how different it felt being on the arm of her husband than when she arrived all those years ago in a troupe of orphans. The first thing Rhoda noticed was how the city had sprawled out; there were more sawmills and factories and houses as far as the eye could see. Then the stink of rotting clams hit their nostrils. There'd always been a fishy smell but never this strong. Clam shells were piled high along the riverbanks and clammers with their wooden boats and nets filled the waterside jostling alongside barges and log rafts. It was a noisy hive of industry.

Martha was waiting on the jetty to greet them, waving a hanky. Rhoda rushed to meet her.

'Lordy, you've grown.' Martha hugged her. 'I wouldn't have recognized you 'cept for that hair. I've been telling folks that know you that you's back in town and Mr James has invited you to dine at his house.'

'What is that smell? I thought the Ouse was foetid but...' Hamer put his hand over his nose.

'It's the clam shells piled up to be stamped into button blanks. Buttons is big business now. Brought plenty work for folks,' Martha replied, pointing to boats filled with clam shells. 'Then they crush what's left to take to the vegetable-growing fields. Nothing is wasted but it sure does foul up the air. Mr James is big in buttons now,' she added.

Rhoda laughed at her words but Martha shook her head. 'You'll find him much changed. I never told you how his wife died in a tragic accident. Don't mention her name in his hearing. He can't bear to talk about it.'

'What about the little boy?'

'Hamish's fine, you'll meet him and see for yourself. He's just like his pa. He can ride a pony like a savage.'

Rhoda turned to Hamer to explain their connection. 'Martha's employer was our landlord. He was very kind when Greta's husband drowned and I was ill. He and Greta were quite friendly before we left.'

'The less said about that the better,' sniffed Martha guiding them across the street to their

404

lodgings. 'You get settled, have a look around the town. Mr James will send a cab for you this evening. You will dine with him. I'm making pot pie like old times.' With that she left them to register at their hotel.

'It all sounds very intriguing. A captain of industry invites his tenant's maid to dine in his mansion house?'

'I can't believe Martha never wrote his wife had died. I've told her all about Persie being born early and all about the shop and she forgets such important news?'

'Perhaps she thought it wasn't her place to tell you,' Hamer offered. 'I was young when we lost our mama. My father went silent for months. He worked and worked but when he was reconciled with Edmund, things got better for him. Mother so wanted Edmund to be a lawyer but he refused so I took that place. Families are strange beasts, don't you think?'

'I never knew a family until Greta took me in. Her husband was mean and hated me but she made up for him. I was glad when he drowned.' Rhoda put her hand over her mouth. 'I've never said that out loud before.'

'Speak the truth in love.' Hamer hugged her. 'So here we are, back in the very place where it all began for you both.'

'It holds strange memories though. Miss Greta hit Mr Slinger with a skillet and knocked him out when he attacked me. The miser hid his pearls in his clothes and when we found them by accident, we danced around the room with relief. We had the chance to leave.'

'You make my life seem so dull after all your adventures.'

'Sure but the Lord in his wisdom found me someone who would be an anchor to hold me steady.'

'Shall I hold you steady now?'

'No, no.' She laughed. 'Hold me rough and keep me close.'

Jem went onto the veranda to greet his guests as they stepped out of the cab. He saw them looking up at the white portico and shuttered windows with admiration. Could this really be little Rhodabel, the gawky kid he last saw recovering from fever? By her side was a fair-haired young man with a full beard in a sombre black suit. She seemed too young to be married but then Effie was little more than a schoolgirl ... but no more of that.

In the year since her passing he had gotten used to the silences. It was enough to hear factory noises thumping in his ears, the clatter of the stamping machine that Boepple was using to produce the buttons. Little Hamish brought his own welcome noise and chatter. They had horses and rode out together. It was a blessing he didn't look like his mother. There was no reminder of Effie's fair beauty to choke him with regret.

Everything he touched seemed to turn to gold: business investments, property leases, a new lumber mill where Jake ran the show. Marcella stayed away and that suited them both. The garden was kept immaculate as a memorial to his wife. Not a blade of grass was out of place and the flowerbeds were magnificent but he never went in the garden. He had a boat on the river so he could go fishing for catfish and sometimes he went clamming. He wanted Hamish to delight in the things that he'd enjoyed as a child in Perthshire. He showed his son pictures of Scotland, promising they would return one day and visit Glencorrin once more. The boy was too young to understand but he liked playing on the shoreline and pearling.

Jem hated the weeks when his son went to stay in Clinton. The silence of the mansion was oppressive and he drowned his sorrows in the saloon bars or visited Madame Honorie's establishment to relieve himself of all the frustrations of living a bachelor's life but somehow that left him lonelier than ever.

There were discreet matchmaking overtures among the wives of his business acquaintances but their wholesome hearty daughters held no appeal. He wanted to spend time with no one apart from Hamish. One day his son would be wealthy but he wanted him to know just where he came from and never to be ashamed of his humble origins.

'My father was a tinker, they said, a travelling man and a pearl fisher, and my mother was the kindest soul who filled his heart with love and tamed his wandering soul.' How many times had he rehearsed this line knowing the laddie was too young to understand his meaning. No more of all that, he thought, watching Martha bringing his guests up the steps to the porch.

'Welcome to Rosemount,' Jem held out his hand to his guests. 'We are so glad to see the wanderer return.'

Rhoda introduced her new husband and he felt a flicker of envy for the couple looked so happy together.

'What a view!' Hamer Blake said shaking his head in disbelief 'I've read *The Adventures of Tom Sawyer*. I never thought to visit this mighty river. Thank you kindly for this invitation.'

'Nonsense. It's just old-fashioned hospitality and Martha would never forgive me if we didn't show off her house.'

'We are sorry for your recent loss,' Hamer continued bowing his head.

Jem nodded and moved them into the drawing room. 'Come and meet my son who has been allowed to stay up late to meet you.'

Hamish looked up from his jigsaw puzzle and smiled. He was in pyjamas and dressing gown.

Hamer stared at him, shaking his head. 'Goodness me, doesn't he look just like–' Jem saw Rhoda nudging her husband hard.

'He looks just like you with those dark curls,' Rhoda replied blushing, a puzzled look on her face.

'Would you like a tour of the house? Most people seem to find it an interesting design. It was only a dream when you lived here, Mrs Blake.'

'Rhoda, please,' she insisted. 'I am very curious.'

He rang a bell and Martha sprang into view. 'Let them loose while I take this young man to his bed.'

'Why did you elbow me when I nearly remarked on Hamish looking like Persie?' Hamer pushed his wife up the stairs.

'Because he doesn't know about Persie but

Martha does and Greta was insistent no one should know.'

'Well they could be twins they look so alike, that's all I'm saying.' Hamer paused on the landing until Martha was out of earshot before asking, 'Are you saying what I think you are saying?'

'Shush not a word, the less said the better. I did wonder when she was born so early but it was never spoken about. But after seeing the boy...'

'Does James not know then? Shouldn't he know?'

'It's none of our business. The two of them were very friendly. I once thought I saw them kissing but I could've imagined it. I was such a greenhorn I never thought ... oh heck!'

'He ought to know if he has another child, for the child's sake. It affects inheritance...'

'Trust you to see the legal side of things. Perhaps in time but he's lost his wife and Greta is settled with her business. We can't interfere or break a confidence. What you don't know can't hurt you, can it?'

'What you don't know can destroy trust if the truth is withheld between good friends and then you find out later. We must hold this matter in prayer to the Lord and ask for guidance,' Hamer suggested. 'Perhaps we were guided here to find this out.'

'Are you two coming or not?' yelled Martha. 'Come and see the marbled bathroom.'

'Coming... Lead on Macduff.' Rhoda wasn't going to spoil this sociable evening by worrying about their strange discovery. After all it might be just a coincidence. Although she had often wondered how a man who died in October eighty-eight could father a child born early nearly a year later.

60

Greta couldn't believe her daughter was now four years old and attending a little dame school close to the Minster. She always felt the draught of her absence however busy she was. Rhodabel was living across the river in Mount Vernon so Greta now ran the shop alone and life fell into an ordered pattern. There were regular visits to auction rooms in Leeds and Harrogate where, after eyeing up jewellery pieces, she'd let a steward bid for her so she retained an air of mystery. The 'Widow from Goodramgate' was easily recognized by local competitors in her smart black suit and jaunty hats. She was good at rooting out bargains.

Yet Greta was beginning to feel cramped and restless in the upstairs living space. Persie had Rhoda's bedroom now but there was still not much room for the two of them. They took walks around the city and the park and visited the Blakes so that Persie could play in their large garden.

Rhoda's honeymoon was still a talking point and Greta was pleased to hear that the couple had visited Muscatine. Their meeting with Jem troubled Greta especially when she heard about Euphemia's tragic accident. 'I didn't know a bee sting could kill you,' Rhoda added. 'The poor man looks so sad and his little boy is almost as old as Persie. Hamish looks like his father too.'

Greta looked at the photograph of Martha holding a small boy's hand and tried to stay calm. 'Did you tell James about Pearl?' she said, not lifting her eyes.

'Of course not, Hamer nearly spilled the beans when he saw Hamish but I stopped him.'

'Why's that?' she replied, sipping her tea, her fingers rattling the saucer.

'It's not our place to tell him he has a daughter, is it?' Rhoda looked her straight in the eye. 'She is James's child?'

Greta bowed her head feeling defensive. 'And what good would that do for the world to know? Persie belongs to me, to my family. I am a widow. That's all people need to know.'

'But it's not honest. It might cheer his spirit to know he has a little girl too. He's very wealthy now,' she added.

'Is that all you Quakers think about, money and business? I am successful too.'

'Of course you are but Pearl thinks her papa is dead. One day she should be told the truth...'

'What's brought all this on? My affairs are my own business not yours. You have a husband to attend to. Please don't tell me what I should be doing.' Greta banged her cup and saucer down, spilling its contents all over the cloth.

'We just wanted you to know that we know, that's all, but if you saw little Hamish—'

'Well, now I know you know and I will never see his son, will I?'

'But lies have a way of unravelling themselves.'

411

'Don't preach at me, Rhoda. It doesn't suit you.'

'That's not fair. I have kept silent but how can I stand by and let someone I love do a bad thing? I'm speaking the truth in love.'

'Rhoda, you are preaching at me. Let me tell you how hard it was to leave when we did but there was no choice and I didn't realize my condition until we came home. How could I destroy their engagement by making demands on him? Better to let things be, and if you want honesty here's something else to chew over. Persie wouldn't be here today if you hadn't been so sick and at death's door. Jem came to comfort me while you were all those weeks in hospital. That's when it all began. There you have it.' Her heart thudded with the memory of that time. 'And perhaps we wouldn't be here if he had abandoned Effie but he made his choice and it wasn't me.' Greta paused. 'I'd better go before I say anything more.'

'I didn't mean for us to quarrel. I owe you so much.'

'You owe me nothing. What I did suited me as well as you. Come on, Persie!' she yelled from the French window. 'Time for home.'

Persie dawdled over in a sulk. 'Do we have to?'

'Come when you are told.' Greta was in no mood for arguments.

'Oh, please don't leave on a bad note,' Rhoda begged. 'I didn't mean to hurt you.'

'Well, you have so you must live with it.'

Greta was furious as they stood waiting for the horse tram. Persie was sulking and it was hot and sticky. Her mind was racing at the thought of Jem's

412

young wife, cut short in life leaving such a small child. She had never borne her any malice, or had she? Was there jealousy that Jem's wife was richer, prettier and younger? Would it be proper to write to him with her condolences? Should she renew their friendship with a view to … she paused … to what? Should she tempt him with news of his other child? Should she slip a portrait of Persie in the letter for him to see the likeness to his son; a resemblance so obvious that even the Blakes were struck by it? Now she had rowed with her dearest companion. How could she be so ungrateful and mean to her? What was the matter with her these days?

As if to punish her more, the week got off to a bad start. The pavements of York were steaming; the stench from the river had seeped into the narrow streets and with the result that custom was slow. Pride made her unable to write a postcard of apology to Rhodabel. Let her sit in the shade of her garden and contemplate her sermon for all I care, she thought. Greta snapped and sweated with bad temper and fear, keeping herself busy by cleaning out the shelves and cupboards. Despite wearing as thin a dress as she could find, the heat was oppressive and her hair stuck to her forehead.

To her surprise Sam Broadhurst arrived. It was not his usual market day. He had a grey look to him she'd never seen before, as if he had not been outdoors for days. He looked awkward in his black serge suit and he was carrying a bowler hat.

'Have I missed the day?' she laughed.

He stood four square. 'No, lass, but I thought

413

you ought to know I've just buried my lass.'

Greta stood in shock at this news not knowing what to say. 'Oh, Sam, I'm sorry to hear that. Please come in. I had no idea.'

'Aye, well, Letty's been badly for months. We kept hoping but it allus were a poor job. Summat to do wi' a weakness of the blood, they said at the hospital. She were only nineteen but that pale and tired, she just faded away before my eyes. Tell me, Mrs Costello, what did a lass like her do to deserve such like?' There were tears in his eyes.

'I'm going to make us a brew. You shouldn't be out in this summer heat. I am so sorry.'

'They say she were too good for this world. They say the good die young and she'll be in a better place now but I want her here with me, not over there.' The anguish was so raw as he wiped his eyes with a grubby hanky.

Greta shut the shop. 'Come upstairs and tell me all about Letty.' It was the least she could do. She knew just what it felt like and thought of Kitty. The poor man had all the stuffing knocked out of him. Blow having tea, what he needed was a stiff drink. She had some brandy in the cupboard for when they were ill. There was almost a full bottle so she poured two glasses and they sipped it as he poured out his sadness.

'It means, I'm afraid, I'll not be needing them pearls. I'd be grateful if you could buy them back. It took a lot of brass to give her the best send-off. I'd such plans for her to marry and take over the farm. It'll have to go one day as I've no heart in it any more.'

Greta nodded and let him talk and drink. The

brandy loosened his tongue and she heard all about his late wife, his stock, his struggle to build up his herd. The pearls would have to be sold on. None of that mattered when this poor man had lost his most precious girl. This must be what Jem felt after losing his wife. How could she have ever thought of contacting him again?

Broadhurst fell into a snooze and started snoring so she left him in peace, knowing rest was what was needed. It would soon be time to collect Persie from her school.

Feeling the effects of the brandy, she half tumbled down the stairs to open the shop. Edmund was waiting on her doorstep. 'I've been to the printers in Fossgate to collect these posters. There's going to be an exhibition of Arts and Crafts. What do you think?' He spread his poster on the counter. 'I'm sorry, I've got to dash, but I'll look in later to collect them and to see what you think.'

Just at that moment Sam Broadhurst staggered down the stair with the smell of brandy on him. Edmund took one look at the barrel-chested farmer and scowled. 'Oh, you've got a visitor. Sorry to spoil your little party, have I interrupted something?' He didn't wait for a reply but dashed out into the street and Greta was too stunned to call him back.

'Thank you, lass, for your listening ear. I just wanted you to know the situation. You don't have to rush about buying them back. They're only pearls after all. What I've lost is beyond price, beyond my understanding.' With that Sam staggered forth to the nearest public house to drown

415

his sorrows.

It was only when walking Persie home from school that it dawned on her that Edmund thought she was entertaining a man upstairs in private. How could he ever have thought such a thing? Did he think she was a widow on her own finding comfort where she could?

She waited anxiously all evening for him to collect his posters so she could explain. He didn't come that night or the next but then the following evening she caught sight of him staggering out of the Cross Keys in the direction of the shop. 'There you are. I want a word with you.'

Edmund raised his cap. 'Has your fancy man stood you up?'

'Come inside, you're drunk. How dare you think such a thing of me? You're like all the rest, women are good only for one thing. That poor man lost his only child and came to tell me before drowning his sorrows. We had an arrangement to buy her pearls that she will never now wear so I gave him some brandy to cheer him up and you assumed that I was whoring on the side, did you?'

Edmund looked shocked at her angry words. 'I'm sorry. It's just the way he was staggering and there was spirits on your breath too.'

'I kept him company. I just want to put the matter straight.'

'You cared that I thought badly of you, does that mean...' He looked down at her with hope in his eyes.

'It means I care for my reputation, that's all. You and I have always been good friends.'

'Then it's time it was something more, Greta. I

could give you a good home and love Persie as my own.'

'Please, not now, don't let's quarrel again. Give me time. I'm not ready to give up my independence or my way of doing things. I had enough of that in my marriage.'

'But it wouldn't be like that with us,' he protested. 'I can make you happy.'

'But I fear I would make us both unhappy. There are things in my past...' she paused knowing honesty was needed now. 'You don't know all my story.'

'I don't care about all that stuff. Ever since you were a maid in the house, you showed such spirit. What happened with your husband in America is history. Promise me you'll think about a life with me.'

Greta nodded. 'I just want to be straight with you. I'm not a silly servant girl or any man's bride now and Persie belongs only to me. I don't want to talk about her father so let's leave it there. Let me make you some supper. You can't go back to Mount Vernon smelling of stale ale.'

'I can stay here with you then?' he asked.

'Edmund Blake, have you not heard a word I've just said?'

In the morning she found Nellie Webster from next door on her doorstep. 'Have you heard?' she rushed in with her sleeves rolled up.

'Heard what?'

'They're going to pull us down, all of us...'

'Pull what down?' Nellie was talking gibberish.

'These houses, shops and the pub will go to

417

make a street up to the Minster,' she said.

'What street might that be?'

'There's talk about turning out all of us so they can pave a road up the side.'

'Talk, it's just talk, Nellie. You know how people like to make up stuff. It'll never happen in our day.'

'But John heard from the Todds and the other shop that there's plans afoot to widen the street and to pull down the Cross Keys.'

'Is there anything on paper? Surely it all has to go to meetings and committee. You can't just pull down shops. It won't be in our lifetime.'

'I tell you, our livelihood's under threat.'

'It's my landlord's under threat. I'm only a tenant. I don't own anything.'

'Makes no difference, though, does it, love? We'll have to up sticks and shift to another place. We'll lose customers and the street will be a mess of rubble.'

'I'm sure it won't come to this, not so soon anyways.'

'Mark my words it will come and we'll all be the last to know.'

Nellie flounced out of the shop leaving Greta winded by her threats. Could it be true? Could she ask the vicar? Erasmus Blake might know about town plans. He was always her ally but she had fallen out with Rhoda and upset Hamer. She didn't want Edmund championing her corner once again.

To lose her livelihood now was unthinkable. She felt the sure ground of certainty shifting beneath her feet, a rumble of change in the air, a storm on

418

the horizon. Perhaps her mother would lend her an ear but not even Sadie could take this unexpected fear from her. Never had she felt so alone.

61

1895

Dear Friend,

After much thought and prayer we feel it is our duty to inform you of the following circumstance which we omitted to divulge last year when you were so gracious as to give us such kind hospitality.

Both my wife and I remarked on the likeness between yourself and your son but we also noticed a remarkable likeness between Hamish and the child of our dear friend Margaret Costello.

A recent portrait of the said child is enclosed. The child was born in York in September 1889. It was a miracle of God's grace that she survived being so premature. Her survival was due to her mother's devoted care.

Now she is nearly six years old and delights us with her reading. Her name is Kathleen Pearl but within the family she is known as Persie. My wife is her godmother because at that time she had not become a member of The Society of Friends who do not hold with such ceremonies. We perform our own duty of care to the best of our abilities and for this reason feel we must speak out on Persie's behalf.

She thinks her father to be dead as, of course, do

most of Greta's family. Margaret expressly told my wife not to speak of such delicate matters and not inform anyone outside the family.

However, it is in the light of truth that a friend must sometimes intervene in the interests of mother and child. Bearing in mind your recent sorrows we feel sure you would want to know of this child's existence. Be this at the risk of losing the friendship of our most valued sister, we are taking this unusual step.

How you respond to this letter is entirely up to you. It will no doubt be both a shock and disappointment that Margaret did not inform you herself. It is a measure of her courage and discretion that she prefers to soldier on alone being a most excellent mother.

Pearl as you can see is a delight to the eye and heart. I am sure she would be thrilled to know she has a half-brother but, of course, this will be your decision.

We hold all of you up to the light in prayer and hope that one day this might be resolved.

Your Friends in Christ
Hamer and Rhodabel Blake

Jem read the letter in disbelief. He read the letter twice over just to be sure then he stormed into the kitchen waving the paper in Martha's face. 'Did you know about this child?'

Martha looked up from her baking and put down her spoon. 'What child?'

Jem shoved the photograph in front of her. 'Oh my, what a little beauty. Yes, Rhodabel let slip something about a birth in one of her letters but it was said in confidence. It was not my place to share.'

'You never did like Mrs Slinger.'

'No, sir, it ain't for the likes of her to claim your attention when you is already taken up with another. She should have looked the other way.'

'You were wrong to sit in judgment on her. I would have married her and gone out west to start over,' he replied. Better to tell her the truth.

'But you didn't, sir. You stayed true to your girl in Clinton.'

'Only because Mrs Slinger left before I could tell her my plan.'

'How would I be knowing that?'

'There's a lot of things you don't know about Greta and her husband and the life she endured with him. She did the honourable thing and sent me away and left to bear her burden alone.'

'Pardon me for saying, seeing as I got it all wrong, but you's free now to do what you please. It ain't too late now Miss Euphemia is passed to her Glory.'

'No, it's too late. I am sewn into this city so tight now with the mills and the new button company. I can't just go swanning off.' He banged his fist on the table. 'I can't believe no one said anything.'

'Then forget this letter and get on with your life here.'

'How can I, now I know about Pearl? She's my flesh and blood. Look at her...' He pointed at the picture in her hand. Martha held it out at arm's length to allow her eyes to focus.

'Lordy, she do look like you and the boy. Take time to think before you do anything rash, sir. I know how you is when you go chasing an idea.'

Jem sighed. 'What would I do without you to cut me down to size?'

421

'Outta my kitchen with your soft talking... Don't rush in like a fox in a barnyard.'

'I've a good mind to take you with me,' Jem added seeing the look on her face.

'Oh no. I ain't going on no ship across an ocean to some cold city. I can go visit my folks while you is gone.'

Jem kept looking at the picture of Pearl. She was wearing a white dress and staring hard into the lens. He knew that glare. He had seen it plenty of mornings in the mirror. Now he knew of his daughter's existence, how could he stay away?

Months later he sat down and wrote the following letter.

Dear Hamer and Rhodabel Blake,

Thank you for your letter. Forgive my silence but I have had a lot to consider in the light of the startling revelation you shared with me.

I have given the matter much thought these past months and have decided that the occasion of Queen Victoria's diamond jubilee might be a good time to take my son across to Scotland so he might see for himself the splendours of the old country and learn that not all Scots are born in castles.

We will sail from New York to Southampton to visit London and Edinburgh but I wondered if we might impose on you for a short visit to York so we may discuss these delicate matter further. Furthermore, if you might convene a meeting with Greta and her daughter in a way that appears impromptu, I would be most obliged.

I realize this is burdening you with some element of secrecy and duplicity. If you feel this is not suitable,

please advise me further.
  Yours sincerely,
  James Baillie

62

The news about future street developments was true but it was not going to happen immediately as it was still at the planning stage. Greta had looked at the proposed changes and her premises would be one of those properties demolished to make way for the new road. It was unsettling to know she would have to move one day.

Over the years that hard shell she had grown to protect her reputation had softened to a thin veneer of confidence. Business was brisk enough to make a modest living. Yet in her heart she knew something was missing in her life, an absence that even Persie couldn't fill. Edmund's offer had unsettled her. Rhoda had Hamer. Mother had Bert but there was no one to share her worries with at the end of a long day. Time she could fill: visiting the theatre, listening to bands in the park, checking her suppliers and visiting auctions but there were still moments when she felt alone.

She was reading to Pearl Mark Twain's *Adventures of Huckleberry Finn,* although it was a little old for her child. Twain had been a reporter on the *Muscatine Journal* long before her time, living close to Walnut and Front Street for a while. His great success was the pride of the city. As she sat there reading his story she could see the mighty Mississippi in all its glory and recalled those wonderful sunsets, the icy chill of the winters, those great expanses of corn fields, and she felt herself yearning for something long lost.

For the first time in years she was no longer content to be solitary. If truth be told she was lonely, yearning for the physical warmth of a man's arms around her, a shoulder to lean on. Was that why she so looked forward to Edmund's visits to her shop? They had patched up their misunderstanding and she had visited his workshop with a view, she paused, with a view to something more? He was kind and generous, artistic, talented and, like her, he was an individual who was not afraid to step out of line. She smiled knowing together they would make a good team. They could share a workshop and outlet like Norman and Irene. She could raise Pearl in the countryside with fresh air and fields. It could work and she could grow to love the idea of this life together. She tried to put thoughts of Jem out of her mind but reading to Pearl, a vision of Jem's face came into her mind's eye. Would she never be free of him? Perhaps though Edmund might be the answer to this.

Next day she visited the Arts and Crafts exhibition where she knew Edmund was showing furniture and Irene and Norman had their stand. She browsed along the stalls with their tapestries, pewter tableware, trinket boxes and beautiful wall hangings before going to see Irene sitting at their jewellery stall.

'I hoped you might call in. How's it all going?

Do you need some more brooches?'

Greta glanced over the stall admiring Irene's work. 'Not just at the moment. Trade's quiet. Have you seen Edmund? I've not seen him for ages.'

'He's been lecturing at the art college. He was here a few minutes ago. Ask Alice.' Irene pointed to a pretty girl minding his furniture exhibition.

'Who's Alice?'

'One of his student acolytes and by the looks of her, it's more than the carving she's interested in so get yourself over there... That's what you've come for, isn't it?'

'I don't know. I just wanted to see his work.'

'Pull the other one, Greta. Edmund is yours for the taking but don't wait too long. You've kept him dangling for years. Time to reel him in.'

Greta stepped back shocked. 'Oh, don't say that, Irene, it sounds so calculated and cold. I don't know what I want, if the truth be known. It's not that he isn't kind and clever, it's just... I can't feel for him what I know I should.'

'And what might that be, girlish flutterings and romantic passion? There's more to marriage than all that stuff. You should know.'

'But I don't know, not now. I'm not sure.' How could she explain her misgivings?

'Then leave him be, don't torture him with hope but make sure you know what you're doing, my girl.'

Greta shrugged her shoulders. 'I'd better go and see him, now I'm here.' Irene's words had chilled her. She strolled across to inspect his display. There was a dresser with carved panels that took her eye. The young woman called Alice was guarding his stall as Greta inspected the dresser.

'It's good, isn't it?' said the girl, smiling. She had the greenest eyes that lit up as she spoke. 'He's such a marvellous designer.'

'Is Edmund around?' Greta asked.

'Oh he's just gone to fetch some luncheon.'

'It's a bit wide for my staircase but I do like the design,' Greta continued, determined to wait for his return.

'Most of our work can be ordered to your specific dimensions.'

'You work there too?' She had assumed Alice was a temporary assistant.

'I do some carving. We met at art school, he's a lecturer there. If you bring us some measure-ments– Oh, look he's back... Edmund, there's a lady...'

Greta smiled. 'Oh we are old friends.'

Edmund smiled greeting her warmly. 'This is Alice, and this is my dear friend Greta Costello.'

'Oh, I've heard so much about you and your shop in Goodramgate,' Alice added, shaking Greta's hand as she looked her up and down. Any-one could see the girl adored him. 'Mrs Costello was asking about the dresser.' Alice was eager to make a sale.

'I'm glad I've seen you, we've been so busy. Alice is such a help.'

I bet she is, thought Greta with a brief flicker of jealousy towards her rival but for some reason eager to leave. 'I'll send you the measurements but I must dash now.'

How close had she come to making a fool of herself? She had made one mistake in marrying

426

Eben to please her family and for her own convenience. How could she think of marrying Edmund purely because she was tired of living alone? His admiration was always a comfort but she didn't really want him in the way she had wanted Jem. Marriage to Edmund would be yet another mistake and cruel to her dear friend. Better to live alone than make yet another mistake. She fled from the building into the street, stumbling through the crowds in her confusion.

You are thirty two years old, a business woman and a mother. What more do you want? You do not love Edmund for himself but to satisfy your own neediness. Pull yourself together and be satisfied that you have your little shiny shop, which was always your dream. Just get on with it. As she pushed her way back to Goodramgate there was no comfort in the familiar buildings around her. Everything was old and shabby, blocking out light and air. Why was she feeling trapped? Why did her home city no longer feel a safe haven? When did this refuge suddenly become like a prison?

63

June 1897

For months now, since the arrival of James's letter, Rhoda had been worrying about how best to prepare for his coming visit to York. His reply sent her into a flurry of anxiety as to whether it was a good idea to allow them to stay at Mount Vernon but how could they not extend the famous hospitality of Friends to strangers when the whole city would be en fête with jubilee celebrations, pageants and military parades. The streets and bridges were already festooned with banners and flags.

It troubled Rhoda not to be able to warn Greta of the coming visit but Greta was busy with her own patriotic window display and local trade meetings. They must find a way to lure her up to the house for this 'chance meeting' with James but how would she react? Rhoda feared she might refuse at the last minute, saying she was too busy. There was nothing for it but to make her way down to the shop to give her a formal invitation.

'We've got friends coming soon from America, ones we visited on our honeymoon trip. I would love you to meet them as they've heard all about what you did for me in Muscatine and they are curious. I thought we'd make a First Day luncheon after meeting in the garden. There's a child so Persie will have someone to play with.'

'I'm not sure. I usually visit Mother on Sundays.'

'Oh, but they'll be invited too. We'll make it a real family occasion. It's not often we get everyone together. I want to show them all the decorations and flags on Lendal Bridge. You are always busy on what should be your day of rest.'

Greta was wavering. 'Why do they want to meet me? You can show them round the city without us trailing behind you.'

'Yes, I know, but I'd like you to come too. To be honest, you look as if you need a good luncheon.

428

You're nothing but skin and bone these days and I would appreciate your company as I don't know them all that well, and we hardly see you these days.'

'You can talk.' Greta smiled. 'With all your meetings and charity work. Besides, these friends might find me a little too worldly.'

'Nonsense, they don't belong to a Friends' meeting house. You'll have much in common.' Rhoda put on her pleading look which never failed with Greta. 'Promise me you'll come?'

'You've twisted my arm.'

'Wonderful. I promise you won't regret it.' Rhoda shot out of the door before Greta could change her mind or ask why.

At least with friends like Rhoda and the Blakes, Greta needn't dress in finery for a Sunday luncheon. Not that she had much in the way of fancy dresses and hats. Her workwear consisted of a plain black skirt and smart lace shirts secured with a firm belt around her waist but today it was summer and sunny. She would make an effort to be more colourful for these American guests, choosing a blue candy-striped cotton dress with puffed sleeves and a frill round the neck. Her summer boater trimmed with a blue ribbon would have to do.

'Is it time?' Persie kept pestering, eyeing the wall clock as it chimed the hour. 'Do we have to walk all the way?'

'We can take the tram.'

'Can I sit upstairs?'

'We'll see.'

'You always say that.' Persie loved dressing up and visiting Aunt Rhoda's. She was wearing her Sunday best white cotton dress with a deep satin sash around the hip. Her shoes were patent leather with little ankle straps and her pretty straw bonnet was dressed with rosebuds and leaves.

They took the tram across the river and up to Micklegate and walked past all the fine houses on Blossom Street, a trek she knew so well from her time as a servant. What would the late Serenity Blake have made of this gathering? Hilda the housemaid opened the door and pointed to the garden. Persie rushed ahead but Greta hung back, feeling nervous now to be meeting strangers. She drew a deep breath to make her entrance and stepped into the sunshine. A boy in a sailor suit was whipping a hoop and Persie was chasing after him. 'Can I have a go?' They ran off down the garden together.

Greta shielded her eyes looking for the other guests, blinded by the brightness. She saw the back of a tall man wearing a linen suit and a wide-brimmed Panama hat. Then he turned round and stared and she went cold.

'Oh, there you are.' Rhoda rushed to her side seeing the shock on her face.

'What's this?' Greta whispered. 'Why is he here?'

'He's our guest, your old friend James Baillie. They are en route to Scotland and called in to see us. Isn't this a lovely surprise after all this time?' She heard the quiver in Rhoda's voice and wasn't fooled, realizing now that this meeting must have been carefully planned behind her back.

Jem marched forward holding out his hand.

'How good to see you again, you look well.'

What could she do but nod and shake his hand as if they were old acquaintances, her heart thudding at the sight of him. 'Our children have already met.' He smiled. 'Hamish is glad of a playmate. It's been a long journey for a seven-year-old. I've walked him all over London, but how are you?' His voice still retained that soft Scottish lilt.

'Fine,' she replied briskly, her eyes refusing to connect with his. 'Have you met my mother?' She pointed to Sadie sitting in the shade.

'Not yet, it's you we came to see,' he said quietly, his eyes blazing into hers.

Greta wasn't ready for this shock encounter and backed away, seeing her mother staring and smiling. 'Excuse me, I must speak to her.' How could they have ganged up on her like this? She felt everyone was looking at her. Frozen with shock, trapped by politeness, friendship and courtesy, she must now play the grateful guest. How dare Rhoda do this to her?

The luncheon was a lingering affair; a roast with all the trimmings, a beautiful meringue, elderflower cordial and iced lemonade. The children raced around until even they faded in the heat. Greta glanced at Jem who was sitting next to Erasmus at the other end of the table. Did anyone suspect the tension between them as their eyes locked in silent combat?

Then Erasmus Blake retired to rest. Bert and Mother departed early and Hamer and Rhoda made a feeble excuse taking the children indoors which left them alone at last.

'Why have you come?' Greta demanded.

'To see my daughter,' he replied coolly. 'How could I pass by my own flesh and blood? When exactly were you going to tell me?'

'I didn't know myself until I came back to York and that's the truth of the matter.' She hesitated, not knowing how to explain. 'You were engaged to be married. What was I to do?'

'But if I had known...' He gripped her arm tightly.

'I chose to tell no one. Everyone thinks she's Eben's child. She has his surname.'

'I came to find you to tell you I couldn't go through with my engagement but you'd left. Things could have been so different, if only you'd waited an hour longer...'

'Oh, what's done is done.' She was in no mood for if onlys. 'I'm sorry about your wife, such a terrible accident.'

He ignored her sympathy and the change of subject. 'I had to see Pearl for myself. News of her gave me hope for the future.'

'It's eight years, Jem. Our lives have gone in different directions. I am settled here. You have your businesses back home. Better to keep things private. Persie need never know her mother's disgrace or Eben's disgrace.'

'Why do you say that? Shouldn't a girl have a chance to know her real father? I could do so much for her, if you'd let me.' His dark eyes were pleading.

'I can provide for her. My shop does well.'

'I'm sure it does but is that enough?'

'What do you mean?'

'It must be hard for her without a father's guidance.'

'That's not for you to say or judge. Did you turn up here out of the blue and expect me to fall into your arms and pick up where we left off? How dare you assume such a thing after all these years. What happened between us, happened. We are both different people now.' The angry words shot out of her mouth like bullets from a gun.

'Of course I see that, Greta, but I hope we are still friends enough to be able to come to some amicable arrangement.'

'My life is here and I am content enough. I wish you both well and a wonderful trip north but how could Rhoda deceive me in this way? It takes some stomaching.'

'She did not. Keep her out of this. It was my idea to find some way for us to meet.'

'And now we have met...' She tried to turn away from his gaze but he could see she was in a turmoil of indecision.

'I would like to spend some time with Pearl. Hamish has been looking forward to meeting her. Surely you'll allow them to play together? Don't deny us that. I never thought you'd be selfish.'

'A woman alone learns to put her own needs and her child's first above others.'

'You sound so bitter.' Jem was pacing. He was not getting his own way. 'Please let's meet up with the children. We still have a few more days here to fill. I'd like to take them on a picnic up the river.'

'It's not the Mississippi, just a Yorkshire river full of coal barges.' This was all she could muster in her anger. 'I shall have to think about it.'

433

'Oh, don't play games with me. It doesn't suit you. Either come out with us or not, Rhoda can bring Pearl. They are being so kind.'

Greta sighed shaking her head. 'We'll come but it'll have to be after I close the shop. The city is thronged with visitors for the jubilee. I have to keep open.'

'Of course, business first, thank you, it looks like we'll have to take whatever crumbs you throw for us then.' She could see he was disappointed and angry at not getting his own way.

'Now who's being bitter? I can close early,' she offered. The two of them were like children spatting in a street game, neither of them wanting to give in.

Jem stared across the garden. 'Effie would have loved this English garden with its roses and wildness. You know our marriage wasn't easy but I never wished it to end in such a terrible way. Ah well, that's life, the best laid plans gang aft agley.' He sighed, turning away from her. 'Best go inside or they'll be sending out a search party.'

He was trying to make light of their meeting but she could see the frustration written all over his face and felt mean as he returned to his hosts. Greta sat outside watching a bee buzzing in and out the flowers and thought of his wife. How could everything have gone so wrong? Perhaps tomorrow they might find some way to relax with each other if they were together in company.

Rhoda slipped out to join her on the bench. 'Well?'

'Well what? Did you expect some romantic reunion? How could you give me no warning and trick me into coming?'

'We thought it was the best way to introduce him to you.' Rhoda was pink and nervous.

'You told him about Persie, didn't you?'

'I had to in all conscience, the poor man.'

'You and your conscience, this is a disaster. I wish you'd stop interfering in my life. Persie and I were quite content the way things were.'

'That's not what I see, Greta. I see a woman driven by the need to prove her success to others, but at what cost? Don't you want to have a family and give Persie better chances in life? I know what it's like not to know who my parents were. At least give Persie a chance to know her own father. Don't be selfish.'

'If that's what you think, I'd better leave now.' She jumped up.

'What's got into you? We just wanted to help two lonely people find each other again. Is that so wrong?'

'And you've just made things ten times worse with your meddling. Please leave me alone in future.'

'Don't worry, I shall do just that.' Rhoda turned on her heels and fled in tears.

It had all gone horribly wrong again between them. There was no point in stopping to make small talk now. Greta grabbed a reluctant Persie from her game with Hamish and shot out of the side door in tears of rage and frustration, determined not to give anyone the satisfaction of saying a goodbye.

64

First thing on Wednesday morning, Sadie came into the shop and plonked herself on the stool in no mood for pleasantries. 'What's all this to do, my girl? I've had Rhoda in tears on my doorstep. Just what have you been up to now? I could only get half a story from her about the American and his son?'

'It's nothing for you to get involved in. She went behind my back and broke a promise. I told her a few home truths. This Quaker business is making her holier than thou.'

'That chap didn't come all this way to tour the Minster. I gather he was here to renew his friendship with you and, by the looks of him and his son, it were Persie he had his beady eye on. You kept that quiet, didn't you? Anyone with half a brain could see she were never Eben's bairn. She's far too bonnie.'

'So you knew?'

'What do you think? But I wouldn't shame you in public so I said nowt. I gather you never even gave him a fair hearing. That's you all over, lass, Miss Know-it-all.'

'Oh leave off, Mother, I had enough yesterday with them springing him on me like that with no warning. I'm not made of ice.' Greta stood her ground, arms folded.

'Rhoda were only trying to do you a favour and

you spit it back in her face. Look at yourself, Greta. You've changed that much I hardly know you. All you think about is this blessed shop. You've hardly time to blow your nose or have any fun with your own kiddie.' They glared at each other.

'That's not true. I'm doing this for Persie's future. I've never neglected her welfare.' How dare her mother criticize her mothering like this?

'You've lost your way since you came home. No one dare speak to you but you clam up tight. What happened to my happy lass?'

'Life happened. Kitty died, or have you forgotten?' Greta was shouting. 'I let that awful man into my life and he killed her.'

'And the Good Lord took him from the world and gave you another chance at happiness. What went wrong there then?'

'He was never mine to have. I wanted to be fair to his fiancée.'

'He's come all this way on a chance meeting and you treat him like dirt.'

'Oh shut it! I don't want to hear another word about him.'

'I'm not finished with you yet. You need telling.' Sadie was giving as good as she got. 'I see you driving yourself into an early grave and now you turn on your one true friend. That lass would walk on water for you.'

'Rhodabel interfered.'

'How many times did you interfere to get us housed proper, to get Kitty fixed with a job?' There was no answer to that. Greta shrugged her shoulders, leaning on the counter for support.

'And look where it ended. It was all my doing bringing her into our home. Eben never loved me.'

'And you never loved him and to my eternal shame I encouraged him to court you. We are all to blame for what happened to Kitty, not just you. It suited us to go along with your wedding and I blame myself there. None of us knew his real schemes. None of us are perfect, we all make mistakes. Do you recall what Mr Abrahams used to say when I gave him the wrong laundry? "My dear, your mistakes are pearls to be cherished." You have to learn from them so you don't get in a fix again. So don't go putting all the blame on your shoulders.'

'Jem is only here because his wife is dead and he is free to come and see his other child. Yes, I loved him once but he chose to stay and honour his obligation to the Allisters. My life is here now. I am proud of this business. It came from nothing, like me.'

'Is that all that matters to you? Aye, it'll put a bit of brass in the bank but it won't warm yer toes of a night. It won't wipe yer tears. Persie will grow up one day and leave home. What then, lass, will you sit with your cash ledger for company? Think on, Greta. Don't make another mistake.'

'I'm a big girl. I'll do things my own way. Any road I couldn't go back to Muscatine after what happened. I could never belong there.'

'So you have thought about it then?'

'How can I think of anything with you lot ganging up on me?'

'Oh, there's no talking to you when you are in this mood. I just thought I'd come and hear your

438

side of things but I don't like what I am hearing.'

'Tough but it is the truth.'

'No it is not,' said her mother. 'It's fear and anger talking. You were allus our thoughtful lass. Without you we would have been left to rot in Walmgate. I know your worth. Give that man a chance before someone else jumps in. If a mother can't speak her mind, it's a poor do, but I won't keep you from your work.' She stood up. 'And thanks for the cuppa I never got.' With that she left.

Greta went into the back room and wept. The truth cut deep and she was so confused and tired of being told what to do by others. They just couldn't spring this unexpected arrival on her at the busiest time of the summer and expect her to down tools and jump to their wishes.

Later when Rhoda came in a cab to collect Persie for the picnic Greta was in two minds whether to swallow her pride and go along, but she just couldn't face any of them after her tantrums yesterday. Jem was here in York and she couldn't bear to see him again even though she felt the same old attraction. She made her excuses, explaining that she was too busy to take the time off. There was a local auction she wanted to view in case there were any decent lots to bid for. If there was time she would pick up Persie herself from Rhoda's house and make her peace before the Baillies left for Edinburgh.

She recognized she was being a martyr, but she was too stubborn and too proud to let anyone know her mother's words had stung her. The tongue searches out the sore tooth and she kept reliving her row with Rhoda who, Greta knew, had meant well. Her heart was in the right place. It was her own heart that was frozen.

The auction house was on the edge of town, a regular haunt on half-day closing. She liked time to browse and examine pieces, to check the hallmarks, look for any hints of fakery. Once in a job lot of paste jewels she had discovered real diamonds. Greta had a nose for a bargain, for something out of the ordinary that could be redesigned and made up to sell on again. Her training under Eben had not gone to waste. The staff knew her and often bid on her behalf but she liked to make time to visit herself to be sure of her lots.

As she browsed along the cabinets she noticed something familiar that made her gasp. Her heart leapt in recognition when she saw Adah's pearl necklace lying on a velvet pad looking up at her. After all these years to see it again brought tears to her eyes. She hovered over the display, her eyes fixed on her quarry, trying not to shake with excitement. This must be a sign. If she had gone out on the river picnic today and missed the viewing, missed this auction, she would have missed what was surely hers by rights.

She marked the catalogue with care, knowing there would be no upper limit to what she would pay to make sure of the pearl. There was nothing quite like the chase, being in at the kill, securing your lot. No one must have Saul's gift but her, nothing and no one would stop her retrieving what was hers.

It was the symbol of all she had achieved so far.

440

Saul gave it to her as a mark of friendship and trust. He had opened her eyes to beautiful objects, taught her to thread, to assess fine-quality items. How could she not retrieve it? How could she explain her excitement at this discovery to anyone?

Rhoda had no interest now in such fripperies. Persie was too young. Mother would see only a waste of money but Jem would understand. After all, he once was a pearl fisher before he became a button manufacturer. She must share this news with him. It gave her a valid reason to return to Mount Vernon to collect Persie from their picnic. She could make her peace with everyone and tell Jem about her find.

The party were late enough home to make her anxious. It was a relief to have them safe off the river. The children were mud-stained and tired. 'We went fishing,' Persie said to her. 'And then we went to our shop but you weren't there.'

'I'm sorry to miss it all but Mama had a busy day too. I must tell you, I found a very special necklace in the auction rooms. Isn't that good, after all these years? I'm going to bid for it.'

'That's nice for you,' Rhoda replied with a coolness that Greta knew was her own doing.

'Look, I'm sorry about yesterday. It was such a shock to find Jem here. Don't worry, my mother's given me a dressing down. I am really sorry but I had to tell you all about the necklace.'

'So what's special about this necklace?' Jem added.

'It was given to me by an old jeweller as my very first piece of jewellery. I was so proud to own it but I had to let it go for tickets to America. I pawned it but was never able to redeem it. You see I promised Saul I would never sell it. I've been looking for it ever since. It belonged to his dear wife and has a beautiful pearl baroque drop. You just have to see it.'

'Sounds interesting, sure, but tomorrow we'll be off to Edinburgh and then to Perth. I'm going to take Hamish to Glencorrin to see where we all began.'

Greta felt a stab of alarm at this news. 'So soon.' She sighed.

'Could I see you alone before we leave?' Jem replied, taking her by the elbow and steering her away from the others. 'There are things to discuss. Please?'

She turned and smiled. 'What's wrong now?'

'In private,' he muttered. 'Or are you afraid to be alone with me?' He gripped her arm even tighter.

'No, of course not,' she replied, her mind still on the pearl necklace. 'When Persie's gone to bed, come to the shop. You can say whatever there is left to say there. I'd like to show you the shop. Though for how much longer I will stay there if they go ahead with alterations in the street, I don't know. It's all so unsettling. I don't want to move.'

'Can't you talk of anything other than your shop?'

Greta looked up at him with surprise. 'When you run your own business, there's always something on your mind. I'm sure you button kings are just the same.'

Jem shrugged his shoulders. 'Suppose so but I am on vacation. Don't you ever take one yourself?'

She shook her head. 'Persie and I take days out to visit Irene, my friend in the country. They live in a colony of artists and workshops. I wish you could see how they live. I'll have to tell her I've found Adah's jewel.'

'There you go again.'

'You don't know what it means to me. It's a sign. I just know it... Now I must take Persie home. We can talk later.'

She didn't give him time to reply, she was so excited about her find that she was even looking forward to Jem's evening visit. She would show him all her stock and perhaps she could order some fancy pearl buttons and buckles from his factory. He had brought cards of samples to give to all the ladies as gifts. Soon she would be hanging Adah's pearl around her neck once more. She would pay whatever it took to secure it for herself once more.

65

Jem dressed with care for this last visit. Tomorrow they would leave for Scotland on the train. The journey that had begun with such hope now had fallen flat. Greta was ignoring him, avoiding him as if he were no longer important in her life. Eight years absence changed them both. She looked gaunt, her features were sharper and she was distracted by her business concerns and as tense as piano wire but he could not take his eyes off her. She found it hard to look him in the eye.

Was that a good or bad sign? At least she wasn't indifferent to his arrival.

What was he expecting, a hero's welcome, an embrace? York was a fine city but there were no hills and it was too English for his liking. He couldn't wait to see those rolling Scottish hills and glens again, to breathe fresh mountain air and reconnect with his homeland.

The Blakes were being kindness itself, trying to make up for Greta's coolness. They were a serious religious couple and he felt he had imposed himself on them to no avail. There was one last thing to do before he left, something he had decided to do months ago should this very situation arise, hoping against hope that it wouldn't.

Perhaps within the confines of her own home Greta would relax and be with him as she once was, a friend if nothing more.

The picnic by the river at least gave him time to know Pearl. She was a singular child, curious and friendly, a bright button. She played alongside Hamish, bossing him as girls of that age seemed to do but also guarding him close to the water's edge. 'It's a dirty river and there's dead bodies in it,' she announced with pride.

'Where, can I see one?' said Hamish.

'My Aunt Kitty was found in the river but she's in the churchyard now.'

'Can I see her?' At this point Rhoda called them back and they skipped off to the next activity.

Jem wondered whether Kitty's murder at the hands of her own husband was the root cause of Greta's tension and drive? Was all her determination to be successful just a way of proving her

444

worth and to make up for their terrible loss, to wipe the slate clean in some way? If so she might be better to make a fresh start, letting go of the past, but who was he to lecture her? Look how he reacted to Slinger's own drunken confession. He had caused the man's death. Why should she care what he thought or did now? Who was he to judge anyone?

He took a cab to Goodramgate. It was still light. After the wide American streets built on a grid system, he felt hemmed in by these dark, poky, cobbled streets. These were the ancient, medieval routes through the town but on this hot sticky night they felt oppressive.

The lamps were lit in the shop window and he saw her waiting before she saw him, her arms folded, anxiously staring out of the shop window. He was impressed by her window display, all the trinkets and cabinets of necklaces neatly displayed to lure in customers. They climbed the steep stairs to the living quarters which Greta had brightened with candles and pictures and colourful drapes. The table was covered with an antique lace cloth and laid with a silver teapot and china cups. There was a bought cake and a hunk of local cheese, napkins and forks.

'I thought you might like a bite,' she offered, her voice wavering with tension.

'Thank you, you've gone to a lot of trouble.' He sat down. 'Just some cake will be fine.'

'But you have to have cheese with fruitcake. It's a good Wensleydale from the market.' Greta handed him a slice of both. 'They say round here that cake without cheese is like a kiss without a

445

squeeze...' She laughed.

'Really?' He looked across at her. 'Is that an invitation? It's the first time I've seen you smile all visit. Let me just say, before you clam up on me, that your daughter is a credit to your loving care. Hamish thinks she's swell and that's quite a compliment from him. Wouldn't it be good if they could see more of each other? I had hoped to invite you all to come and join us in Perthshire. We're renting a large house with staff. It's close to Glencorrin where I grew up. I want to show Hamish where my father and I used to fish for pearls. Would you consider coming for a short holiday so the children could play together and I could show you my wonderful county?'

Greta sighed. 'Sounds lovely, but with all the jubilee celebrations next week, I'm not sure I can. I'm helping at a special feast for the poor in the park. I can't just down tools and swan off without leaving someone in charge here. I haven't got round to training anyone up yet. Wages are a burden for a small business.'

'I could help you there if it's money stopping you from coming,' he offered but she bristled at his words.

'I don't want charity. Haven't I made that plain enough? What I do, I do for myself. I made that vow when I was on the ship coming home.'

He would have to try it from another angle. 'Doesn't Pearl need a break with you, time alone away from the smoky city?'

'Thank you but when we need a break I know where to take one. Now is not the time. I appreciate your concern for our welfare but we're fine

446

as we are.'

He held up his hand. 'I get the message. There is one other thing I have to say. Even if you are not prepared to let me back into your life as a father or friend I can not, in all conscience, leave my daughter unsupported. I've thought long and hard but she must have something of mine as a token of my continuing presence; a "wee tochar" as we say in Scotland, a little legacy.' From out of his waistcoat pocket he produced a small box and placed it on the table. 'I had hoped one day that Hamish would have a sister for me to give this to but of course now it belongs to Pearl.'

Greta opened the box to see the large pearl nestled in a silk cocoon. She looked at him puzzled. 'Is this what I think it is?'

He nodded. 'The last pearl my father fished out of the river, the last pearl he dreamt was there waiting for him to find. It was his final act. He hoped it would change all our lives.'

'Is this the pearl Eben stole from your mother?'

'He didn't steal it, he just cheated her of its real worth.'

'And this is the pearl he thought you threw into the Mississippi?' she added.

'Aye but it was a pearl too far for even him to reach.'

'And you want to give our daughter such an evil thing?' She snapped the box shut. 'Pearls for tears they say. This one has a lot of death on its conscience,' she added.

'Not at all, it is for her to sell to give her the best of education or to make into a fine necklace if she so chooses. It is pure and undrilled. It will fetch a good price on the open market. Please take it.' He pushed it back across the table.

Greta pushed it back. 'I don't want it.'

'I'm not giving it to you,' Jem bellowed in exasperation at her stubbornness.

'What good has it ever done but cause death and sorrow?' she argued staring him in the face.

'It brought you to my side or have you forgotten?'

'We want nothing to do with it. I can provide for my daughter when the time comes.'

Jem was losing patience now. 'I don't understand you. What have I done that you won't even let me give my daughter her due legacy? I didn't know of her existence but now I do she is part of me and my family. I had hoped you would let me back into your life. I came back to claim you and planned to start out west with you all those years ago but you never even left me the courtesy of a letter.' He didn't want to hear any more excuses, rising to leave he banged his head on the low beam. 'But I see I am wasting my time. Have no fear, when Pearl comes of age, I will find her and give her this gift. No matter what you say. She can decide then if she wants Hamish and me in her life. You, my dear, will have no say in the matter.'

As a parting shot he paused to try one last time. 'You and I are alike in some ways, proud and stubborn, but I can see your mind is closed and bitter so I won't take up any more of your time. You know where I am if you change your mind. Please give my love to Pearl. Don't feed her any more lies about her father being Slinger. Give her the chance to know that once we loved each other and she was born from that passion or it might haunt you that you couldn't be honest with her.'

Jem careered down the stairs and turned. 'I'll see myself out. Enjoy your shop. I hope it is everything you wish for, Greta. Goodbye!'

She followed him to the door but said nothing to halt him. He walked off his fury getting lost until he found a cab. How could that woman be so pig-headed she could refuse such a precious gift? To part with his father's Queenie, that very last pearl, was a wrench but his gift was about love and duty and it was given freely. If Greta thought she had the last word then she was mistaken. One day Pearl would have her tochar with or without her mother's consent. She was his flesh and blood and he was never going to let his child down.

66

How dare he come and throw his wealth in her face? Greta tossed and turned unable to sleep. He was so tall and his very presence had filled the room as once it had done in the shack in Muscatine. All those old feelings were churning her guts as she mulled over every word they'd exchanged. It was like a sword fight, parry and thrust from both sides, but he had wounded her none the less.

How could she forget his kindness in America? His loving had brought her back to life. She could still feel the pull of those dark mysterious eyes, the curve of his lips and the touch of his fingers on her skin but he didn't fit into York, into the safe little world she was building around herself and their child. How could she let him into her life again?

Jem had offered his precious pearl to their daughter as a gesture of love and she had thrown it back in his face, confident that Persie would soon have another pearl, the one she'd spied in the auction room. It might not be as large or as beautiful but it was just as meaningful and had been given to her by an old friend. It was Saul's wife's last pearl, once lost and now found. So while Persie went to school, she would secure its return.

There would be no time to see the Baillies off on their travels north. Rhoda would do that adequately. Yet to part on such bad terms with Jem did not sit easy with her. Jem had made such an effort to find them and she knew in her heart she had treated him with less than respect, unable to relax her guard and enjoy what little time they had together. There was real shame in her mean behaviour and she needed no mother to tell her that.

The auction room was packed as bidders rechecked their catalogues before the sale. She knew most of the dealers by face. They often outbid her but not today. Everyone was cruising down the aisle giving nothing away. She had to see if there was any interest in Adah's jewel. She tried to put in a pre-emptive bid to secure it but it hadn't been accepted and that worried her. She felt nervous, conspicuous in her black workwear. There was an older couple hovering over the cabinet that housed the necklace, pointing out her item with interest.

'That's the one, Herbert,' she heard the woman say. 'But is it real?'

One of the dealers pointed to Greta lurking behind them. 'If Costello's looking, it'll be real enough. She's the one to ask.'

They turned round smiling. 'Thank you. We're after that one there for our daughter. How much do you think it will be going for?'

What could she say? 'It's a fine piece. It will be a popular item. But have you seen any of the others down the row?'

'Yes, but we're set on that one. She'll love it.'

Could she be tactful and head them off? 'It's not for a wedding, is it? You know what they say about pearls on a bride.'

'Stuff and nonsense, we don't hold with that, we're Methodists. It's for her passing into college. She passed her exams with such flying colours and we're that proud. She's going to university in London. We know she'll need summat special to wear for evening dos. That'll do the job nicely, we reckon.'

Greta didn't want to know all this. She wanted a clear path to her necklace and no serious competition. It was hers not theirs.

This wasn't fair so she tried another tack. 'I was thinking of bidding for it myself. I do have some other similar pieces in my own shop. I could let you have one at a good price?'

The woman looked at her sharp. 'Then you'll be looking at other stuff to bid for. We just wanted to know it was genuine. Thank you.'

It was time to play on their sympathies. 'It's genuine all right. It came from the family of a jeweller in Aldwark who taught me so much. It was his wife Adah's jewel.'

'Ooh, do you hear that? What a coincidence, that's our daughter's very name. Now I know we're meant to have it. Come on, Mr Briggs, let's get to the front so we can be seen. It's going to be our lucky day. We love auctions, you never know what you'll find or who is bidding against you.' She gave Greta another fierce look, a look only a mother could give, which every daughter knew meant the battle was on.

The auctioneer was almost ready to start. It would be a long morning before her lot came up to the stand. She felt sick with apprehension. She would have to bid against that formidable woman, up and up as far as her funds could go. Why had she told them Adah's name? Why hadn't she confessed her own story and played on their decency? Why was it so important for her to take it home for Persie? The thought of it going to someone else was unbearable.

Had they been just dealers it would be a fair fight, but parents wanting a special gift for their daughter was another matter. How could she bid against them knowing that as a mother she would have done just same? Why was everything going so wrong? Last night she had glibly turned down a pearl worth hundreds of pounds out of pride and cussedness. Now this?

'My dear, it's just a pearl. It's served its purpose. Why can't Adah Briggs have the joy of it?' She whipped around to see who had whispered in her ear but there was no one there. With a shiver, she realized the soft voice with its foreign accent was Saul's.

452

Greta sat rigid as the auction began, her eyes firmly on her catalogue, waiting for the moment of decision. Still his voice kept whispering in her ear... *'So what if they beat you to it? Nothing changes, you still have your shop. There will be other pearls to chase if that is your heart's desire.'*

'No!' she cried out and the room went silent, everyone turned to look at her as she slumped down in her seat puce with embarrassment. Will I spend the rest of my life chasing pearls? Have I become like Eben? Pearls before people, is that what this is about? What's got into me? Pearls are just pearls, cold to the touch. They can't breathe or sing or dance but in the wrong hands they are objects of lust and envy as well as beauty. Once they lived within a shell, a foreign body, forcing the oyster to protect itself with layer upon layer of nacre until they form a pearl. Then all we ever search for is the pearl, throwing away the living thing that created it.

Suddenly she was panicked by a worrying thought. Has the journey of my life been like a pearl in a shell? All those layers of sorrows, murder, betrayal, grief, layer upon layer, have they hardened the heart of me? How could I have become so bitter when I have my family and good friends and the love I found with Jem? Have I thrown everything away?

Surely the most precious pearl in her life was her own daughter and time spent with her was the best gift she could give. How long was it since they had had fun together on the river, sailing boats in the park, chasing butterflies down country lanes? Was it true that their lives were full of dull stuff?

Greta felt faint at such thoughts burning in her mind. Have I lost sight of what really matters in life? There's nothing wrong with shiny things but they are not worth losing your very soul for. Lay not up for yourselves treasures upon earth where moth and rust doth corrupt... How many times had she seen that embroidered on samplers in Sunday school?

The lot containing the necklace came and went but Greta never raised her hand, instead she stood and slipped out of the room as if suddenly waking from a strange dream. The sun was shining, the gaudy jubilee bunting fluttered, all the brightness of the day lay ahead of her as the city went about its bustling business. Why did she feel such relief to be out of that stuffy atmosphere? Why did she feel so free? How could losing that bid feel like the best day's work for months?

Suddenly she looked at her little timepiece and knew the Baillies would be leaving soon and she must say goodbye and make her peace. Hailing a cab to the station, she prayed there was still time but the streets were crowded with carts and trams. She wanted to scream with frustration, hoping against hope they would still be on the platform. She fled through the archway and onto the platform in time to see the Edinburgh train chugging away in the distance. Rhodabel and Hamer turned to see the look of despair on Greta's face. 'You're too late. They waited hoping you would arrive. I'm afraid you've missed your chance now.'

67

'Are we there yet?' whined Persie looking out of the carriage window onto the wild moorland already purple with heather.

'I told you it would be a long way to ride.' Greta smiled 'Have another sandwich. Isn't the scenery grand? I never thought a country could be this empty.'

The two of them were off on holiday. The shop was shut with a notice on the door. It had all happened so quickly but she was determined to heed Saul's words not to become like her husband and the first thing she'd decided to do was to take Persie out of the soot and grime of the city.

Now sitting back and watching Persie chomping on the bread, dressed in her new navy sailor suit and skirt, she knew she was trying to change their life around. But it was not easy. Her first step had been to make peace with Rhoda, apologizing for spoiling the Baillies' visit and thanking her for all the trouble she had gone to, promising she would try to find a better balance in her life when they returned. How could she fall out with her dearest friend? 'I'm sorry,' she wept. 'My thoughts have been all higgledy piggledy lately.'

Rhoda just hugged her and smiled. 'I knew you'd come round. It's the heat, it's so draining. I owe you too much to bear a grudge. What changed your mind?'

They sat in the cool of the house as she told Rhoda about the auction and the strange experience there. 'Do you think he spoke from the grave? It was his voice.'

Rhoda shook her head. 'Saul Abrahams has always been in your heart as are all the people we love and respect. His words came out of that love at the right time. You recalled them because you were ready to hear them, that's all. I don't think it was anything spooky. It's why we sit in silence at our meetings to listen within. It never fails.'

Greta felt a great weight lifted off her chest knowing she and Rhoda were reconciled. She was determined to make Persie's holiday full of fun and adventure. Childhood was short and their time together was precious. She looked across at her daughter, looking forward to their first proper holiday together. Sadie had encouraged them to go and had pressed coins into Persie's hands. 'To spend for your fairing,' she'd said, winking, giving her daughter a hug. 'You do right, lass, to have a break.'

Everything that mattered was within her grasp, and to think she'd nearly missed what was most important in her life. She hoped that couple won their bid and that Adah's pearl was now resting on the neck of another Adah. Was it possible that such a necklace had a life of its own, a jewel given in love to be shared and passed on? Only people and love mattered and she had come close to losing them both.

For too long her heart was clammed shut through fear and hurt. She'd set her eyes on being a success, being respected and a little feared but

456

that was then. Now she felt opened up and aware that she was no longer in control of what might happen next. She was taking a risk, trusting that what she was about to do would work out for the best. No wonder she was afeared it was all too late...

Jem led his son each day to the secret fishing place in the pine woods. Hamish loved playing in the river, splashing as he learned to swim, collecting cones and pebbles from the water's edge. Cairn Lodge was a little big for just two but it was quiet and just outside Glencorrin.

Once back in Perthshire, Jem's Scottish lilt had returned. He and Hamish trawled old haunts and visited folk who still remembered Jem's family and himself as a young lad. He took Hamish to see the loggers and visit the pearling camps that had set up for the summer. It was a journey of nostalgia tinged with sadness but having moved so far away from the little cottage of his birth, it was strangely comforting to find it all so little changed when he had altered so much.

He recalled that first dramatic meeting with the Allisters. How chance had changed his life with that rescue and the losing of the pearl. Crossing the ocean he had found wealth and opportunity but his heart was still embedded in these hills and rivers.

The sun was setting down for the night when, dirty and hungry, they made for the lodge where Mrs McKinnon the housekeeper would have a roast in the pot for supper. The vacation was coming to an end but he wanted Hamish to find his very own mussel pearl, if they were lucky. It was then that Jem saw the pony and trap parked outside the drive and wondered who had come to call.

Mrs McKinnon stood on the doorstep. 'You've got visitors, Mr Baillie, all the way from York,' she said, looking worried. Then a flash of blue and white shot past her.

'Hamish, it's me ... I've come to play,' announced Pearl.

Jem felt such a spark of hope as he saw Greta following behind smiling at him shyly.

'You did invite us. I hope we're not too late?'

Jem raced up the steps to greet her, clasping her hands to see if she were real. 'Come away in,' he shouted to the children, gathering them in from the dark and closing the door.

Later they sat silent by the firelight, enjoying the quiet after the excitement of this arrival, the bustle of unpacking and settling the children upstairs as the housekeeper and maid prepared the extra bedrooms. Greta watched Jem stoking the embers, sitting on the floor beside her.

'I never thought you'd come. What changed your mind? I'm glad I gave Rhoda my address, just in case.' He looked up at her, smiling.

She told him about what had happened at the auction. How she had let the necklace go to another owner, realizing it no longer belonged to her. 'But there were other things too. I was so confused when you arrived in York. It brought back all those memories of what happened with Eben. I was so wrapped up in chasing the lost necklace that I was blind to what was really going on. I was becoming like Eben chasing pearls at the cost of everyone else around me. The sight of you was such a shock. I thought that part of my life with you was over.'

'And is it?' He leant up to kiss her.

'No, how could it be but I was so rude to you and ungracious, please forgive me.'

'You're here and that's all that matters. Who is looking after the shop?'

'No one, it's closed for a week. You were right. All work and no play...'

'Just makes a body tired and scratchy.'

'Just so, so we'll make the most of the time we have together before you leave us.'

'Now I've found you again, would you consider coming back with me or is that a step too far?'

Greta felt his rough skin on her cheek and the dizzying warmth of his breath. 'It's not that simple. I have the shop. It may seem small beer to you but I built it up from nothing. How can I let it go before they pull it down? Then there's mother. She loves Persie too.'

'I know. I understand. It's too far for you to leave her again but there must be a way for us to be together, to build a new life. We'll think of something. Where there's a will and all that.'

But how? Greta lay awake in her narrow bed staring out at the starlit sky. The blissful silence was broken by the hoot of an owl. Jem had made them so welcome and she had felt the warmth in his kiss. There was such a certainty that she had made the right decision in following after him but why had she left it so late? Could she contemplate closing the shop, walking away from York and crossing the Atlantic again?

459

She thought of all those months with Eben, travelling, arguing. How could she trust that the two of them would find common ground together? What if it failed again? Tiredness from the long day's journey was drowning out her doubts as she sank into the pillow. There must be a way for this reunion to work but she was too exhausted to fathom one out just now.

Jem lay staring out at the moon in its full quarter, remembering how he had camped out under the stars as a boy. Now all who mattered to him were under his roof. He smiled recalling that look on Greta's face, blushing, uncertain but triumphant at battling with her pride and winning. His mind was racing with possibilities. Did he really have to return on the intended ship? Did he have to return at all? Selling Rosemount would in many ways be a relief. His investments in the button company were sound. There were fast liners back if he was needed. Hamish could be educated here.

It was always the plan to return home. Scotland was booming with its steelyards and shipbuilding. There would be a future here for a man with his experience and contacts. He was still young enough to make change happen and he was not without means.

He sank back into the pillow with relief. There was always an answer if your heart wanted something enough. There must be a future together for all of them. He would sleep on it and trust for the solution to come.

They spent the next day gathering blueberries

on the hill. The sun was high and the children scoured the moor, their fingers purple with juice. It was wonderful to be among such beautiful scenery, and there were trips to the coast and castles to look forward to but where would they go from here? Greta sighed as they laid out the picnic basket on the tartan rug.

'I've been thinking. Hamish and I don't have to rush back yet,' Jem suddenly announced chewing on his mutton pie.

'You don't? What about his school?'

'A few weeks away won't harm his studies at his age. In fact, I think he'd do better over here.'

'You want to stay on?' Greta could hardly believe what she was hearing.

'You wouldn't mind if we did?' Jem seized a brief moment of privacy to pull her down on the ground beside him so they lay side by side staring up at the clouds.

She leant over and kissed him. 'What do you think?' She laughed. 'But I can't let you sacrifice your business.'

'You won't. I'll find other opportunities back here, start up somewhere closer to Glasgow or Edinburgh perhaps. We could visit each other until such times as you thought fit to join me. I don't want to put pressure on you.'

'If you sell up then I must do the same. It's only fair but where would we live?' Greta felt the excitement of thinking up a whole new scheme.

'Somewhere between York and Glasgow or Edinburgh or in the Borders on the Tweed perhaps,' he replied. 'I'd love to build another house.'

'Then you must see the work of George Walton

461

and the Grainger estate. You have to see it before you leave. I'd love to support those sort of craftsmen. I've always promised Edmund that one day I would buy his furniture. I've seen what they can do with wood and stained glass. We would need a large garden for the children to play in.'

'Hey, steady on, not so fast. I'll build it only if you'll help me. We would have to start from scratch and raise funds here but the country sounds like a good place to bring up our children,' he whispered, his hands roaming under her dress. 'And others to come, I hope.'

'Two's enough for now, James Baillie,' she replied, pulling his hands away, her eyes smiling with love for him. 'It's nearly the close of this century, think how different our children's lives will be then. I want Persie to have all the opportunities I was never able to get, college, the vote, to become independent through education. They will be the next century's children but the most important thing will be for them to grow within the love of family and friends. That's what really counts the most.' She sat up and looked down at Jem who was lying with his hands behind his head. 'Could we really make this happen or are we just daydreaming?'

'Have faith in yourself, Greta. Look how far we've both come through hard work and big dreams.'

'And luck,' she added.

'That too but between us is surely enough love and courage to make our life together happen. Besides we have Queenie. She will see us right.'

'You would sell her?'

'Her work with us is done, don't you think? From now on we build our future with our own hands. That way Hamish and Pearl will see that money doesn't drop from the sky into their lap as of right.'

Greta laughed. 'Someone once told me that my fingers were my fortune.'

Jem kissed each one of them in turn. 'Then tomorrow we'll all go pearling. Perhaps there's another Queenie lurking in the riverbed waiting to make our fortune and these bonnie fingers can fish her out.'

Christie's Auction House, London, 1898

'And last but not least in today's catalogue of superior gems, we come to lot seventy-three.' There was a hush of anticipation as the last pearl was brought out on a velvet cushion for a final inspection.

'Behold this rare specimen of finest lustre, a unique and perfect example of the Scottish fresh-water mussel pearl, undrilled and without a blemish, fished from a tributary of the River Tay over twenty years ago. Who knows when such a national treasure will ever grace us again? This queen of the river attains over eighty-five grains to almost paragon size. Who will start the bidding at two hundred guineas...?'

At the back of the auction room the two newly weds clasped hands tightly as the bidding began, hardly daring to breathe as the price of their pearl rose over the reserve, knowing that every extra guinea raised would help make their dream come true.

'Would your father mind you letting her go?' Greta whispered, knowing how much Queenie meant to him.

Jem shook his head. 'It was always mine to do with as I pleased so no regrets and she'll give delight to some collector, no doubt.'

Greta felt so grateful that against all odds they had found each other again. 'I wonder if she'll end up on a fine necklace. I think that jewels like Queenie have a life of their own and belong only to themselves. We have to pass them on to others to enjoy or we'll end up like Eben.'

'Too true, if we cling on tight to things, the having of them begins to possess us but ... the gavel's gone down. Glory Hallelujah.' Jem whistled. 'Was she really worth that much? To think I carried her inside my jacket and nearly lost her in the Mississippi! What a life she's had with us.'

'Then let's wish her well wherever she ends up.' Greta smiled with relief that the waiting was over. The proceeds of this sale would help them build their new family home in the Borders. Muscatine was in the past, her lease on her own shop in York was sold on. The journey from the Old World to the New and back again had ended for both of them but a new adventure was already beginning. There were no certainties given their two strong wills but there was love and hope. Surely that was enough for now?

Acknowledgements

I've never seen myself as 'a girl in pearls'. But my husband's surprise gift of a necklace changed all that and I began to read up about their history. When I came across a facsimile copy of *The Book of The Pearl* by Kunz and Stevenson (1908), the journey of this story began.

I would like to thank Judith Milnthorpe, late of Mary Milnthorpe and Daughters of Settle. (The original 'shiny shop') but alas no longer there. She gladly recounted anecdotes about life in the jewellery business. I am also indebted to Roger Mitchell for suggesting other details and showing me some early instruments used in assessing pearls. I also would like to thank Linda Prout of The Archive Office at York Library for helping me discover more of old York. Once again my friend, Kate Croll, came to the rescue with a wonderful album of family postcards of York and some ancient history tomes about the city.

It was on a visit to Perth, Scotland that Martin Young of *Cairncross Jewellers* trusted me to handle some of their rarer pearl items and added more anecdotes about the pearl fishing industry in the area before it was disbanded years ago.

The journey of the book then took me to Iowa to the *Muscatine Heritage and Industry Center* by the Mississippi river where Mary Wildemuth and Terry Eagle gave me a warm welcome and a wonderful tour of the clamming and pearl button industry there. There is nothing like seeing a place through the eyes of local experts. Thank you, Josh, for driving us around, pushing the boat out and finding the best steakhouses in town.

My story and characters are fictitious but they live among some real events and locations. Any mistakes therefore are entirely my own.

To my editor, Joanne Dickinson, and copy editor, Louise Davies, and the team at Simon and Schuster, I wish to say a big thank you once again for your sensitive editing and suggestions.

Finally I dedicate this novel to my granddaughter, Cicely Darling Evans, who is dying to see her name in print in one of my books.

Leah Fleming, 2015.

The publishers hope that this book has given you enjoyable reading. Large Print Books are especially designed to be as easy to see and hold as possible. If you wish a complete list of our books please ask at your local library or write directly to:

Magna Large Print Books
Magna House, Long Preston,
Skipton, North Yorkshire.
BD23 4ND

This Large Print Book for the partially sighted, who cannot read normal print, is published under the auspices of

THE ULVERSCROFT FOUNDATION

THE ULVERSCROFT FOUNDATION

... we hope that you have enjoyed this Large Print Book. Please think for a moment about those people who have worse eyesight problems than you ... and are unable to even read or enjoy Large Print, without great difficulty.

You can help them by sending a donation, large or small to:

**The Ulverscroft Foundation,
1, The Green, Bradgate Road,
Anstey, Leicestershire, LE7 7FU,
England.**
or request a copy of our brochure for more details.

The Foundation will use all your help to assist those people who are handicapped by various sight problems and need special attention.

Thank you very much for your help.